Decadent

Decadent

SHAYLA BLACK

HEAT
NEW YORK, NEW YORK

THE BERKLEY PUBLISHING GROUP
Published by the Penguin Group
Penguin Group (USA) Inc.
375 Hudson Street, New York, New York 10014, USA
Penguin Group (Canada), 90 Eglinton Avenue East, Suite 700, Toronto, Ontario M4P 2Y3, Canada
(a division of Pearson Penguin Canada Inc.)
Penguin Books Ltd., 80 Strand, London WC2R 0RL, England
Penguin Group Ireland, 25 St. Stephen's Green, Dublin 2, Ireland (a division of Penguin Books Ltd.)
Penguin Group (Australia), 250 Camberwell Road, Camberwell, Victoria 3124, Australia
(a division of Pearson Australia Group Pty. Ltd.)
Penguin Books India Pvt. Ltd., 11 Community Centre, Panchsheel Park, New Delhi—110 017, India
Penguin Group (NZ), 67 Apollo Drive, Rosedale, North Shore 0632, New Zealand
(a division of Pearson New Zealand Ltd.)
Penguin Books (South Africa) (Pty.) Ltd., 24 Sturdee Avenue, Rosebank, Johannesburg 2196,
South Africa

Penguin Books Ltd., Registered Offices: 80 Strand, London WC2R 0RL, England

This is an original publication of The Berkley Publishing Group.

Copyright © 2007 by Shelley Bradley, LLC.
Cover photo © Mark Adams/Taxi/Getty Images.
Cover design by Marc Cohen.
Text design by Tiffany Estreicher.

First edition: October 2007

Library of Congress Cataloging-in-Publication Data

Black, Shayla.
  Decadent / Shayla Black.—1st ed.
    p. cm.
  ISBN-13: 978-0-425-21721-4
  I. Title.
  PS3602.L325245D43   2007
  813'.6—dc22   2007019285

PRINTED IN THE UNITED STATES OF AMERICA

20   19   18

My special thanks to two great women and writers:

To Jaci Burton for always saying "Why not?" or "It rocked!"
or "Dayum, that's hot!"

To Rhyannon Byrd for her infectious enthusiasm and incredible
insight and lots of "OMG!"

You both kept me going and assured me I wasn't crazy.
Thanks for your time and talent, your awesome books . . .
and for being great friends.

Chapter One

NORMALLY, Kimber Edgington didn't have problems asking for a favor. If her father happened to be in town, asking him to pick up dry cleaning didn't disturb her. Or bugging one of her brothers to stop for milk, no problem.

Today, she wasn't asking her family for their help. And this favor she planned to request was anything but average.

Deep breath. She could do this. No, she *had* to do this if she wanted to fulfill a seven-year fantasy.

Easing out of her car and into the humid afternoon, Kimber studied the red brick house. From the outside, it looked well-groomed with a riot of colorful azaleas and a well-manicured lawn. Elegant with its partial stone façade, pristine white trim, sweeping balcony, and Doric columns. And without a single noise disturbing the green East Texas countryside, the place appeared sedate.

No one would guess exactly what depravities went on here. In fact, Kimber had come to discover them for herself.

And see if she could embrace them.

Curling her shaking hand in a fist around the strap of her purse, she gathered her nerve and approached the heavy oak door. Sparing a passing thought for the beauty of the inlaid stained glass window of a seascape, she knocked.

Perversely, she hoped Deke Trenton wouldn't answer.

Ugh! She hadn't seen the man in . . . what? Five years? Maybe more. Kimber wished like hell she could go for another five—at least—without having contact with him. His crass, in-your-face way of doing everything made her want to grind her teeth and take him down a peg or two—or ten. When she'd been seventeen, he'd roused a curiosity that scared her, yet she'd been unable to ignore it. The one time she'd tried to act on it by starting a simple conversation, he'd rudely rebuffed her. For a long while, she'd hated him for it.

Now, instead of avoiding him, she was going to have to ask him for the favor of a lifetime. And she'd do whatever it took to make him say yes.

Tossing a stray auburn curl behind her shoulder, Kimber resisted the urge to check her lip gloss again. Her mascara wasn't smudged; she'd glanced just minutes ago. The olive cargo pants had been a stupid choice, but one that brought her comfort. She'd offset the look with a prissy, breast-hugging white eyelet top. The low, rounded neck ought to snag his attention. She'd polished off the look with strappy white heels she knew men loved, but damn it, they made the balls of her feet ache.

There wasn't any reason to put this task off for another minute.

With a hard swallow, Kimber knocked.

"Coming . . ." A muffled male voice announced.

Deke? It had been so long, and she'd blocked out as much of the grating man as she could. But she'd never quite forgotten his rough, gravelly voice.

A battalion of butterflies jostled in her stomach as she heard the sound of padding footsteps approaching the door. She'd rehearsed this speech. Multiple times. Deke was cut from the same military cloth as her father and brothers. They didn't want stalling or sugarcoating. So she'd just throw it out there, hopefully without screwing it up.

Abruptly, a man jerked the door open.

He wasn't Deke. Not even close.

Inky hair hanging loose around lean shoulders. Soulful dark eyes.

A strong jaw dusted with a five o'clock shadow. A tight charcoal gray T-shirt and scrumptiously faded jeans hugged a tall, swimmer's sort of body. The man could model and make a fortune. He looked oddly familiar, so maybe he did.

"Can I help you? I'd be glad to." His amused smile said he was aware she'd been checking him out and didn't mind in the least. He'd done some reciprocal scoping.

Kimber laughed. Clearly, she hadn't been subtle, or good with her directions.

"I'm sorry. I think I'm at the wrong house. I'm looking for Deke Trenton. And I guess I've taken a wrong turn . . ."

"Nope. You're at the right house. Cousin Deke will be back soon."

"Deke is your cousin?" That possibility nearly made her jaw drop.

In terms of looks, the two men were night and day—literally. The one before her was a sultry, sexy midnight, all dark and wanton looking. Deke was tawny hair and skin, all discipline and hustle and hard noon.

He shrugged. "Second cousins. There are times I'd like not to claim him, but he does pay half the bills so he has a place to crash in between assignments. I'm—"

"Luc Traverson. Ohmigod! I recognize you from your pictures. I have several of your cookbooks."

"I'm flattered."

She sent him a self-deprecating smile. "Oh, wow! I love them . . . even though I'm still a disaster in the kitchen."

Luc's hearty male laugh resonated in a warm echo in her belly. She liked him right away. He was good people, down-to-earth, despite his success.

"What's your name, sweetheart?"

"Kimber Edgington." She held out her hand. "You're really Deke's cousin?"

"Whether I like it or not." Luc took it, caressing her hand more than shaking it. "I don't mean to keep you out on the porch. Do you want to come in and wait for him? I'd love your beautiful company while I finish tonight's roast."

The man was full of southern charm. Kimber felt immediately at ease. "Thanks. Do you expect him soon?"

"Yes. He called a little bit ago to say he was on the road." Luc stepped back and opened the door to admit her.

Kimber wandered into the house, eyes wide open. Everywhere she looked classical and Italian influences reigned . . . but with an interesting mix of rustic cabin and modern technology. Distressed hardwood floors with warm-shaded plaster walls. Cognac leather chairs with wrought-iron tables—and a fifty-inch plasma TV. Tasteful and plush . . . but still very masculine.

"I suspect he'll be here in ten minutes or so." Luc sent her a sly grin. "Just enough time to bribe you with raspberry iced tea and fresh peach scones, so you'll tell me what on earth that asshole has done to earn a surprise visit from a beauty like you."

Her smile fell. The mission. How quickly a pair of magnetic dark eyes and a few suave words nearly made her forget . . .

A part of her could hardly believe her reason for coming here. It was wild. Crazy. Gutsy.

Imperative to her future.

And Luc wasn't worming the truth out of her, no matter how delicious his scones were. Deke would probably tell Luc the minute he laughed her out the door, anyway.

"I'm just teasing. No need to be grim. You don't have to tell me a thing," he assured, his voice smoky and intimate. The teasing expression had been replaced by the comfort of his dark, solemn eyes.

"Sorry." Kimber did her best to smile. "I'm a little . . ."

"Nervous?" he prompted, leading her into a bright kitchen.

"The house is gorgeous, especially the kitchen," she observed, happy for a reason to change the subject.

Rich cherry cabinets with furniture detailing, a European feel, and stainless hardware, backsplashes, and appliances. A gorgeous mix of the old and new. The six-burner gas stove, granite countertops, and double ovens made this a chef's dream. Luc looked perfectly at home here.

"Thanks. Deke didn't help me decorate, in case you were wondering." He winked.

Deke decorating? The very idea made her laugh. Deke would hang gun racks and litter the floor with shell casings. In his eyes, infrared binoculars would be the perfect coffee table conversation piece. TV trays, any old couch, and a bank of security cameras, period. He'd never need anything else for entertainment.

"That, I'd believe. You did this?"

"With a little help from a friend who's an interior decorator."

"It's really lovely."

He sent her a considering smile. "Glad you like it. Raspberry tea?"

What the heck was that expression about? "Sure. Thanks."

Luc placed his hand at the small of her back and guided her to a wrought-iron chair with plush, mossy-shaded cushions. His touch warmed her. Kimber had no doubt that plenty of women found the well-known chef sexy. He was. But something about him also set her at ease. He cooked and decorated and made her feel immediately comfortable. Maybe he was gay. Another glance at him, and she revised that thought. *Doubtful.* He was just naturally polite and easygoing.

Totally unlike his cousin. Deke had always set her on edge, even before hello.

"So you know Deke?" Luc asked, handing her a tall glass.

"Oh, yeah." She gave him a tight smile. "He and my father are in the same line of work. In fact, he used to work for my dad." Kimber took a sip of the tea and moaned. "Wow. This is great!"

Luc frowned, then recognition dawned. "Ah, you're Colonel Edgington's daughter?"

She nodded. "Deke's mentioned me?"

"Not by name. Mostly he's talked about your father. I'll have to kick his ass for that oversight. You're a doll." He sat in the chair beside hers and smiled, dripping charm. "If he was hoarding you all to himself, I'm going to be very unhappy with him."

A heated feeling crept up her neck, to her cheeks. *A blush?* She never blushed. Ever! But Luc and his smooth tongue weren't something she'd ever encountered in her years of dealing with nothing but military men.

"I'll bet you flatter a lot of ladies right out of their panties."

A ghost of a smile hovered around his lush mouth. But he didn't answer. "Did Deke know you were coming today?"

"He didn't. And he hasn't been hoarding me. Trust me, I haven't seen him in years. I think I was still in high school the last time we met."

Surprise flashed across Luc's dark, sensual features. "So out of the blue, you decide to surprise a man who, unless I'm totally off base here, you aren't really fond of. Anything wrong?"

Kimber paled. Damn, he'd figured that out quick. "I—I just need to talk to Deke. It's . . . urgent."

* * *

DEKE hovered just outside the kitchen, jaw clenched.

Damn, he'd know that sweet, little-girl voice anywhere. High-pitched, lilting, usually delivered with a hint of mischief. Kimber Edgington. She made his dick itch for action. Always had. Every day he'd worked for the Colonel, he'd seen her. Just the sound of her voice had been enough to send a mad rush of blood straight to his cock. One glance from those sweet hazel eyes made him as ready as a jackhammer.

Adjusting himself, Deke grimaced. Damn it, she still had that power.

At least she wasn't seventeen anymore, tempting a man who was old enough to know better and nearly too horny to care.

Five years ago, he'd quit working for her father before he'd done something stupid. Something he was sure he'd regret every bit as much as she would.

But why the fuck was she here now? *Hell, only one way to find out . . .*

She gasped as he stepped into the kitchen. Deke leaned against the kitchen island to hide his raging hard-on. By Luc's amused smile, he knew he wasn't fooling his cousin.

But it was Kimber's face he focused on. More mature lines. Fuller lips. The freckles had faded. She wore a hint of makeup. The air of innocence remained, still begging corruption.

Deke would bet every last medal he'd ever earned that she was still a virgin.

Crazy. The girl had to be twenty-two, twenty-three. In his gut, though, Deke knew he was right. *Shit!* He had to get her the fuck out of here. Fast. Head-spinning desire and virginity were a bad combination.

"Kimber." His voice sounded like ground-up gravel. He resisted the urge to wince.

"Deke."

His name fell from her glossy, rosy lips. The husky sound only made him harder. Then she bit her cushy lower lip, and all he could think about was watching his dick slide over that lip, then deep inside the wet silk of her mouth while she looked up at him with those innocent eyes.

If he didn't stop thinking like this, he was going to have to go into the bathroom and jack off before he could have a decent conversation with the girl so he could send her on her way.

"Hi," she murmured into the awkward silence.

"It's been a while."

She nodded. It was jerky, nervous. He hadn't heard much of Luc's conversation with Kimber, just enough to know his cousin had some whacked-out imagining that he'd been keeping the beauty to himself. And that Kimber thought she had an urgent reason to be here.

Since they only had one acquaintance in common, this had to be about the Colonel.

"Is everything all right with your dad?"

"He-he's fine. Thanks." She pasted on a smile. "He says some psycho ex-convict he helped bring in for a client is out now and threatening him, but that's nothing new."

In their line of work? "No, it's not."

Finally, his erection abated enough for him to cross the room and plant himself at the fussy Italian table. A smile still tugged at the corner of his cousin's mouth, and Deke sent him a warning glare.

"I heard you tell Luc you had something urgent to talk to me about. It's not about the Colonel?"

"No. It's . . ." Kimber's lashes swept toward her cheeks as she looked down, bit her lip again.

Damn it, her unconscious, innocent flirtations were making him hard all over.

Her gaze bounced back up, and he saw fortitude there. *Interesting . . .*

"It's personal."

Personal? Deke had no idea what to say. She'd come to *him* for something personal? He'd done his best to be an ass to her when he'd worked for her father. Not too difficult when he'd been knotted up by sexual frustration on a daily basis.

A moment passed in silence. A pause.

Luc rose and approached Kimber. "I'll give you kids a few minutes alone. I have to make a phone call, anyway. There's more raspberry tea in the fridge. Don't let Mr. Glower scare you off." He grabbed her hand and kissed it. "And don't leave without saying good-bye."

Deke watched the exchange, and realized that he was grinding his teeth. *Bastard.* Kimber was everything his cousin pursued with single-minded vigor: the promise of sweetness, white lace, and innocent sighs. The fact she had a healthy hint of red in her hair was just a bonus.

Not this woman. Not this time. If Kimber was off-limits to him, Luc wasn't getting a piece of her ass, either.

The muted slam of a door down the hall let Deke know his cousin was safely ensconced in his office. He turned his attention back to Kimber.

"Go ahead. I'm listening."

"I came to ask you for a favor. I realize this is odd but . . ." She drew in a shaky sigh, then raised her chin, seeming to take her nerves in hand. A moment later, she sent him a direct stare. "Would you teach me about sex, the way you like it?"

Generally, Deke's expression conveyed none of his thoughts. His line of work made a poker face essential. But Kimber had his jaw dropping on this one. He couldn't have been more stunned if she'd asked him to dig a hole the size of the Grand Canyon with his bare hands.

"*What?*"

"I want to learn about the way you like to have sex."

The way he liked to have sex? Like it was some foreign fucking planet?

Something here was wrong. Very wrong. Virginal Kimber couldn't possibly want what he wanted. It shouldn't even be in her vocabulary.

Hell, maybe it wasn't. She probably didn't have the faintest idea what she was asking for.

With that sobering thought, irritation doused his manners, and he shook his head. "Why the fuck would you want that?"

Kimber didn't bat an eyelash at his language. Deke gave her credit for that—and having the guts to come here in the first place. Growing up with the Colonel and two older brothers, likely she'd heard every four-letter word known to man, and a few they'd probably made up on their own. He wondered where she'd come up with the fortitude to ask him to . . . what? Be her sexual tutor? He damn near snorted at the thought of all the things he'd like to show her.

"I think it's time I expand my horizons," she explained in a breezy, practiced manner. "And for all your brash attitude, you're an honorable guy. You'd never hurt me—"

"Which is exactly why I'm going to say no to you before you get any further in that little speech."

"I haven't finished."

"You shouldn't have started."

"I need your knowledge. I have to know how to please a man with your wants."

His wants. As if it was easy. As if he could just draw her a picture. He held in a bitter laugh.

"Let me get this straight: You want to learn how to fuck me, but you have no clue what that means, do you?"

She bristled. "I do. You're into ménage."

How the hell had she learned that? Surprising. Perplexing. Disturbing. So damn arousing.

But the way she said the word *ménage*, like it scared the hell out of her. Deke laughed. Long and hearty, out loud and totally at her expense. "Kitten, you're in way over your head."

"Please don't treat me like a child. I'm not the most experienced woman. So what? Everyone starts from scratch. I'm trying to learn. I'm not asking you for a commitment or a lot of your time. I'm talking an evening or two. What's your hang-up?"

So the little kitten still had claws. He found that wildly exciting. She'd look mighty fine spread out on this gleaming round table, parted legs dangling, swollen pussy open to him, while she mewled, a pant away from orgasm . . .

He cleared his throat and forced himself to focus.

"Forget for a minute that you only have a vague idea what you're asking for. Let's get to the bigger question: Why? Why do you want to learn about ménage?"

Kimber folded her hands in front of her and hesitated. She was trying to decide how much to tell him, formulating and discarding plans. He gave her a minute to get her head together. He could wait. It wouldn't take long for him to get to the bottom of all this shit.

"You may be aware that, shortly before you came to work for my father, he had been guarding Jesse McCall."

"Yeah." He shrugged.

"Jesse and I . . . became very close that summer. We shared a special connection. You could say our romance blossomed. We've both dated other people, but it's just not the same. And our relationship has only grown stronger over the years. We've kept in constant touch via e-mail and phone calls. We share our hopes and wishes and dreams. I've had a lot of years to think about him, about us, and I believe he's the one for me."

Someone hand him a barf bag. She honestly believed that, while Jesse was churning out hits and banging a different woman on every stop of his concert tour, their friendship had some special significance in his life? He supposed it was possible—on the twelfth of never following a blue moon right after hell froze over.

"I see," he drawled. "So what do I have to do with all this?"

"Well, about six months ago, we talked about our relationship at length. I told him I thought he was the one." She bit her lip, hesitated. "He told me that he cares for me very much, but that his . . . lifestyle would shock me."

Based on what the tabloids printed? "It would."

"I've seen the pictures of him with different women. I've heard the rumors that he's been into this whole ménage scene. I know what I need to do to have a future with him. He says he doesn't want to taint me and thinks I couldn't cope. I need to prove to him that I can be everything he needs."

Holy shit. Was she completely out of her mind? She wanted him to tutor her in pleasuring the pretty-boy crooner and some unknown asshole. Did she really still have a teenage crush on the celebrity, the kind that made her squeal each time she heard his name? An immediate denial bit into his gut.

"So you think I'll teach you, you'll snare him, and we'll all live happily ever after?"

Kimber bristled. "I think it's wise to go to Jesse prepared to please him and prove I can be that special person in his life."

"How is this urgent?"

"He's been in Europe for the last few years. I've missed him terribly. But he's finally coming back to the States. Back to Texas, but just for a few months. We've made plans to see each other, find out where our relationship is going. It's my chance to prove to him we still have that special connection."

Special connection? What the fuck was that supposed to mean?

"First of all, the guy is an international pop star. He's had something like three number-one albums in the last two years. He's got women falling all over him. And you know it."

She raised her chin. Pride. She had it in spades. Just another thing that made him hard for her.

"Which is exactly why I can't afford to go unprepared. I'm aware of the competition for his time and attention. I'm aware that I'm not as worldly as the groupies who hang around him. But there *is* a connection between us. I want to take it to the next level. I think he does too, but is afraid of hurting me."

"Second of all, you're way too innocent for this."

"That's why I'm asking for your help. I refuse to go to him and run the risk of seeming like a child. Why the interrogation? How difficult can this be?"

"You think I can draw you a fucking picture, and that's going to tell you all you need to know about ménages?"

"I was prepared for an explanation, maybe a demonstration . . . depending."

Un-frigging-believable. "An explanation would do jack squat for you, kitten. It wouldn't help you prepare the way you'd need to. A demonstration would blow you away."

She frowned, her frustration clearly rising as fast as his arousal. "If that's the case, I need to know it now, before I commit to Jesse. A small demonstration—"

"Would make you run screaming out of here so fast, it would set records. You couldn't handle this."

"Why? Does it include bondage or whipping?"

Deke's eyes widened in surprise. Kimber even knew about such things?

"Don't look so damn shocked. I'm not a child anymore."

"Maybe not. But you're a virgin. I'd bet my life on it."

"Yes. So what? I've saved that for Jesse." She tossed a glossy curl behind her shoulder and acted as if a twenty-something woman announcing she's a virgin was the most normal thing in the world. "Deke, I know you don't owe me anything, but I'm asking as nicely as I know how for your help."

"Fuck how you asked. Yeah, it was nice. Whatever. It's a damn stupid request."

"If you're worried about my father being angry—"

"Hell, yes, he'll be angry. But that has nothing to do with why I'm saying no. Kimber, this isn't the sort of sex a virgin has."

She paused, pondering. Then she stood. "Okay, I get it. I don't . . . light your fire or whatever. Fine. I'll figure something else out."

He should let her believe that and let her go, but Deke couldn't. She had to understand that she lit his fire—and was now playing with it.

Deke stood and blocked her path. "You think you don't light my fire?" He looked down toward his cock, thick and hard and straining the front of his jeans. A moment later, her gaze followed suit. Her little gasp only made him harder. "Kitten, you have no idea the thoughts that have been running through my mind since your request that I teach you all about sex fell out of that pretty, fuckable mouth. I doubt you want to know."

Fresh color stole up her cheeks. She glanced at his crotch again. Bit her lip. She did that when she was nervous and thinking.

"Yes, I do, if it has anything to do with sex the way you like it. The way Jesse likes it."

Annoyance spiked in Deke. *If* he ever touched Kimber, big if, she wouldn't be thinking about that pansy-ass pop star. She'd be too damn busy coming.

But saying no to her felt like he was turning his balls inside out. Hell, she was serving herself up on a platter for his lust. The lust he'd been harboring for over five years. Lust that created a nagging ache in his cock and clawed at his gut to be quenched.

Innocent. Virgin. Danger!

Time to put a stop to this now. She thought she was adult enough to handle ménage? Yeah . . . He could scare her off in about two seconds. And he'd better, before he did something crazy like grab her, touch her, drive her to the brink, then stuff her full of cock.

"The sex I like isn't sweet or pretty or romantic, kitten. It's raw, sometimes a little painful for a woman. It can require a spine of steel and a lot of stamina."

Kimber tensed, swallowed again. She was nervous—but intrigued. Curiosity swirled in those pretty hazel eyes. Finally, she nodded. "Go on."

Deke stepped closer. He couldn't resist. Now he could smell her. Peaches and brown sugar and a hint of female arousal. Were his words making her hot—or was it knowing she could turn him on that got her wet?

Another foot forward, and he leaned into her personal space, putting his lips near her ear. "In my bedroom, *ménage* means two men simultaneously pounding a woman to orgasm and driving her so insane, she forgets her name and screams the roof down."

Deke leaned away to gauge her reaction. Her mouth opened on a silent gasp, but no sound came out. Her eyes widened, pupils dilating just as quickly. *Oh, shit.* On some gut level, the idea appealed to her? His cock was ready to do the tango, despite his brain doing its best to shut off the music.

"Help me understand. For you, why ménage?" she barely managed to whisper. "Why not make love to a woman, you know . . . just the two of you?"

"Two men can make a woman come so utterly undone, she's willing to do *anything* for her lovers' pleasure. And I get off having a front-row seat."

More color bloomed in her face. The scent of female arousal now hung heavy in the air. Her nipples peaked, even as her tongue danced nervously across her lips.

"I understand."

His gut clenched at the sight of that little pink tongue. "Do you?"

"I've heard about such things. Read them. Physically, I understand how that works. Um . . . what—what about emotional bonds?"

"Emotional bonds?"

He must be from Mars, because that question was definitely from Venus. What about the curiosity he'd expected? Stuff like: Where did the cocks go? How did a woman handle two men at once? Those he could answer. In detail. He'd love clueing her in about the dueling slide of dicks, one in her tight pussy, the other in her untried ass.

Damn, he had to stop thinking like this before his jeans strangled his erection.

"How do you make relationships work without petty jealousy interfering?"

"There's no relationship. Just sex . . . any way it can be accomplished in threes."

"Oh." She blinked, then looked away. "I should have realized . . . you're not the relationship type."

"Lust works just fine for me." Anything more had catastrophic potential. Been there, done that—and he didn't want to think about the nightmare that had happened next.

"Well, with you, lust works fine for me, too. I—I just want to learn whatever you can teach me."

Still? "Are you serious?"

Kimber clutched at her purse and squared her feminine little shoulders. "I drove over a hundred miles today to talk to you, a man I haven't seen in five years. One who's never liked me much. I swallowed my pride to admit to you why I want this and the fact I'm still a virgin. Would I have bothered if I wasn't very serious about learning to please Jesse and deciding if this is something I want in my life?"

Jesse. There was the prick's name again, right from her mouth. Stupid Backstreet Boys copycat son of a bitch. He and his melodious falsetto constantly topped the charts. Deke couldn't imagine why any man wanted to sound like a female with the whole world listening.

"I'm not the man for the job, Kimber. I'm not doing it."

Her lips tensed. Her fingers tightened around her purse strap. "Why not?"

"A million reasons. I don't do virgins. Period."

"I didn't ask you to *do* me. In fact, I want to save my virginity for Jesse. I don't know why you'd say no to at least some explanations of the . . . acts involved."

"Because explanations aren't going to cut it, kitten. You won't know what you've gotten yourself into until you're getting pounded by a pair of hard cocks."

"Tell me what you mean. Pounded where exactly? In what way? With the intent to create pain?"

His assertion hadn't shocked her in the least. Her questions stunned the hell out of him. Wasn't she freaked? He sure the hell was.

"I'm not having this conversation with you. You want to learn about ménages, keep reading."

"As you pointed out, words aren't a substitute for real experience."

"Then let the girl-voiced pretty boy give you the experience. It won't be me."

"Fine." She maneuvered around him. "If you don't want to help me, let me think . . . Who did you hang out with when you worked for my dad? Oh, Adam Catrell. I remember hearing whispers about him. He lives near here, doesn't he? I'll just go look him up. And if he's not interested, wasn't Justin Wheeler a friend of yours, too? He might be willing to help me. See you later." She bolted toward the door.

Deke bristled. Oh, yeah. Both Adam and Justin would be more than happy to help her—right out of her clothes and right onto her back. But neither was known for being gentle. Virginity wouldn't mean a damn thing to either of them. They'd see fresh, sweet meat and dive in, teeth bared, like hungry dogs.

It's her choice . . . her problem. Deke tried to tell himself that.

Yeah, but if he just let her walk out the door now, she'd get mauled by that pair of ravenous rottweilers. The thought really pissed him off. She'd be overwhelmed in minutes . . . and for some damn reason, he just couldn't let that happen. Residual loyalty to the Colonel or something.

Damn. He was going to have to dissuade her from pursuing this path before he sent her on her way. Grinding his teeth together, he mentally sorted through the ways in which he could do that. They were, unfortunately, limited. And so far, talking hadn't done jack shit.

Time for action.

Deke grabbed her arm and pulled her against him. Her breasts, sweet and firm, burned his skin as if his shirt didn't exist. He hissed at the contact. *Fuck!* The girl had always gotten to him. Five years later, her effect was only more pronounced.

Kimber gasped as their bodies brushed. Her gaze skittered up to his. Awareness burned across her face, glowed in those dilated hazel eyes. From her expression, Deke wondered if this was the first time she'd felt something for him beyond annoyance.

The possibility wasn't comforting.

This plan better take three minutes or less . . .

"Wait." His fingers tightened on her arm before he forced himself to relax his grip. "I get that you're serious. I'm reconsidering your request. But it has to be all hands-on demonstration."

She swallowed. Her pulse jumped. God, she had no idea how perilously close she was to being laid out on the kitchen table for his afternoon snack.

"Okay. Who would, um . . . join us?"

Luc took that cue to saunter into the kitchen, with a sultry smile and a hard-on that was impossible to miss. So his good ol' cousin had been listening? Deke turned Kimber to face him.

"Hi, sweetheart," Luc drawled.

Deke felt Kimber tremble in his arms as she met his cousin's stare. He fought an instinct to soothe her. The point was to show her exactly what she was getting into, make it so fast and furious, she'd dismiss the plan on her own. Comforting the girl was the last fucking thing he should do.

"You and Deke share . . . ?" Her voice shook.

"We do."

Even her exhalation trembled. She was nervous. *Good.* Finally, something had gotten to her. Now it was time to ramp up her hesitation into a full-blown *no*.

Deke glanced up at Luc, sent him a warning expression and a nod. His cousin responded with a ghost of a smile, then strolled toward them.

Chapter Two

KIMBER shook, despite Deke's huge hands on her shoulders, steadying her. Burning her.

The idea of two men seemed wild, daring—something out of a sexy novel. Now about to become her reality. Could she handle it? Could she accept it as a permanent part of her life?

Luc strode slowly in her direction, wearing a shark's smile and a hungry stare. Excitement and erotic fear sucked the air out of her lungs. Deke was right: Words couldn't possibly prepare her for the reality of these two men. He had barely touched her; Luc was still two feet away. The testosterone oozing in the room was already overloading her senses, making her brain buzz. Her nerves sizzled so hot, she trembled.

Being a virgin, Kimber was a bit intimidated. But not scared. Nervous . . . yes, but it wasn't going to stop her. She had to know if she could be the woman Jesse needed, if she could deal with the touch of two men at once. Her calm was probably the result of being raised by mission-minded men. Fear wasn't an option. Just do it.

But curiosity . . . yes. Suddenly. What would it be like to have Deke's raw power and Luc's playful finesse devoted to her pleasure at the same time? She burned to know that answer. Want churned in her belly, along with curiosity and fascination, to create a potent brew.

Stop. She swallowed, remembering why she was here. The answer to her question was irrelevant. It didn't matter how Deke and Luc made her feel. She was here to learn for Jesse, so he would see her as a woman. Someone he could make *his* woman when he held her and shared her with . . . Who did he share with? Band members? Other fans? Jesse had refused to give her details about the sex life the tabloids all called *lurid* and *beyond shocking.*

Then Luc touched her, his hands sliding onto her hips. The question dissipated under the slow burn of his fingers as he gripped her gently and turned her back to Deke. Over her shoulder, her gaze collided with Luc's. With his hold on her, he eased her against him, her back to his chest—his very healthy erection nudging her.

She barely had time to react with hot shock and a blistering curl of desire in her belly before Deke's fingers tangled in her hair and he dragged her gaze back to his blue eyes, the mesmerizing color of barely washed denim.

"Kimber," Deke growled. "You're playing with fire, little girl. Get ready to burn."

His fists tightened. Without further warning, he descended.

With one touch of his mouth, he breached and invaded her lips, dazzling her senses as he slid his tongue inside and dominated everything he touched. A languorous sweep, a lingering slide.

She'd expected Deke's kiss to be harsh, to the point, with no concession to her inexperience. Not so. Hungry and demanding, yes. But good. *So good.* A wild tangle of lips and breaths and hunger.

Kimber had been kissed, but never like this. Never without hesitation or an invitation. Deke didn't bother with either.

Suddenly, he retreated, leaving behind an ache she already couldn't fight. *Oh, God.* And his taste. Spicy and male. Addicting. Kimber craved more.

In a single kiss, he stripped her defenses, turned her body inside out, stole her control.

His lips brushed hers again, and Kimber opened to him a little more. He sank in, deeper than before. He tasted, teased, withdrew. *No!* She needed more, and pressed her palms up the solid slabs of his chest, where she felt his heart beating wildly under her palm.

Deke rewarded her with another flirty caress of his lips, which melted over hers into a firm taking, a wild possession. Though she'd been expecting him, the spiced slide of his tongue still blindsided her defenses. Her hands rose from his chest to his hair. She tried to grab the very short strands with her fists and pull him closer, but his hair, like the man himself, was elusive. She craved. She clawed. Barely breathing, dizzy, she reveled as heat curled in her belly. Her nipples tightened. Wild. *So good . . .*

A hot palm curled around her arm and slid upward in an unhurried caress. Luc. She'd almost forgotten . . . But when he moved closer, the heat of his chest blanketing her back, his hardness still pressed against her backside, he became impossible to ignore.

With a sweep of his hand, he brushed the hair off her neck. The gentle press of his warm mouth and hot breath fell there next, like soft rain on sensitive skin. Sensations exploded, tingles skittered. She shivered, but Luc continued. Her ferocious response stimulated her senses right in concert with the soft, ragged demands of Deke's kiss.

Strong hands slid up her ribs. Luc again. Teasing fingers brushed the sides of her breasts. Unexpected sensations bolted straight to her nipples, making them beyond hard. She moaned—right into Deke's next kiss. He took the sound into his greedy mouth, tilting his head, positioning his lips over hers perfectly and delving deep for a long, lingering stay.

Kimber melted, mewled. She burned, just like Deke warned. As desire swamped her, her blood heated to blistering temperatures. And she ached. *More. More!*

Clutching her hips, Deke arched into her, pressing his impressive erection into her in a move deliciously suggestive of sex. It didn't soothe her—only inflamed. She moaned.

Bending at the knees, he grabbed her thighs and lifted her off the ground. Kimber barely had time to gasp before he pushed her back into Luc, whose dick now pressed even tighter against her. But he wasn't done . . .

Deke tore off her pants and her thong, then spread her legs, holding them wide with his huge hands. Luc helped him by supporting her knees in the crooks of his arms, which held her open to his cousin. Heart pounding so fast she couldn't hear anything but its frantic beating, Kimber watched as Deke looked at her, all spread out like a living, breathing invitation before him, those dark blue eyes shimmering with scorching heat.

He paused, waited. Stared. Drove her crazy with anticipation and broiling want.

"Deke . . ."

"Keep her open," he told Luc.

Then he slipped between her spread thighs and notched his denim-covered cock right against her wet folds. Intimately. At the contact, her clit jumped, then pulsed greedily. Deke grabbed her hips, taking her from Luc's grip. He wrapped her legs around his hips and he rocked against her again. Kimber cried out. Masturbation was never this sharp or intense. Decadent. Overwhelming.

Before she could assimilate or think beyond their next touch, Luc's hands slid from her rib cage to her abdomen, then up. Straight up. He enveloped her breasts in his hot palms. Kimber melted on a long moan. His thumbs and forefingers pinched her gently, but the jolt of desire jumped all the way to her clit. Her nipples sprang to painful tightness at his touch, and he rasped at them with his thumbs.

It took Kimber a moment to realize that Deke was watching Luc fondle her, his stare nearly black with hunger. A quick glance up, and those burning eyes promised to devour her. Thick need slid through her belly, punching her gut with a sharp spear of arousal.

"It's got to come off." He reached for the bottom button of her shirt with one hand.

"Now," Luc agreed, and together, they set her on the counter.

A moment later, Luc grasped the top button and tore into it. Male hands worked at her little buttons, cursing, exposing her to their devouring gazes so rapidly, she could barely assimilate. She watched, dazed, her skin too tight on her aching body until all the buttons came free of their moorings. As Luc pulled the shirt off one shoulder, Deke peeled it off the other and raised his gaze to hers.

Intense. Ferocious. Determined. A fist of desire clenched in her belly, closing off air, rational thought . . .

With his hot breath on her neck making her shiver, Deke reached behind her and unclasped her bra in a single pinch of his fingers. *Oh my! Oh, damn.* Stark naked. This was getting serious. And overwhelming . . . felt too wonderful. She couldn't stop. Not yet. Soon . . .

"Oh!" she cried as Deke's mouth covered one breast, teeth lightly scraping her nipple until tingles screamed along the nerve endings between her breasts . . . all the way to her begging clit. The sensation doubled when Luc pinched the other sensitive nub at the same time he nudged her lips apart and leaned in for a kiss.

He more than kissed; he seduced without words. Luc was an artist, a master. He didn't rush or demand. He cajoled, toyed, promised with a hot sweep of his tongue, only to back away and leave her needing. His kiss alone would be enough to make her lose her head and melt like hot wax. Coupled with the erection against her thigh, the sensations were downright combustive.

Deke continued to lave her nipple, switching to the other, pushing Luc's fingers away to take the sensitive bud inside with a hard suck, a gentle bite, a flat-tongued lick, at the same moment he pressed that iron-hard ridge of flesh right against throbbing clit.

This time, Luc's mouth absorbed her cries. The hot tease of his kiss took the sound and asked for more. And she gladly surrendered another gasp when Deke nudged her in just the right spot again while suckling her nipple with a hard ferocity. Then Luc moved in for the kill, a kiss of soft demand that infused her with a sublime jolt of pleasure. Her lips tingled when they backed away to take harsh breaths. A line of electric pleasure darted between her breasts and her vagina, lighting up her entire body.

"You're like sugar on my tongue," Luc praised, nuzzling her neck, one thumb scraping the distended nipple still wet from Deke's sucking. "Sweet as you dissolve."

That talented mouth swept across her jaw, over her cheek, pausing to seize her lips again and sink deep. He inflamed with his kiss, sending her hotter, higher, silently promising each time he touched her that he'd deliver satisfaction—in his time. In his way.

To add to the mounting sensations, Deke continued to ride her clit in steady, friction-furious strokes, igniting everything from the waist down. He pinched her nipples, twisted, turned, engorging them further, lifting her senses high. When she panted and clutched at Deke's arms and swore she might come, he backed away. Luc did the same.

Kimber cried out in frustration.

Deke flashed her a merciless smile and scraped her sensitive nipple. "You want more, kitten?"

He was toying with her. *They* were. But at the moment, Kimber didn't care. She'd never felt anything like the pleasure Luc and Deke were saturating her with. Sensations were like quicksand, drowning her. The more she writhed, the faster she went under. And she loved it.

"Please." The word slipped out of her mouth on a pant.

Luc slanted one of his devastating kisses across her mouth in his next breath. Deke continued his rhythmic friction of his cock against her clit, the merciless nips of his mouth at her nipples.

Every time they touched her, fresh sensations poured over her like warm honey—that quickly became liquid-hot lightning. She was floating, sinking, begging . . .

"More." The word slipped out, breathy and urgent.

Deke kissed his way up from her breasts, breathing over her neck. She shivered, and Luc pinned her with another haunting kiss. The man's mouth seemed to say with every swipe of his tongue that he wanted something only she could give him. Deceptive, but oh so effective. Once he got his mouth on a woman, Kimber bet they never said no.

As wonderful as it was, when Deke nibbled on her earlobe and wrapped his arms around her, the sensation was even more intense. She arched into his hard-hewn chest, suddenly hating his shirt—any shirt—that stood between his skin and hers.

Kimber had never imagined that she could so badly want a man she thought annoyed her so much. But she did. *Why?*

"What more do you want?" Deke's silky whisper slid down her spine, then seemed to caress the very wet spot that ached most for him.

How did he do that? With just a whisper, how did the sound seem to go straight to her clit?

Luc lifted his head to hear her answer.

"It feels so good . . ." was all she could whisper in return.

She doubted she could give either of them any details they didn't know for themselves.

"It can be better," Luc whispered into her other ear.

Better? God help me . . .

Usually, Kimber was made of stronger stuff. The only sort of contest she'd never won at least once against her brothers was a pissing contest. Pain, drinking, speed, endurance—she'd beat them at least once.

Yet this pleasure was crushing her will.

"If you want more, we'll give it to you. I want to lay you facedown on the kitchen table and watch Luc eat your pussy while you suck me off."

Through pleasure-hazed eyes, Kimber glanced at the kitchen table. She could picture the scene. Too easily. She'd never given a man a blow job, but she'd try. In fact, she'd love to make Mr. Tough weak at the knees. And if Luc's kiss was heaven, she could only imagine how fabulous he would be with oral sex.

But the challenging tone of Deke's words bothered her. Did he still think she was afraid?

"Okay," she whispered.

"You'd better wait to hear all you're agreeing to."

"Deke," Luc cut in, frowning.

The hunk and a half of blond muscle stopped him with a raised hand. "She should hear everything."

Zeroing in on her again, Deke grabbed her cheeks and forced her gaze to his. "Then I want to take you to bed and watch Luc sink balls deep into your pussy while you gasp and scream and come. While he's at it, I'll work into your sweet little ass so we can both fuck you. Together. Hard. All night. Until you're sore and wrung out and exhausted."

Heat and alarm tore through her at once. The idea appealed in a forbidden way. She'd never really fantasized about two men . . . but she just might now. These two could give pleasure, no doubt. But she wanted to preserve her virginity—no matter how badly her body ached otherwise.

And still, something about Deke's words bothered her. He sounded like he wanted to just . . . use her. Like she could be any woman he picked up in a bar and brought home for a quickie.

"Then we'll fuck you again," Deke went on in his smoky voice. "Sleep an hour and fuck you once more, so hard and deep you won't walk or sit for a week. How about it, kitten? Wanna say yes now?"

The look on his face was pure predator. He wanted. To fuck. Nothing more. He could give a shit about helping her.

She swallowed, trying to process through desire and anger and confusion. *Separate fact from emotion.* Dad had taught her that. From where she stood, Deke looked like an asshole, proving that maybe first impressions were right.

"I came to you with a genuine request for a favor, and you act like you're just looking for an easy lay you can abuse."

Deke shrugged. "Favor . . . fuck. It's the same thing in this situation. If you can keep up with Luc and me for a night, you might be ready for whatever your pretty singer can dish out. You game?"

"First, I plan to keep my virginity for Jesse. I told you that."

"Fine. Guess your ass and your jaw will be extra sore, but I can live without pussy. How 'bout you, Luc?"

Kimber flipped her gaze to the tall, dark, seductive one. He paused a long moment. "I'd never take anything Kimber didn't want to give."

"See?" Deke sent her a tight smile. "So it's all settled. Hop up on the table."

She watched him settle his fingers around the top button of his jeans and, with a flick of his wrist, open it, revealing a hint of the bare golden skin of his rippling abdomen.

Nerves set in. Bullshit. They bit her like a pack of half-starved wolves, nipping mercilessly at her bravado. He just . . . expected her to hop up on the table like she was offering herself up for an afternoon snack? He thought she'd just spread her legs and shove his dick in her mouth and—no.

She hadn't come here for happily-ever-after. But she'd thought they would explain how this sort of sex worked. If there was touching involved, that they'd go slow, make sure she was comfortable. That pleasure would be something she'd give and receive. Not be crude, rude, and try to scare her off.

Kimber understood Deke's point about words not sufficing. But now that her body was cooling—more with every word he spoke—logic was reasserting itself.

"Second," she went on, "I don't like your attitude. You act like I could be anyone. Like, as long as I have a . . . wet hole of some variety that you can get into, you're going to be happy."

Deke paused, seeming to think it over. "That's pretty accurate. You get to learn. We get to come. It's a win-win. Get on the table."

Now he thought he was going to order her around?

Kimber watched as Deke reached for his zipper. Luc ripped his shirt off over his head and threw it on the floor, exposing swirls of dark chest hair and miles of firm olive-skinned muscle.

Her frantic heartbeat and wild breathing signaled something deeper. *Fear. Yeah, there it was now.* Vicious and unrelenting. No matter what her father had taught her, this wasn't going to simply be pushed aside. She couldn't keep going forward in the face of it. If she let them, they'd lay her out, use every part of her damn near to exhaustion, then send her on her way without a backward glance. They'd overwhelm her and expect her to keep up. They'd be fast and furious. Strike, pound, fuck. Luc might care that she was inexperienced, maybe; she didn't know him well enough to say for sure. Deke had made it perfectly clear that he only saw it as the loss of pussy, and he'd work around it.

Bastard!

She grabbed her clothes from the counter, hopped into her pants, and slung her shirt over her breasts. She clutched her undergarments like a lifeline. "I came to you for a favor."

Damn, she hated the trembling in her voice.

"And we've got two hard cocks ready to grant your favor," Deke assured. "You scratch our backs, we'll scratch yours. Get on the table."

"No. I came to you because I thought"—she shook her head—"you were always a bastard to me when you worked for Dad, always aloof. But you never seemed heartless and mercenary. Was I ever wrong."

Luc stepped forward. "Kimber—"

"Stay there!" She retreated. "He treated me like a worthless whore, and you were going to let him."

"I—"

"You offered yourself like one," Deke broke in. "What did you expect?"

"Go to hell!" She turned her back on them and thrust her bra and thong in her pocket.

"I'm there, kitten. I'm so hard, I'm losing blood in the rest of my body. You sure you don't want to stay and help me out?"

The nerve of the unbelievable asshole! "You've got a palm and five fingers. Figure it out."

She marched to the front door. The sound of the door slamming reverberated into the peaceful East Texas afternoon until she laid rubber on the road and sped away.

* * *

"DID you find her?" Luc asked, his annoyance coming through loud and clear. Damn the perfect digital cell phone signal. In the old analog days, he could have pretended he hadn't heard.

"Yeah."

Deke had found Kimber, all right. And just like she had at seventeen, she'd tied his gut up in knots so crazy an Eagle Scout with Houdini ancestry couldn't get them undone.

"You're going to apologize for scaring her off and make sure she doesn't get into trouble," Luc reminded.

Deke didn't want to. But as Luc had rationally pointed out, scaring the crap out of Kimber was only a temporary solution to a problem that wasn't going to just go away because he wanted it to. Kimber was too tenacious to simply give up. She'd track someone else down to help her in her quest to catch Jesse McCall—someone who, at best, would cause her discomfort because they didn't know what the hell they were doing. At worst, they would take total advantage of her and hurt her.

The Colonel would kill Deke if anything happened to her because he'd had his dick in a knot. Her old man was scary, too. Tough SOB. Mean when he needed to be. Not that he'd condone Deke and Luc introducing his baby to the joys of anal sex . . . but somehow he figured the Colonel would pick that over Kimber picking up a very minor acquaintance in a bar and doing—he couldn't think about what she might do with two other guys. He gripped the thin wooden table in front of him and didn't let go until he heard it crack.

But it wasn't his old boss who motivated him now. It was Kimber herself. He'd had vivid fantasies about her once upon a time, great for jacking off to. But reality was far stronger, like comparing a gust to a category-five hurricane. She'd tasted like sugary innocence. Sweet in his mouth. So damn perfect. Bright in his arms, like a summer day. She was white heat and soft skin and . . .

God, listen to him. Fucking pathetic, going on about the girl like he was Keats or something. *Hell.*

One fact he couldn't escape, however: Kimber was the sole temptation that, as much as he hated to admit it, might be stronger than his self-control. He should be pushing her away as fast as he could, before he swallowed her whole, like a snake does its prey. Before he destroyed her. But she wasn't going to give up her quest, and he wasn't going to let anyone else tutor her.

Blowing out a breath with a short, ugly curse, Deke lifted the longneck to his mouth and swallowed. And he stared.

Kimber was currently on the dance floor at Adam Catrell's bar, The Hang Out, swaying her sweet hips to a Shakira song about that very part of her anatomy. With thighs bared by a skirt so short it neared indecency, a strip of pale belly bared, she danced—sandwiched between Adam and his brother, Burke. The club was smoky and crowded and just getting loud. And despite all that, Deke couldn't mistake the lust on either brother's face.

"Are you listening to me?" Luc ranted.

He gripped the phone tighter. "You made yourself real clear last night, cuz. I'm going to play Sir Galahad and ride in to save the day."

"Don't forget the apologizing part."

"Back off."

Luc sighed. "Tell her we'll help. Nicely. No mention of using her ass so harshly that she won't sit for a week."

Deke winced. He'd treated her badly, hoping to dissuade her from this foolish, reckless idea. Luc knew that, but admitting it out loud would only give him more ammunition. He already had right on his side . . .

"You're pushing it."

"You're the one pushing. You're shoving Kimber away when she's done nothing but ask for a favor. And it's a favor we're both dying to grant."

"Hell, yes, I pushed her away. She's a virgin."

"She isn't Heather."

That was just dirty pool. Deke gripped the phone, pissed at how low this conversation had become in the space of a heartbeat. "She has nothing to do with this. Kimber just isn't my type."

Luc laughed in his ear. "Really? Who is your type?"

Deke paused. Hell, he could barely remember another woman's name for thinking about getting inside Kimber. "Alyssa Devereaux."

"That blond strip club owner with the Tupperware breasts?"

"She's not a whore," Deke protested, knowing from previous discussion that's exactly what Luc thought.

"Maybe, but you don't really want Alyssa. She doesn't want you."

"She wants you." A fact that had pissed Deke off when he'd last seen Alyssa a few months ago.

"And I'm not interested. Besides, you're only telling yourself that you want her because you think she's 'safe.' "

"I want her because she's hot and I hear she gives a killer blow job."

Luc snorted. "You want Alyssa so bad that you jacked off last night and moaned Kimber's name. I heard you through the wall."

Deke felt a flush crawl up his face. "Invest in some fucking earplugs. Yeah, Kimber got me hot. So what? She's a virgin. Man, I'm telling you, they're bad news."

"I've been with a virgin. It was a beautiful experience. They're not bad news; Heather was."

"Leave her out of this."

"No! You pushed Kimber out the door with a slew of ugly words yesterday because of Heather. Deke, you weren't responsible—"

"We all know I was. I live with that fact every fucking day. Drop it," he growled. "Now."

"I think you're wrong." Luc sighed. "But I'll drop it if you'll go talk to Kimber. Apologize. Tell her we'll help."

He took another long swallow of his beer and stared as Burke Catrell grabbed Kimber's hips and gyrated his cock against her ass. The bastard apparently wanted to wear his nose somewhere in the middle of his forehead. Deke would be happy to make it happen if Catrell didn't get his fucking hands off her. His blood was beginning to boil, and the fury rising in him was about up to his eyeballs, ready to overtake his brain.

"She looks otherwise occupied," Deke snarled into the phone.

"But she came to you first."

Yeah, she had. Damn Luc and his logic. And Kimber was putting on this show for his benefit, he'd guess, given the way she kept sneaking glances in his direction.

"Get over whatever snit you're in," Luc said, "and do the right thing."

"If I bring her home, I'm going to end up fucking her. We both are." He sighed heavily. "You know it."

Deke wanted inside her. Bad. Damn bad. Not just her ass, though he'd enjoy it. Not just her mouth, though he was sure a blow job from Kimber and her lush pink mouth would be mind-blowing. He wanted her—all of her—and suspected that bypassing her pussy just wasn't going to be an option.

"We'll respect whatever her wishes are. If she changes her mind, great. If not, we'll live with it. And you're making excuses."

In a way, he supposed that was true. They were truths, in his book. He didn't have any business teaching Kimber anything about sex. He would want in her pussy if she came back to their house. She drove him out of his ever-lovin' mind with desire, and his self-control would be shattered. And she scared the hell out of him. What if the past repeated itself? She wasn't Heather . . . but close enough.

Given all that, he still couldn't stay away.

Refusing to dwell on that reality, Deke lifted his bottle and emptied it. Then slammed it down on the table.

"All right, I'm on it."

"Bring her home."

Home. As if she belonged to them. As if they could just claim her like some stray kitten. Luc wanted to. His cousin was hearing wedding bells and babies crying, which made a nice little soundtrack for his picket fence fantasy where he and Luc and the girl of their dreams lived happily ever after. Deke snorted.

Still, he pushed his chair back, stood, staring as Kimber did an X-rated rumba with the Catrell brothers. With a glower, and hoping for a fight, he crossed the room.

Chapter Three

ON the dance floor, the elder Catrell brother reached for her again. Kimber gyrated, turned, hips swinging, as she edged away from him. She'd forgotten his name. Oh, he was handsome. Damn good-looking, in fact. Blue eyes, sandy hair, ripped body. Once upon a time, she might have been attracted to him, but now learning how to please Jesse so they could live happily ever after was her mission. Determining if ménage was something she could handle was key.

But another man, one with military hair, hungry eyes, and a furious stride, had seized her attention in some darkly fascinating way, much like he had five years ago.

Uh-oh. Deke was definitely headed her way. What the hell did he want? At his house yesterday, he'd gone out of his way to humiliate her. Was he here for round two?

Suddenly, Adam Catrell wrapped his arm around her and dragged her close, lowering his head toward her. Kimber's first instinct was to panic. Did he intend to kiss her in the middle of the dance floor? She didn't know him. As she discovered about thirty seconds into this dance, she didn't want him. Especially not with everyone—with Deke—staring.

"You got something going on with Deke?" he shouted in her ear over the music.

"N-no."

Not that she could manage to forget her afternoon in his kitchen, when he and Luc had kissed her and . . . Better to forget it. Or try to. Lord knew, she hadn't had much luck with that so far.

In a way, it was her own fault. In retrospect, she realized that military men weren't built for eloquence, but brute force. He'd tried to say no to her request. When she'd pushed, Deke had stopped talking and simply acted, intentionally scaring her off with his crude words.

Damn if it hadn't worked.

Then she'd compounded her mistake by coming here and assuming that if being with Deke and Luc had aroused her while being "educational," then being with Adam and . . . Brad-Brian-Brock-whatever his name was—would be equally enjoyable.

Nope. Almost since this dance started she'd wanted out. But running away like a coward with Deke looking on just wasn't an option. With her thoughts whirling like a salsa dancer on speed, Kimber tried to decide her next move.

Then Deke had risen from his chair and marched her way, looking more than ready to take the decision out of her hands.

She risked another glance in his direction. God, he was close now. Close enough that she could see a muscle ticcing in his jaw as his sharp gaze zeroed in on Adam's hand, now riding low on her back, almost on one cheek.

"You're not involved with Deke? I'm guessing he doesn't see it that way." Adam lifted his head—but didn't move his hand—and turned to greet their mutual friend. "Hey, Trenton. What brings you to The Hang Out, man?"

"An unfinished matter with Kimber." He directed that disconcerting denim-blue stare at her. "Can we talk outside?"

Deke had phrased his words into a question, but his glare said he wasn't asking at all.

Kimber swallowed. Wearing a pair of fine-fitting jeans, black boots, a khaki T-shirt with the word *Army* stretched in black above his solid left pectoral, and a demanding glare, Deke looked like a man on a serious personal mission. Everything about his demeanor seconded that. He hadn't greeted his buddy and had barely answered Adam's question. He hadn't said hello to either of them. No pleasantries; just down to business.

What more did he have to say that he hadn't said to her in his kitchen yesterday? In a few words, he'd both annoyed and spooked her, and she'd run like a girl in over her head. Just like he claimed she was. Since nothing in his expression looked remotely apologetic, she couldn't imagine what he had in mind, other than more humiliation. *No thanks.*

"You said plenty yesterday. We don't have anything left to talk about."

"Yes, we do."

"I'm busy dancing." She turned away to engage Adam's brother again—Brett? Buck? Something like that.

She flashed the blond club owner a smile and swiveled her hips—all too conscious of Deke's gaze drilling into her back.

As soon as the nameless Catrell brother smiled back, the song ended. The DJ announced a JELL-O shot special and his intent to take a break.

Deke grabbed her wrist and whirled her around to face him, golden brow arched. "You're not dancing now."

Damn it! Kimber fisted her hands on her hips. "Say whatever you came to say, then."

"Outside."

The command in his tone raised her hackles. "Is this going to take long?"

"No."

"Then just say it and be gone."

He hesitated. "I don't think you want an audience."

Or he didn't. For reasons she could only guess at, he didn't want the Catrell brothers, each now staring at Deke intently over her shoulders, to hear what he was about to say. If he said more of the filth he'd spouted to her a mere twenty-four hours ago, then he'd come off smelling like shit. He should know that . . . but maybe he didn't. Deke was hardly a master of the social graces. The chance to give him enough rope to hang himself made her smile.

"I don't mind. Shoot."

"Okay"—he shrugged—"yesterday, when Luc and I had you naked and spread across our kitchen counter with our mouths on your—"

"Stop!" she gasped, feeling furious heat dash up her cheeks.

The brother whose name she couldn't remember chuckled in her ear.

Deke smiled smugly. *Bastard!* He'd come to fight dirty and had gone straight for the jugular. Why hadn't she seen that coming?

"She belong to you and Luc?" Adam asked Deke.

"Yes."

"Hell no!" she blurted at the same time.

That muscle in Deke's jaw began working again. "Come outside with me so we can discuss this."

Did the man just not know when to quit? "I don't belong to you and your cousin, I'm not coming near your kitchen counter again, and I'm certainly not going outside with you."

"I came here to say something I think you want to hear."

"I'm not interested in being just another wet hole to you, and I'm too pissed to care."

One second, Deke stood two feet away, not touching any part of her. A blink later, he crowded in and hovered toe-to-toe with her, one arm around her waist, the other tangled in the hair hanging halfway down her back.

"I'm not going to ask again. Come outside and talk with me or I'm going to find the nearest chair, pull that little skirt up over your ass, and spank your pretty cheeks red with the entire crowd watching."

Kimber didn't waste the breath necessary to say, "You wouldn't." She knew better.

Irritation poisoned her thoughts. He was a high-handed SOB. Even as she thought it, though, her belly fluttered with something . . . No, that could *not* be arousal.

"You have no right."

He shrugged. "I'll sure enjoy it."

Adam shoved his way between them. "As much as I'd like the view, there's no violence or nudity in the club, y'all. You'll have to take it outside."

She whirled on him, jaw dropping. The jerk was letting her go and feeding her to the wolves all in one sentence? Figures the men would stick together.

"You know what? Go screw yourselves—all of you. I'm going home."

The Catrell brothers laughed. Blood raging with fury, she stormed toward the exit.

Assholes, the lot of them! And she wasn't stupid enough to believe that Deke would leave it at that. He was following her; she felt him about two steps behind. Damn the man.

As she reached the club's door, the music started up again. Kimber found the biggest, meanest bouncer of the trio clustered around the door and smiled his way.

"Can you escort me to my car? I'm being followed." She sent a nasty glare over her shoulder at Deke.

"Aw, honey," Deke crooned and wrapped an arm around her. "Don't be mad."

Before she could tell him where to shove his comment and inform the bouncer that he was an annoying stranger, deranged stalker—something—Deke hauled her against him, dropped his head, and trapped every furious word on the tip of her tongue with a blistering kiss.

She struggled, but within moments, all she knew was Deke.

Warm male, ripe with persuasion, soaked in sin, invaded her senses. His mouth coaxed her. Kimber resisted. She really tried. Despite the fury swirling through her, Deke incited a familiar leap of pulse, a surge of want, that doused her protests. With a brush of his lips, a slow caress of tongue, the soft slide of his palm down her back, he enveloped her in desire—and not just hers. His own was so tangible, she tasted the tang of his arousal on her tongue.

His kiss melted her with the restrained urgency of his own need, softened into a tangle of lips, breaths, and tongues she would never have imagined Deke Trenton capable of. Timeless, weightless, thoughtless, Kimber let herself float away into the heart-racing, heat-pooling power of his kiss.

Until he nipped at her lip, soothed it with a tender lick, then slid a soft brush of his mouth over hers. Without thinking, she leaned into him, seeking more kisses, more contact, more him.

Deke grabbed her shoulders. "I'm sorry about yesterday. Come home with me, kitten."

"Have a good night, y'all," said the bouncer with a teasing smile.

While she tried to think of a good comeback, Deke took her hand and led her outside, into the humid summer night.

A car spilled into the parking lot, headlights bobbing up and down on the dirt road, and cruised to the far end. Somewhere near, a pair of frogs croaked to one another. Crickets sang and mosquitoes buzzed as the parking lot's halogens combined with the full moon to rain silvery light down on them.

Now that Deke's persuasive mouth wasn't obliterating rational thought, Kimber rolled her eyes at her stupidity. Damn it, she hadn't intended to heel after Deke kissed and stroked her. She may as well have been doing her own imitation of a bitch in heat.

Well, she'd wanted to leave, anyway. Now was her chance.

She fished into the hidden pocket of her skirt for her car keys. "Okay, I'm not staying with the Catrell brothers. You got your little way. Happy?"

A sly smile quirked up the side of his mouth. Before she could wonder what mischief he was up to, Deke snaked out a hand and snatched the keys from her fingers. They disappeared deep into the pocket of his jeans. The only way to get them back was to slide her hand into his pants. *Lovely.* Considering the erection bulging the front of his jeans, she didn't think he'd be at all opposed to having her hands fishing around in his pockets—or anywhere else down there.

"No, now I'm getting my way," he said, patting her denim-covered keys. "Now you're not going anywhere until we finish this chat."

Kimber sighed with frustration. "Look, you high-handed son of a—"

"Hang on before you start name-calling. I've come here to offer you my help. If you still want it."

She paused. Did he mean what she thought he meant? "You came here to say that you'll teach me about sex? You and Luc?"

He paused, not looking terribly happy. "Yeah."

Relief or irritation—they ran a close race for her reaction. Relief eventually won, since she wasn't going to win Jesse's heart without an education. Letting the Catrell brothers teach her, despite how willing they'd seemed, wasn't something she wanted.

But she wasn't about to let Deke know that.

"Maybe it's too little, too late."

"You didn't look too comfortable with Adam and Burke."

So uncomfortable that she'd blocked out the older brother's name apparently. "Who cares? Not me, since you purposely tried to scare me off the other day."

Deke chuckled. "Figured that out, huh?"

"I'd have to be a moron not to. You would never have talked to me like that when you worked for my dad."

"No."

Kimber snorted. "You would never even have thought about me in a sexual context if I hadn't come knocking on your door."

He stilled. "You're naïve if you believe that."

Who was he kidding? Kimber frowned. Big, bad Special Ops man turned bodyguard couldn't have thought about her sexually before Luc had invited her into his kitchen.

"Oh, c'mon," she scoffed. "Before yesterday, you never imagined doing the wild thing with me. I was what, eighteen? Nineteen?"

"Seventeen." His lips twisted in a grim smile. "And a half. And everything that ran through my head back then was illegal in every state, Kimber. My thoughts haven't changed. I'm just damn glad I won't go to jail for acting on them now."

Deke looked serious. Dead serious, with those dark blue eyes burning her.

"All those years ago, you wanted to . . ."

"Fuck you? Oh, yeah. And anything else you would have let me do. I wanted you. Bad."

Kimber sucked in a shocked breath. *Oh my God . . .*

She sent a long stare toward the obvious erection about to burst out of his zipper. "So you still want me?"

"Haven't I already said that?"

She licked her bottom lip. As his hot gaze zeroed in on the action, her belly clenched, her nipples tightened. Fantasy flashed her a vision:

Deke leaning over her, sliding into her with hard insistence. She'd come under her own fingers last night to that mental picture. Heat flooded her cheeks. It made no sense, being aroused by a guy who was nothing more than a tutor to her. Temporary insanity, she supposed. Stress after a hectic school year or lingering adolescent curiosity. It would pass.

But suddenly, a few things made sense.

"So you wanting me, that's why you barely talked to me when you worked for Dad."

"Yeah."

"And the reason you've changed your mind about my . . . favor."

"In part. The other part was Luc. He nearly tore the skin off my back with his sharp tongue."

"Because he didn't want you talking to me like that?"

He nodded. "And because he wants you as badly as I do."

"And you tried to scare me off because you think I'm in over my head."

Deke nodded. "I still do. But as Luc reminded me, you're an adult."

"I have been for some time now. I have my own place. I've put myself through nursing school. I'm not underage, and I'm not an idiot."

"I'm not convinced you really understand what you're getting yourself into, but it's your life."

Kimber gnawed on her bottom lip, suspecting that he was right. She understood—in an abstract way—what being involved in a ménage à trois would mean. She'd read an erotic book this morning and found herself aroused by the story of one woman loved by two men totally devoted to her pleasure. What red-blooded woman wouldn't be?

But, despite what Deke had said about emotion easily not being a factor in a ménage, Kimber knew better. Already she felt a tug toward Deke that made no sense. Probably because she'd always been curious about him. He'd repelled her as much as he'd compelled her back in those days. The bigger factor was Jesse. She really missed him after his nearly four-year absence. Even though they didn't look alike, she was probably using Deke as a subconscious substitute. That, and Deke had already done more to her sexually in fifteen minutes than Jesse had in years. Kimber sighed.

"I'm also not convinced that Jesse McCall is the right guy for you."

Deke would think that. To Mr. Practical here, she would look like a groupie chasing a star, like a teenybopper with some silly adolescent, happily-ever-after fantasy. He couldn't possibly understand how her relationship with Jesse had grown and evolved in the last few years through faithful e-mail and telephone conversations.

Kimber shrugged, trying not to be annoyed. "You're entitled to think that. But like you said, it's my life."

"It is, and you want to learn about ménage. So here's the deal," he went on. "Come back to the house. Stay with us for two weeks. We'll show you what you need to know."

Relief slid through her. She'd won. It was tempting to tell Deke to shove it, but her pride wasn't going to solve her issue with Jesse. He'd insisted she couldn't be what he needed, was too innocent for his lifestyle. She was going to prove him wrong by learning everything. It was the only way to secure a future with the man she adored.

And despite the crappy way Deke had acted yesterday, she knew he was a man of his word. He would teach her everything necessary.

Still, she had questions about his plan . . .

"Stay with you? As in move in for two weeks?"

Deke nodded. "Part of learning to deal with a ménage is satisfying two horny men. Sex with two men at once isn't easy. Some men also have individual demands they'll want you to fulfill. Some guys are partial to morning sex. Others to midnight sex or anything in between. You'll have to learn to deal with two sets of demands."

His explanation made sense. Two men would definitely be more taxing than one. Odd to be thinking about having sex multiple times a day when she'd never had sex at all, but this was Jesse's reality.

"Let me guess, Luc is a midnight man. Your favorite time for sex is in the morning."

Deke shook his head. "Luc is a morning man. My favorite time for sex is every time Luc is in the mood and you're willing. I won't fuck you alone. Ever."

Like before, he was totally serious. He wouldn't have sex with her if Luc wasn't there and participating. What was that about?

His face gave away nothing, but his expression was too empty, almost painfully blank.

Was he trying to hide something? With Deke, who knew?

"Anytime I say yes, you'll want to . . . ?"

Lust glowed bright and blue from his eyes. "If Luc is ready and you say yes to us both, I'll be there."

The suggestion of his words created a heady, melty feeling that swirled delicious heat through her and settled a dangerous ache right between her legs.

"So I'm not just another wet hole?

He grimaced. "No."

"Okay, um . . . I just finished nursing school, so I'm free. I'll need to study for my exams, but I can do that anywhere. Let me grab a bag tonight. I can leave a note for my dad that I'm visiting a . . . friend. He's out of town right now, anyway. I can be back tomorrow and—"

"Wait. We have one rule."

A rule? There were rules about a three-way? "Like . . . ?"

"I don't do virgins, so there won't be any fucking your pussy."

Kimber bristled. She didn't like his blunt language, but was used to that. What bothered her more was his tone, as if virginity made her a lower life-form.

"I think I made it clear earlier that I wanted to save my virginity for Jesse. So that won't be a problem."

"I just want you to remember that when things get hot." He grabbed her face in his hands and leaned his taut body closer. The intent glow of his eyes said that he was desperately resisting the urge to kiss her. "And Kimber, they will get hot."

A sizzling shiver stole through her. "I won't forget or change my mind."

"I won't give in when you beg."

Kimber tore away from his grasp. "When I beg?"

My, someone thinks a lot of his prowess.

Deke's grim smile went straight to her nerves. "One of the joys of a ménage. We can make you willing to do anything. But since we're agreed now that there won't be any straight sex, then there won't be any risks."

What sort of sex would there be, then? Oral. Anal. She hadn't done either. In two weeks, she'd become a pro at both. The thought made her suck in a sharp breath at the dangerous jolt of desire.

"Risks of what? Pregnancy?"

Deke's mouth tightened. "That and entanglement. Taking virginity is accepting a responsibility, in my mind. A man shouldn't fuck a virgin he doesn't intend to claim and keep. And I'm not in the market to claim any woman, not in the forever sense."

Amazing. The old-fashioned and commitment-avoidant all in one breath.

"Somehow, I'm not surprised," she remarked, hearing her own sarcasm.

Deke merely crossed his arms over his chest and stared, his expression closed. Unreadable. Taut jaw, unapproachable body language. His mouth flattened into a grim line. And those deep blue eyes of his, they looked flat, matter-of-fact . . . at first glance. Kimber looked again.

Bleak. Everything about him screamed it. A stiffness in his posture, coupled with some yearning she glimpsed the longer she looked.

Deke blinked, shifted his weight, took a step back. Whatever she'd seen was gone.

Kimber frowned. Lord, she was losing it. It wasn't possible to see that much from a single glance. And Deke was the last man she should attribute any real emotion to. That look . . . she'd probably just mistaken his annoyance that he had to wait until tomorrow for her to ease his hard-on or that he wouldn't be getting any vaginal sex from her. The subject of virgins and claiming didn't actually upset him. She doubted much ruffled him, in fact. He'd probably thought next to nothing about the "risks" of vaginal sex, except to decide that declaring "no virgins" gave him a better shot at no commitment.

"Should I tell Luc you'll be back to the house in time for dinner?"

His dead expression was back, and this time, Kimber didn't look any closer. She doubted Deke was sensitive enough to have any demons, but if he did, she didn't want to know them.

"And pass up his cooking? I'll be there."

Deke didn't smile. In fact, he looked as cheerful as a man facing death row. "We'll be ready."

* * *

DEKE nursed a beer just inside the kitchen as he watched Luc open the front door. Kimber stood on the other side, looking so damn innocent in a white lace shirt and flirty flowered skirt. He gnashed his teeth.

Having her here had "bad news" written all over it. *Damn.*

The hint of mischief in her eyes didn't make him hard—just the thought of her had managed that twenty minutes ago. But the excitement flushing her cheeks slammed a fresh rush of blood to his cock as Luc invited her into the house. She accepted with a smile and stepped her strappy-sandaled feet into the hall.

His good ol' cuz had been like a panting puppy with the promise of a new toy all afternoon. He'd sweet-talked Wiletta, their old housekeeper, into a midweek sprucing up. Luc had also spent the last four hours preparing some gourmet chicken dish Deke couldn't pronounce. And dessert—some complicated chocolate torte thing with strawberries. Deke shook his head. Luc had bought four cartons of the berries and handpicked a mere few for the confection.

Deke doubted they'd make it to dessert.

He didn't have to ask why all the effort on Luc's part. His cousin wanted to believe they'd finally found the woman who could complete them, discounting the fact that no sane woman would want to play house permanently with a former Army Ranger and a temperamental chef. Apparently, Luc had also forgotten the thousands of times Deke had insisted he didn't want a permanent relationship.

Still, his cousin persisted in hoping Kimber was theirs. Who knew why? Deke had pointed out repeatedly they wouldn't be sinking their cocks into Kimber's sweet pussy. That she was, in fact, coming here merely to experience a ménage so she could be prepared to please another man.

None of that mattered. Luc was still convinced Kimber could be The One. Sweetly curious, soft on the outside with a tough inner core,

Kimber was everything Luc insisted was perfect for a life with two difficult men.

Deke snorted. Yeah, this sure was headed for a fairy-tale ending. *Not.*
But Luc would have to figure that out for himself. Deke was tired of
pointing out the obvious.

Still, he admitted privately there was something about Kimber that
utterly flipped his switch.

Grimacing at the hard-on straining the fucking slacks Luc had insisted he wear, he lifted his beer for a long swallow. Hell, he was as hard
as he could ever remember being and he'd done nothing more than
watch Kimber walk through his door with a hesitant smile.

"Hi."

Her voice was breathy, soft, a little shaky. Good. She had every reason to be nervous. He was. His insides were like a lit powder keg on a
short fuse. What would happen to his restraint and self-control after he
and Luc laid her out on the bed? *Kaboom.* He was all jacked up on adrenaline, just as he was after a mission. He needed to fuck, and he could only
deny it for so long. Worse, the need seemed fixated on her.

It wasn't a matter of *if* she begged to be fucked, but when. And when
she begged for a hard cock in her pussy . . . could he keep to his vow to
leave her a virgin? Despite his tough talk, he wasn't sure.

Could he fuck her, claim her, and risk the consequences?

Hell no! No more risks where virgins were concerned. Abso-fucking-
lutely not. Never again. She'd learn what they could teach in two weeks
and be gone. He'd resist . . . somehow.

"Come in," Luc said, taking the duffel bag that weighed down her
slender arm and setting it in the hall. "We're glad you're here. I'm thrilled
you've agreed to stay with us."

And if Luc had his way, Kimber would never leave.

"Thanks for changing your mind."

She looked self-conscious, tucking her silky reddish hair behind one
ear, her hazel eyes darting around the living room and into the kitchen.

Her gaze found his, and their stares connected. At the visual jolt of
electricity, she sucked in a breath. He felt her gaze like a sucker punch to
the gut and a hard tug on his cock.

Oh, hell. He was in major shit here.

Luc tucked Kimber's hand in his and led her to the kitchen. "My mind never needed changing. As far as I'm concerned, you've always been welcome."

Thanks for the public hanging, cuz.

"Deke." His name trembled from her lips.

The sound went straight to his dick.

Not trusting himself to keep quiet every dirty thought screaming inside his head, he just nodded.

"Wine?" Luc asked her, leading her deeper into the house, into the middle of the kitchen.

"Sure. Thank you. Do you have any white?"

"I have a great chardonnay."

"Perfect."

Luc slanted a chastising glance his way. What the fuck did his cousin want him to do? Deke didn't like wine. Luc was the slick one with all the verbal skills, so Deke was letting him do the talking. It was smart, since Deke only spoke caveman. Besides, he had nothing to say. If he touched Kimber at all right now, Luc would only hear two sounds: him ripping her clothes away from her body and her scream as he covered her clit with his mouth until she came.

"Everything smells delicious," she murmured and slanted a shy glance in Deke's direction.

Smiling with all the charm of a damn talk show host, Luc handed her a glass of wine. "I hope you'll enjoy it. Make yourself comfortable. Or, if you prefer, hit Deke up for a tour of the house."

Kimber took a sip of the chardonnay, then cut another anxious glance in his direction. Her tongue dragged along her plump lower lip—nearly sending him to his knees.

"I'd love a tour."

What he'd really love was to see that tongue sliding across the head of his cock. He swallowed at the image gnawing across his mind and right through most of his self-control.

"Sure," he said, trying not to grimace at his scratchy voice.

He made his way across the kitchen and, because he couldn't stand not touching her for another minute, he molded his palm to the small of her back. Warm, firmly curved. Responsive. Deke glanced her way and couldn't miss the fact that her nipples hardened the instant he touched her. And her smell . . . He inhaled peaches, brown sugar, and cinnamon. Homey, spicy, comforting, and arousing. Another sniff. Holy shit, if he got any harder, his zipper was going to leave permanent indentions on his dick.

With a gentle push, he took his hands off her and urged her out of the kitchen, back into the living room, then down the hall, grabbing her bright blue duffel bag.

Hoisting it on his shoulder, he looked back at her. "There are two bedrooms and an office at the end of the hall. Luc's is the larger, since he lives here full-time. I'm only here when I'm between assignments or, like now, recovering from an injury."

"What happened?"

Deke couldn't mistake the concern in her voice or the way it made him want to pin her to a wall and kiss her. Not just fuck her. He still wanted to—bad. But her little show of care lured him in a way he wasn't familiar with, but was still every bit as effective as a top-of-the-line rod and reel.

If he wasn't careful, he would fall for her hook, line, and sinker, to quote a cliché. He'd been there, done that with Heather, and he'd love to burn his souvenir T-shirt, but his memories wouldn't let him. Instead, he hung it in his mental closet, determined not to fuck up again.

"Some asshole with a knife wanted to demonstrate his Zorro impression using my ribs. Twelve stitches and a tetanus shot later, I'm good as new."

"You and Dad are in a dangerous business."

"Beats the hell out of sitting behind a desk."

"Depends on your perspective, but I know you men of action always need some ass to kick."

Deke couldn't help the smile tugging across his mouth. "Damn straight."

A few steps later, he shoved a door open to reveal a smallish bedroom with white walls. It held a double bed, a chair, a reading lamp, and a desk with a laptop. It would never win interior design awards, but it worked for him.

"This is your room." It wasn't a guess; she knew it.

"Yep."

"It looks like you."

"Dull?" he baited.

"Hardly." She laughed. "I could call you a lot of things, but never dull."

The slightly breathy pitch of her voice was still going straight to his cock. He'd never been much for peaches, but right now the smell of her was rushing all his blood south. Damn, Luc always made dinner with company a grand affair. How the hell would he make it through the whole meal without throwing Kimber up on the table and eating her instead?

"It's functional, clean, uncomplicated. You'd appreciate those qualities."

Oh, shit. She'd guessed a lot about him when he wasn't looking. That dangerous feeling of wanting to kiss her returned, along with an urge to hold her close just for the pleasure of feeling her against him. *Bad. Stupid. Wrong. Not happening.* He'd taste her sweet kiss before he fucked her ass, but affection—out of the question. Kimber would take it the wrong way.

Hell, he might, too.

"Exactly," he murmured and shut the door.

Across the hall, he eased open the door to Luc's office. With its deep burgundy walls and dark woods, etched glass and brass accents, it resembled an elegant gentleman's establishment of old—but with a cutting-edge desktop, speaker phone, and a printer/scanner/fax machine. A tobacco-colored desk chair in leather presided over a masculine walnut desk and bookshelves, inlaid with lighter woods on the top and sides with something Luc had called a medallion.

"Wow," Kimber breathed. "This is gorgeous. Luc has wonderful taste."

Why did women always say that? Normally, men with "wonderful taste" were gay, but he knew firsthand that Luc was as straight as he was.

For the first time in ages—no, ever—Deke regretted Luc's hetero-sexuality. If not for that and his interest in Kimber, Deke might find a way to have her all to himself, legs spread from one end of the bed to the other while he alone climbed between them and fucked her.

No! In all the ways that mattered, she was his worst memory come back to life. Not that she actually was Heather, but . . . close enough. Like he had for the past twelve years, since that terrible summer, he was going to share the woman and just be happy for the great sex.

"Luc enjoys decorating and cooking and shit."

"He's wonderful." Her hazel eyes lit up as they traveled the room.

Deke shoved aside a prickle of irritation. Luc was damn good with cooking and decorating, so of course, she was going to be impressed. But she'd come here for sex, and he vowed that when it came to that, he'd impress the hell out of her.

Pivoting, he exited the office and made his way to the end of the hall. He shoved the door open and tossed her duffel bag in. "This is Luc's room."

Spacious, an eclectic blend of modern and Tuscan, technology and Old World. Taupes, olives, and gold with a splash of red, along with a cozy king-sized bed, invited women to come in and get . . . comfortable.

It bothered him like hell that Kimber wouldn't be the exception.

She glanced at her bag on the floor of Luc's room, then at his bed. "I'll be staying here?"

Deke swallowed and tried not to picture Kimber naked on Luc's bed, tried not to picture the two of them alone sleeping, touching, fuck-ing, while a few walls separated him. The thought charged a violent surge of fury all the way to his fists. He clenched them to keep still.

Kimber sleeping with Luc . . . it was better this way. Less temptation. Luc slept like the dead most nights. Deke didn't have that luxury. And if he wasn't lying right next to the woman who'd most revved his libido in the last decade when the next sleepless midnight rolled around, he couldn't caress her silken skin, whisper naughty suggestions to her, and sweet-talk his way into her pussy. And he'd want to. Hell, he wanted to now.

Bad, bad sign.

"Yeah. Luc has the bigger bed. I sometimes have trouble sleeping. I wouldn't want to keep you awake."

Kimber turned slowly and shot him a considering stare. "I know you think I'm making a mistake, and that you're not thrilled about helping me . . ."

She was both right and wrong. Her being here, learning from him and Luc, it was a double-edged sword. Deke did think she was making a mistake. Kimber just didn't strike him as the kind of woman who could make ménage a way of life. But to indulge his purely selfish need to touch her, he'd give her a thorough education. Still, he hated like hell that she wanted to learn all about ménage so she could please pretty-boy Jesse McCall—a rock star who likely had a willing hoard of groupies in every city around the globe and would eventually break her heart. Hell, as long as he was being honest, he didn't even want to share her with Luc.

Whoa! They were more like brothers than cousins, and since that disastrous summer with Heather, he and Luc had shared damn near everything, damn near every woman. And here he was admitting that he wanted Kimber all to himself.

Confession couldn't be good for his soul, Deke decided, since he felt like shit.

Kimber reached out, touched his arm, making him want to crawl out of his clothes and put her flat on Luc's bed. *Fuck dinner.* Some crazed part of him was nearly ready to ditch his resolution never again to take a woman to bed alone.

"But," she murmured, "I'm not trying to make your life difficult. I promise. I know you don't really want me here."

No, he really did want her here, way more than he should. And Kimber was a smart girl; she'd figure that out before too long.

"It's fine."

He shut the door to Luc's bedroom—and the disturbing images of his cousin and Kimber entwined alone together—then stomped back down the hall. They passed through the living room again, then down another hall.

"Game room." He pointed to the spacious room with a minibar and a pool table that, thanks to Luc, managed to have enough class to avoid looking like it belonged in a bachelor pad.

"Den." Deke pointed to another room that held a big-screen TV, a pair of leather sofas, a couple of gaming consoles—and perfectly masculine window treatments.

Leave it to Luc to think that a man's domain needed freakin' drapes.

"We chill here. There's a library of both books and movies on the shelves along the back wall. So if you're ever bored . . ."

"Thanks. Right now, I'm studying for my nursing exams so I imagine a lot of my time will be devoted to that, at least when we're not . . . busy."

Color flushed her cheeks again. Her perfectly pale skin didn't allow her to hide from much. The thought thrilled him. The more aroused she got the rosier her skin would turn. Damn, what a fucking turn-on.

Deke ducked behind one of the sofas to hide his erection and grimaced. How the hell was he going to hold it together through the two-hour affair Luc liked to make out of dinner? At the moment, he'd give anything for fast-food burgers—as long as everyone was willing to eat them naked.

"During most days, it's quiet in here, so it will be a good place to study. Now you've seen pretty much the whole house. There's a hot tub outside."

She frowned. "Dang it, I didn't bring a suit."

"Even if you had, you wouldn't be wearing it."

"Oh. Well"—sexual awareness dawned, brightening her hazel eyes—"I see."

She sipped her wine, then bit her lip again, and Deke was damn near ready to leap over the couch, pin her to a wall, and get her out of her clothes.

"That makes sense." She sent him a flustered smile. "You're going to see everything, anyway."

Yeah. He was going to do a lot more than see it. That moment couldn't come soon enough for him.

"Dinner!" Luc yelled from the kitchen.

Thankful to commence the next two hours of razor-sharp anticipation so they could get on to the big show, Deke walked Kimber back to the center of the house. Luc waited there for them, with a full spread. His cousin seated Kimber, pushing in her chair like a gentleman. Damn, why hadn't he thought of that?

Trying not to sulk, Deke dropped down into his seat, watching as Luc dished up her food, refilled her wine, smiled, flirted, casually touched— and made him mad as hell. Kimber blushed and smiled and hung on his every word, which only pissed him off more. He needed to get a grip and get over her. She was here for sex. Period. Who cared that he wasn't Sir Galahad?

But later, when they got naked and in bed, Deke intended to prove that while Luc's nicer qualities were all well and good, they weren't going to flip her switch. Deke was tuned into her. He could damn near see her eagerness escalating, clawing through her body.

He'd use her desires to make her come so many times she'd lose count. And he vowed that his name would be the last word on her lips.

Chapter Four

DINNER was scrumptious—and entirely too long.

Luc could cook, no doubt about that. He'd mastered an art that amazed Kimber, since she could barely boil water. Most of the "feminine arts" had escaped her. The by-product of growing up with men always on top-secret missions and paranoid about safety. Honestly, she was shocked that the lace top and skirt she'd worn tonight hadn't given her hives. But the reality was, she knew more about firearms than couture. More about martial arts than makeup. That had made romance everything from challenging to a big joke in the past. She only hoped that, since Deke and Luc were tutoring her, not dating her, that they wouldn't mind the same way Jesse didn't mind.

"Did you like dinner?" Luc asked.

Like it? She was totally impressed by Luc's culinary expertise. He'd earned his international reputation.

But after nearly two hours of rich food, small talk, and everyone avoiding the unspoken topic hanging heavy in the room—the coming night and what it would bring—Kimber's nerves were sharper than any of Luc's fancy kitchen knives. She couldn't take the anticipation building inside her, the bubbling testosterone all around, the thick heat sliding between her legs.

Based on the monosyllables Deke had replied with for the past hour, she guessed he was more than ready to adjourn to the bedroom.

Either that or he still wasn't happy to have her there.

Kimber shrugged off the unpleasant thought. "Dinner was wonderful. Thanks for a lovely meal, Luc. Everything was truly spectacular."

"More wine?" The words formed a polite question, but his eyes . . . they danced with mischief, as if he'd asked the question merely to toy with her.

"No thanks. Two glasses is my limit or I fall asleep."

"Sherry, then?"

A ghost of a smile curved that full, sinful red mouth of his. Luc was beautiful, sensual, playful, easy to talk to, cultured, curious. Shocking that some bright woman hadn't snapped him up ages ago.

But right now, she wanted to strangle the man for prolonging her agony.

"No more for me."

Luc stood and cleared his plate, setting it on the counter and reaching for some decadent chocolate confection. "Dessert? I can make coffee, if you want. I have cinnamon hazelnut, French-roasted vanilla—"

"I appreciate your effort, but I'd just like the two of you in bed."

Luc stopped in the middle of the kitchen, dishes in hand. Deke sucked in a sharp breath. Neither moved.

Oh, no. Had she misread the vibes? They'd seemed interested. Deke had barely managed civil conversation, and those burning eyes of his had damn near charred her appetite. Luc had flirted, touching her hands, bumping her knee, feeding her from his fork.

Kimber glanced across the kitchen. Luc had hardened, damn near bursting the front of his slacks. To her left, a chair scraped across the floor, disturbing the dead silence. Deke stood, and she discovered he was in the same state as his cousin—tense, erect, ready.

That meant she hadn't misread the situation, right? Or maybe not . . . Maybe Deke's desire hadn't totally tackled his reluctance. Maybe Luc was having second thoughts.

Damn it, she didn't know. Inexperience wasn't helpful just now.

"I-I'm sorry if that's too blunt," she apologized. "I'm not used to tempering what I say, since my family never does, so I—"

"Let's go." Deke grabbed her hand and tugged on her arm, nearly dragging her out of the kitchen in his haste.

"To bed?"

"Hell, yeah!"

Deke did want her. Excitement jolted her, screaming through her blood.

Now. The time had come. She was going to learn about men and sex and something beyond self-pleasure—and she was going to learn it at the hands of two of the most gorgeous men she'd ever seen. With the arousal bubbling in her body now, she didn't think accepting a ménage would disturb her in the least. She'd learn all about it so that when Jesse returned to Texas in a few weeks, she would know exactly what he needed and how to give it to him. He'd race to pursue deepening their special connection because she'd no longer be too innocent to deal with his lifestyle.

Luc tried to look put out. "I spent a lot of time making this torte."

Kimber tossed a teasing glance over her shoulder. "It'll make a great midnight snack."

"It will if you let me eat it off your breasts," Luc murmured, stalking closer.

She sent him a giddy laugh. "Only if you promise to lick off every crumb."

Luc said something and started after her, but she couldn't hear, since Deke was already pulling her down the hall, toward Luc's wide bed. In less than thirty seconds, she was flat on her back, with Deke's big body covering hers, his knees spreading her legs wide.

His mouth swooped over hers before the bed stopped bouncing. He nudged her lips apart and plunged deep into the kiss, engaging her, igniting her. Kimber threw her arms around his neck and lost herself in his spiced flavor and his touch. Demand tinged with desperation; she tasted it. His impatient lust flowed with every hot swipe of his tongue against hers, every bunching of his hard shoulders under her fingers.

He urged her legs apart even more and settled his cock directly against her. Oh, he felt good. No, more than good. Wildly arousing. He fit as if he'd been made to occupy the cradle of her thighs. And when he pushed against her, bumping her clit, she gasped into the kiss, stunned that he could raise such sexual havoc in a handful of heartbeats. He swallowed her response, and with another grind against her, demanded more.

To her right, the bed dipped again. Heat blasted her, coming closer with each second, until another hard male body plastered itself against her side. Luc. Shirtless, she discovered as she reached out to touch him.

Her fingers encountered skin as soft as suede over steel-honed muscles. Then his midnight hair, gloriously loose and hanging around his wide, bronzed shoulders.

Luc planted a series of soft kisses on her cheek and down her neck as he worked a hand in between her and Deke, until he found the hard point of her nipple through her shirt and caressed her. A sweet ache pooled there, tingling, lingering. Moisture gushed between her legs. *Oh wow!*

Deke tore away from his possession of her mouth long enough to taste the skin of her neck, nibble on her collarbone.

A shaky sigh escaped her lips. Her eyes fluttered open, settling on Luc and his chocolate eyes melting her, watching her, inviting her to sin. She threaded her fingers through the loose, inky hair. Luc looked like a gentleman pirate—barely tamed, sensual, promising pleasure—willing to take whatever he wanted. Kimber's breath caught as he moved closer.

Then Deke distracted her as he plowed into the buttons of her lacy blouse, swept both halves of the flimsy garment aside, then shoved her bra up, exposing her to his ravenous gaze. He covered her breast with one huge palm. Kimber sucked in a sharp breath at the lightning contact. Deke didn't pause to let her catch up. He simply lifted her breast, testing its weight, then brushed his thumb over the taut tip. Tingles erupted again.

Kimber had almost no time to be overwhelmed by Deke's fondling before Luc's mouth settled over her own. Like a maestro, he played her with his kisses. Soft strains at first—a gentle brush of lips, a teasing lick of her bottom lip, a sexy sigh as he pressed her mouth open, taunting her with the notion that he might take the addicting kiss deeper. But he didn't.

Moaning restlessly, she lifted her mouth to Luc. He merely smiled, then nipped at her bottom lip with a playful bite. He was gentle, teasing building the anticipation, filling her with a tender swell of want.

Still at her breasts, Deke didn't build a gentle anything—and made it clear he didn't intend to be overlooked or overshadowed. Instead, he sucked her nipple into his mouth with a hard pull, drawing desire directly from the aching point, which hardened like a rock against his tongue. Then he bit down, enough to sting. Enough to send a fireball of want through her breast, jetting down her belly, to crash right between her legs. She whimpered and arched up to him in offering.

"She's beautiful, Deke," Luc whispered against her mouth. "Better than a fantasy."

Kimber warmed under the praise, but found herself holding her breath, waiting for Deke's response. Would he agree? It didn't matter, really. Learning for Jesse was the goal. But somehow, it did matter. Though it was hard to decipher why when Deke lifted his mouth, transferred it to her other breast, and created another fireball of need, which had her gasping and wet.

"Isn't she, Deke?" Luc prodded.

Am I? Why did his opinion matter, damn it? Maybe because the thought of the man teaching her about sex not finding her attractive was distasteful. She wanted him to see past the tomboy. That had to be it.

"Yes," he groaned across her breast, his breath striking her wet nipple, cooling it, hardening it more. "Like a fucking wet dream."

His words vibrated deep inside her, straight to her swollen folds. God, she wanted. She throbbed . . .

Then Deke's hands were at her skirt, pushing, lifting, sliding the soft material across her skin. The sensations didn't arouse half as much as the sheer knowledge that Deke's rough palms followed. From her calves, to knees, to thighs, up her hips. The touch of his calloused skin over her sensitive flesh lit her up even more. The fireball multiplied and settled between her legs, right under her clit. Luc unhooked the front clasp of her bra and laved at one nipple, while Deke tore off his shirt, sat back on his heels, and stared.

"These have to come off." He glared at the flesh-colored thong underwear she'd bought this morning so she'd have something sexy to wear.

Before she could take hold of the waistband and peel them off, Deke grabbed one side. With hot male eyes in a face shouting that he was strung out on lust, he wrapped the wisp of fabric around his fist and pulled. A surprised gasp and a soft rip later, and Kimber was basically naked. Luc made *basically* a fact by pulling the blouse and bra down her shoulders, then sliding the skirt down her hips, to the floor.

Deke hissed in a harsh breath as he looked down at her, his stare unabashedly focused between her legs, on the sparse dark reddish curls. A glance to the right showed her that Luc was taking the scenic route to the same view, as his gaze traveled over her dips and swells, starting with her breasts, down to her waist, over the flat of her belly. Then lower.

Luc looked ready to savor every moment. Deke . . . those glowing blue eyes of his told her that he was ready to dive into the feast. Now.

Kimber's breath hitched. Her heart pounded, pulsing through her body, making her clit throb madly.

"Deke?" Luc asked softly beside him.

This pause of Deke's, it must be unusual. Kimber could see Luc's confusion under his lust. She didn't have time to ponder or frown before Deke's gravel voice vibrated inside her, stroking her desire a notch higher.

"Damn, she's wet."

"Very," Luc murmured. "Why don't you find out just how wet?"

Yes, please! If Kimber hadn't already known she damn near dripped with desire, Deke proved it by sliding his thumbs up her swollen labia and parting them wide, the pads sliding over her slick skin. His touch was electric as he forced her flesh apart for his and Luc's gazes.

Knowing the two of them watched and wanted her sent Kimber's desire soaring, almost hurtling her beyond her ability to breathe.

One of Deke's thumbs slid closer to her weeping opening, and Kimber felt her emptiness acutely. She ached for him to fill her empty sex with the stiff length of his cock—badly. Dangerous, yes. And wrong. But with every touch, her body fell under his spell until it was his to control, not hers. Of its own accord, her body raised its hips to him in silent pleading.

"Don't," he warned her. "Do *not* tempt me to fuck you."

Denied but more feverish because of it, her thoughts whirled. Was he annoyed by her attempts to experience more of what he could give her? Or that his unraveling self-control was already hanging by a thread?

Lovely thought that she, inexperienced Kimber, a girl whose pigtails and karate classes he used to ridicule, could test him so thoroughly. A glance at Luc proved he was in no better shape.

Eyelids half closed, she sent the men a slumberous stare, then focused on Deke's penis. It tented his slacks. Hard, thick—and growing, even as she looked at him.

Kimber sent them a kittenish smile, and before she thought better of it, she lifted her hips to Deke again.

He snarled at her and reached for his zipper. "You're begging for what you don't want me to give you. Stop now."

"Just make her come," Luc whispered, the voice of sanity. "She's needy and doesn't know what she's asking for."

She frowned. She did know what she was asking for—relief! Deke wanted her; his unflagging erection made that clear. But he was saying no, just like he'd said no to vaginal intercourse during their conversations. Why? He liked women, she knew.

Jesse. She couldn't forget Jesse. She needed to experience sex his way, but still come to him a virgin, as she'd said she would. Deke had vowed that he wouldn't take a virgin. He didn't want to claim anyone. Now she recalled . . . Somehow, his stance disturbed her.

Deke's fingers curled into fists. He swallowed. The effort to resist her was costing him dearly.

"Right," he said finally, his voice like gravel in a blender. "I'll make her come."

"We talked about this earlier," Luc assured her, leaning closer to lay a soft kiss across her mouth, then the side of her breast. "For tonight, you'll just take pleasure from us, get used to the sensations of two men pleasuring you at once. When you're ready, we'll teach you about pleasing us in return. No rush. No pressure. Okay?"

She sent him a shaky nod, barely able to focus her thoughts away from Deke and his promise. He was going to make her come. Kimber had no doubt he could. In about thirty seconds. Or less.

Would it erase the aching emptiness inside her?

Swinging her gaze back over to Deke, she took in his flushed cheeks, the harsh rise and fall of his heavily muscled chest, the sinew and veins roping his thick forearms. Sleek, powerful, all male. Fresh want pulsed in her belly, in her sex.

No. Think about Jesse. Whatever pleasure Deke gave her was for instructional purposes. It would have to be enough. No big, pulsing, more-than-ready-to-do-the-job cocks inside her.

"Just touch me." The words fell from her lips, soft, imploring.

"I will, in any way I can. I'm going to find out every way to make you come and get you off until you beg me to stop."

Oh, God. Did he mean that? Her body hoped he did, every word.

She swallowed a burning lump of lust. "Please."

Unable to stop herself, she lifted her hips to him one more time.

Deke didn't turn down the invitation to touch her.

He slipped a thick finger into her wet depths, swiping his thumb over her clit with the other. Electric sparks blended with pure magic to brush her skin with want, fire her blood with pure need. She mewled. When he repeated the process, and Luc bent to take her mouth in a kiss ripe with sensual demand, her mewls became low moans.

Luc swallowed the sounds and lifted his hand to cover her breast, fingers toying with her nipple, gently pinching, turning, awakening. He sent more bolts of lust south, down low, to join the heavy pulse of demand her body pumped out at each brush of Deke's thumb over her clit.

Legs taut, back bowed, Kimber felt the edge of climax drawing near. And they'd what, touched her for less than two minutes? She was drowning, flying, aching desperately—and didn't want it any other way.

Deke pushed a second finger inside her, fighting to slide his thick digits in. A sting became an ache as he muscled his way deeper inside her. Finally, her flesh swallowed him up and clamped down on him. He swore.

"She's burning me alive."

Luc nodded, breathing against her neck as he took her earlobe between his teeth. "Tell me how she feels."

Hedonistic Luc was encouraging Deke, trying to drive her over the edge with wicked words, flirting dangerously with Deke's ragged control.

"She's so damn tight and hot. Her pussy is gripping me. Clinging. Rippling. Fuck!"

"Pump her with your fingers."

Deke gasped and began to slide his fingers in and out of her tight passage. "Can't stop. Too fucking good to stop."

"Come for us, sweetheart." Luc whispered in her ear, brushing his thumbs across so-sensitive nipples.

Kimber felt swollen everywhere. Strung tight. Ached inside her own skin. Damp with perspiration, wet with need, blood raced through her body. Her heart pumped. Her skin tingled. And still Deke kept that incessant, merciless thumb strumming her clit. His fingers slid in and out, plying some sensitive spot inside her sex she'd never found on her own.

Luc whispered against her mouth, "You look beautiful. I can't wait to watch you scream in climax."

Then, with insistent fingers, he plucked at her aching nipple.

Too much. It was all too much to resist. Holding out wasn't an option.

Heat built. Blood roared. Kimber held her breath, whimpered, moaned—before the pleasure condensed between her legs into a concentrated burst of energy that exploded like a supernova, sending her hurtling deep into a realm of ecstasy she'd never imagined.

"Yes!" Deke's fingers stayed lodged in her, and she could feel her sex clutch him, squeezing, releasing, caressing him again. "Yes. Again," he demanded. "Come again."

She moaned. "I don't think I can."

Luc laughed, low and amused and thrumming with sensual promise. "We'll take care of you."

"But usually after once, I'm . . . spent."

Deke shook his head with sharp military precision or anger—or a bit of both. "Not with two men. You come repeatedly, until you're so exhausted you're nearly unconscious."

Unconscious? Kimber opened her mouth to argue, though she really didn't have the energy. And couldn't quite focus with his thumb continuing to play over her clit, making her twitch and pulse, prolonging her pleasure until her head spun. Until it slowly built to more. Until she ached again.

"That's right," Deke murmured.

Then he bent down to her. No preliminaries. No waiting. No warning. His tongue lashed her clit, assuming the same teasing movements as his thumb.

The sensations matched those he'd incited before, but felt more intense. Kimber filled with need, as if she'd never come at all. Only this time, the pleasure was stronger. Her body was primed, his mouth determined, and his will iron. She *would* come for him again. He would *not* take *no* for an answer.

And she watched, the visual of him feasting on her aroused her nearly as much as his actual touch. Within moments, the question of whether she'd come again ceased to be, morphing into a question of when. Kimber knew from her tensing body, the thickening pleasure, the way her legs spread wider all on their own, inviting Deke in deeper, that the *when* would be soon.

"Her taste?" Luc asked his cousin against the underside of her breast before he dragged her nipple into his mouth for a long, sensual suckle.

Kimber's breathing climbed, hitched.

"Fucking sweet," Deke muttered, lapping at her again like a treat. "Christ!"

Elation soared at his words. He approved. No, he enjoyed. His rough voice and uninhibited devouring told her that. He wasn't going to stop until he'd wrung every drop of pleasure from her that he could.

Luc rose above her then, his gaze penetrating her. Desire hardened his features. Dangerous. Predatory. He wasn't content to just watch. He expected his turn.

Her pleasure climbed, ratcheting up, every lick ramping her euphoria higher than before until it strung her so tight, she felt her clit fill with blood, pulse, moments away from incredible orgasm . . .

"Look at me when you come," Luc demanded.

Kimber did, her gaze helplessly fixed on his black stare.

Grabbing the sheet, Kimber arched up as the pleasure began to overwhelm her. "Luc . . ."

"Soon, I'll lick you. Suck you. Make you come."

"Yes," she panted.

Then Deke's tongue flicked her clit, devastating her control. "Oh, God. Oh . . . *Deke!*"

Ecstasy ripped the sound from her throat as light, color, sensation, and heat all rushed inside her, detonating through every nerve in her body. She jolted with the force, shook, perspiration making her body damp, her muscles turn as liquid as water.

As she lay back, trying to catch her breath, struggling to recover, Deke looked up from between her legs, his mouth red and wet and set in a determined line. "Once more, kitten."

Then he licked her again.

She didn't want to say no. Could she, even? Kimber doubted it. But she was so tired, turned inside out, and spent after two monster orgasms. And Luc still hadn't had a turn to send her flying into pleasure. And he wanted his chance. The way he stared at her even now told her he was done waiting.

"My turn," Luc insisted. "Before sweet Kimber passes out. And you have other things to prepare her for."

Other things? Kimber couldn't make her exhausted body support her lethargic thoughts so she could ponder what those other things might be.

But Deke apparently agreed—reluctantly—as he slid off the bed and disappeared to the other side of the room. She began to tip her head back and follow him with her gaze, but Luc snagged her attention by caressing a pair of elegant fingertips through her steamy, swollen slit, then slowly, so slowly, sliding them deep inside her.

"Lie back and enjoy," Luc murmured.

Tingles erupted, shocking her with their insistence, flaming to bright new life. She'd never believed that she was very sexual. She masturbated, yes, but rarely came more than once. Who knew she had two hard orgasms in a row in her? And the way she felt now, a third wasn't out of the question.

Kimber's eyes slid shut, and she let out a shuddering breath of tortured pleasure. *Lie back and enjoy.* Luc wasn't taking no for an answer. And she wasn't inclined to say it, anyway.

He prodded that sensitive spot inside her that Deke had quickly found as well and plied it—softly, yes, but without mercy. The need spiraled again, faster, hotter. The walls of her sex tightened, tingled, ached.

"Your vulva swells and turns rosy when you're aroused. It's fascinating to watch," Luc murmured.

His words made her clench with helpless arousal. Then he stimulated her clit with a long, lagging drag of his tongue.

Kimber cried out and clutched the sheets again.

"You smell . . ." He breathed deeply, taking her in through his nose. "Amazing. Spicy and hot and addicting. Which only makes me want to taste you more."

"Luc . . ."

Kimber didn't know if she was saying yes or no to the man. She only knew that he and Deke had managed to take her to a place where rational thought ceased, sensation ruled—and drove her completely out of her head.

"Stay where I can taste you," Luc said. "Take the pleasure I give you."

Kimber braced herself for another crash, for something even bigger, more powerful. The undertow of this one might knock her unconscious, but suddenly she was sure it would be worth it.

Then Deke muttered something low and unintelligible near Luc's ear. Her lashes fluttered open in time to see Luc nod. Then Deke's hands disappeared between her legs.

Her gaze connected with his. He burned, broiling her with the demand in his expression. He wanted to see her come again, under Luc's tongue. It was all there in his harsh stare. And he was going to help push her over the edge.

Not that Luc needed help, she thought, as he sucked her swollen clit into his mouth. Kimber clenched her teeth against the rush of sensations, but one piled on top of the other. The coming orgasm packed power, gnawed into her composure with sharp teeth, and began to unravel her. Then . . . oh, Luc's tongue flirted with the ultrasensitive tip of her clit, now peeking out from its protective folds. She screamed at the sensations, nearly climbing out of her skin.

They weren't done.

Sensing that her climax hovered moments away, Luc released her clit and backed off. "Not yet, sweetheart. Soon. There's more. And I want to savor you."

"No," she panted, so close now that sweat burst across her brow, between her breasts. "No. Now."

Luc chuckled. "Have a little patience."

"No," she repeated, looking between the two men.

"Yes," Deke insisted.

She focused on him as he leaned closer.

"Do it," he commanded Luc.

With a slow nod, the dark-haired hedonist reached for her legs, caressing his way up, up. "With pleasure."

Do what? They weren't going to make her come again. Yet. No matter how badly her body ached and needed, arched and yearned and turned to fire.

Luc answered her question when he curled his palms under her knees and lifted her legs, spreading them high and wide until they were folded against her body, resting above either hip. Leaving her wide open. For anything.

She breathed harder at the thought.

"Hold yourself here," Luc said, bringing her hands under her knees.

They both stared at her exposed sex, eyes hot, determined. No doubt, they were up to something. Something new. Wondering what that something was tied her stomach into knots of apprehension and need.

"Luc . . ."

"Don't beg him for mercy. He doesn't have any. I have even less. You wanted to learn about ménage, kitten. You want your virginity intact. That means we're going to invade that delectable ass."

Anal penetration. Now. She could see that fact in their eyes as their stares tumbled across her body, lingering on the swollen flesh between her widespread legs. Secretly, she'd wondered after overhearing one of her brothers wax practically poetic about anal sex. Yes, of course Deke and Luc were going to penetrate her there. How else could she take two men at once?

"Will it hurt?"

"Today will be simple," Luc assured. "Enough to give you the sensations without opening you too much."

Deke cut to the chase. "We won't fuck you here. Yet."

But soon, they would.

Kimber felt faint at the very thought of taking them into her body in the most primitive way possible and giving herself completely to them, letting the pleasure—and likely, the pain—drown her.

She sent them a shaky nod. "Okay."

"I wasn't waiting for your consent. You gave that to us when you walked through our front door, suitcase in hand."

Deke, again. And he sounded angry somehow. Or maybe he was just on the edge. The enormous erection still tenting his slacks had to require attention . . . And he was still staring at her sex hungrily, savage need lighting his deep blue eyes.

A part of her wanted to protest his arrogant speech. The presumption. Kimber bit her lip, logic telling her that he was right. And that his sexual frustration was doing the talking.

"I know."

Some of the tension left his body, then he looked down at Luc with a nod. "Finish it."

"She won't last long," Luc commented.

"Kimber may not respond to it." A shrug of Deke's massive shoulders was meant to give her the impression that he didn't care. But she sensed that he did care. Very much.

They didn't leave her wondering for long if she would respond. Moments later, she felt something cool and slippery nudging her back entrance. She tensed, having second thoughts. No, make that third and fourth thoughts. What were they invading her with? What if she didn't like it?

"Don't tense," Luc urged. "Push down just a bit. It isn't big . . ."

Biting her lip, Kimber tried to relax and push down on the invading object, clearly coated in lubricant. She was only half-committed to it, hedging her actions.

Until the fire in Deke's eyes skyrocketed. Until he was forced to rip off his pants, take his cock in hand, his stare all the while glued to Luc's gentle probing.

That she could get to him, force him to stroke his own flesh because she aroused him so much, made Kimber want to give him more of a show. She'd imagined she'd be hesitant and shy around Luc and Deke, but the feminine power of knowing she drove them to undeniable arousal burned away any timidity. She wanted to tease them.

Concentrating on Luc's instruction, she did as he suggested, and suddenly, something slender slid up, up, up into her ass. A gentle click later, and that something began to vibrate.

Oh my God!

Pleasure wound up again in seconds, tearing through her, soaring, shoving her hard toward ecstasy. Luc slid the vibe in and out of her gently, letting her adjust to the feel of the little wand rapidly destroying her sanity as she watched Deke stroke his own cock in a harsh fist. When Luc bent his head again to take her clit back into his mouth, the blaze between her thighs roared into an inferno, streaming fire into her belly, down her legs.

Her back arched as she panted. This climax was big. Huge. When it swelled over her, she feared the loss of consciousness they'd forewarned her about would suck her under and leave her there for hours. Days. She'd never imagined pleasure so consuming she couldn't take a breath, couldn't stop the black edges from closing in on her vision.

"She responds," Luc said with a hint of amusement as he slid his fingers into her waiting sex. "You ready to come?"

Kimber couldn't answer, couldn't do anything but whimper as the climax began to steamroll her.

"Fuck!" Deke cursed.

Through half-opened eyes, she watched him lean over her. He fused his mouth to hers, plunging his tongue inside, deep, then deeper, as if trying to get closer. Moments later, he stepped back to gasp in a desperate breath and continued to pump his cock. The sight was unbearably erotic. Totally arousing. Then Deke leaned in and kissed her again like a starving man, with savagery and demand, licking her deeper into the flames.

Knowing he couldn't stand not to stroke himself while he touched her filled her with erotic fascination and a heavy pang of need.

All the while, Luc was driving her mad with the vibe in her ass, his fingers inside her, and his mouth on her clit. Along with that kiss of Deke's . . . He possessed her, urging her on, silently begging to give him her cries of passion—all while driving himself toward ruthless orgasm.

And it was so much, too much. She couldn't stop it, couldn't fight it, and didn't want to.

She screamed into his mouth as the world blasted into tiny pieces all around, detonating her body, blowing her mind. The hard slam of contractions clenched the walls of her channel again and again, and she clamped down on Luc's questing fingers, making her moan into Deke's mouth all over again.

Suddenly, Deke broke the kiss, panting, frantically fisting his erection with a tight jaw and taut abdomen. Then he threw back his head and roared so loud, the sound bounced off the walls. Then warm jets of semen splashed on her belly, and another wave of sensation slammed her at the thought that she could make him come so powerfully.

"Deke!" she screamed.

* * *

KIMBER'S cry of pleasure was still ringing in Luc's ears when she closed her eyes and her body gave way to an exhausted sleep. Grimacing at his painful erection, he gently extracted the vibe and withdrew his fingers from her swollen, rippling sex. She felt exquisite and tasted better. But she'd had all the excitement she could handle for one evening.

And she'd called Deke's name out in her passion. Not his. Deke's.

Swallowing a boulder-sized lump of envy, Luc reminded himself it was all for a good cause and turned to gaze up at his cousin.

Deke stood frozen over Kimber's prone body, half-hard cock in his fist, satisfaction relaxing his features. He let go of himself on a long sigh, his shoulders falling, his breathing returning to normal, his eyes damn near rolling into the back of his head. Still, he stared at her.

He'd come—hard—holding nothing back, which was unusual in itself. But if Kimber could do that to Deke without his dick actually being somewhere inside her, Luc could only imagine the fireworks that would ensue if Deke allowed himself to make love to her. To admit that Kimber was more than a play toy. To confess that this woman mattered to him. And she did. Luc could see that all over his cousin's face.

"What the fuck are you staring at?" Deke snapped.

"Nothing."

Luc looked away, turning his attention back to Kimber's sleep-soft form. Sweet, beautiful woman.

Kimber was *it*. The One. The woman he and Deke had been wanting for years. Luc hid a smile of sheer joy. He *knew* Kimber was everything they needed: soft and yielding in bed, take no shit when she was angry, smart, warmhearted. She responded to their touch beyond his wildest fantasies. The fact she was a virgin would be cathartic for Deke.

As for the rest of the issues that could trip up their future . . . she'd understand—eventually.

But he'd deal with those later. First, he had to convince his cousin that happily-ever-after wasn't a cross between toxic waste and bullshit. Slowly. Luc knew that if he started his campaign tonight, it would be too obvious. Deke wasn't stupid. He knew that Luc wanted them to share a wife and children someday. If he focused too much on Kimber now, Deke would run screaming in the other direction. Best to move slowly and give Deke a gentle nudge here and a sharp nip there . . . then let nature take care of the rest.

"I was checking to see if you're in any shape to clean her up," Luc lied. "My legs are as stiff as meringue, and my dick isn't much better."

Deke grunted, glanced at Luc's tented slacks, then Kimber's silvery-wet abdomen.

"If it's a problem, I'll take care of her in a few minutes," Luc added.

Jaw tight, Deke cursed. "I'll take care of her."

I thought you might. "When you're finished, tuck her in, will you? I'm going to shower."

Deke hesitated, then finally nodded.

"Oh, and stay with her until I come back. She might wake up disoriented and be afraid."

"She's a grown woman."

"Who's had a very big night. I'm only asking for fifteen minutes, okay?"

Deke growled, "Make it ten. Unless there's sex involved, I don't want to be near her."

No big surprise there. Luc had his work cut out for him if he wanted to create a big, happy family.

"Sure, ten minutes."

Luc turned and left the room. He didn't look back, but had no doubt that Deke was already reaching out a hand toward the forbidden fruit of Kimber's pale skin—just for the pleasure of touching her. To remind himself he could touch her. To fantasize about touching her again.

Smiling, Luc eased the door to the bathroom shut, knowing deep in his gut that Deke wouldn't be able to resist doing far more than touching her for long.

Chapter Five

SWEAT filmed Deke as he rolled out of bed, gray fingers of dawn pushing their way beneath his shutters, mocking him. A night gone without sleep, spent alone, knowing that just down the hall, Luc and Kimber had shared body heat—and probably a lot more—without him.

Something ugly and hot surged inside him, cramping his gut. Deke didn't want to identify it. Then again, he didn't need to. Jealousy was damn near impossible to mistake.

Rolling from his bed, he crept down the hall, toward Luc's room. Stupid. Torture, self-inflicted no less. But he had to see. Had to know . . .

And now he did. *Fuck*. He grimaced at the sight of Kimber curled up on her side, her back cuddled to Luc's front, their legs entwined. The pair of them were tangled in soft white sheets, and Luc's sleep-slack palm rested just under her breast.

They looked peaceful. Domestic. Content.

Three things he would never be. Not that he deserved it. He'd destroyed Heather, so innocent—

Breaking off the thought with a curse, Deke stalked back down the hall to his room. Exercise. This day was like any other, despite Kimber's presence here and his crappy mood.

Push-ups first. He dropped down and started his first fifty. Sweat coated him as he counted out each one, then he rolled to his back for a hundred crunches. All the while, he could hear every rustle of sheets down the hall, every murmured good morning, every lazy stretch Kimber and Luc made. Every forbidden intimacy that Deke didn't dare partake in.

Don't whine. It's done and past, he told himself.

True, except . . . Luc always woke up horny, so Deke knew what would happen next. Why the hell hadn't he ever bought an iPod or put even a simple radio in his room, so he wouldn't have to hear it?

Deke grabbed free weights and quickly worked through biceps, triceps, lats, and pecs, reminding himself that Luc deserved any happiness he found with a woman. Luc always saw the good in people, always tried to help, took time to laugh, put his heart on the line to love time and again. And Deke . . . Well, he knew better.

Suddenly, Kimber laughed. The soft lilting floated down the hall as Deke dropped down for another set of ab crunches. He gritted his teeth. Then Kimber's sighs reached his ears. First one. Then another, deeper, longer—one that went straight to his cock and felt like a stab in the gut at once.

The twisted surge of jealousy gouged him again, doing absolutely nothing to improve his mood and everything to multiply his desire to hit something and do damage.

Focus. Squats and hamstrings in alternating reps. The usual drill. But concentrating on the usual felt impossible when he imagined Luc's hands caressing their way up the sleek lines of Kimber's torso to toy with her flushed rosy nipples, while he inhaled the peach-spiced fragrance of her skin and waited with his signature patience, whispering a few well-placed words that would make her beyond wet. Then, with tongue swirling around the hard buds of her breasts, he'd smooth his way back down her abdomen, urge her to spread her sweet thighs for him, then slide his fingers into the slick haven of her pussy to feel her tight walls close around him like paradise.

Deke's gut clenched. Doing squats while his cock was hard enough to pound nails wasn't happening.

Especially when Kimber's sighs suddenly became cries.

Fuck this. He stripped off his sweat-drenched clothes and headed for a cold shower.

Ten minutes alone in the Italian-tiled box with water just shy of freezing and a healthy lather perfumed with Luc's fussy-scented soap only pissed him off more.

Growling, Deke stepped out, praying they'd be done in their quest for a morning orgasm by now. He hadn't even finished toweling off the beaded moisture on his chest and abs when he heard Kimber cry out in a sound lush, sensual, tortured. Pleading. *Well, hell. There went all the benefits of a cold shower.*

Deke finished drying off, concentrating on the pattern of the Venetian plaster wall. But he couldn't block out the sexual sounds of the pleasure Luc was giving Kimber.

The door between the bathroom and Luc's adjoining bedroom was ajar, and Kimber's needy moans invaded mercilessly. First breathy, then keening. She was getting close.

"Please, Luc . . ."

Fuck.

And that's exactly what he wanted to do to her, settle right between her sweet thighs and be the first one to sink deep inside her. That wasn't going to happen. She didn't want that; he couldn't let it happen.

But you can join them.

Damn if he wasn't sorely tempted. He had every right. Full and equal sharing; he and Luc had agreed to it over a decade ago, and they'd never wavered. So why was he begrudging Luc his one-on-one pleasure with Kimber? He'd never minded this before. And why turn down the chance to join in this morning?

Kimber Edgington was too tempting, too sweet and responsive. Too innocent and vulnerable. Too dangerous for his peace of mind. Too . . . everything he'd wanted for years. If he marched in Luc's room, all naked and demanding, he'd get sucked into her allure and start drowning. Last night, the urge to spread her legs, settle between them, and claim her had beat at him relentlessly. If anything, that urge had grown, like some freaking weed in a perfectly manicured garden. He had to get control of it before it took over. Before he touched her again and lost control and did something crazy and irrevocable. Fatal.

Snarling, Deke reached for sweat shorts and a T-shirt, then tossed them on over his unrelenting morning erection. Coffee. He needed it now.

He started down the hall, then faltered as he passed Luc's room. The sight of them punched him like a battering ram to the gut. Luc with his dark head bent in the crook of her neck, his long hair trailing over her porcelain pale shoulders and breasts. His artistic fingers toyed between her spread thighs. From Deke's viewpoint, Kimber's arousal was obvious, considering her slick, swollen, nearly red folds.

"I'm dying to make you scream," Luc murmured. "Once you ache so badly you're ready to beg."

"Luc, now. Please." She groaned and clutched her fingers in his hair. "Please!"

"Soon, sweetheart. Let it build."

Her head thrashed from side to side. "Can't take more."

Kimber's pleading clawed at Deke's gut.

"You can. A little more . . ."

Luc withdrew his fingers from her wet, swollen pussy to caress her thighs, her abdomen—and ignoring her hips when she thrust them his way. Deke couldn't ignore it. Wouldn't.

He took a step into the room, hand pushing at his sweat shorts, shoving them down to his hips, intent, savage with hunger.

Fuck her. He needed to—had to get inside her and sink deep. Be the first one.

Now.

"Luc . . . touch me."

Her throaty cry seared Deke, bringing him out of his daze of desire. She'd asked for his cousin to touch her, not for him to fuck her. *Holy shit.* What was he thinking?

Nothing he should be thinking.

In fact, he shouldn't be here, wanting to be inside her. Claiming her. Worse, hoarding her and taking her from the man whose name she called. Only bad things would happen if he had sex with Kimber. He'd taken a virgin before and knew that for a fact.

Deke yanked up his shorts, turned, and stalked down the hall, barely holding in an ugly curse. Two weeks with Kimber here . . . He'd never last without fucking her, without destroying her.

The kitchen tile slapped cool against his bare feet as he entered the room and grabbed the coffee grounds from the pantry. He glanced at the bag. Chocolate caramel truffle. Pansy-ass flavored coffee. Whatever happened to just coffee? He slammed the pantry door.

Tossing the bag on the counter next to the coffeemaker, Deke paused. "Luc!"

Another plea from Kimber. *Hell.* He squeezed his eyes shut and let out a ragged breath.

A moment later, he flipped open the coffeemaker's lid; it cracked and popped off, making a plastic crunch sound that couldn't be good. Then the damn thing tumbled to the floor. Cursing again, Deke grabbed the edge of the counter. Every muscle in his body was tense, all the way from his brows slashing down over narrowed eyes to his toes curled into the Italian slate beneath them.

Get your shit together, he castigated himself and fit the lid back on the coffeemaker, filled it with grounds and water, then flipped the *on* switch.

At the same time, Luc apparently flipped Kimber's switch.

"Oh, Luc!" she cried out, followed by a long, tortured groan.

So she'd come finally—under Luc's hands, fueled by Luc's touch.

Why the hell did that make Deke want to hit something? Or someone?

He'd be better off not examining it too hard.

Instead, he watched the coffee drip, doing his best to keep his mind perfectly blank and focused on the task at hand—nice little Special Ops trick he could thank the army for.

A few minutes later, Luc emerged from his room in crisp jeans, shirt in hand, and wandered down the hall, his posture relaxed. And no visible raving hard-on. "Morning."

"Did she get you off with her hands or mouth?"

The question was out of Deke's mouth before he could stop it. It wasn't any of his business. Knowing wouldn't change Kimber's moans of pleasure still ringing in his ears or the visible satiation softening his cousin's face.

Luc propped his hip against the kitchen counter, crossed his arms over his chest, and quirked a dark brow.

Before Luc could answer, Deke said, "Never mind. It doesn't matter."

He busied himself grabbing cups in the cupboard above, then retrieving the sugar and cream for Luc. All the while, he felt his cousin's gaze on him, sizing up the situation, deciding how best to reply. Crafty bastard.

"Neither."

Something of a nonanswer. And damn it, Luc's face gave away nothing. All of Kimber's pleading . . . Luc hadn't been working his way inside of Kimber when he'd peeked in on them—but he also hadn't stayed for the grand finale. Had he . . . ?

"You didn't fuck her." Deke stated his question as fact, hoping that could somehow make it true.

"What's eating you?" Luc asked. "If you want her this morning, she's all soft and rumpled and wet. And she's still in bed. Go. I'll babysit the coffee."

Deke hesitated. Show that he could resist or march down the hall— by himself—and get as much of Kimber as Luc had? If he could, he'd take even more.

He'd take everything.

The coffeemaker beeped, and Luc extracted the fresh pot off the burner and poured a cup, wearing a faint smile, as he knew exactly the options Deke was weighing.

This game playing was bullshit, and he didn't want to be on either team.

"Fuck! This isn't going to work. Kimber has to go."

"Keep your voice down or she'll hear you," Luc whispered, irritated.

That would be for the best. He didn't want to hurt her feelings, just make her go away.

"Why do you think she has to go?" Luc asked in low tones. "You can't think she's unable to learn what we have to teach her."

Deke rolled his eyes. "Don't play stupid. She can learn. Obviously. I know she's not scared. She should be, but for some crazy reason, she isn't. But that isn't the issue."

"Hmm. I think I know what the issue is, but why don't you explain it to me in your words."

"Remember? She's a virgin."

"Whose name isn't Heather."

"She has nothing to do with Kimber. We're not rehashing the past again."

Luc cocked his head and slid him a considering stare. "We never hashed it in the first place, which is part of the problem. But fine, you don't want to discuss Heather. Tell me another reason you have for avoiding Kimber."

Deke hesitated, then realized he wouldn't be telling anything Luc didn't already know. "Nothing I didn't warn you about before. She's blowing past my self-control. If she stays, I'm going to disrespect her wishes. Sooner or later, she'll beg, and I won't have the will to say no. I will fuck her."

"If Kimber begs, we'll reevaluate the situation. Maybe it would be in everyone's interest if we give her exactly what she asks for."

The idea of Luc being the one to take Kimber's virginity made him feel as if his guts had been churned in a blender then spit back out. But he could never take her, especially not alone. Ever. "You think she's ours."

Luc responded slowly. "Anything is possible. I'm hard-pressed to believe that a woman would respond so perfectly the very first time if, in her heart, she belonged to someone else."

"Has it escaped your memory that she's here to have us train her to accept the touch of two other men, one of whom she thinks she's in love with?"

"No. I merely think she's trying to find her future and hoping that Jesse McCall is the right path. I also don't think it will take her long to sort it all out for herself."

"Which is Luc-speak for you think that Kimber belongs with us and she'll come to that conclusion quickly." *Freakin' amazing*. Deke shook his head. "You're delusional, you know that? At best, Kimber is really applying herself to learning all about ménage so she can live it with someone else. At worst, she's just horny. But you've got to get rid of this idea that there's some perfect woman out there who wants to play house with us until death do us part."

"She's out there." He sounded confident. "But that somewhere may be miles away or just down the hall. We don't know yet."

Deke shook his head, poured himself a cup of coffee, and counted to ten. Which did absolutely no good. The frustration still boiled up inside him, rising, drowning good sense and restraint.

"I don't want a wife. I don't want anything but a good fuck, and she isn't it."

Luc said nothing for a full ten seconds. "Then you have nothing to worry about except keeping your word. She's overcome her anxiety about being here and forgiven you for the terrible way you treated her when she first arrived."

Shit. Luc didn't just state that they couldn't go back on their promise to teach her all about ménage. But he implied it in every syllable.

"Besides," Luc added. "It's not as if we're her only options. Have you forgotten the Catrell brothers?"

No. The sight of Adam and Burke with their hands on her was burned into his brain.

"I don't think she wants them."

"But she may be determined enough to learn to go with them, anyway."

True. Deke sighed. Kimber had him by the balls—in more ways than one.

"Think of it as keeping her occupied so we can protect her from the Catrell brothers, whom we know far too much about to kid ourselves," Luc said.

Yeah. They were hard on their women. The tag team that never quit. They'd use her, grind her into little pieces, and spit her out when she couldn't keep up.

Basically, he was screwed if he let her stay and screwed if he let her go.

"Fine. She's here for the next thirteen days. Not a minute more."

Luc smiled as he shrugged on his shirt, took another swig of his coffee, and shuffled over to the sandals he kept by the back door. "I have to run to a local radio interview. We'll have this chat again in thirteen days. In the meantime . . . Kimber is all sleep-soft and very sweet this morning"—he licked his lips—"help yourself."

As Deke watched his cousin grab his car keys and head out the door, he restrained the urge to hit walls, blocks of wood—Luc's head—and cursed.

Help himself? Deke would love to. But it wasn't going to happen. There was way more at stake than Kimber's virginity and sophomoric crush on Jesse McCall. Way more than petty jealousy. And damn if Luc didn't know it and plotted to tempt him.

He might as well start counting the days, probably on one hand, before he wound up breaking through Kimber's barriers—mental and physical. It was inevitable.

And when it happened, everyone was going to suffer, Kimber most of all.

* * *

SHE woke for the second time that morning alone in Luc's cozy, downy bed, tossed on someone's discarded shirt—Luc's?—and padded down the hall. Heavy-limbed and flushed, Kimber made her way toward the smell of fresh coffee. But she couldn't pretend anxiety didn't claw her.

When she reached the kitchen, the sight of Deke hunched over a cup of coffee, lost in his thoughts, brought her to a stop. Especially since they didn't look like happy thoughts.

Of course they weren't. She was underfoot, and he didn't want her here. She hadn't heard any other part of his argument with Luc, but that sentiment had come through loud and crystal clear.

Which explained why she'd fallen asleep last night with Deke by her side, only to awaken twenty minutes later to find him gone. And why each time she'd awakened during the restless night, she'd found only Luc beside her. Not only had Deke chosen to sleep elsewhere, but he'd refused to come within five feet of her this morning after Luc had devoured her. The *why* behind that pressed sadness and shame down into her chest with crushing intensity.

Despite Deke's seeming eagerness last night, after the orgasm he'd apparently lost interest in her. Because he still saw her as a teenager? Because he liked and respected her dad too much? Maybe. But those hang-ups would be easy. A little nudge from her would get him past either. He wouldn't be staring morosely into his coffee about those issues. The real problem would be harder to get past, especially if it was the one she'd had her entire dating life.

"Hi," she murmured.

His head snapped up, and he drilled her with a stare that seemed at once hot and accusing. He drew in a deep breath. Bracing himself?

"Coffee?" he asked finally.

"Sure. I'll get it."

"Cups are in the cupboard above the coffeemaker."

Kimber nodded and retrieved her cup . . . and wondered what to say next. What was there to say? Should she apologize for the fact her tomboy ways seemed to turn him off? Once the skirt and lacy under-things had come off and he'd seen the real her, maybe it had been too . . . masculine. He wouldn't be the first guy in her life to think that—just ask her prom date.

Cursing reality wouldn't do a bit of good. She couldn't escape the fact that after being raised motherless by military men, the Colonel and her two Navy SEAL brothers had been her role models. She liked fatigues, enjoyed a good five-mile run at o-five-hundred, hated panty hose, lace, and makeup. Most guys swore she had testosterone running through her veins. But the fun of flipping one over her shoulder and straight onto his back or drinking him under the table had lost appeal long ago. She wanted men to see her as a real female, not one of the guys who happened to have breasts.

With Deke and Luc, she'd been as girly as she knew how. By all appearances it hadn't been enough. All that want Deke said he he'd been harboring for her for years . . . More than likely, she'd cured him of it last night.

Changing wasn't an option. She liked herself. Screw anyone who didn't, Deke included. Yes, he turned her on. A lot. A hell of a lot. Even when she'd been seventeen, he'd fueled some dark fantasies in her adolescent brain. But in two weeks, she'd be with Jesse. He accepted her tomboy ways, even told her he found it adorable. This . . . fear eating at her hardly mattered.

So why couldn't she shake it now?

"Sleep good?" she asked into the thick silence.

"No."

She noticed he didn't ask her in turn. Probably didn't care. "Me, either."

Deke grunted and sipped his coffee. He avoided looking at her.

Damn, she had to get this off her chest. Stewing in self-doubt wasn't her style.

Taking a fortifying sip of her own coffee, she sank into the chair across from him. "You didn't sleep with us last night."

"So?"

"Why?"

"We covered why last night." A muscle in his jaw ticced.

"And your insomnia is the only reason?"

He paused, and those deep blue eyes flashed with something—anger?—but he dropped his gaze to his half-full coffee cup before she could be sure.

"Kitten, don't dig into my psyche on this. You won't like the answer."

That, she didn't doubt. If she dug, she'd probably find out that he'd once wanted her but realized last night that she was nothing like whatever feminine fantasy woman he'd conjured up in his head. And now he wanted her gone because he didn't want to repeat last night. His honor, along with Luc, had bullied him into letting her stay.

Fine. Just fine. She could live with that. Revel in it, in fact. All she cared about was what he and his cousin could teach her. Deke didn't have to actually desire her. It was probably better if he didn't, since she was responding to him more than physically.

But she couldn't just leave it. Not her style. "I probably won't like the answer, but if it's going to affect your ability to live up to your end of the bargain to teach me—"

"I'll keep up my end. You'll learn everything you need and probably more than you want."

"Good."

But Kimber's relief was both uneasy and short-lived.

"Don't be too happy." Deke picked up his coffee cup and stared at her over the rim. "Luc has this fucked-up notion that you're going to fall in love with us and want to ditch your pop star boyfriend to marry us and have our babies."

Marriage? Babies? Kimber gasped. She did want those things some-day, but she was set on Jesse. He'd known the real her for years, accepted her as is. That wasn't true of Deke or Luc. "Seriously?"

Deke nodded sharply. "I don't want to encourage that notion. You shouldn't want to, either. So that means, unless there's something sexual going on at the moment, stay the fuck away from me."

No one would ever fault Deke for beating around the bush. Kimber had known from the start that he was anti-relationship. Not that she wanted one with him, but if she was going to allow him incredible inti-macies with her body, touch him skin to skin, and live under his roof, shouldn't they at least be able to talk?

"Is Luc here now?"

"No."

Kimber frowned. "He can't get the wrong idea if we talk while he's gone."

"I don't want to talk. You came to learn all about ménage. We're go-ing to teach you. But we're not best friends, I don't give a shit what you think about, and I've got nothing to say."

Defensive and *closed*. Those were the best words to describe Deke. Oh, the offense came through, but that was his defense. He wasn't just morning crabby; she knew him well enough to know that he liked morn-ings. He hadn't been troubled by anything last night.

He hadn't been troubled until he'd gotten a firsthand taste of how feminine she wasn't.

His instinct had been to refuse her request. Now he was probably kicking himself for letting her and Luc manipulate him into this arrangement. He was probably thinking it was going to be the longest two weeks of his life.

Her brothers often congratulated her on being one of the few females they knew who could contain their emotions, but the unruly things snapped up and bit her now. And she felt wretched. Hurt. She hated it.

"Fine. I've got nothing to say, either. Be an asshole. As long as you're a good tutor, I don't care."

Kimber stood and waltzed past Deke, toward the exit.

He grabbed her arm and pulled her down damn near into his lap. "Kitten, I'm going to be the best tutor you could possibly imagine. Don't you doubt that."

"Glad to hear it." She yanked free of his grip. "I'll respect the fact you don't want me to talk to you when we're not in bed, as long as you don't touch me unless you're teaching me. So until tonight, you leave *me* the fuck alone."

Deke hesitated, a bitter smile lifting the corners of his mouth. "Kitten, that's the best idea you've had since you walked through that door."

* * *

DINNER passed in silence, despite the fact Luc had grilled damn fine pork chops and brushed them with a delectable maple-cranberry glaze. Luc shrugged off the chilled silence. The army had taught Deke to eat anything—mess hall grease, MREs, the side of a raw goat—as long as it kept him alive. Luc's palette was a bit fussier. And Kimber . . . The way she darted venomous glares at Deke through the meal told Luc that she and his cousin had exchanged unpleasant words earlier that day.

And the way Deke watched her told Luc that his cousin's hunger wasn't going to be sated by scrumptious pork or the blackberry-peach crisp he'd baked earlier.

Behind his napkin, Luc smiled. Cross words aside, everything was falling into place perfectly. Time to add a little fuel to the fire . . .

Luc reached across the space separating him from Kimber and caressed his way up her arm, which was bared by a small spaghetti-strapped tank top. Then he brushed the back of his knuckles over her cheek. *Hmm, soft. So sweet.* And so pissing Deke off, a slanted glance in that direction told him.

"More salad, sweetheart?" Luc asked.

"No." She relaxed enough to smile at him. "I'm stuffed. With all your wonderful cooking, I won't fit into my pants soon."

He leaned in to steal a slow, gentle kiss right on her lips, still tasting faintly of the tangy glaze he'd prepared with the meal. Across the table, Deke tensed. His fork clattered to his plate. Luc ignored him.

"With the two of us around, you really don't need pants. Isn't that right, Deke?"

Luc curled his hand around Kimber's naked shoulder and softly stroked her, all the while watching her nipples peak under the little white shirt and his cousin's gaze heat dangerously.

"Is everyone done eating?" Deke barked, standing, hovering over the table.

Kimber pushed back and shot Luc an uncertain glance. Worry; he saw that in her gaze. Uh-oh, what the hell had Deke said or done to put her on edge?

"That's up to Kimber. We can sit for a bit longer, if you'd like, sweetheart."

Deke tossed down his napkin. "If you want your tutoring tonight, kitten, it's now or never. I've got better things to do than sit here and chat."

Luc registered Kimber tensing under his hand. *Oh, the fireworks are about to begin.*

"You've made that clear. I don't want to be a bother to you. Maybe I should just follow Luc down the hall to his room. You can . . . run along."

Chin held high, Kimber stood and, despite wearing a fatigue-print mini skirt and a tank top sans bra, breezed past him as regally as a queen.

The stunned look on Deke's face was priceless.

His cousin spun around and followed Kimber down the hall. Luc scrambled to follow them. He wanted them riled, but not so furious they'd fight, rather than fuck.

Kimber nearly made it to Luc's bedroom door before Deke grabbed her, shoved her back to the wall, and covered her body with his.

"I promised we'd teach you all about ménage, kitten. That means three. I'm not going anywhere except to bed with you."

She opened her mouth to protest—no, more likely to issue a scathing retort—but Deke preempted her with a scorching kiss, covering her mouth with his, invading and devouring. Hell, just the sight of them turned Luc on, especially since he could see Kimber's tense rejection changing and softening with every lash of Deke's tongue against hers. She moaned when one of his cousin's hands sailed down her back, curled around her ass, and lifted her hips right up to his.

No doubt, Deke wanted inside her—bad. *Perfect.*

He tore his mouth away, but his body still covered hers, drilling her into the wall. And he stared, panting as if he'd run twenty miles. He didn't look away.

Luc forced his way between them and put an arm around each, filing them through his bedroom door. "Let's go inside and get comfortable and naked so we can enjoy ourselves, shall we?"

Around him, Deke shot Kimber a tense stare. What the hell was going on?

"Sweetheart, is that okay?" Luc asked.

Her gaze skittered to him before going to back to his cousin. At that point, her skin was flushed, her nipples like enticing hard candies. Luc did his best to focus on the long-term goal, rather than rushing Kimber out of her clothes now.

She visually clung to Deke, eyeing him with reluctant hunger. With every moment that passed in thick silence, Deke grew more tense. *Very interesting . . .*

"Okay," Kimber finally whispered.

That one word was all it took to send Deke into action. He snaked a hand across Luc's body and reached for Kimber. One arm he wrapped around her waist and brought her against him. The other he used to push the spaghetti straps off her shoulders and shove the garment down her torso.

Leaving her breasts and rosy, swollen nipples bare to their gazes.

Luc had been hard before, almost uncomfortably so. This pushed him firmly into unbearable territory.

Deke looked back at him with eyes so burning with sexual need and frustration, they were damn near glowing. "Now."

His cousin couldn't wait to touch her and wouldn't waste his time stating the obvious. And as much as Luc enjoyed savoring a woman, something about Kimber and the way Deke responded to her simply didn't allow for the sort of cool distance that made patience possible.

Instead, Luc sent his cousin a terse nod.

As he approached, Kimber gasped, her eyes wide and dilated. Hesitation stamped her face, but need followed, as if sensing it was too late to stop the hungry seduction her body was about to endure. Tonight, they'd take her further, push her harder.

Eagerness sang through his bloodstream like good wine.

When he reached Kimber's side, Deke had positioned himself at her right. He settled on her left.

"Luc?" she whispered, looking for reassurance.

Did she feel the barely leashed violence of their need hovering in the air? He bet she did. And that it frightened and thrilled her at once. She had good reason for her fear. In the decade plus that he and Deke had been sharing women, Luc had never seen his cousin more intense, more driven. He would take everything she was willing to give. Right now. And push for more.

Deke's need fed his own, until Luc felt primal and deliciously aroused.

"Buckle up, sweetheart," Luc whispered. "This is going to be one amazing ride."

He'd barely finished the sentence before Deke bent down, cupping her breast in one hand and lifting it to his descending mouth. Luc followed suit, sliding her other nipple against his tongue. He glided gentle fingers over the curve of her hip to counteract the tingle of hard pulls and nipping teeth he knew they were both unleashing on her turgid nipples.

Kimber gasped, back arching. She stood on tiptoes as if she was trying to absorb the sensation or get closer to their suckling mouths—or both. She reached a fist into his hair, grasping, holding him against her breast. Luc reveled in the little sting on his scalp, her fingers clutching at him, helpless against the onslaught of pleasure.

The sounds of constant laving, voracious sucking—her hard breathing—punctuated the still air. She was perfect, her nipples hardening against his tongue with every fresh lick . . .

Suddenly, at his side, Deke snarled, "Let's get on with this."

Ah, the plan, the one they'd worked out while Kimber had been holed up in the den studying and Deke had been pacing the kitchen, acting as if he were about to crawl out of his skin with impatience, while Luc cooked.

Reluctantly, he lifted his head from the sugared perfection of Kimber's breast. There would be time later. If things worked out, a lifetime of it. As soon as he appeased the hungry beast beside him. Truth be told, the thought of what could happen tonight roused the beast in him, too.

Knowing it was way too soon for that, he pushed it back down.

At the loss of their touch, Kimber moaned, the sound small and pleading. Luc risked a glance at her breasts. He swallowed. Already her nipples were deep red, visibly swollen, and so damn hard. The sight made him want to forget his plans and instead spend his night giving her beautiful breasts constant attention.

"Now." Impatience resonated in Deke's demand.

Down, boy, down. Luc sent his cousin a warning stare before turning back to Kimber. Gently, he eased off her miniskirt and removed her thong. God, she was gorgeous. Slender, but with curves. Lean and athletic without looking masculine. Tall enough to be graceful, but not so tall that she looked awkward. Just . . . perfect.

Luc smiled at the thought and took her shoulders in his hand. "Sweetheart, last night was all about getting you accustomed to accepting the touch of two men."

Despite dazed, slightly dilated eyes, she nodded. "I know."

"You did well. Really well. Tonight is about seeing how much pleasure you can dish out. This will be more challenging since you want us to leave your virginity intact and you're not yet ready to accept one of us in that sweet backside."

Kimber paused, clearly puzzling his words out. "I don't know anything about oral sex."

He smoothed a hand over her shoulder, soothing her. "We'll work through it together."

Biting her lip, she sent him a shaky nod. Then she smoothed her tongue across her bruised lip, and the sight punched Luc with a fresh bout of pure lust.

Beside him, Deke appeared to lose all patience—and self-control. He put his hand on her shoulder and urged her to her knees before him. Kimber fell slowly, an uncertain inch at a time, her gaze never leaving Deke's. It traveled up as she went down, and the sight kicked Luc with a jolt of lust.

Then he sighed. Guess that settled the question of who would partake of Kimber's silken mouth first.

Kneeling behind her, Luc tore off his shirt, watching as Deke ripped off his own and tossed it across the room, then began to unbutton his old-school, button-fly jeans, one button at a time. Luc settled in behind Kimber, easing his hands on her shoulders, observing her as she watched Deke reveal a wedge of muscled abdomen, a strip of light brown pubic hair, then, as he shoved his jeans off, the entire length of his cock.

Deke stroked his erection, as if he couldn't stand another minute without stimulation. Luc related to that. He grimaced as he adjusted himself, sat behind Kimber, and touched his hands to her bare hips, then roamed her soft flesh.

"Touch him," Luc murmured.

"What?"

Luc couldn't keep his hands from wandering, across her hip, around to her belly, up to her breast. He flicked his thumbs across her pebbled nipples. Still hard. He'd love to know exactly how wet she was. Soon . . . *Patience, damn it.* Right now, he couldn't distract her.

"Take Deke in your hand and stroke him, just like he's doing to himself."

So slowly Luc could feel his sweat drip, Kimber reached out and grabbed Deke's hard flesh in her hand. Up, up . . . until she clasped the tip, ran her thumb across the head. Deke groaned so loud, his entire chest rumbled with sound.

"Good instincts," Luc praised. "Down and up again."

Kimber repeated the process once, twice, faster, coordinating her movements a bit more.

"I can hardly get my hand around him."

She frowned in concentration and brought her other hand up to Deke's cock to join the first, wrapping her slender fingers around his girth. Now she totally encompassed him, stroking him with more vigor, watching Deke's face as those blue eyes women drooled over slid shut and he threw his head back in brilliant pleasure.

"Good," Luc muttered. "Now lick your lips. Yes, like that." He couldn't resist kissing the side of her neck, nibbling on her earlobe. "Lean in, open wide, and take him in your mouth."

The look she shot him over her shoulder, of hot curiosity, of naughty anticipation, just about unraveled Luc. Damn, simmering under that seemingly straightforward surface lurked a tease. A vixen. He'd bet if they gave her a little control in the bedroom, she'd come out and play.

"Now!" Deke demanded.

"Say please," she taunted.

Luc couldn't quite hold in a laugh. Apparently, she already got the idea that when she held a man in her palm, the promise of her mouth ripe in his fevered mind, she had all the power.

"Fuck!"

"Wrong word . . ." Kimber shot him a kittenish smile.

Deke swallowed. His fists tightened at his sides as he drew in a bracing breath. "Please."

The word sounded gritty and unused. But it worked for Kimber.

Slanting one last challenging glance up at Deke, she put her hands on his hips and leaned in.

Tilting around her, Luc watched with both raging need and envy as Deke's cock entered her mouth, cushioned by her slick tongue. He slid in, more and more of his length disappearing into the depths of her virgin mouth.

God, the sight alone was killing him. Deke's long moan vibrated pleasure in his gut. His desire multiplied. He could only imagine how fabulous Kimber felt.

When she'd taken as much of Deke as she could, she drew back and repeated the process, taking another inch. Deke loosed another groan, clutching at her hands as they held him steady.

"Yes," Luc breathed. "Now suck him. Hard. He likes it hard."

Her cheeks hollowed on the next upward stroke. And the one after. Deke gritted his teeth.

"Fighting the urge already?" Luc asked him.

"Fuck off."

Deke had barely managed to choke out the words. Kimber was getting to him—fast. Luc had never seen anything like it. Usually, his dear cuz could be bathed in a woman's mouth for twenty minutes and look unmoved. Everything was so been there, done that with Deke.

Except when Kimber touched him. The telltale tightening of Deke's abs and the flush crawling up his cheeks told Luc just how close his cousin was to losing control.

Time to finish him off.

"You're doing great," Luc whispered to Kimber. He noticed the cadence of her bobbing head and instructed, "Now a little slower. Make him suffer. Good. Cup his balls in one hand."

Kimber did exactly as he said, fondling Deke's testicles, which were drawing up toward his body with every sweet suck of her mouth. Even watching them made breathing damn hard—to say nothing of his dick.

Reaching out with a blind fist, Deke grabbed Kimber by the hair. Luc nearly stopped his cousin and broke the hold, but she moaned—and not in pain.

Ah, so she liked a little edge to her pleasure. Luc smiled. He'd definitely be able to provide some for her, but Deke was especially well equipped to give her a sting here and there.

As soon as Kimber got Deke to come.

"That's it, sweetheart. Suck him. Hard and slow. You're getting to him," Luc whispered. "He can't last against the sweet temptation of your mouth. Lick the head with your tongue. Perfect. Yes."

Deke groaned, as if lending credence to Luc's assertion. His thighs tensed. His fist tightened in Kimber's hair. "Holy . . . I can't stop it."

Luc smiled. "Good girl. Now, drag you teeth lightly across the head."

"No," Deke groaned in protest.

"Do it," he urged. "Then suck him hard again. He'll come for you."

Supporting the thick stalk between Deke's legs with one hand, Kimber eased up on him and dragged her teeth across the head. The sight even had Luc hissing.

"Shit . . . *Kimber!*"

"Now suck him deep and hard, and you've got him," Luc whispered.

She did, and Deke roared, tossing back his head and shouting out his ecstasy, the sound rumbling around the room, echoing off the ceilings.

Kimber froze, eyes widening with uncertainty and panic.

"Swallow, sweetheart. It's okay."

She did, and Luc watched her swollen mouth and throat work. Need and envy shot through him. God, she was beautiful and amazing. And, thank God, he'd feel her mouth next.

Slowly, Deke pulled away. She moaned as she continued to lick him, as if not quite ready to let go.

At this point, Deke usually gloved up, went straight for a woman's ass and left Luc to either partake of her mouth or pussy. He often left arousing and toying with a woman up to him, which was fine with Luc. To him, women were sweet, soft, perfumed creatures meant to be explored, charted with fingers and tongues, every secret crevice and sensitive spot learned by sight and feel.

So Deke kneeling in front of Kimber to stare at her, like she was something as precious as hope, as confounding as an ancient riddle, surprised Luc enough. Him easing to his back, grabbing Kimber's hips and nudging her up, up and over his face shocked Luc.

"Have to taste you," he muttered. "Know how wet . . ."

The moment her thighs bracketed Deke's head, he lifted his mouth to her wet cunt, and delivered an open-mouthed assault. He clasped her hips and threw his entire torso into the intimate kiss. A startled moan ripped from Kimber's chest, and she reached out for something, someone, to steady her.

On wobbly legs, Luc rose and made his way to the bed to watch them. He'd join the show soon, but watching Kimber come apart a little more with every lash of his cousin's tongue and, now he could see, every demanding swish of his fingers inside her, made Luc beyond hot.

Deke turned his head to nip at Kimber's thigh. "The vibe."

It took Luc a moment after hearing the snarled words to realize what Deke was saying. Yes. They needed to start that. They'd enjoy watching Kimber squirm and flush and come while they used it, knowing it served a greater purpose they'd all enjoy.

After a quick jog to the nightstand, Luc grabbed everything they'd need, prepped it, then headed back toward them. Kimber, eyes closed, fair skin all rosy and covered with a thin sheen of moisture, nipples beckoning, looked like a goddess as she moaned and accepted every stroke of Deke's tongue.

Luc's blood boiled. He had to have relief from Kimber soon. Very soon. Masturbating in the shower wasn't going to ease his need tonight.

Settling behind her again, he touched a palm to her back, right between her shoulder blades. Damn, she was soft everywhere . . .

"Sweetheart, lean forward. Hands and knees."

She did, and Deke didn't miss a beat. Luc would guess, in fact, the new position brought new sensation, given the way Kimber moaned.

Luc caressed her hip, peppered kisses up her back to whisper in her ear, "Just relax. I'll try to make this good for you. Tell me if it hurts."

She merely grabbed at the comforter in front of her and panted as if she couldn't get enough air. And he was about to drive her even closer to the brink.

Parting her cheeks, he slowly—so slowly—began to insert a new vibrator in her ass, a larger one than last time. About six inches, an inch in diameter. Closer to the real thing. Luc hoped with all the fever of the knot of lust in his gut that she liked this. He was dying to get inside her soon.

The vibe was halfway in when he began to sweat. Just watching it disappear into her body was setting him ablaze. He kept inserting, watching it slide deep, deeper. Almost to the hilt.

Suddenly, she arched, tensed, and whimpered.

"Hurt?" he asked.

"A little." She could barely get the words out.

"Take it for us. Can you?"

She nodded, her shoulders tensing. Luc gently slid in the vibe the rest of the way. As she cried out, he flipped it on. Almost instantly, she gasped. Moments later, she began thrashing, grabbing for the comforter again.

"Yes!" Kimber cried out. "I need—Oh, God . . ."

"We know." Luc kissed her shoulder, then stood, shucked his pants, and rounded the pair of them on the floor. Settling on the edge of the bed in front of her, he eased the auburn curls away from her rosy-cheeked face. Her dilated hazel eyes settled right on his cock.

Cupping her nape in his hands, he urged her forward. "Suck me."

Thankfully, she didn't have to be told twice. She lunged forward and damn near swallowed him whole. Luc sucked in a sharp breath. The rush of sensation sizzled up his cock, darting down his legs, shooting thick desire all through his body. Her head bobbed up and down as she took him nearly to the back of her throat, her eager tongue sliding over every sensitive spot he had and discovering a few he hadn't known about. She didn't bring teeth, as if she somehow knew that was Deke's thing and not his. Instead, she gripped his thighs and set a monster-fast pace that ensured he wasn't going to last long. But given the way she was moaning around his cock and the sounds of Deke devouring her pussy, neither was she.

Kimber laved Luc, loved him, her mouth enveloping him like heaven, her tongue providing a constant caress that urged him on and up. Desire swelled inside him, grew faster than he could assimilate. Breathing short-circuited. He fisted his hands in her hair, trying to slow her down. Luc wanted to savor each slick flare of sensation, every searing tingle. Watching her with Deke, then feeling the silken suction of her mouth for himself, knowing this was the first time he would come with the woman who could complete him and Deke . . .

Ecstasy burned in his gut and clawed up his cock, overwhelming and undeniable. Luc tried to stave it off—reciting recipes in his head, thinking about the master chef he'd hated in culinary school—but only the shimmering heat of his skyrocketing need came through. The background music of Kimber wailing with building pleasure told him she was about to orgasm in a big way.

Luc just couldn't hold the pleasure in anymore. The base of his spine tingled. His balls drew up. *Oh, God.* The heat was burning him, inch by inch up his cock, taking liquid fire with it. Then he erupted on a shout, long and agonizing and gritty. And all the while, Kimber's mouth worked on him, her frantic, uneven sucking drawing every ounce of pleasure out of him.

Drawing in a ragged breath, he pulled out of her mouth and found her gaze, unfocused, frenetic need tightening her face. Her body was taut, like a bowstring. Her heart beat wildly at the base of her neck. He reached around her and pumped the vibe in and out of her ass once, twice.

"Come, sweetheart. For us."

She didn't need another word of urging. Hugging his thighs, she clung and mewled out her satisfaction, body thrashing, convulsing with every ripple of pleasure dominating her. Her cry echoed, and under her, he could hear the faint whispers of Deke praising her reaction, her flavor.

As she came down, Luc extracted the vibe slowly. Kimber moaned and crumpled to the ground at Deke's side. She looked at him, eyes soft with something so womanly and profound. He couldn't place it, but the impact of that expression hit him square in the chest. Then she turned that expression on Deke. It amplified, until it was like a sound, a call, a plea.

Then she burst into tears.

Deke tensed.

"Oh. Oh my—What . . . ? I can't . . ." Kimber drew in a huge, heaving sob.

Luc dropped to his knees next to her. "Sweetheart?"

She laid a comforting hand on his arm, but she opened hazel eyes drenched with tears, still ripe with a woman's knowledge. That gaze clung to Deke as she reached out to him, too.

"You make me f-feel. It's . . . I've never felt more turned inside out or more alive than when I'm with you."

Luc rejoiced. Kimber knew this was right, too. She felt it, somewhere deep down. He smiled and reached for her.

But one glance at Deke had Luc's stomach plummeting to his toes. His cousin looked both elated and sick. He had a tight rein on some emotion, not fury, but something damn close.

"No emotion," Deke growled at her, as he rose to his feet and grabbed his clothes. "Just sex. Nothing but sex, damn you."

Then he stalked to the door and slammed it, the finality of the sound echoing all throughout the room.

Chapter Six

"I want to talk to you," Kimber said the following morning as she seated herself at the kitchen table where Deke sat nursing his coffee.

She looked good in red cotton shorts and a tank top. Her glower, however, wasn't as appealing.

"Luc is asleep," she went on, "so he can't get the 'wrong idea.' But I have to say this."

Deke tensed. She had confrontation on her mind, pure and simple. "I don't want to talk."

"Okay, then listen."

When even the sound of her voice gave him a hard-on, that wasn't good. But this morning, he heard a trembling quality to her words. Not a surprise, since he'd been an utter bastard to her yesterday morning and again last night.

But it was either keep distance between them or fuck her. Claim her. He knew she wanted him at arm's length—not between her thighs. Smart girl. He'd just fuck up her life.

"You got three minutes."

"This will take less than two." Now she sounded pissed, which was better. Pissed he could handle. If she was mad, she'd be all right. It was her vulnerability that shredded his guts.

Her tears last night . . . God, listening to her cry in Luc's arms had nearly done him in. Luc had soothed her, whispered to her. Those soft sobs and torn breaths had eaten at Deke, gnawing on his resolve. *He* wanted to be the one to comfort her. Dangerous want. If he'd held her, caressed her last night, he would have ended up making love to her. Not fucking her. The kind of sweet, soft loving meant to reassure. The kind that would bond them together.

For her sake and his sanity, he'd resisted.

First jealousy, now this. What the hell was wrong with him?

Kimber drew in a bracing breath. "After yesterday morning and last night, I can't stay. You don't want me here, and I know why. Thanks for the help you've given me. I'll get my things and be gone by ten."

What the . . . ? Gone by ten. Her words should have been a relief, but Kimber was a fighter. Why would she suddenly concede and retreat? And why did the thought of her leaving take a gash out of something inside him that felt suspiciously like his heart?

She turned away from him. Even so, he couldn't miss the vulnerable expression tightening her face as she rose and crossed the kitchen and exited the room. He could just let her go, should let her walk out now . . . *Woulda, coulda, shoulda.*

Deke stood and scrambled to block her path. "You know why I don't want you here, huh? What do you think you know?"

A frown of incredulity wrinkled her brow. "I know what men have been saying about me since puberty hit. I rarely wear makeup and I don't own a dress. I hate lace and I think fatigue pants are a great fashion do, despite what magazines say. I never mastered the fine arts of giggling and eyelash batting. I like fishing, loathe cooking, and can drink a six-pack of beer in under four minutes, if challenged." She tossed back her head, fighting tears, and her face said that she was annoyed because of it. "I'm a tomboy. And I know for a lot of guys—for you—it's a turnoff."

Her comment was so wrong, Deke almost couldn't process it. "You think I'm turned off by you?"

The *duh!* expression would have made him laugh if this wasn't so serious. "When I first came here in lace and heels, you wanted me. But then you saw through it, and like in high school, you came to view me as one of the guys. It turned you off, so you told me to leave you alone unless we were in bed. There, you intended to live up to your promise. That proves my point."

Was she serious? "That proves you know jack shit, kitten."

She planted a hand on her hip and sent him a challenging stare. "I've been down this road. More than once. You don't have to shield me from the truth. I can take it."

Suddenly, Deke wanted to pound the face of every high school creep who'd made her feel less than female. But it was an out, an easy one. Letting her believe the lie would get him off the hook.

But it would be chickenshit. And he couldn't hurt her on purpose.

He sighed, defeated. "Have I done anything yet to baby your feelings?"

Kimber hesitated. "No."

"Exactly. I wouldn't pretend you turned me on if you didn't. And this shit about you not being . . . feminine enough. It's crap. It isn't makeup and giggling that makes a woman. It's her smarts, her moxie, the way her sexuality flows through her."

"What are you saying?"

Reaching for her hand, he squeezed it. "You've got it all, kitten. I like that you're straightforward. You don't get freaked out by my profession. You've got a killer sense of humor when you're not tense. If I'm grouchy, it's because you turn me on *too* much."

"Too much?" Skepticism shot from her hazel eyes. "You want *me* too much?

Tugging on her hand, he draped it across his fly, covering the unflagging erection he had whenever she came within ten feet of him. "Does it feel like I'm lying?"

Through his sweat shorts, she gripped him, stroked her nimble fingers up and down his rigid length. "No."

Deke grabbed her wrist to stop her. Between his crazy urge to hold her and the lust she was inciting with her every touch, she was treading dangerous waters. "Don't start something you can't finish."

With her free hand, she grabbed at his shorts and began to push them down. "I can finish you. Didn't I do it last night?"

Her mouth. *Oh, hell.* Yes, she'd totally finished him. The wet, silky heaven had been paradise. Luc had told her exactly how to unravel him, and she had. Slow, hard, a little bite—and he'd been a goner. The thought that she might do it again, here and now, made his cock pulse under her hand. She gripped him even harder in answer.

He grabbed her fingers, which were pushing at his shorts, with his free hand and his last bit of wits. "Don't."

Kimber didn't pause. She stopped and jerked her hands away. "You want me but you don't want me to touch you? And since when does a man who wants a woman too much turn down a blow job?"

"If you push me right now, I'll want more."

"What does that mean?" she snapped.

"Your virginity is off-limits. Don't test me, or you'll find yourself naked and impaled on my cock. It's all I can fucking think about. If I get inside you, I'll stay inside you—all damn day if you let me. And I'll come back for more tonight. And Luc will want to be next in line."

A sharp intake of breath. A sudden flush staining her cheeks. A softening of her combative posture. "Oh."

"I'm on a short fuse, so I'd get the hell away from me if I were you."

But Kimber didn't move. For a long moment, she just stared at him. Deke resisted the urge to squirm uncomfortably. There was something going on in that pretty head of hers. God help them both if she gave any indication that she wanted to have sex with him. He didn't have much self-control left. He'd drag her back to Luc's bed, wake his cousin up and . . . do something he'd regret.

A long silence later, she stepped closer, placing her hands on his shoulders and stepping on her tiptoes to reach him. She settled her lips over his and gave him a soft, almost chaste kiss.

"You didn't want to admit any of that, but you did it to spare my feelings."

Perceptive. He'd give her that.

"That's really . . . decent of you. You could have let me believe I wasn't feminine enough for you, but you didn't take the easy way out." A relieved grin broke out across her face. "Thank you. I really respect that."

Deke shrugged. He was stupidly pleased to have put a smile on her face. "Just being fair."

"I should be fair, too, and admit that I'm off balance. You and Luc are a potent pair. Both of you turn me on, but"—she released a shaky breath—"I respond to you a lot more than I thought I would. When you touch me, I melt and ache. I've never felt this way."

He got to her, more than Luc? More than Jesse? Euphoria and lust blasted him in a potent combination, raced through his veins like a drug. In the snap of a finger, he was high on Kimber.

Shit. He shouldn't. He knew he shouldn't—

Too late.

Deke was already grabbing her, thrusting his fingers into her hair, cupping her jaw, then dropping his head to ravage her mouth. With a little gasp, she opened to him, met his possessive kiss.

Curling his tongue around hers, he breathed in her heat, swallowed her moan. He held her tight. And his brain began to shut down.

Now. Sooner than now. He had to taste her, be as close as possible. Deep, deep into her mouth. Her flavor knocked him on his ass. Like heaven.

Then she molded her body against his, arched into him and pressed those sweet breasts right against him. *Touch them.* He had to. *Get them bare.*

With one hand, he swept her tank strap down one shoulder, then the other. He pushed it low enough to free her breasts and run his palms over the firm mounds. Not large, not small. Just right. And those nipples, hard. Always ready for his mouth. *His.*

Soon . . .

Focusing on the remaining barriers, Deke yanked the tank down her waist, then grabbing the waistband of her shorts and panties, dragged it all down her hips and legs.

Naked. Perfect. Boiling him with want.

Raking a pair of fingers through her slit, Deke confirmed his suspicion. She was wet. Very wet. Hard breathing, eyes dilated and begging, she gripped his shirt in desperate fists. Thank God she was aroused.

So was he.

Deke lifted her by the waist, ignoring her gasp, and set her on the kitchen table. He'd fantasized many times about having her spread across it like his next meal, his sustenance. The reality ratcheted up his need. His heartbeat soared. His cock throbbed.

Pulling his shirt over his head, he tossed it away. Then, chest heaving, he pushed his shorts down his legs until Kimber could see nothing of him but bare skin and naked want.

With rapt eyes, she took him in, unblinking, unwavering. *Unbelievable.*

Gripping her thighs, he dragged her hips to the edge of the table and leaned over her, blanketing his body with hers. Searing heat. Peachy, sugary smell. She drove him insane. His gaze sought hers. Found it. Wide, aroused, trusting.

Want seared him, sizzling his blood. On fire.

Touch her. He had to. He kissed her flat belly, dipped his tongue in her navel. She sucked in a breath. He stepped closer, so near her heat. She spread her legs wider, gaze still clinging to him. Silent, open, drowning in want.

Her nipples were hard. Standing up, thick and swollen. Irresistible. He swooped down and took one in his mouth. Devouring it. *Like candy.* Better, actually. He swiped his tongue over it, nipping the tender flesh when it hardened even more. *Hmm. Perfect.*

Kimber panted, little whimpering sounds peppering the air as she curled her hands around his head, trying to get her fingers in his military-short hair and tug him closer.

"Deke . . ."

That note in her voice, pleading. It forced him to look up again. Her stare singed him.

Claim her mouth. Her sweet kiss, all accepting and impassioned, kicked him with another jolt of lust.

Fuck. Her. Now.

He enveloped her hips in his hands, loving the way his palms nearly swallowed her, the way she was open to him, and he could see the wet, welcoming cream of her pussy, her swollen folds.

Taking himself in hand, he positioned his cock against her entrance.

Steamy. Hot. She scalded the head of his cock as he savored the moment before he'd push into her, make her his.

Jesus, he was shaking. Desire piled on top of desperate need, wrapped in the harsh demands of his body. And something else . . .

Take her. Claim her.

"Deke," she pleaded, both for him to push forward—and to stop.

Stop? No. Hell no! Why should he stop?

Because he shouldn't do this. To her. To himself. The reason escaped him. She was open, wet, laid out on his table like a freakin' banquet of delight, eyes shining.

With tears.

Tears? The sight, the question, snapped him out of his lust-induced haze.

He looked around. Clothes strewn across the floor. Sunlight filtering in through wide-open windows, slanting across her breasts. She was spread out across the same damn table they'd eaten dinner on.

She was a virgin.

He swallowed, knowing he should back off, leave her the hell alone. Right now, he was one thrust from changing their lives forever.

Maybe . . . maybe it would be different this time. Kimber wasn't a teenager. She wasn't from a troubled family. She wasn't Heather.

If he thrust into her, she'd be his. *His.* Completely. His to hold on bad days, his to share smiles with, his to surprise, to tease, to please, to fuck . . .

His to care for if something went horribly wrong.

The lust jacking up his system iced over at that thought. He took a half step back.

"Weren't you going to stop me?" His voice creaked. For chrissake, he sounded like he was a hundred.

Kimber hesitated. "Yes."

But he wasn't convinced. "When?"

"Well, I—I meant to. I tried."

Deke pulled up his shorts, tucking his erection back inside with a grimace. "Do you actually love this pop star you're chasing?"

A blink. A glance away. A boulder of unease settled in his gut. Was she skittish because she didn't love McCall or because she was trying not to throw her feelings for the pop star up in Deke's face?

She sat up, covered herself with her arms, drawing her legs up to her chest. "Would I be here trying to learn all this if I didn't?"

"Only you know why you're really here. But I know you don't comprehend the fire you're playing with, little girl. Next time, say no. If Luc had been here, I might not have stopped. Next time, I might fuck you—and fuck the consequences."

* * *

LATE that night, Kimber dozed on Luc's shoulder while they snuggled to an old black-and-white classic. His warmth curled around her. Safe. Comforting.

By unspoken agreement, they didn't discuss Deke, but her thoughts kept drifting back to him. Where was he?

Somewhere in the house, a door slammed. The sound jerked her fully awake.

Sitting up with a yawn and a stretch, she looked around in confusion. Still just Luc and the old movie.

"Kimber!" A voice bellowed. Then she heard stomping in the rest of the house.

A bolt of gladness and relief struck her. "Deke?"

She had only to say his name once and he appeared in the doorframe, filling the space with his massive shoulders and huge presence. His breath rose and fell in heavy, angry pants. He swayed on his feet. Those blue eyes of his zeroed in on her wrapped in Luc's arms. They stripped her clothes off with a glance. Immediately, her nipples beaded. She swallowed.

"You're drunk," Luc bit out in disapproval beside her.

"I wish. But not for lack of trying. If I was, I could have drowned out all desire to touch her." Deke pinned Kimber to the sofa with a hot stare.

"Then I could have passed out into oblivion without needing to feel her around my cock."

Kimber's stomach clenched at his words. So did her sex.

Why did this man get to her, despite being so dangerous and difficult, so angry? Luc was gentle and understanding, charming, seductive, talented. The desire he roused was gentle and beautiful.

And nothing like the hot blast of need that scalded her every time she experienced Deke's demanding caress.

"Not when you're in this mood." Luc stood and crossed his arms, half standing in front of her protectively. "You know what we had planned next, and you're in no shape to carry it out. You'll hurt her."

"I won't." He stared, then sent her a smile that glittered with danger. "Look at her. Those pretty nipples are hard. Her hot hazel eyes are eating me up. And her pussy . . ."

Deke pushed past Luc in the small den and fell to his knees. Before Kimber had any idea what he had planned, Deke had pushed up her miniskirt and ripped out the crotch of her panties.

"Damn things," he muttered. "Naked. You should always be naked."

"But—"

He spread her legs wide, slammed two fingers inside her wet sex, and bent his head to her clit, consuming her in a devouring sweep of his tongue.

"Deke!"

Immediately, fire sizzled down her legs, roaring into an inferno low in her belly. Tight and aching, hot and out of control, the sensations slammed into her. She couldn't breathe. Definitely couldn't stop him.

Didn't want to.

Kimber curled her fingers around his head and gasped. His greedy licks were shocking to her system. He was eating her alive—all her passion and yearning, all her doubts, hopes. Her indecision.

Why did Deke reach her on such a deep level? Because she sensed he was wounded and wanted to heal him, as any nurse would? Why did he rule her body more than any other man? Why had some part of her fantasized about him, even before she understood sexual fantasies?

The question dissipated in her mind, dissolving like sugar in wine, as

Deke's fingertips stroked the sensitive bundle of nerves inside her. Luc sank onto the couch at her side and watched, arousal fierce across his face.

"I won't let him hurt you."

"He won't," she gasped.

"He's arousing you?"

"Yes." She threw back her head and closed her eyes. "Yes."

Luc's thumb suddenly swiped across one nipple as he pulled her summer top down, anchoring it beneath her breasts. "I'm going to arouse you, too, sweetheart."

His tongue flicked across the beads of her tight nipples, followed by a nip of his teeth. Deke mirrored the action, clamping down on her clit, then manipulating it with the tip of his tongue.

Relentless, one swipe after the other, he made her burn. The fire spread, injecting its way through her body, shooting up to her nipples, down her legs, sizzling across her skin. Building, building . . . Her heart careened out of control, the sound of its beats roaring in her ears, blocking out everything else except the hungry sounds of Deke's mouth and Luc's moans.

In seconds, the need grew and towered above her until she hovered right on the edge of wildfire pleasure. Totally beyond her control, her body jerked with every hard flick of Deke's tongue.

The fire gathered, coalesced, peaked. Then it erupted, bursting behind her eyes until black spots clung to the edge of her vision. Her back arched, and she screamed, gripping Deke's head, his shoulders.

Enormous. Huge. Had she ever orgasmed so hard?

She struggled to catch her breath, to right her crazy, tilting world.

Deke merely pushed her thighs wider, stabbed his tongue into her core, and demanded, "Again."

Sensations assailed her faster than her body could process them as his tongue stroked across her clit again. Too much, all at once. "Oh . . . Wait. Slow down."

"No," Deke barked, lifting his head from between her thighs, his lips wet with her juice. "You're here to learn how to accommodate two men. I told you things would get hot. Sometimes, they're fast and furious. Adjust."

Continuing to caress her breasts, Luc sent him a stern stare. "She's inexperienced. We can moderate—"

"Why? She's a big girl. An adult, she keeps saying. In the next five minutes, she can be gripping your cock in her ass. And don't lie; I know how bad you want it."

"I'm sure it would be very enjoyable, if that's what Kimber wants."

Deke flashed him a bitter stare. "You smug bastard, always hiding behind the good image, the chevalier to my caveman. Don't forget, I was there when you had sex with that flight attendant in Memphis last year. You went at her for over three hours. Do you think Kimber could keep pace in one of your marathon sessions?"

Kimber stared at Luc in a whole new light. Sweet-tempered, gentle Luc? He flushed guiltily, lending credence to Deke's assertion.

"She wasn't complaining. Besides, you participated, too."

"Once. The rest was all you, buddy boy. And she's not the first one to get that treatment. Don't pretend you don't have a dark side. You want to win Kimber over? You'd better show her the real you."

Luc swallowed. "She knows the real me. I'll always be as gentle as possible with Kimber."

Deke snorted. "Sooner or later, you're going to have to give her a taste of that killer stamina or you'll be doing nothing but lying to her."

"Shut up."

Kimber watched the byplay with astonishment. The anger. The secrets they'd both been keeping from her. Did they keep things from one another, too? Stunned didn't begin to describe how she felt.

Clearing her throat, Kimber cut in. "Luc, really, I'm—"

"Here's the deal," Deke said to her, as if Luc hadn't growled at him, as if she hadn't spoken. "We work well together because Luc has patience and likes to get a woman all hot. I strike fast, make sure she gets off a few times. Somewhere in the middle of it all, Luc moves in." Deke slanted another ugly stare at Luc.

"Shut up, cousin."

"When his dark side takes over, he'll fuck a woman for a good three hours. More, if he's on a real tear. Never say die. Isn't that your motto?" The bitter words hung in the air.

Mouth open, Kimber watched as Luc dragged Deke to his feet and curled a fist in his T-shirt. "You're scaring her."

"I'm telling the truth. And she should be scared. She's a little virgin playing with grown men. I damn near fucked her sweet pussy this morning on your kitchen table while you slept."

It was Luc's turn to send her a sharp stare. "Are you okay?"

What could she say? Kimber nodded. Embarrassment didn't count as harm. She'd been stupid, allowing her good sense to be overwhelmed. It wouldn't happen again. She hoped.

Deke scoffed. "What, you think I would have forced her? Raped her?"

"Normally, I wouldn't think so, but you're awfully pushy today," Luc growled.

"*If* I had fucked her, it would have been because she aroused me and didn't have enough control of her faculties to say no. *I* put a stop to it."

Luc hardly looked impressed. "You don't want the responsibility of taking a virgin."

"I don't want to hurt Kimber, and I have very little control with her. We all know it." He paused. "Is your dark side wailing at you tonight, cuz?"

Kimber watched as Luc released Deke's shirt and shut his eyes, refusing to look at anyone. She had the distinct impression that he was embarrassed by his occasionally extreme behavior. Oddly, she wasn't afraid of Luc's answer; she just wondered what caused him to need to fuck a woman so . . . thoroughly.

"No," he murmured finally.

"Good. Since you have all the patience and no whiskey in your system . . ." Deke reached into his pocket and pulled out a condom and a tube of lubricant. He tossed them on the table right in front of her. "You know what we had planned tonight. You do it, all gentle and shit, so it will go down smooth. Or I will. And heaven help us all, then."

Luc let out a shaky breath.

Mr. Calm? Mr. Never-Ruffled? Wow . . . There was far more going on here than she'd ever suspected. What the hell was brewing in this place? She didn't want to answer her own question the hard way, not when she knew what the condom and the lube meant for her.

"Guys, if neither of you is sure—"

"I'm sure," Luc cut in quietly. "As indelicately as Deke might have said it, he's right to push the issue. This is part of your training, and one of us has to do this. Deke is in no shape. You know what we're discussing, right?"

A glance again at the items on the table didn't lead Kimber to any other conclusions. The thought of it happening to her—right now—both alarmed and aroused her. Would it hurt? Get her off?

It didn't matter. This was part of Jesse's world, a big part of what Jesse would probably want. She was here to learn if she could accept it, take it, like it.

"Anal sex," she finally answered.

"Yes." Luc's voice, usually smooth as brandy, was like a rough drag over gravel. "Are you going to be okay with that?"

"It's necessary to take two men at once. It's part of what I signed up for."

"But tonight? It's late and we've argued—"

"You two argued. I'm fine. Are you . . . up for it?" Kimber glanced down at the crotch of Luc's shorts.

Even as she spoke, his erection rose. "I'm always up for being with you."

"It's settled, then," Deke said as he plopped down on the sofa arranged perpendicular to the one she occupied.

Kimber frowned as he reclined and looked at her with a cool smile. If Deke wanted her too much, why didn't he want to be the first to do this? He'd said he had very little control with her. Did he think he'd go wild and hurt her? Or push his way into the wrong orifice?

"Apparently." Luc shot his cousin a puzzled glare. "And what are you going to do?"

The stare Deke sent Kimber damn near sizzled the flesh off her bones. "Watch."

That one word set off a detonation of hot longing inside Kimber. He wanted to watch Luc take her anally, planned to enjoy every moment of watching her writhe in ecstasy. A quick glance down proved the mere thought of it made him hard.

The thought of his arousal made her ache. Her sex clenched, and fresh moisture drenched her already-wet folds.

"Eventually, you have to participate," Luc pointed out to his cousin.

"Eventually." He leaned back, crossed his ankles, and clasped his hands behind his head. No one could mistake the enormous erection jutting against the front of his jeans. "Get started. I'm ready."

Arrogant bastard. But a sexy one. Kimber tried to form some pithy comeback, but then Luc touched her arm.

"Sweetheart?"

He was asking her if she was ready for this, for him. *No. Yes.* She sighed. *Maybe.* She was curious, but afraid. She needed to be able to accept a man anally, but worried it would hurt. And if Deke wasn't going to touch her, she wanted to drive him crazy, make him so insane for her that he couldn't stay away.

Stupid and reckless, Kimber knew. But after this morning on the kitchen table when he'd refused her because she hadn't had the willpower to say no . . . He'd mustered the self-control to put a stop to disaster and left. Clearly, he hadn't wanted her half as badly as she'd ached for him. He'd done the right thing, she supposed, and part of her thanked him for it. But it still hurt.

Why did his opinion matter? She was here for Jesse. *Jesse*, damn it. Not Deke.

But he'd said no this morning, and now he'd given up the opportunity to be the first one to take her anally. Instead, he'd deferred to Luc. The devil of doubt rode her hard. Kimber was determined to make Deke regret what he'd passed up. He'd had better get ready for a hell of a floor show.

"I'm ready," she whispered to Luc, sending him what could only be called a saucy, fuck-me smile.

For a moment, Luc just stared, as if he wasn't sure what to make of her smile or what to do first. She took the decision out of his hands.

An odd bravery, feminine resolution—pure need to tempt Deke—flowed through her as she reached for the hem of her top and pulled it over her head, completely baring herself to Luc. Deke got a great side view. Then she pinched her nipples, ensuring they were hard.

"I'm more than ready." She hoped those husky words went straight to Deke's cock.

They sure went to Luc's. Staggered by them, he sank to his knees. "Stay on the sofa."

Casting a challenging glance Deke's way, Kimber wriggled, rolling her hips and making a great show of getting comfortable. Then she primly crossed her legs, imitating her best ladylike posture, and wasn't it lucky for her that the pose thrust her breasts right into Luc's face?

Yanking out the elastic band restraining his midnight hair, Luc tossed it on the table. Waves of inky hair fell around his strong face. His shirt came next. Off and onto the floor, exposing the taut lines of wide shoulders, the ropes of muscles straining up and down his arms. Abs rippling with every breath. He worked out, no question. And he looked damn good. She shivered.

"What can you take off next?" she taunted, glancing at his shorts. "I have something you can touch if you strip down for me."

Kimber parted her legs enough for Luc—and only Luc—to see her all wet and swollen. Luc moaned, his gaze fixed on her damp curls.

Out of the corner of her eye, she saw Deke unzip his pants and take his meaty cock in his hand. He began to slowly stroke every long inch, grasping the width of it in a harsh fist, his eyes glued to her. She loved having the power to drive the taciturn Deke to such desire. And she wasn't close to done.

Where the inner vixen had come from, she had no idea. But she wasn't about to put a stop to her right now.

"You do want to touch me, don't you?" she asked Luc, toying with her own clit and gasping for effect.

"Yes," he panted. "Do that again."

"Get naked, and I will."

Luc shucked off his shorts in less than two seconds to reveal his long staff with its thick veins and vivid purple head, and Kimber tried not to laugh. The power she had over them was heady. She was drunk on it. In the end, Luc or Deke—or both—would take it from her. But in this moment, she owned them.

"Very nice," she murmured.

The inner vixen goaded her into slipping her finger into her mouth and making quite a production of wetting the tip. With a feline smile, she dropped the wet digit to Luc's cock and rubbed the moisture all over the head, adding to the leakage seeping from the tip. He hissed, the tendons standing out in his neck as he fought for control.

"You're being naughty," Luc scolded.

"Me?" Kimber was all innocence.

"Very naughty. Lift your skirt and touch yourself again. I want to see you do it."

A surprising request coming from the usually gentlemanly Luc, but after tonight, Kimber guessed there were hidden depths to the man. A demand that she masturbate for him—for them—definitely shocked her. And thrilled her.

Pushing self-consciousness aside, she leaned back and lifted her skirt higher with slow hands, very slow. She ended at the top of her thighs, and with Deke sitting on the sofa to her right, she knew he could see just enough to tease. His muttered curses bespoke frustration.

To add a little fuel to the fire, Kimber wiggled her ass and moaned, closing her eyes and licking her lips.

"Now, Kimber."

She opened her eyes. Blinked. That commanding tone came from Luc? The usually gentle encouragement on his face had been replaced with something severe and impatient.

His fingers wrapped around her thighs—not lightly. "Now!"

When his entire demeanor made her wet and the edge of fear zipped through her to create a thrill she didn't quite understand, what choice did she have? Canting her hips forward, she lowered her hand to her sex and rubbed her clit.

Usually, when she was alone, she started in leisurely circles, spinning some fantasy in her mind. Tonight, she had no need to dream up any sexual circumstance. She was living it. And those slow circles? No way. With two sets of burning eyes roaming every inch of her flesh, caressing hard nipples, smoothing over her abdomen, probing her pussy, slow circles were not possible.

Sensation mounted hard and fast as Kimber manipulated her clit.

The burning pressure became an ache as she watched Luc's cock bob with every harsh breath he took. Deke leaned in. He tried to peer closer, then sniffed.

"Oh, hell, I can smell how close she is."

Luc gave a shaky nod. "Stop."

Pleasure bubbled inside her, thick and roiling. Kimber heard Luc speak. He said something she didn't want to hear, so she ignored him.

"I said stop." He grabbed her wrist.

She whimpered at the loss of stimulation but ceased because he forced her to. She blinked once, twice. Twin flags of color flushed his face. His long, artistic fingers gripped her wrist with startling force.

"Don't push me," he warned, looking unrelenting. "I'm close to my edge."

In other words, if she didn't want to be sating him with her ass for the next three hours, she'd better back off.

"Okay," she whispered.

He released her and nodded, his expression looking grateful. "Slide off the sofa, knees on the floor in front of me."

Kimber didn't even think of teasing him. She simply complied.

"Good," he praised as he gripped her hips and turned her away from him.

Then she felt his palm between her shoulder blades giving her a gentle push. "Lean forward and brace your elbows on the sofa."

Oh, God. This is happening. Really happening.

She could say no. Kimber knew she could. But it wouldn't serve her purpose. And she ached for what Luc could give her now, for what Deke would see and be aroused by. There was no stopping tonight.

Swallowing hard, she did as Luc demanded. The scents of leather and her own cream wafted around her. Luc handled her, caressing her hips, lifting her skirt, stroking her ass.

"You're beautiful here." He smoothed his palm over one of her cheeks. "Round, firm, pale. And right now, all mine."

She moaned. His words, his touch, aroused her even more.

"This will work like the vibes, only I'm flesh and blood. And larger than the last vibe you took."

Yes, he was larger, and not by just a tad. "Will it hurt?"

"I'll ease in, minimize the pain."

"It's best this way. Luc's got the patience, kitten. I'm going to love hearing you scream."

Deke.

Frowning, Kimber turned to him. Those denim eyes flared with passion, yes, but now tenderness also lurked. His face said that he feared he would hurt her if he tried to be the first to take her anally, but he was right there with her, hadn't abandoned her. And she saw longing. He wanted to be in Luc's place.

Her mind raced as she heard Luc ripping foil behind her. Deke had given up this opportunity because he wanted it to be good for her? Had he goaded Luc into this on purpose?

"This will be a little cold and slippery," Luc warned.

A second later, Kimber felt his fingers probing her back entrance, spreading the cool lube in and around her puckered opening. She shivered.

Doubt assailed her suddenly. Luc, while always gentle with her, was not a small man. Maybe she wouldn't be able to handle him. Maybe it would hurt too much. Maybe—

Luc caressed her cheeks gently, then parted them. "Relax. Remember to push down as I push in. You'll be fine. I'll make it good."

He placed a tender kiss at the small of her back, and Kimber knew he'd do everything in his power to give her pleasure, minimize the pain. She exhaled.

Then she felt him, slick and hard against her back entrance. He pushed in a fraction, and his head entered her. Pressure but not pain. *Good.*

Gripping her hips, Luc whispered, "Now, push down."

Kimber did, gritting her teeth. He thrust once, twice, blocked by the ring of muscle there.

He cursed, his fingers digging into her hips. She whimpered at the sharp edge of pain slicing into her.

Instantly, Deke was there in front of her, on the sofa. "Shh. It's okay, kitten."

"Damn. I need to push harder," Luc said.

She gave them both a shaky nod. Deke gripped her hands.

A slight withdrawal, a fresh grip on her hips, and Luc surged forward, the head of his cock popping past the resistant ring of muscle. She gasped as pain burst, then slowly dissipated. Fullness took its place. Jumping nerve endings awoke with new possibilities.

"Is it done?" she whispered.

"About halfway," Luc croaked. "The hard part is over. Are you okay?"

Was she? Experiencing something new, not sure if she was feeling pleasure or pain or something in the middle, opening herself to an act she'd scarcely thought of, was she okay?

Once glance at Deke's face told her *yes*. Taut with pleasure and expectation, he loved it. Watching? Or just knowing that when it was his turn, the slide in would be easier? Either way, the fact that she was submitting to Luc now both pleased and aroused Deke and somehow made it okay. More than okay.

"I'm good." She nodded. "Go."

"Damn you're tight, sweetheart," Luc ground out. "I won't last long."

There was no opportunity to reply, and Kimber supposed he didn't need one, not when he shoved forward again, easing in another few inches. The pressure increased, and she mewled, arching her back. He slid in another inch. She gasped.

"Almost there . . ."

With a last, frantic grab of her hips and a growl, Luc thrust inside her ass to the hilt.

Kimber cried out at the sudden, sharp sensations. Not pleasure, not pain; somewhere in the middle. An odd feeling of suspension, even as her knees became numb. And a total feeling of being mastered.

Deke brushed her hair away from her face. "God, you look sexy." Then he glanced up at Luc, and she could see that their eyes met over her back. "Fuck her."

Luc didn't answer; he simply drew back, all the way to the ring of muscle, then slid home. The friction made her gasp. Again, the pleasure/pain, the fullness and pressure, they made her writhe, toss back her head, and struggle to take it. Even as she knew she'd take it again gladly. Everything about her felt . . . alive.

"Touch your clit." Luc's voice sounded strained. "I want to feel you come."

No chance of her not coming, really. The newness of it all, and the rapture on Deke's face as he watched her reaction to being all pumped full of pleasure. And Luc's cock, strong but gentle, slowly picking up the pace. Slowly driving her toward oblivion.

Being obedient appealed at the moment, and she touched her fingers to her clit. Not just wet but soaking. In fact, cream dripped down her thighs. Had she ever been this aroused? Deke and Luc were a powerful one-two sucker punch to her self-control. *Amazing*, she thought, feeing the sexy chef thrust into her again.

Her clit pulsed under her fingers, and she rubbed. Tendrils of pleasure spread like the parts of a spiderweb, delicate and far-reaching. Shocking. Kimber heard moaning, and realized the sound had come from her.

The sweet ache of Luc's invasion and the sharp edge of pleasure she gave herself was about to send her into the stratosphere.

"Oh, hell. She's rippling around me."

"You gonna come, kitten?" Deke whispered in her ear.

Kimber could only cry out and arch her back a bit more. Luc slid deeper and hissed, digging his fingers into her hips. He fucked her harder. Her nerve endings jumped in approval. God, she'd never imagined this would be so consuming.

"Suck his cock," Luc ordered.

Deke's gaze bounced up to meet Luc's. Whatever he saw there calmed him. When he lowered his gaze to her, those blue eyes pleaded with her. He took his cock in his hand and eased himself closer to her mouth.

Yes! Full at front and back. It was . . . perfect.

Luc's rhythm was now deep, slow, and hard. Kimber set her tempo the same. She knew Deke liked it.

"Oh, fuck yes!" he cried out in approval.

Her fingers faltered on her clit, and Luc came to the rescue, batting her hand out of the way and taking over.

Oh, much better. He was so damn effective. The ramp-up to ecstasy multiplied. Spinning, tumbling, flying. Almost . . .

"Come, sweetheart."

She moaned around Deke's cock, and an explosion rent her body, tearing through her soul, rearranging her. Shaken, broken and remade, stunned and amazed, she convulsed, her back rounding as rivers of white-hot pleasure streamed through her body.

Behind her, Luc stiffened, gripped her hips again, and let loose a guttural cry.

Kimber felt joyous, triumphant. She'd done it! And she'd gladly do it again.

But she wasn't finished, Deke reminded her by thrusting into her mouth.

Determined to share her bliss, she took him deep and slow, sucked hard, tongue swirling, teeth scraping. His hands made their way onto her face and cradled her. "Yeah, kitten. Suck me. So fucking good."

Knowing she could do this to him, yes. It *was* good. And she wanted him to come, needed to know he felt the ecstasy, too.

Luc withdrew from her backside slowly, carefully. Kimber moaned at the odd sensation of his withdrawal, of the ache of sudden emptiness.

He leaned over her body and planted a kiss on her shoulder. "You keep amazing me. That felt incredible."

Behind her, she felt Luc rise. Vaguely, she heard him peel off the condom. Then his padded footsteps left the room.

And she focused her attention on Deke, on the muscled thighs beneath her fingers, the thick stalk her tongue cradled.

Instantly, Deke tensed. "Get the fuck back here!"

Kimber lifted her head, puzzled. "I'm here."

"I meant Luc," he growled.

Deke needed Luc . . . why? Certainly Deke could come without him.

"Back in a minute," Luc called from across the house.

"I want your ass back here now."

Luc didn't answer. Deke's hands became fists, and he jumped to his feet and cursed, something mean and ugly that shocked even her.

Curiouser and curiouser.

"We don't need him," she whispered. "I'm more than happy to finish what we started all by ourselves."

Deke's gaze left the empty portal and he raked a hot stare over her body. At the sight of her wearing nothing but a little skirt, his cock flared, swelled. Another frantic gaze around the room. "Oh, shit. No! No more condoms . . ."

Trying to smooth the puzzlement from her face, Kimber took his hand. "It's all right. Sit down. We don't need a condom. I'll finish you—"

"No. Not without Luc here. I won't do this without Luc in the room."

"What?" Shock reverberated through her body. What he was saying . . . did he really mean it? Every muscle in his body taut, the denial of his pleasure, the screaming obscenities at Luc at the top of his lungs? Yeah, he meant it.

"You can come without Luc in the room, I'm sure. He's not going to help you."

"No, but he's supposed to help you, keep you safe. And if he doesn't get back here, I swear to God, I'm less than two seconds from throwing you to the floor and fucking you."

Chapter Seven

*T*EMPTING. It was the first word that popped into her head. Kimber had never thought of herself as being sexually driven, but a few days with Deke and Luc . . . and she could think of little else, especially with Deke's pants hanging low around his thighs and his thick, ready cock right in front of her.

Stupid. It was the second word to burst into her head. She hadn't come here to be with him, but to learn how to be with Jesse. But that wasn't what made her pause. For some reason, Deke would not engage her sexually without Luc in the room. And judging from Luc's lack of surprise, she didn't think this was a new development. Which implied that he had hang-ups unrelated to virgins, but to sex in general.

Kimber heard the clink of pipes that signaled the shower running in Luc's bathroom, and she knew he wasn't coming back, not quickly enough to intercede. She was flying blind in a situation that was clearly touchy for Deke. And she was going to have to wing it.

"Take a deep breath," she suggested. "We can wait for him to come back or continue as we were. Your call."

"Don't touch me right now. You'll be sorry if you do."

Between his tight jaw and ground-out words, Kimber believed him.

He was riding a razor-thin edge of control. One move the wrong way and he'd snap.

Just this morning she'd believed she was too tomboyish to seriously arouse Deke. He'd quickly proved her wrong and made her feel both alive and feminine in the process. Amazing the perspective a few hours and a little conversation could give a person.

Unfortunately, none of that helped her now.

"I'm in better control of myself than this morning. We can work this out. I'll say no if things get too hot."

His hands slid into her hair, his fists gripping her. Indecision and craving warred on his tight face. His harsh breaths fell across her cheek. "Kitten, you just don't know all the reasons that's a bad idea."

"Then tell me the reasons. Maybe I can help."

His fists tightened in her hair. His tawny brows slashed down over eyes so blue, they nearly looked black. Torture. The emotional kind. It was all over his expression.

"Despite the fact I've been a total asshole to you, you still offer to help me. If I was a better man—" He stopped, apparently not wanting to finish that train of thought. "You can't help, kitten. I dug my own grave twelve years ago."

And he'd buried himself emotionally ever since. He didn't say that, but Kimber knew it. He wouldn't come without Luc in the room for the same reason he engaged in ménages, she'd bet. Something had happened to him as a teenager that had changed everything.

"Tell me what happened."

He scoffed and looked at her as if she'd lost half her brain. "A regurgitation of the past is not going to change a thing."

"Maybe it will. I've had time alone with Luc. I want some with you, just you. But this . . . *thing* is between us."

"It always will be. If a small army of therapists couldn't erase the problem, you sitting there in nothing but a fuck-me skirt and listening to me talk about my past isn't going to 'fix' me. You'll only be tempting me to take what I know I shouldn't, and as heavenly as sinking down deep into you would be, it won't raise the dead."

She didn't understand his reference at all, but quickly grasped that somehow, somewhere along the way, sex and death had tangled together, and he felt responsible, like some Greek tragedy. Luc had been his watchdog and crutch since.

With a curse, Deke shoved his cock back in his jeans, yanked up his zipper, and made for the door.

"Stop!" Kimber cried, without even knowing what she would say, what she even could say.

For a moment, she swore he would keep going. But he turned back.

"What?" He whispered the word, almost as if all the shouting of the last few minutes had never been.

Kimber stared straight up into his tormented gaze. Grief and guilt swirled together on his face to create a picture of total misery. He needed someone to care, someone to hold.

Someone to give him a second chance.

She swallowed hard but never looked away as she pinned him with a solemn gaze and lay flat on her back. She lifted her skirt and parted her legs slightly, then let her hand drift up her abdomen to rest on her breast.

Those blue eyes flared to life, and she smiled.

"Make love to me."

* * *

FOUR words. That's all it took for Kimber to wrap around his cock and squeeze. She did the same thing to the murky feelings inside his chest he'd been battling all evening.

"You don't want this." He didn't have a better argument for not taking her up on her offer. With her spread out at his feet, naked, lush, lovely, Lord knew he was ready to give up breathing to have her.

"Yes, I do," she murmured

"I'm not gentle."

Her smile said she understood. "I'm not made of glass."

Deke shook his head. "You wanted to save yourself for Jesse."

"I wanted to give my virginity to someone who would care that I gave it to him."

"What makes you think I'd care?" He tried for snide and dismissive.

"Things you've said to me." She reached up for his hand and started to pull him toward her. "The look on your face right now."

Closing his eyes, Deke tried to block out his expression, shut out his view of every bare inch of her skin. But she tugged on his hand, pulling him close, and the vision replayed itself over and over in his mind, as if burned on his brain. Damn, it wasn't just her body that made him hard. Right now, it was that honest, giving nature of hers reaching into his pants—into his chest—and making him wild.

"You're hallucinating."

"You're lying," she whispered.

He glared at her. "Why the hell would you offer yourself to me?"

"I want to help you."

"I don't want a pity fuck," he growled.

Her gaze seared him as it drifted up his body, settling right into his eyes. "I don't pity you. I want to comfort you, but I'm not being totally altruistic. You make me feel female, like a woman. When I'm with you, I don't feel tomboyish or awkward or inexperienced. I feel . . . desired. I care. I want more. I think I've always wanted more of you."

Oh, hell. He could have easily turned her down when he'd believed she was just tossing her virginity at him as some sort of Band-Aid for his emotional boo-boos. But refusing her now would mean hurting her, scraping raw her insecurities to shield his own.

Better her feelings wounded than permanent physical harm—or worse.

Would it really be a risk? Kimber was so much stronger than Heather . . .

"Deke, honey, don't try so hard to protect me. I'm a big girl, and I know what I want. That's you." She squeezed his hand. "Just give me you."

She might think that, but she didn't know. Damn it, he shouldn't give in.

Still, he dropped to his knees between her spread legs. Frantically, he searched his pockets, his wallet, praying . . . *Yes!* A condom. One. Lubricated. Letting out a ragged breath, he dropped it on the table beside them.

"You are prepared." She smiled.

"Thank God." He gave her a shaky nod, then tore at his shirt.

Her fingers wandered in hungry strokes across his abdomen. Tingles, huge jets of them, jolted his gut, his spine, his cock. He groaned, his erection now so damn hard it could drill holes in metal. Could he actually get any blood to his brain? Felt like it had all rushed south.

A tug on his zipper and his cock sprang free, relieved of pressure. He fell into the paradise of Kimber's waiting hands.

She stroked him, softly, encouraging. He didn't need more persuasion—or arousal. He needed to stop this somehow . . . someway. But with his blood churning and desire dousing common sense, firing his senses, Deke had no idea how he was going to resist something he wanted so badly.

His hand shook as he shoved his pants down to his hips. He covered her with his body and captured her mouth in a kiss of crushed lips, harsh breaths, and moans. Kimber welcomed him, throwing her arms around his neck, stroking his back, his shoulders. Lifting her hips up to him.

The condom lay mere inches away. A tear, a roll, a thrust—and he could be totally surrounded in her heat, and he could have a part of her that no other man would ever have.

Just the thought made a vicious hunger flare in his gut.

Stop. Stop now!

He broke off their kiss, then groaned at the feel of her eager little mouth kissing its way up his shoulder, to the side of his neck.

Somehow, his hands drifted down and he settled his cock against the steamy, forbidden flesh of her cunt. Damn, she was wet. And so hot. She damn near burned him alive. When she wriggled against him . . . *Jesus!*

"Stop me." He sounded like he'd been on a steady diet of gravel and sandpaper.

All she did was smile and raise her legs up around his hips.

Sweat broke out across his skin—forehead, back, chest. Kimber was killing him here, taunting him with everything he wanted and should not take.

Unable to stop himself, he ground against her, nudging her clit with his length. Her little gasp went straight to his dick. It didn't take much imagination to picture her legs totally wrapped around him, her nails in his back, as he plunged deep inside her and surrounded himself with her heat.

Deke swallowed against the vision. Why the hell was this happening? In twelve years, he'd never been seriously tempted to fuck a woman by himself, in her pussy. He'd never had sex unprotected. Yeah, the condom was inches away, and right now, he thought it might take a Herculean effort to grab it and put it on.

He'd need at least that much effort and double the willpower to simply get up and walk away.

Where the hell was Luc? Propping his upper body up on his arms, he stared down into Kimber's flushed, welcoming face. He was in deep shit here. And he suspected that if Luc was here, he'd only encourage Deke to do the stupid. *The unthinkable.*

Gritting his teeth, he backed away and grabbed the condom. He was *so* going to hell. He didn't deserve Kimber and her innocence. But here she was, laid out in front of him, and he had to get inside her— somewhere, somehow—now.

But if he took her virginity, made love to her now . . . what if he ruined her life?

He rolled the condom on and stared down into her sweet face again. She wasn't afraid, and she should have been. His control was hanging on by less than a thread as he grabbed her bent knees from underneath and pushed on the backs of her thighs, tilting her hips up.

His greedy gaze wandered over her breasts and their swollen nipples, the soft skin of her belly, the needy red flesh of her pussy, a hint of the puckered flesh of her still-slick back entrance coated in lube, increasingly visible as he tilted her a bit more.

"Deke?" Luc called from the door.

His cousin was asking what he planned to do. Deke whipped his head around to meet Luc's dark, inquiring gaze. What the fuck could he say? The temptation to break his every rule gnawed at him. Kimber wasn't someone else's woman. If he fucked her now, she wouldn't belong to another man who would take responsibility if something went bad.

At least in this moment, she belonged to him. Only him.

"I offered," Kimber explained softly. "I asked him to make love to me. To be the first."

Luc's smile was damn near blinding as he entered the room, sat on the sofa, and grabbed Kimber's hand. "It's a lovely gift. If Deke hasn't said it yet, he's touched and honored."

Deke shot his cousin a dirty glare. "I didn't accept."

Brow raised, Luc took in their position, the way Kimber was all spread out and welcoming, Deke's cock gloved up and ready.

Deke let out a shaky breath. The fact was, he hadn't turned her down, either.

He had to do something. *Now.* The need bubbling in his gut was about to spill over. A feral desire pumped through his system, like a pure shot of adrenaline to his cock. His chest was so tight with need, every fucking breath was a struggle.

Trying to block out all the voices, the doubt, the fear in his head, Deke took his cock in his hand and leaned closer, closing his eyes.

His. She could be his. In the next ten seconds.

He hesitated. Swallowed. His mind raced.

And then, once he'd taken her, claimed her, what would happen? What if . . . No, he couldn't even think it.

"Fuck!" he snarled.

He tilted her up again, her legs now resting on his shoulders, and positioned himself and began to push.

Into her back entrance.

Kimber drew in a great, shocked gasp, her hazel eyes wide. "Deke?"

"What the hell are you doing?" Luc barked.

Tensing a little more with every inch he pushed inside Kimber's tight passage, the tendons in his neck standing out, the muscles in his arms shaking, assailed by the amazing sensations of being slowly enveloped by her tight, ready flesh, Deke could barely form a word. "Fucking her ass. Saving her life."

Luc looked like he really wanted to chastise him, but he didn't. *Good damn thing, too.* The more he tunneled into Kimber, the more his brain short-circuited. Would he even hear over the gong of his rampant heartbeat? She was like a hot fist around his cock, clamping down more with every nudge into her.

"Deke!" she cried out.

"Almost in."

Sweat rolled off him now. The urge to pound into her with long, punishing strokes assailed Deke. He refrained, determined to slow down and enjoy the heaven of being inside Kimber.

Quick pants punctuated her breathing. "Stop. I can't take more."

"Please. *Please*, kitten. Oh, God!" He was going to die if he couldn't bury himself into her, to the hilt.

But a look at her grimace, her closed eyes, had him backing away. Before he could withdraw, she reached out and grabbed his shoulders. Lowering her legs to his sides, she tilted up and wriggled. Unable to resist the hot promise of her, Deke thrust hard.

He slid in all the way on a long, dark groan.

"Kitten, yes. That's it. Take me. Take everything I have to give you."

Kimber's head fell back on a whimper, her auburn hair spreading out all around her. Damn, she looked like some fiery goddess of temptation, a siren luring him to doom, and he just didn't care. At least he'd die happy, because as he thrust in once, twice, Deke realized that fucking her was one of life's best experiences.

Then she reached up to toy with his nipples and whispered, "I feel you inside me, so hard. Yes. Oh . . . It's like you're going to split me in two. But the pain is so . . . wow." She gasped as he crashed into her again. "You make me feel so alive."

That's about all it took for him to lose control. He started pounding into her like a wild man, reveling in the exertion of his body, the yielding of hers, the little moans she made every time he sank in, sank deeper. The urge to come started broiling in his balls. *Dear God . . .* He *never* fought off the need to climax this quickly. He prided himself on staying a good twenty minutes or more, but with Kimber, after three minutes, he knew he couldn't stave off the inevitable.

More blood rushed south, engorging his cock, increasing his sensitivity.

"Deke," she pleaded. "On your knees. I need you to touch me . . ."

What? He couldn't process her words for the tingles racing up and down his spine, the roaring in his ears. The imminent loss of control would be sweet—with an edge of intensity that would blow the top off his head.

"Please . . ." she pleaded.

"Back away and balance on your knees," Luc snapped. "Kneel and pull her hips up to you."

Their words finally registered. He changed positions, refusing to break stride.

"Luc . . ." Kimber turned to him, her fingers closing around her nipples to pluck at them.

Oh, fuck. The vision of her fondling her own breasts pushed him closer, to the place where need ruled every thrust.

His cousin slid to the ground beside them and palmed Kimber's breasts, pinching the hard nipples that looked so red, so edible. Deke wanted to lean in and suck them, but he couldn't, not if he wanted to keep fucking her. And he needed that. Kimber was addicting. Knowing how heavenly it felt to be inside her ass, if she ever offered her pussy again, he'd take it. No questions asked. No hesitation. He'd plow right into her sweet, grasping folds and claim her.

Luc leaned in and sucked one, then the other of Kimber's nipples into his mouth. Even as his hand drifted south to thumb the hard knob of her clit and plunged two fingers into her sex.

"Yes!" she cried out.

Instantly, Deke felt her tighten on him, begin to ripple. Oh, hell, he couldn't last through that, not for two seconds.

"Now, Deke. Now! Fuck me hard!"

The wild man inside him broke free of his last bit of restraint. His fingers dug into her hips as he lunged into her, one punishing stroke after the other. His cock leapt. She moaned. He absorbed the fluttering pulses of her body, the hard squeeze of her walls.

Kimber screamed, her body spasming. Then, with a roar, Deke shoved into her one last time and came apart, exploding into a million pieces until he began soaring, light-headed. He saw white . . . and Kimber's flushed face, mouth open as she cried out in satisfaction.

The ejaculation went on and on, the pleasure multiplied, magnified. It had never been like this. Deke felt suspended, like these timeless moments of ecstasy would last as long as he could stay inside her. Keep her close.

But reality quickly intruded.

He withdrew slowly, and the moment he did, emptiness beat at him, urging him to get hard again, get right back inside her, and never leave. Kimber was what he needed.

Take her. Claim her. Keep her.

And then what? He'd seen what happened next. Lived it. Still had nightmares about it.

Shuddering, Deke backed away and removed the condom.

He made the mistake of looking at Kimber's face. Her uncertain smile tugged at him. *Bullshit.* It tore a huge hole in his chest. She wanted to know if he was okay. She wanted to know if she'd rocked his world.

No and hell yes, in that order.

And if she stayed another hour, she wouldn't be smiling anymore. She'd be fucked—literally.

Now that he'd been inside her, staying out of her pussy *really* wasn't an option. If she was still here in an hour, she'd be flat on her back. He'd be buried balls deep. And it would be a huge mistake.

Sex with a virgin, even one as practical as Kimber, usually led to visions of romance and white lace and matching monogrammed towels. It brought heartache, pain, and tragedy. She had no way of knowing that. She'd offered herself to him spontaneously, and a terrible thought occurred to him: she had feelings for him, maybe even believed she loved him. She probably thought she could "fix" him. Impossible. He wasn't equipped to give her the sort of happily-ever-after she deserved.

Deke sighed. God, he felt like he was a thousand years old as he stood, snapped his pants, and put on his shithead hat. It was the only weapon he had to make sure he didn't ruin her life.

He turned to his cousin. "You know, she's a hell of a fuck, gives a killer blow job, can handle the needs of two guys, and barely break a sweat. Who knew that under that virginal façade and those fatigue pants there'd be a red-blooded woman?"

Kimber stiffened and stared at him as if he'd transformed into a three-headed alien.

Luc frowned. "Watch your words."

Oh, he'd watch them, all right—and make them as vile as he could stand to. Kimber could *not* stay here. Or at least she couldn't stay here and stay a virgin.

"Oh, no offense, kitten. I appreciate the offer of your virginity, but you should really save it for someone who wants it. You're just not my type, you know."

She blinked, struggling to understand. "You said you wanted me. Too much."

Deke shrugged. "I had you. Your mouth, your ass. I ate your pussy, fingered it. I can live without fucking it."

God, had he ever told a bigger lie?

Hurt seeped into her eyes as she reached for her clothes and covered herself from his crude gaze. That expression gouged a hole in his chest. *Damn!* But she wasn't packing her bags yet, and she needed to be.

"I know we told you to stay with us for two weeks, but I think you're ready for whatever Jesse throws at you. I mean, if you want to stay to perfect your blow job, I'll never turn down the chance to come in a woman's mouth. Or if you want your ass opened wider so you can take more cock, I'm game to help with that. Otherwise . . . I'm not sure why you'd stay."

"Because she's beautiful and special and we don't just see her as another warm body," Luc growled.

Deke tossed them a flippant gaze. "Sure. Yeah. I just figured . . . I felt done and assumed it was mutual."

"Mutual?" Her mouth gaped open. "I just offered you my virginity! You said sinking into me would be heavenly."

"That just shows your innocence. A guy will say anything to get laid when he's hard." He shrugged. "I get that your virginity is some sort of prize to you, and I'm sure it will be to Jesse. I just don't like being the one to break a woman in. It's messy, there's always pain—not the good kind. They're always too sore for round two anytime soon, and you spend the rest of the time in their mouth or their ass, then they complain about being sore all over—"

"Shut your filthy mouth!" Luc grabbed his arm and squeezed. He looked ready to throw punches, and Deke welcomed the thought of pain.

He tossed off his cousin's hold and watched as Kimber put on her clothes like someone dressing to escape a fire. She couldn't get dressed fast enough. "And that's all I am to you? When you look at me, all you see is a virgin?"

"Now? Yeah. I've had every other part of you. What else is there?"

Kimber fisted her hands at her sides, her face flushed and incredulous. "What happened to a woman being about her smarts and her moxie and her sexuality?"

He reached out to test her, to touch her, and was not surprised when she jumped away. "You're smart and you've got backbone. You arouse me. Deep down, you're a sweet girl."

"You say that like it's a bad thing."

"I like raunchy," he said apologetically. "I've been chasing this stripper. Ask Luc, he knows her. She's got enormous tits. Ah, and she wears garter belts. That's so fucking sexy—"

"And you're not interested in tutoring me anymore?"

"What do you think you don't know? What else do you want us to teach you?"

Deke watched her thoughts race across her face, like she was searching for something to say, something that would make him take it back and eat his words.

Finally, she sighed. "You're trying to run me off because you're afraid of my virginity."

"Why would I be? It's not going to reach out and bite me."

"I meant emotionally," she said tersely. "I'm getting too close to your defenses, aren't I?"

Luc sidled up to her and put his arm around her shoulder. "You're right, sweetheart. He's being an ass, and he'd better stop now."

"Look you two, I'm being honest." He turned to Luc. "Didn't I tell you before she came that I was hot and heavy after Alyssa?"

"Of the two of us, Alyssa does not prefer you. And I have no desire for her."

"With you out of the picture, she'll have to look at me." He tried to smile brightly. Damn hard when Kimber looked crushed. "I've heard she has a waxed pussy. Sweet!"

She flinched, then tears glossed her eyes, gathering at the corners, threatening to spill. Yeah, he'd caused it, but he couldn't bear to look anymore.

Making a great show of straightening the pillows on the sofa, he was unprepared when Kimber tapped him on the shoulder. He turned to her, and she smacked him across the face. Hard.

"If all this vile shit you're saying is the truth, then you're a first-class asshole and I wish I hadn't come here in the first place. If you're saying it so you can leave your precious scarred heart wrapped in ice, then not only are you an asshole, you're a coward. Unless you get over the past, you'll be alone for the rest of your life, because Luc will someday meet a great girl, get married, and leave you to rot alone. Enjoy your misery; it's well deserved."

She spun and stormed away. *Victory*. And yet he'd never felt more wretched.

"Kimber . . ." Luc called after her departing figure, auburn hair curling around her back. "Sweetheart!"

She didn't hesitate, much less stop. Instead, Kimber just marched out of the room, across the house to Luc's room, then slammed the door.

Deke flinched at the angry sound of the door reverberating, shattering the tense quiet.

"You stupid son of a bitch," Luc snarled. "I hope you're happy."

"No," he said heavily. "But it's for the best."

"For who? Not me!" He pointed at his chest. "She was the best thing that happened to us, and you fucked it up. Why? Because you wanted her, and you wouldn't take a chance that she wasn't like Heather. She's right; you're a coward."

Luc tore out of the room, his heavy footsteps tracking toward his room and Kimber.

Deke hung his head. He *was* a coward. And he hated it. He'd taken missions all over the world, assassinating power-hungry generals in third-world shit holes, extracting hostages from fanatical terrorists, diffusing bombs ticking away their last ten seconds.

Kimber frightened him much more.

"No, sweetheart. Please. Unpack and stay." He heard Luc's pleading words. "Deke's just being an ass. Stay with me. *I* want you. I'll—"

"Luc, it won't work. I—I need to go . . ."

The tears in her voice were shredding Deke's guts when he heard her lift her car keys out of the dish in the foyer and open the front door. He walked to the corner and peeked around.

"Don't leave." Luc tried to soothe her with a soft touch.

"Tell me why he does this." She swiped at the tears on her cheek. "Why he tries so hard to push me away? What's eating at him?"

Deke tensed. Goddamn it—he wouldn't put it past Luc to spill all his secrets to soothe Kimber and make her stay. And then she'd see him for the monster he was . . .

"That's Deke's secret to tell," Luc said reluctantly.

"Then I can't stay." She marched for the door.

Luc grabbed her arm. "Don't go. Please. Ignore him. Stay with me."

"Deke doesn't want me here. He made that obvious from the start, and I shouldn't have barged in. Lesson learned." Kimber caressed his arm, stood on her tiptoes to kiss his cheek. "Thank you for all you've done. I think I know enough to please Jesse, and that was the point."

"He's a pop star with a transient life and a wild reputation. You're a settle-down kind of girl who deserves a stable home and love. I care about you and I want to—"

Kimber kissed his words away, softly. Deke could almost taste her regret and pain as he watched. Then she drew in a teary, shaking breath. "Luc, I've got to go. I care about you, too, but I can't be here with him. It hurts too much."

Oh, shit.

She opened the door and turned back. Deke's gaze connected with hers, and it felt like a battering ram crushing his chest. His cheek burned where she'd slapped him, and he knew that would be the last place she ever touched him. Hell, he was going to implode from the pain. He hurt so fucking bad.

Kimber didn't say a word. She just shook her head, stepped out, and slammed the door behind her.

His knees nearly crumpled. Deke turned and braced himself against the wall, closing his eyes against this hell.

Luc cursed softly, an ugly string of words Deke doubted his cousin had ever uttered in his life.

He was in major trouble, no doubt. Luc had every right to be pissed. Kimber had every right to hate him.

She couldn't hate him anymore than he hated himself right now.

Chapter Eight

KIMBER smoothed down a ripple in her jeans, flipped her hair over her shoulder, then knocked on the door.

Nearly five years. That's how long it had been since she'd actually seen Jesse McCall in the flesh. She'd seen dozens of pictures. They'd talked on the phone, written countless e-mails. They'd shared parts of themselves over the years—what it had been like for her to grow up without feminine influence after her mother's death, what it had been like for him to be thrust into sudden stardom. Her difficult classes. His demanding schedule. Her wishes. His dreams.

She'd planned for months to be with him so they could share all that together in person finally, maybe for the rest of their lives.

Now, she'd come here with mixed feelings, no longer certain what her future held. She'd wanted to be with him for so long.

But Deke, his anguish and need, his hunger and denial, haunted her.

Kimber's stomach twisted with pain. She pushed it down, hoping to achieve the numbness that had blanketed her for the past forty-eight hours.

Clear the mind. Deep breath. A little calm, but will it ever be enough?

For days after she'd left East Texas, Kimber had hoped that Deke would call and apologize, beg her to come back, tell her he was sorry for humiliating her. God, the hours of tears she'd cried . . . Jesse had been the last thing on her mind.

From Deke, there'd been silence. Utter, hellish silence. Luc had called to check on her, and attempt to cajole her into returning. He'd even pleaded. But Deke wasn't going to beg her to come back. According to him, he had a stiff dick for her, nothing more. Kimber didn't believe it. She'd gotten too close to him emotionally; Deke had shed her in an attempt to protect her from something she didn't understand. But he was also protecting himself.

After he'd thrown the offer of her virginity back in her face and all but announced he was tossing her over for a stripper was a hell of a time to realize that she loved him.

She shoved the thought and the chest-crushing pain aside as footsteps approached the door. She took a deep breath. The blessed numbness began to return.

Deke expected her to move on. So here Kimber was, at Jesse's door, determined to follow through with her plan. She still adored Luc, but she had to get over Deke and carve out a future. What else could she do?

The hotel room door opened. A stranger with a boyish smile stood in the doorway. Wavy brown hair. Blue eyes. He would have been white bread and apple pie—except for the big tattoo of a skull and crossbones on his biceps, his black eyeliner, and the bullring through his nose.

"Hi, I'm here to see Jesse."

He stuck out his hand, pale and artistic. "You must be Kimber. I'm Ryan. I do backup vocals and write songs."

She took his hand, shook it. "Oh, yes. He's mentioned you many times. Nice to meet you."

Ryan's gaze roamed over her with subtle appreciation. "You, too. He said you were a gorgeous girl, but he was wrong. You're a gorgeous woman, and he's going to be surprised."

Sending him a nervous smile, Kimber looked around the room. A suite. A very nice one in tasteful taupes and creams—and a view of Houston's skyline that went on forever.

"Thank you. Is Jesse here?"

"Just getting out of the shower. He asked me to greet you since he got out of rehearsals a bit late and had to take an unexpected radio interview." Ryan shrugged narrow shoulders. "Goes with the territory."

"I'm sure."

Kimber tried not to be let down, tried not to fidget. Surely, Jesse would have greeted her personally if he could. Still, she'd waited five years and she really, really needed a friend. Couldn't those people wait ten minutes?

"Have a seat," Ryan invited. "Drink?"

He pointed to the half-empty minibar. Lots of little bottles missing. The soda shelf was mostly full.

She shook her head as she sank onto the empty chocolate brown sofa. For a moment, she was tempted to lose herself to whiskey oblivion, but she'd tried last week and endured the hangover from hell. "No thanks."

Ryan sat beside her. "Jesse has talked so much about you, I feel like I know you. He always brags about how kind you are. How sweet."

Kimber frowned. She wasn't a saint. Look at the things she'd done with Luc and Deke. And in retrospect, she hadn't done them strictly to learn for Jesse. Or to see if she could handle a ménage. Once she'd identified her lack-of-experience problem and realized Deke was a solution, she'd jumped—hell, leaped, hopped, and skipped—at the chance to see him. To satisfy a dark fascination she'd had for the hard soldier since she was old enough to understand and too young to indulge.

"Jesse may have exaggerated my goodness."

"Him? Nah. He's as jaded as they come. He never gives praise unless it's due. Trust me."

"I see." But she didn't. Not really.

The Jesse she'd connected with that special summer had been optimistic and eager for the future. True, in the last few years, he'd seemed . . . a little more skeptical about people. Less trusting. But didn't that come with stardom? Having to protect your identity and privacy? All that crap would affect anyone's outlook, she supposed.

"It's great to meet one of Jesse's friends. I know you two are pretty close," she offered, fishing for information to discover exactly what role Ryan played in Jesse's life.

"He probably told you; I've been a member of the band for the last three years." He leaned in, gave her a direct stare. "We do *everything* together."

Including have sex. So *he* was the third in Jesse's ménages. Ryan's pale blue eyes communicated the gravity of the information without saying a word. As far as he and Jesse knew, Kimber had no notion about their kink, but she understood the other man's message. And his stare made it clear that he expected to jump in on the action.

The thought was unsettling. Would Jesse want her to have sex with this person she barely knew and wasn't sure she liked? The thought made her grimace. Wasn't she different to Jesse than other women? More special? He'd always said so . . .

But that wasn't her problem. Deke and Luc—*they* were the issue. They haunted her. Yes, spending time with them had shown her firsthand how arousing ménage could be. Kimber was sure that Jesse craved the excitement, the forbidden thrill. Lord knew, after those few days with the cousins, she more than understood. But now, the thought of anyone else touching her made her queasy. When Ryan looked her over, she recoiled and nearly lost her lunch.

Run! a part of her screamed.

Ever practical, her mind pointed out that she had no future with Luc and Deke. She had to move forward, and she'd planned for years to be with Jesse. She had to follow through, to see where their years-long rapport might lead. Maybe her first love could help her recover from her last mistake.

"I understand what you're saying," she murmured.

Ryan's smile faded, removing the boyish quality. One brown brow quirked up. "Do you?"

"Jesse may have last seen me as a seventeen-year-old girl, but while I've retained a certain amount of innocence, I can assure you I've grown up."

"Beautifully so, I'd say," boomed a voice from behind her.

Kimber whipped her gaze around. *Jesse?*

He looked so much the same from a distance. Tall, shaggy brown hair liberally laced with sun-streaked gold, olive complexion, dark eyes, and a smoking hot bod, as evidenced by his tight black T-shirt and jeans. Jesse.

She jumped up from the sofa at the same time he moved toward her. When he grabbed her in a big hug, wrapping lean, strong arms around her, she sank against him—just like she had that summer they spent together. Her head didn't fit exactly under his chin anymore, but he kissed her lips tenderly, as he always had. Kimber waited, but . . . Where was that shiver his kiss had always given her? The smile he flashed her didn't look complete.

Maybe he was just tired. And distracted. Lord knew, she'd been completely preoccupied after leaving Deke and Luc. And it had been five years since she'd seen Jesse. Things changed. People changed. She'd learn his new ways. She and Jesse would reconnect.

Holding out hope that Deke would call and apologize and ask her to come back was plain stupid.

"Wow!" He stood back, holding her at arm's length, and stared. "You look great."

"You, too."

He waved her compliment away. "It's easy when you have a hairdresser, a personal trainer, a chef, blah, blah, blah. Sit down. It's great to see you!" He tugged her to the sofa and she sat beside him. "Since we haven't had the chance to catch up in a couple of weeks, tell me how your dad has been."

"You know the Colonel. Always busy. Always running a tight unit. He's been all over the world lately. He'll be heading home next week for a mini-vacation. He hasn't had one in over a year."

Jesse nodded. "That man was always driven. Remember that week at the lake we all spent the summer he guarded me?"

Remember? That's where she and Jesse had fallen for each other, and they'd started talking about the possibilities of a future together.

Nothing had changed since then. Yet everything had. Jesse had drifted into a wild lifestyle, according to the tabloids. Now, Deke kept intruding on Kimber's thoughts. Her stomach was in a constant knot of pain. Standing in front of Jesse with Ryan looking on, one big question hit her: Even if she managed to push Deke and Luc out of her heart and started a new future, how could she fit into Jesse's life?

The details of how Jesse had become attracted to ménages—and where he got the women—should probably trouble her. It had several months ago. But since her involvement with Deke and Luc, she hadn't thought much about it. Certainly, she couldn't expect celibacy when she hadn't seen Jesse for so long. And she had problems of her own.

Besides, the last time she and Jesse had talked, he'd said he was ready to give up his partying ways. More than ready. She wasn't exactly sure what that meant. Giving up ménages? No matter what, she'd have to forget Deke and Luc enough to handle being with Jesse if they were going to have any sort of future.

"Sure, I remember," she murmured. "I have fond memories of that week."

"You know that was my attempt to force your dad to take a vacation." He had the good grace to look sheepish.

Really? She'd thought—hoped at the time—it had been his ploy to get some extra alone time with her.

Kimber reminded him tartly, "All he did was complain for a week that the cabin was too hard to defend and that any psycho fan could get out on the lake with a sailboat and a high-powered rifle and pick you off."

Jesse rolled his eyes. "Yeah, he never mastered the fine art of kicking back."

"Nothing has changed."

"So you're still working on your nursing exams?"

She shook her head. "I just finished my state exam yesterday. Once the results are in, I have to figure out where I'm going to work. I've got a couple of offers I'm considering, of course contingent on passing the exams."

"You'll pass." He frowned. "You're going to get a job? How soon?"

"Six weeks." She shrugged. "I won't get my test results until then."

Something pensive crossed his face. "That gives us a little time—"

A sudden hard rap on the door startled Kimber. She and Jesse both turned toward the sound as Ryan opened the suite's door. An older man dressed in a camel-colored sport coat and an overstarched white shirt stood on the other side and entered the room. As he moved under the light, Kimber saw his hair was dominated by salt more than pepper. Sagging jowls puffed up an otherwise thin man.

He scowled. "Jesse, you've got press coming in an hour. Don't forget." He turned a sharp stare to the half-empty minibar. "And damn it, don't get drunk. They spot that shit a mile away, and your reputation isn't exactly squeaky clean."

"Cal," Jesse supplied. "My manager. The soul of kindness."

A deaf man wouldn't miss the sarcasm in Jesse's tone.

All gruff and rumble, Cal blustered out, "I keep you from self-destructing. Without me, you're one party away from has-been."

"Thanks for the pep talk, Dad."

His manager turned his watery blue gaze on her. "We haven't met."

The greeting wasn't warm, but it wasn't unfriendly, either. She wasn't sure what to make of him, since she didn't disagree that Jesse needed to tone down the partying. But if she was delivering the message, she would have done it with a little more finesse.

She stood and held out her hand. "No, we haven't. I'm Kimber Edgington."

Cal's blank expression as he shook her hand said he'd never heard of her. *Odd.* Then again, Jesse had only hired the seasoned veteran about eighteen months ago. Jesse and Cal weren't close, and their relationship was strictly business.

"I've known Jesse for years. We're old friends."

"And since we've got a little break, Kimber and I are going to catch up," Jesse chimed in, now standing beside her and wrapping his arm around her shoulder.

"Just remember your priorities, Romeo. We've got a lot riding on this next album and upcoming tour." Cal frowned.

"Got it." Jesse shoved Cal toward the door. "I'll be down in an hour. Thanks for the heads-up. Good to see you. Buh bye."

Kimber frowned. "You're going back out on tour?"

"Mostly we're finishing studio work. There's a mini U.S. tour, but it's only ten cities," he assured, still pushing Cal. "You'll come with me, won't you? You said you'd spend at least a few weeks with me. Does it matter where we are?"

"She's a distraction you don't need," Cal warned, digging in his heels just short of the door. "It's not the image we've been pushing to the press.

Single bad boy with a voice like an angel. Chicks dig it, and it sells records. Word gets out that you have a girlfriend on tour with you, and you watch. The album won't do as well."

"If you leave in the next ten seconds, I'll do an extra press junket in the first three cities."

With a scowl, Cal dashed out, slamming the door behind him.

Jesse leaned against it with a groan. "He's got great business smarts, but he's so single-minded, he drives me crazy. So, you'll come with me on tour, right?"

Kimber had cleared her schedule so she could be with him. But a tour? Everything between them right now felt a little awkward. Having Cal and Ryan hanging around wasn't helping. Or maybe this . . . weird feeling was all in her head because she couldn't get Deke out of her thoughts.

Did he regret rejecting and insulting her? Did he miss her at all? Even now, she itched to pick up her cell phone and call Luc, ask him for some word about the hard-headed soldier. But why? Even if Deke wanted her, he'd never accept his desire. For some reason, she made him vulnerable and he refused to tolerate it.

And damn, it hurt like hell.

Kimber cleared her throat, tried to clear her mind. "I'll have to make sure there's nothing going on, but I'm pretty sure I can go."

"Great." He shrugged and tugged her back to the couch, plopping down on it and pulling her into his lap. "I really want you to go. I've been looking forward to having you around. You're just what I need, babe. Without you here, I can be a really bad boy." Jesse flashed her a thousand-megawatt smile.

Yeah, that's what all the press about him said. With looks, money, and stardom, he was all about the sex, drugs, and rock 'n' roll—pretty much in that order. Sitting on his lap felt weird, since she could only wonder how many other women he'd perched on his thighs and what had happened next. And he didn't rev her up like Deke or comfort her like Luc.

"How will having me here change your bad ways?"

He picked up her hand, rubbed his thumb along the back. "You're a calming influence. My good luck charm. My conscience."

What? The last time they'd talked she wasn't wild enough to live his life, and now she was his conscience?

"Don't frown," he said. "That's a good thing."

Ryan glanced at his watch. "Time to go face Jimmy for the day, toss out the new crop of songs for him to butcher and bitch about for the album."

"Jimmy is my producer," Jesse explained as a quick aside to Kimber. "Dodge a few bullets for me, would you? I want to spend a little time with Kimber."

Ryan's gaze slid over to her, moved over her breasts. She felt somehow touched without permission. Almost violated. She shivered. If he was the third in Jesse's ménages, and *if* she stuck this out with Jesse, she'd have to talk to him about finding someone whose mere stare didn't make her feel the need to shower.

"Sure," Ryan said. "I need some liquid fortification before I go." He peered down into the minibar and extracted a couple of the little liquor bottles. He opened one and chugged it straight, in seconds. "Want something?"

Jesse looked at the bottles in Ryan's hands, then at Kimber. Discreetly, she checked her watch. Two in the afternoon, and he was starting on hard liquor? And drinking it straight?

Kimber felt Jesse's gaze on her, and when she looked up, he shot Ryan a look of faint regret. "Nah. It's early."

"Dude, it's five o'clock somewhere. You always say that."

With a shrug, Jesse pursed his lips, looked away. Then he turned to her with a bright smile. "See, it's Kimber. She's already having a positive effect on my life. Because you're so good, huh, babe?"

Jesse squeezed her hand. Kimber squeezed back almost as a reflex, but his words rattled around in her brain. *Because I'm so good?* When had her life in the slow lane become a plus?

"Then I'm looking forward to getting to know her better." Ryan shot her a smoky look and approached Jesse with a hearty pat on the shoulder, then whispered, "Save some ass for me."

Despite Ryan's low tone, Kimber couldn't help but overhear it. And it pissed her off. The flaming jerk was making a lot of assumptions about what and who she'd say yes to. Deke and Luc had come as a pair, yes. But Luc had been impossible not to adore. All easy, sophisticated charm. Molasses seduction, slow, sweet, and potent. And Deke . . . She'd known him and trusted him right from the beginning, even if he could be a bastard and say terrible, hurtful things for the purpose of pushing away the people who loved him.

"Get lost." Jesse pointed Ryan toward the door.

The band member, four little bottles of booze, and his skull with crossbones tattoo left a moment later. Kimber breathed a sigh of relief.

"Don't mind him. He can be an ass."

Kimber didn't disagree. "He tells me you do *everything* together. He's the third in your ménages, isn't he?"

Jesse squirmed uncomfortably under her waiting stare. "So you know about that?"

"When you said you had a kink and you didn't think I could handle it, I read a few tabloids, asked around. I got answers."

"Ah, babe." He wrapped his arms around her and placed a gentle kiss on her lips. "It's lonely without you. Those girls are meaningless. Ryan and Cal make sure everything that happens on the road is meaningless. And nailing someone by myself just got too . . . common. A twice-daily thing, like brushing your teeth."

Twice daily? With a stranger? And regular sex had become too boring?

"Don't look at me like that. I don't say it to hurt you. I'm being honest. But you . . . you're the one who matters to me. I won't be bored with you. I've thought about it, and I won't share you. You're too sweet. Too good. I need you to stay that way."

Lovely sentiment. But she wasn't up for sainthood or anything. And what would happen if he did get bored?

What would happen if she couldn't get over Deke?

Frowning, Kimber slid onto the sofa cushion beside him. "I'm not too sweet. I'm not totally innocent. After I found out about your ménages, I looked up someone I knew who's into the same thing. He and his cousin . . . trained me."

Jesse's face fell. "Trained you? You let them fuck—"

"No," she cut in. "I told you I planned to come to you a virgin. I have."

Only because Deke had turned her down. Damn, there went that pain in her stomach again, making tight knots into tighter ones. She slept with it, breathed with it, ached with it. Time was supposed to heal all, but the pain wasn't easing or going away.

Kimber had offered herself to Deke not because she'd felt sorry for him. As if she'd give her virginity for a pity fuck. The only thing on her mind and in her heart that night had been her desire to heal him, to bond with him, be meaningful to him. To love him. Somehow, despite his awful words to her afterward, a part of her—a big part—wished that Deke had accepted her offer and taken her. She suspected that him breaking her virgin barrier would help him break through his emotional one.

But now she'd never know.

Jesse breathed a sigh of relief. "So they just talked to you?"

"They touched me. I learned to touch them." She wasn't going to lie. She just wasn't going to tell him she was in love with someone else.

Thunder boomed across Jesse's dark face. "Touch, how?"

"Enough that I understand the appeal of the ménage and what draws you to do it. I never expected you to change your sexuality for me. So I tried to adapt for you."

I tried to find out what fascination a crass, difficult soldier had for me and I got burned.

The answer seemed to mollify him. "That's . . . Wow, you're an amazing woman. But you're not like the whores and bimbos around all the time. I had no intention of sharing you. Not with Ryan. Not with anyone. If I make you bad, how can your good rub off on me?"

His tone was half-joking. Kimber wasn't laughing. They really needed to get past this Virgin Mary image he had of her.

"Thanks for not wanting to share me with Ryan."

Jesse leaned over, pulled her close. "You're mine, babe. We've spent too many years apart for me to only get half of you. You're the only one who really knows me. You're the only one I care enough about to change for."

"I didn't ask you to change."

"But for you, I want to. For you, I want to be a better man. Just being near you makes me one."

His words were touching . . . but confusing. Why did he think he needed to change so badly? When had this all come about? And why had he pinned it all on her?

"Maybe we can compromise. You be a little better, I'll be a little badder. It'll all work out then."

He hesitated. "Badder, how?"

"I hadn't planned on being a virgin forever."

Why not give her innocence to Jesse? She'd saved it for him for years, and Deke wouldn't take it, no matter how badly he wanted to.

Jesse didn't respond to that right away. "That makes sense. I have this plan. Just give me a little time. It'll all work out, babe. You'll see." He finished with that smile he frequently flashed for the cameras.

It wasn't his real smile. His real smile, she remembered from their summer together, was kind of goofy and lopsided. Mischief lurked in one corner, happiness in the other. This smile was symmetrical and phony. Kimber frowned.

"Cut the crap, Jesse. What sort of plan?"

"Nope, you can't ruin it for me. I've had this worked out for a while. Come on the tour and all will be revealed."

"When do we leave?" After five years of waiting and a broken heart, why put their relationship on hold any longer? She wanted to get on with her life, to find some semblance of a happily-ever-after.

And forget Deke. He was past. He'd driven her away, so she was moving forward. Soon, she hoped she and Jesse would find the right footing.

"A week from tomorrow." He grabbed her hands. "It'll be great to have you with me, keep me in line. Everything is going to be different. I'll make the surprise worth your wait."

* * *

"YOU'RE where?" her father boomed over the phone later that night.

Curled up on the couch in Jesse's suite while the band rehearsed, she clutched her cell phone. "I'm in Houston. With Jesse. He's in the States for the next few months, and we're spending some time together."

Her father paused. "You know what the press says about him? About his sex life?"

The man was still a parent, even though she was far from being a child. "Yes, Daddy. We've worked it out." Time for a change of subject, before he asked what that meant, before he asked where she'd been—and who she'd been with—before going to Houston. "Where are you?"

"Watch yourself," he said instead.

So much for the subject change. "I will. I'm a big girl now."

"You are." He barked the words, as if he hated to admit them. "When I look back, I wonder if, after your mother died, your brothers and I sheltered you too much. What do you know about a guy with a lifestyle like Jesse's?"

Oh, she'd learned plenty from Deke and Luc, including heartache.

"Please, don't worry. You did a great job being both a mom and dad. Logan and Hunter were typical overprotective brothers who ran off all my dates and made fun of me every time I put on a shred of makeup, but I'm not too mentally scarred. I'll manage."

Her dad's husky laugh warmed her heart.

"I've known Jesse a long time," she continued. "We've waited years for this opportunity. We just need to figure it out together."

"I don't see you being a superstar's groupie." The frown in his voice couldn't be any more obvious.

Kimber had trouble with that picture, too, in truth. She couldn't live on the road the way Jesse did, but could she just leave him to run off with the band and live the way he always had? Even if he wanted to "change," that would take time. And what would happen if, someday, they followed through on the possibilities they'd discussed over the years and got married?

Could she stop loving Deke, wanting him, enough to say "I do" to someone else? How had that man turned all her plans upside down in a handful of days?

"I'm not going to be a groupie. And right now is our time to figure out what we'll be to each other. Just let me handle it."

"I don't like it. He used to be a good enough kid, but what I hear now . . . I think it's a mistake."

Her gut clenched. Dad said it with such conviction. Still, he hadn't seen Jesse in years, just *heard* about him. Not the same thing.

"It's my mistake to make."

Her father sighed. "Yeah, it is. Just . . . be careful, in more ways than one."

"What do you mean?"

"I'm on my way home from Thailand right now. When I get there, I want to check on you, check your brothers, the house."

"Is someone still threatening you?"

"Yes. Sending creepy e-mails and leaving menacing messages. I don't know who I've pissed off, or how serious he is. You know crackpots, and some never get past the threatening stage. But this one has mentioned you and said he'll hurt you to hurt me."

"This isn't new, and nothing has ever happened to me."

"There's always a first. This one seems tenacious, so I'd feel better if you didn't go anywhere alone right now. Remember your self-defense. I can't persuade you to carry, can I?"

Unease sliced through her, razor-thin but impossible to ignore. Some creeps devoted their lives to waiting for their prey to get complacent and let their guard down. Who knew if this guy fit that profile?

"I'm not getting a permit to carry a handgun. I'll be fine. I'm surrounded by people here."

Her dad growled into the phone, like he wanted to say something more, but knew it was a futile argument. "So, you're going to come visit your old man while I'm home, aren't you?"

"Jesse's tour stops in Dallas on the second night. I'll drive out while we're there. I'm looking forward to seeing you."

"Me, too. Take care, little girl. I've missed you."

He hadn't called her that in years. Hadn't said anything remotely emotional in even longer. "Is there something you're not telling me?"

He hesitated. "No. I just want you to be careful."

Chapter Nine

"How was rehearsal?" Kimber asked as Jesse entered the hotel suite late in the afternoon nearly a week later.

He was shirtless, his longish hair wet from a recent shower. With a towel in one hand, a bottle of water in the other, he strode into the room, all lazy-hipped grace. The sleek bulge of his shoulder moved sinuously every time he swiped at his hair with the towel. His masculine throat worked with each swallow of water. His perfectly symmetrical features pulled into a balanced smile.

In the last five years, he'd definitely grown. No longer a cute boy, quite simply, he'd become a gorgeous man. No wonder he was on posters, billboards, and magazine covers all over the world. After years of sightless communication with him, Kimber was almost stunned anew by his beauty.

She enjoyed looking at him. Just looking. She wasn't moved to touch him. Instead, she ached to see denim-dark blue eyes, razor-short hair, square jaw tensed, and a hard face filled with lust for her.

Damn it, she *had* to stop thinking about Deke. It wasn't helping her here. *Focus!* What would be helpful was a hot ache in her belly that urged her to get naked with Jesse, the way a single glance from Deke had inspired her. The way a tender kiss from Luc could. But that urge to get down and dirty with Jesse wasn't coming. In the last few days, she'd felt occasional bursts of feeling for him, like a camera's flash, brilliant and brief, then gone. Nothing more.

It seemed the urge hadn't hit Jesse, either. He'd kissed her sweetly every morning and tenderly every night, then retired to his own bed, leaving her alone in hers. *Thank God.*

But she did wonder, was there something wrong with her that no man seemed to want her virginity?

Confused by it all, Kimber shook her head.

But the mystery was deeper. In a handful of days, Deke, a man she'd told herself she couldn't fall for, had barged his way into her heart and burrowed in deep. And she felt so stupid. Missing and loving a man who would never return her feelings made no sense. Jesse had been in her dreams, in her plans, for a long time. He was supposed to be her future. True, he wasn't the same carefree teenager she recalled, no longer quick to laugh.

But she wasn't the same woman. And she no longer saw Jesse through rose-colored glasses. What she needed, she feared Jesse didn't have.

"Rehearsal was a regular fuckin'"—he grimaced, as if remembering her presence—"It wasn't smooth. We got some lazy people not doing their jobs. Hung over, the assholes." He rolled his eyes. "And the press crawling around. Like they want to report it as news every time I spit. I wish to hell they didn't follow me everywhere, but Cal encourages them. All for my 'image.'"

"I'm sure he means well. Tonight's show will be great." Kimber did her best to sound supportive, like a friend should be. But she wasn't familiar with the snarling side of Jesse.

"Cal is all for whatever lines his pockets. Greedy son of a bitch. If he wasn't one of the best in the business, I'd shitcan his wrinkled ass and throw him off the gravy train. He acts like I need a damn daddy to keep me in line."

Kimber hadn't seen much of the older man, but enough to know that Cal felt that part of his role was to keep Jesse from self-destructing.

"He's trying to help you."

"He's pissing me off."

"Your only choices are to fire him, put up with him, or ask him to be nicer."

That stopped his tirade. "Damn, you're smart. You're like your dad; you tell people how it is. I knew there was a reason I invited you on tour with me."

Jesse smiled, relieving some of the severity on his face, then he hugged her, kissed her forehead. Kimber did her best to settle into his warmth and bask. But his snarling words were still ringing in her head, distracting her. And though he was gorgeous, everything with him felt wrong.

Kimber knew why. *Damn Deke and his stubborn hide.*

She stepped out of his embrace. "So, you ready for the show?"

"Yeah, we finally got it together. The venue is cool. I've really been looking forward to this."

The look Jesse sent her made no sense. Secretive. Nervous. Eager. Tender. *Interesting* . . .

"Because it's the start of the tour?"

"No. This show in particular. I'm a little nervous."

She smiled and grabbed his hand, reminding herself that he needed a friend. Hell, so did she. From what she'd seen, neither Ryan nor Cal really fit that bill. No wonder he was cranky. And of course he was anxious about this show. As his friend, she could provide a little comfort.

"I'm sure the first show of a new tour is exciting. It's sold out. Fans will be there. They love you. Nothing to be worried about."

"Oh, I'm not worried about that. Sometimes, I think I could sing 'Mary Had a Little Lamb' and they'd cheer their asses off." He laughed, a cynical snort. "It's crazy."

"Then what's up?"

"You'll see . . ."

The singsong taunt was accompanied by that odd look. Jesse definitely had a secret. He was up to something.

"What are you planning?"

"You'll have to wait until tonight to find out."

"I'm looking forward to it." But she lied. A dread she didn't understand settled like a pile of rocks into her stomach. Surprises weren't always good.

"That's it?"

"Um, I'm sure it'll be great." Was he put out because she wasn't jumping up and down to find out about the secret?

"I hope you think so." He stared, those piercing dark eyes looking anxious and confused.

She sighed. "What's wrong?"

"Nothing."

A denial, pure and simple. Damn, the man was so moody. From highs to lows, from mischievous to pensive, all in a snap. Everyone always just adapted, Kimber noticed. Jesse was so used to the world revolving around him. It was so unlike her father and brothers, who only had three modes: work, laughter, and anger—in that order. Jesse was all over the emotional map.

"What happened to the you I used to know?" The question was out before she could stop it.

Jesse's gaze snapped back to her. "What do you mean?"

Kimber fought the urge to fidget and looked away. But they hadn't had an honest conversation in the last week. Passing and superficial, yes. He'd asked about her family, her schooling, scraped a bit of the surface about her wishes for the future. Granted, she hadn't exactly been forthcoming. She couldn't blurt out to the man she'd come to explore a future with that her heart was someplace else. Besides, he was totally absorbed with this tour and hadn't opened up to her. Some days, he hardly talked at all.

Unlike Deke, who'd always connected with her, even with just a glance. He'd told her where she stood, even when he was trying to lie, whether she wanted to hear it or not.

"I think you know what I mean," she whispered, forcing her thoughts away from the iron-hearted bodyguard. "You've . . . changed."

"You have, too. You're more confident and mature and sexy as hell." He leaned in and placed a gentle kiss on her mouth. "When I'm with you,

I feel clearer, more centered. I guess it's taking me a while to adjust to not partying all the time."

Maybe that was true. Who knew? In some ways, Kimber felt like she was talking to a stranger.

"I'm not here to change your life."

"I need to change my life, and I know you're the key. I think back to that summer I spent with you and your dad all the time and remember stuff we talked about, things we did. We found plenty of good, clean ways to have fun." He paused, a glint making his dark eyes sparkle. "Hey, you know what I have on DVD?"

Mischief lurked in that smile. And a hint of happiness. A *real* smile. The first she'd seen in a week.

Kimber relaxed and returned his grin. "*American Pie*?"

"Yep. We've got a few hours before we have to be at the arena. Wanna?"

Watch the movie that had made them laugh so hard they'd cried together that summer? "Sure."

"Hang on."

He clambered over the back of the sofa and grabbed the phone. In seconds, he was demanding popcorn from room service. By the time he found the DVD, figured out how to work the equipment connected to the suite's plasma TV, and had the menu on the screen, the popcorn had arrived.

For over an hour, they laughed at the antics of four high school boys all trying to lose their virginity by prom night.

"Watch this," Jesse demanded, tossing popcorn in the air and trying to catch it with his open mouth.

He missed. The piece hit him on the cheek, and Kimber laughed. "Smooth."

"Okay, so I'm out of practice. And it works better with M&M's."

She mock-punched him in the shoulder. "Excuses, excuses."

"Let's see you do better."

Arching a brow, she plucked up a piece of the fluffy popcorn and tossed it. A perfect landing on her tongue. She tossed him a smug smile.

"Show-off," he grumbled, but tossed an arm around her shoulders as they settled in for the rest of the movie.

And it was comfortable. Friendly.

When it was over, he turned the TV and DVD player off, wearing a huge smile. "That movie always reminds me of the summer we spent together. I don't think I've ever had a better time. No pressure. No groupies. No parties. Just . . . fun."

"I enjoyed that summer, too."

The air had been ripe with the hope of first love. They'd been innocent enough—nothing beyond kisses—but every one of those had seemed so hot and forbidden. And so sweet. The fact he'd bought the very DVD that reminded him of her and carried it with him touched her. Watching it together again had been a blast.

But had watching it helped Jesse to tune in to the emotional connection they'd once shared or just remind him of a happier past? Was he actually interested in her, or was she like the DVD, just another reminder of a better time?

And why was she staying here, giving Jesse false hope, when Deke was so obviously dominating her heart? When she ached with missing quiet times with Luc?

Someone knocked on the suite's door. Without waiting for an answer, he shoved in the key, and strolled into the room. *Ryan.*

He sent them both a long-suffering grimace. "Dang, all clothed again. You two are dull."

Oh, the man miffed Kimber. Annoying, grating, he'd say whatever was on his mind and clearly didn't care a lick if it offended anyone.

"We were watching a movie." Kimber did her best to sound civil.

"I'd rather you get busy and make a movie I'd wanna watch." He leered.

Okay, that made him zoom to the top of her ick chart.

Her annoyance must have shown, since Jesse leveled him a hard warning stare. "Despite how much you like home movies, we won't be making any. What do you want?"

"Showtime is in an hour, kids. I'm just your reminder."

Jesse glanced at his watch, then sighed. "Back to reality." He sent a longing look at the minibar. "Drink before the show?"

Drinking before work? "No, and it's just my opinion, but I don't think you should either."

"It loosens me up." His tone was pure defense.

"Your choice, but I'll bet it makes you less sharp."

Ryan strolled to the minibar and withdrew an armful of the little bottles. "Looks like the old lady still has you on the wagon. You really ought to fuck her and loosen her up. I'll be happy to help."

Before Kimber could flay the man alive with her tongue or Jesse could retort, Ryan left the room. *Bastard.*

"Sorry," Jesse muttered.

"You miss your old life," she said, realizing it was the truth.

"I need to stop living like that. I can't keep waking up every morning hungover next to Ryan and a woman whose name I don't know. I need you to help me."

His dark eyes pleaded, filled with hope and shame and anger.

More alarm bells went off in her head, even as she felt . . . sorry for him. He wanted her to help him save himself. He didn't actually *want* her. And she couldn't rescue someone who wasn't willing to rescue himself.

God, she was so confused. Jesse had been everything to her—or she thought he had been—until Deke and Luc. Until she'd lost her heart. She'd pinned hopes and dreams on Jesse. Now . . . it was clear she just didn't fit here.

"Please help me." He grabbed her hands and pulled her closer.

Kimber smelled his fresh citrus-scented soap and clean skin as he grabbed her suddenly and layered his mouth over hers. Soft. Like the strokes of a paintbrush or the touch of a butterfly's wings. Sweet, like he'd lightly dusted the kiss with sugar. But when he urged her mouth open and slid inside, she tasted the acrid desperation on his tongue and recoiled.

Instead of letting her go, Jesse pulled her closer. His fingers drifted into her hair, fisted around the long strands as he deepened the kiss. Kimber discreetly pushed at him. He resisted, plunging deeper inside. He was . . . taking something from her and begging for more. There was no giving on his part. He thought she had something he needed.

She didn't. Nor did she want him. The kiss didn't make her melt or burn or need. Her heart . . . it wasn't here. He was a friend, but nothing more. And after the show, she'd tell him that.

Quickly, she broke off the kiss. He pulled away with a sigh of regret. "I'd better get dressed." His voice cracked. "You, too. Wear something special."

With another flash of a smile, part excitement, part anxiety, he walked past her, down the hall, and shut the door behind him.

What the hell was that man up to?

* * *

THE roar of the stadium and the decibel level of the music gave Kimber a headache. For over two hours, she'd been sitting backstage, first watching the opening act and trying to ignore the bimbo groupies fawning over Jesse. Now, she watched Jesse and his band winding their show to a close, playing their eclectic mixture of alternative anger and soulful emotion, with a hint of something classical. And he was the perfect singer, with expressive eyes, not just believing every word he sang, but feeling them— whether that was a song about getting down and dirty or embracing eternal love.

Funny, but she was more moved by listening to Jesse than kissing him. She hated to admit why, didn't want to consider the reasons her body had begun to ache desperately. Or why she had dreams—amazing, erotic dreams—all revolving around Deke and Luc.

Kimber missed them both, wished she could throw her arms around Deke and heal him. If she was really honest, she wished she could make him see her as something other than just a virgin, but a woman he could laugh with, smile with, live with . . . The yearning to tell him that she loved him beat strong. Every bit as strong as her need to hear him say he loved her, too.

It isn't going to happen.

Kimber accepted the reality with a sigh. Her future, the one she'd mapped out, was gone.

Sighing, she watched absently as Jesse threw his sweat towel into the cheering crowd of mostly young girls. Several were topless, their breasts bobbing as they danced under the artificial blue light. He smiled and saluted them.

God, she didn't fit in here. She was going to have to tell him. And leave.

"Kimber."

Her name. Someone was calling her name. Loudly. She blinked. Jesse was looking right at her, motioning her toward him.

He wanted her to come on stage? In front of everyone?

Animated now, even a little adamant, Jesse waved her toward him once more.

What the hell? With a shrug, she got off her stool and started out onto the stage. Flashbulbs went off. The crowd quieted.

Microphone in hand, Jesse smiled and said, "It's great to be back in Houston, my hometown!" The crowd cheered as he curled an arm around her shoulders and pulled her against him, planting a kiss on her temple.

Mind racing, Kimber looked out at the crowd, nearly wobbling on her heels. Even though the bright stage lights blinded her from seeing the audience, she'd seen the vast size, the thousands out there, just before Jesse had taken the stage. Why had he pulled her out here in front of all these people? She couldn't sing.

"It's the perfect place," Jesse murmured to the crowd, the tone like a whisper he told just one secret friend, "to announce that my longtime girlfriend, Kimber, and I are getting married."

Chapter Ten

DEKE unrolled the morning paper on the kitchen table, a cup of coffee in hand.

"Any news?" Luc asked tightly.

Those were the first civil words his cousin had spoken in over a week.

Standing as he sifted through the newspaper, Deke set the front page aside and rifled to find the other sections he enjoyed, so he could throw out the rest. So he could focus on something other than Kimber's absence eating away at his sanity. Not that he was having any luck.

Especially not when the headline on the Entertainment page screamed out at him.

Jesse McCall Engaged!

Beneath it was a black-and-white picture of Kimber next to McCall, his arm around her, along with a caption that stated Jesse had informed the crowd at last night's concert that he and longtime girlfriend Kimber Edgington were engaged to be married.

Son of a fucking bitch!

The coffee slipped from Deke's numb fingers and crashed to the kitchen floor.

Luc spun around. "What the hell is the matter with you? Clean the damn coffee—"

"I don't give a shit about the fucking coffee." He thrust the paper in Luc's direction.

After a quick scan, Luc sank into a chair at the kitchen table and swore. "Damn it. Shit! You let her go. Hell, you pushed her out the door."

Luc threw the paper back onto the table with a glare in his direction. Deke found his gaze glued to the picture of McCall with Kimber. The wondering was killing him. Had she slept with the pretty-boy singer? Most likely. And just as likely, McCall had shared her with someone, watched some stranger fuck her to orgasm.

What hurt even more was wondering if she actually loved Jesse. But Deke knew Kimber. She had to believe she was in love with the bastard pop star to agree to marry him.

At the thought, his knees melted underneath him and he stumbled into a chair. Kimber married to someone else. In love with someone else.

Hell no!

But that was reality, and it shredded his guts like a thousand dull razors. McCall had proposed, and she'd said yes. Jesse was happy, if his smile in the picture was anything to go by. Kimber's picture was in profile, but she had to be happy. This was the realization of her little white lace, virgin-girl dream.

While he . . . Hell, he'd been a fucking pissed-off wreck ever since she'd left, wrenching his heart out with her tears.

"She wasn't ours," he managed to croak out. "This just proves it."

"Kimber might have stayed if you'd been decent to her. She offered you her—"

"I wasn't taking her virginity. It didn't belong to me, just like she didn't!"

The fact that the girl and her virginity belonged to the smiling crooner in the picture didn't exactly thrill him. Correction: it made him want to tear McCall apart slowly, with his bare hands, and inflict maximum pain.

Lord knew the army had trained him to do it.

Luc pointed an accusing finger in his face. "You *made* her believe she didn't belong with us. If you had admitted your feelings and just made love to the girl—"

"Yeah, then what? How long before she wound up like Heather?"

"She's not Heather," Luc insisted. "Kimber is stronger and she would have survived. I think she loved you."

Bittersweet. That possibility made joy burst through his chest, even as fear gripped his belly and yanked hard. Damn, he was one fucked-up bastard. He wanted her, but couldn't have her. If she'd stayed, it was only a matter of time before he would have taken her virginity. *Too many risks. Too much at stake.* He'd made the right choice.

It just hurt like hell.

"And then what?" Deke barked back. "Would she have married one of us? Why the fuck do you persist in this stupid fantasy?" Deke grilled his cousin. "And what about . . . later? I know you want her to have our babies so we could all live happily ever after. And you know how I feel about that. Besides, no woman wants to lie between two men every night and wonder which is the father of her children. We can leave petty jealousy out of a simple screw, but out of a committed relationship? Luc, it's a goddamn fantasy."

"It's no more fantasy than imagining you can fuck your way through the rest of your life with a bunch of nameless whores and not care about anyone. I want more." His voice dropped to a whisper. "With Kimber, I know you wanted more."

Shit, Luc knew him too well.

"She's gone. And that's it."

"You don't think we should fight for her?" Luc looked incredulous.

"How? She's going to marry a superstar she's wanted for five years. I don't see her dropping all that just because we come knocking on her door. We need to get on with life."

The words seemed to knock Luc on his ass. "Get on with it, just like that?" He snapped. "Pretend she was never here and that we never cared about her?"

"We tutored her. Period."

"I adore her. You do, too. In fact, I think you love her."

He hesitated. "I don't."

"Liar. That's why you were so vile to her. Anything that might make you vulnerable and force you to face the past has to be destroyed."

"Fuck off!"

"That's going to solve it all, right? When all else fails, yell at Luc. You know what, you're right. Let's get on with life." Luc stormed across the kitchen, lifted the cordless phone, and walked out of the room.

What the hell was Luc doing? Deke almost didn't care, given the fury bubbling in his belly. And the pain, it seared like acid on bare skin at the thought of Kimber in McCall's bed, in his life. But he'd get over it.

He had to. What other choice did he have?

Five minutes later, Luc stomped back into the kitchen wearing a smug grin. "I hope you don't have plans today other than to get on with your life."

"No, it's Sunday. What have you done?"

"I called Alyssa Devereaux and charmed her. I convinced her to fuck us. She's expecting us at three. Get dressed."

With a sharp pivot, Luc left the kitchen and marched down the hall. A moment later, clinking pipes told Deke that his dear cousin was in the shower.

And Deke was stunned speechless.

Holy shit. Alyssa Devereaux. Blond bombshell, strip club owner, with legs encased in sexy stockings and naughty garters that made grown men salivate and beg. She was going to fuck them. After enduring her cutting tongue and apparent disdain, she'd agreed. For Luc, of course. She'd always wanted him. But as a perk, he'd get to sink into that tight, golden body, too. Immerse every inch of his cock into her warm, suddenly willing pussy.

Deke looked down, staring at his surprisingly unresponsive penis through his pajama bottoms.

Shock. It had to be shock. Alyssa was a walking wet dream. Once he got near her, got her topless and had those luscious tits in his face, he'd be ready. More than ready.

Right?

*   *   *

FOUR hours later, Luc pulled up in front of a little white house with climbing roses and southern charm in a residential side of Lafayette, Louisiana.

Deke frowned at his cousin. "We're not meeting at Sexy Sirens?"

"She said to come here." Luc got out, refusing to say another word.

Palms sweating, Deke followed.

How long had he had fantasies about nailing Alyssa Devereaux? A couple of years, at least, since his business partner and friend, Jack Cole, had introduced her to him. He'd tried to entice her. The alpha routine had gotten him nowhere. His nonexistent charm got him knocked on his ass even before hello. Sparring with her got him shut down every time. Usually just the sound of her name got him hard.

Today . . . Well, it wasn't showtime yet. His slow response must be because he still had big, unanswered questions floating around in his brain. Like, what the hell had Luc said to get her to agree to this? And for as many times as Luc had maintained that he had no interest in Alyssa, he was suddenly really eager to be here.

Why?

Deke had no answers—to any of his questions—as he filed up the little brick walkway, past rows of colorful flowers blooming like crazy.

"Gorgeous azaleas," Luc murmured as he rang the bell.

What the fuck is an azalea? Why were his palms sweating?

Alyssa opened the door wearing a classic black skirt with a slit to the thigh and a lace-edged, off-the-shoulder top that showed just a hint of cleavage.

"Hi, guys. Come inside."

Deke hesitated, but stepped in after Luc and glanced at the place. Soothing shades of green with splashes of yellow. Earth tones everywhere. Even one of those Zen garden waterfall things. Black-and-white photos of nature scenes. It all said *peace*.

"Thanks for having us," Luc said. "Lovely place."

Alyssa smiled. Swallowed. "Thanks. I just bought it a few months ago. It was gutted. I've been fixing it."

"It's great." Luc approved. It was in his voice.

Deke couldn't find his.

So now what? Would they sit and sip iced tea and act all civil, or just get down to fucking?

"Do you want something to drink? I have tea, soda, coffee?" Alyssa sent his cousin a come-hither look, her hand resting above her breast, fingers toying with the soft skin at her cleavage.

"No, thanks." No one could miss the sudden strain in Luc's voice or the way his eyes followed her movements across the swells of her breasts.

Luc was tense and sporting a hard-on that looked more than ready for action. Gluing his gaze to Alyssa, Deke searched for some reaction, a stirring, remote interest. *Anything.*

Kimber's face swam in his mind, flushed in pleasure, mottled with tears, sweet with the offer of her innocence.

And he'd turned it down. Like a dumb, stupid prick, he'd let her walk out. No, he'd pushed her out. All but given her to McCall, whom she'd soon marry. And where would he be? Fucking alone. But Kimber was better off. He had to focus on that.

"Deke?" Alyssa sent him a curious glance.

That was the nicest expression she'd ever sent him. Usually, he got complete disdain.

"Drink?" she prompted.

He had to choose. Drink or sex? "You're not going to call me He-Man or steroid boy?"

She winced. "Not today."

Interesting . . . "Um, a drink sounds good. Whatever you have."

She sent him a nod. Or rather, her head bobbed nervously, then she took a deep breath and seemed to collect herself as she walked into the kitchen with a slow-hipped gait that was an invitation in itself, poured him a tall glass of sweet iced tea, and handed it to him.

Her hands shook as she gestured everyone to the living room sofa.

Deke sat. Alyssa sat about three feet from him, the slit in her skirt revealing very naughty black silk garters and sheer stockings. Luc sat right beside her and dropped a casual hand on her exposed thigh. The pulse at her neck jumped.

What the hell is going on here? "You've been saying no to me for about three years. Why yes all of the sudden?"

Alyssa blinked, her gorgeous blue eyes rimmed in smoky gray liner, her warm golden complexion lighting with a little flush. For a stripper who'd seen the seamier side of life for years, she was awfully good at the sweet girl routine.

"Have you changed your mind?"

Her husky voice jolted him. Incredibly sexy. The woman stunned. Soft eyes, glossy lips that pouted as they tempted, breasts he suspected a doctor had provided, rather than God, but enticing all the same. That wedge of thigh bared to his gaze drew his eye.

Something south of his belt buckle began to stir. "I haven't changed my mind."

She turned to Luc with a soft question.

"I'm not going to change my mind." His hand on her thigh tightened, traveled up, taking the skirt with it, until it rested just shy of damp black panties.

"Good." She breathed the word.

"Deke," Luc called to him. "Kiss her. Get that top off."

Alyssa started. "Y-you don't want to go to the bedroom first?"

Luc stood and drew the blinds, toed off his shoes, and ripped off his shirt. "We'll get there. Eventually."

"Oh." She looked dazed, and they hadn't even touched her yet.

Then Luc shot him an expectant look. *Right. Kiss her. Undress her.*

Letting loose a deep breath, Deke reached out and dove into the buttons down the front of Alyssa's blouse. Jesus, his hands were shaking as he parted the material, revealing the bountiful tits barely restrained by a sheer, strapless bra. Gorgeous, golden breasts. He'd bet she sunbathed topless.

He removed her blouse, pausing a moment to set it on the sofa beside him. Didn't want to wrinkle it. It looked delicate.

"Deke," Luc snapped. "Kiss her."

Alyssa gazed at him, her blue eyes uncertain but fevered. Luc turned her away from himself, toward Deke, then his cousin kissed the side of her neck and laid a hand on the underside of her breast. Her nipples pebbled the instant he touched her.

Under Luc's lips, Alyssa's posture lost its starch. She closed her eyes, moaned.

"You smell good," Luc whispered as one flick of his wrist made her bra melt away. "A mixture of sunshine and sin."

Her bare tits were gorgeous. Ripe, juicy, firm. If they were fake, they were a damn fine imitation.

She laid her head back on Luc's shoulder, gasping as his thumb flicked over one of her hard, blushing nipples.

Damn, the two of them were sexy to watch. Luc so dark, inky hair, bronze skin, caressing his way across Alyssa's paler flesh, lifting her platinum hair away from her soft nape so he could breathe in her scent. Seeing her shudder in his cousin's arms made him hard. *Finally.*

One of Luc's hands slid under the slit of her skirt, lifted it higher, and brushed against the black silk covering her mound. Alyssa gasped. Trembled. Moaned.

"Kiss her."

Luc's renewed demand hit Deke like icy water. Which made no sense. Alyssa was the personification of sex. He'd wanted to nail her for years. She was topless, willing, and getting aroused damn fast.

She isn't Kimber.

Pushing aside the insidious voice protesting in his head, Deke didn't just lean in, he charged, covering her mouth and urging her to open wide for him. Desperate. Her tongue did a sensuous dance around his, slow and lazy and promising that she could give a legendary blow job. She tasted spicy and fresh.

But he was hungry for the taste of sugary innocence. Hesitancy. Pure desire to please.

Alyssa was all enticement. Beautiful. Experienced and able to lure a man into wild sin. But for some damn reason, he didn't want her to lead him astray. Touching her felt . . . weird. Wrong. Like he was betraying something. *Someone.*

Kimber's hazel eyes, brimming with tears, splashed across the backs of his eyes.

Frustration burned. The sense of wrongness weighed a thousand tons in his gut. *Shit!* He yanked away from Alyssa.

Luc barely noticed. Instead, he pulled her onto his lap. With one hand, he threaded his fingers into her hair, angled her mouth under his, and sank into her. Deep. Like he didn't care if he came up for air anytime this century.

What the hell?

Alyssa curled her arms around Luc's neck and wriggled on his lap. Clearly, she hit something sensitive, because Luc growled, lifted her until she straddled him, then ground her against his cock. As she threw back her head, a cascade of pale blond hair landed in Deke's lap. Luc's mouth descended, closing around one of her nipples. He wasn't teasing. There was no toying in this touch. It was all fierce intent.

"Luc! Yes!"

His cousin's response? He merely transferred his attention to her other breast, curled a passionate fist into her hair, and grabbed as if he planned to bend her to his will.

"Are these nipples hard for me?" Luc demanded. He stared at her as if she was the only other person in the room. As if she was the only other person on the planet.

"Yes, they're so hard for you," she whispered as she rubbed them against his chest, then rotated her hips, wriggling on his cock again. "I'm so wet for you, too. Feel . . ."

Alyssa made a great show of untying the little bows at the sides of her hips. With a gyration and a wiggle, the little black panties drifted to the floor.

A light dusting of neatly shaped pale pubic hair made a landing strip across her mound. The rest, from what Deke could see, was bare.

Lust fired Luc's dark eyes. His gazed fixed on her pussy as he laid her down over his lap, until her head rested in Deke's.

Alyssa's gaze drifted up, hazy but uncertain blue eyes meeting his.

Aroused. Totally. Luc had done that to her. Both of them had forgotten he was here, and now she silently asked Deke if he was going to jump into the party.

She was damn sexy and was willingly offering her pussy. *Hell, yes!*

But he reached out and couldn't make himself touch her. His hands dropped to his sides.

What the fuck was wrong with him? He'd wanted Alyssa. For years.

A glance down her body told him she more than lived up to the hype. Dimensions like a centerfold, feline movements intriguing to watch.

And he didn't feel much of anything.

Deke met her gaze and shook his head. *No.*

As desirable as she was, he wasn't interested anymore. Physically, he was aroused. Of course. Watching Luc devour her and her loving every minute of it was hot.

But it was auburn hair he wanted to plant his fists in. It was pale, virgin skin he wanted to touch. It was hazel eyes he wanted to drown in as he sank into her body and claimed it.

Deke closed his eyes, wishing like hell he could block Kimber and the fact she was marrying McCall out of his head. *Impossible.*

A sharp, feminine gasp caught Deke's attention. Luc's hands surrounded Alyssa's mound, parting the folds of her pussy, his thumb brushing across her clit in a light, irregular rhythm.

"You *are* wet," he crooned in approval. "But not wet enough for what I'm going to do to you."

"What's that, big man?" Alyssa panted the question, baiting Luc. "What do you want? Maybe I won't give it to you."

Dark determination stomped across Luc's dark face. "You'll give me everything, then give me more. For you, I'm going to be hard all afternoon. All evening. All night. I won't stay out of you. I won't leave any part of you untouched."

"I won't let you leave any part of me untouched," she murmured, spreading her legs wider and lifting her hips to Luc.

His thumb raked across her clit slowly, repeatedly. Her nipples stood up, blushed, begged as she tensed, thrashing her head from side to side.

"*Luc!*" She screamed his name. Her back arched, and she cried out in a long, wrenching climax.

At the sight of her, his cousin lost it—all semblance of normalcy, civility, restraint.

Deke knew exactly where this was headed. Alyssa was about to become real familiar with Luc's dark side, thanks to one of his marathon sex sessions. She looked more than up to the challenge.

"Take everything," Alyssa offered with a sultry blue gaze. "I'll stay wet, keep you hard, give you more than you imagined possible."

With a growl, Luc tore away Alyssa's skirt, leaving her totally bare except for those sexy stockings and lacy garters. Luc's chest heaved as he looked down at her. His cock tented his jeans, and he dived into the zipper, yanking on it viciously, clearly wanting the binding garment off. He pushed the denim down to his thighs, along with his underwear. As his cock sprang free, he grabbed her hips, and prepared to thrust inside her.

Deke reached into his pocket and extracted a condom. "Luc."

His head snapped up. Wild dark eyes. Feral. Unfocused. Indomitable.

Quickly, Deke handed the little foil square to his cousin. He laid another handful on the table.

Luc gave a shaky nod and ripped into it, racing to get it applied. Alyssa tilted her head back and sent Deke a smoky look. Maybe it was an invitation. Maybe not. He didn't care.

Instead, Deke stood and wandered to the front door. He paused long enough to see Luc position himself over Alyssa, the bulge of his strong arms pinning her to the buttery sofa as she curled her legs around his hips in welcome and smiled.

He shut the door behind him, in search of the nearest bar, as the first female moans rent the air.

* * *

"WHAT'LL you have?" A saucy smile in a tight pair of short shorts greeted Deke.

"Whiskey double. No rocks. Bring me two of them."

The bark in his order must have communicated to her. She clicked her heels together and hustled off. He prayed she came back quickly so he could get on with getting drunk and dissecting his fucked-up life.

The little waitress wasn't gone long before she returned with his order and a bowl of pretzels. He shoved those aside and gulped down his first drink. The burning path of the alcohol blazed down his throat, to his stomach. Fire exploded, heavy warmth seeped through his veins, and he welcomed it. How else could he reconcile the fact he'd just turned down the chance to fuck Alyssa Devereaux because he only wanted a woman who was never coming back to him?

From the pocket of his jeans, he withdrew the scrap from this morning's paper. McCall's smug smile taunted him from the black-and-white image. Kimber stood under the singer's arm, looking up at him. What was that expression? Adoration? Excitement? Did it matter?

No. But Deke wondered how the hell she could look at him with such tenderness in her eyes and offer herself so sweetly, then agree to marry someone else three weeks later.

The only available answer stabbed him in the heart. She hadn't loved him. She'd offered herself out of pity, nothing more.

Unfortunately, no matter how much he denied it to Luc, Deke knew he'd fallen hard for Kimber. He'd always wanted her, even when she'd been seventeen, and he'd known better. Even three weeks ago, when she'd been naked and giving under him, he'd known better. And he almost hadn't cared.

But he'd listened to his fear and done the sane thing. *The right thing.* Now, she was gone.

At the moment, Deke wished very much that he'd been reckless and given in to the hot lava of need thundering in his veins, urging him to take her and make her his. Then she'd be in bed with him and Luc right now, wrapped around him, taking the hard drive of his cock and answering with her cries. And he wouldn't be in a bar in Lafayette, horny and hurting and wondering how she could marry a jack-off like McCall. Wondering what to do without her.

What if Kimber had stayed? What if the worst had happened? No, not if; *when.* If she had stayed, it would have happened. Luc would have insisted. How would she have handled it?

Deke grabbed his second drink and tossed it back. Only when his mind was slightly fuzzy did he allow himself to think about Heather.

Complicated. Barely sixteen. Sparkling when life made her high and beyond consolation when life kicked her. Often, she'd shown both emotions in the same day. Deke had tried to keep up. But to someone whose life was one giant bundle of feelings, who believed that all of them should be experienced and expressed, none filtered—he'd just basked in her bright persona.

In the end, that volatility had been her undoing.

He slammed his drink back to the table and signaled for his check. Saucy Smile brought it, took his money, and sashayed away.

Feeling like an old man at twenty-nine, Deke stood and stepped out into the evening air. Humid. Breezy. Summer enveloped him in its cloying fragrance. Pain crushed his insides.

Kimber wasn't Heather. She had better control over her emotions, true, and was far more mature. But she could be hurt. She could emotionally bleed. Deke had seen that the night he'd shoved her out the door with all those vile words. Kimber had been sheltered, unlike Heather. She hadn't seen the worst of life, thanks to the Colonel and her brothers. What would she do if she suddenly found herself in Heather's situation?

Deke didn't know. And even if he felt like a two-ton weight sat on his chest for the rest of his life, he should be glad he hadn't taken a chance to find out that answer the hard way.

* * *

AT nearly nine that night, Deke climbed behind the wheel of Luc's Jeep. His cousin eased in beside him, grim and exhausted.

"You sure you don't want to stay the night?" Deke asked.

Luc turned, gazing back toward the dark, sleeping house. "No."

"You okay?"

Nodding, Luc gripped his thighs.

Luc looked completely spent physically and emotionally. Deke understood the pleasure of fucking a beautiful woman. Luc possessed a certain drive, though, as if his long sex marathons were attempts to banish some inner demons, not merely find the extreme edge of physical pleasure.

"Fine." Luc hesitated. "Did you wait long?"

"Awhile." He shrugged. "No big deal."

"How long?"

"I don't know." Deke focused on the road to avoid the question. The answer would only send Luc into some guilt spiral he didn't need to put on himself.

"How long?" The bleak demand in his voice lashed through the Jeep.

Sighing, Deke caved in. Luc would figure it out sooner or later. "About two hours."

"And you were gone for . . . what? Three or four hours prior to that? Damn it to hell." Even under the streetlights, Deke could see the shame controting his cousin's fluid features.

"Stop beating yourself up, cuz. She sounded like a very happy woman." Luc had made her mindless, driven the woman to orgasm until her cries nearly shook the walls.

Luc sent him a sharp stare. "Did Alyssa say something to you?"

"No. She fell asleep after you bathed her. What I overheard before then made me think she fell asleep with a smile. What happened between you two?"

"You know damn well. It's happened before." Luc whipped a shaking hand through the tangled mess of his dark hair. "I lost my head."

"Why beat yourself up? This doesn't happen every time you have sex. It doesn't even happen often. And Alyssa sounded like she was having a great time."

Luc nodded halfheartedly, reluctantly conceding the point. "This time the need was stronger. Alyssa was amazing. I felt . . . I don't know. Connected . . . or something. I can't explain it." He sighed, then grimaced. "I really wish I'd had more control. Alyssa was so tight. She said she hadn't had sex in nearly two years."

"Really? Then why did she agree to fuck us in the first place?"

After hesitating, Luc shook his head. "It doesn't matter. I'll send her flowers tomorrow and that will be it."

"You're not going to see her again?" Somehow that didn't surprise Deke. Luc never liked to be reminded of his losses of control.

"Why do you ask? Still hot for her?" Luc slanted Deke a sly stare. "If we come back here, are you planning to fuck her?"

"No." Deke frowned as light bulbs went off in his head. "That's why you brought me here, isn't it? You knew I wouldn't fuck her."

"I suspected. It was a gamble. If you'd touched her, I would have known that you weren't in love with Kimber."

Shit, now he'd dug his own grave. Luc had the proof he needed to keep needling him to try and win Kimber back. And he would be relentless.

Chapter Eleven

AFTER the concert, the suite was packed. Band members, press members, roadies, groupies—all kinds of people crammed the hotel room that only hours ago had felt enormous. Alcohol flowed everywhere. White, powdery lines were laid out on the glass-top coffee table a few feet away. A young woman, maybe legal, knelt and sniffed. Around her, a handful of partygoers gathered, waiting their turn. In the corner, Ryan had an inebriated, braless blonde on his lap. Her nipples stabbed her tight turquoise shirt as Ryan fondled them using one hand. His other hand snaked up her skirt, pulled her thong free, and toyed with her sex—in plain view. Kimber looked away when he unsnapped his leather pants.

Jesse lived like this?

Her head throbbed. People she didn't know were grabbing her to congratulate her on her engagement. The engagement that had completely blindsided her mere hours ago, which she hadn't agreed to.

Hurting Jesse's feelings wasn't something she wanted to do, but there was no way in hell she could live this sort of life.

The door to the suite opened, and Jesse sauntered in, bright, perfectly symmetrical smile in place. The little crowd cheered. Ryan paused in banging his blonde to wave. At Jesse's back, Cal scowled and took in the scene, grousing something in Jesse's ear. It caused Jesse's smile to turn to thunder, and he whirled, fists clenched. *Hmm, whatever Cal said, Jesse didn't like it.*

The pair exchanged words. Ugly words, Kimber guessed from their body language. Then Jesse stormed off.

And stomped in her direction.

"Hey, babe." He forced a new smile and grabbed her, hauling her off the sofa and into his arms. "Let's step outside and get away from all this."

More than eager for the opportunity to talk to Jesse, she didn't resist when he grabbed her hand and led her across the room. They headed toward the sliding glass door and the balcony outside, practically stepping over the latest line-sniffer and tripping over an energetically thrusting Ryan.

"Where you going, man?" Ryan asked, then thrust up into the blonde straddling him again. "Don't go far. She's hot."

Jesse's gaze drifted over her. In the last few moments, Ryan had removed the girl's top and her bare breasts bounced with every upward surge he made into her pliant body. She was flushed, eyes hazy and half open. And she looked wasted out of her mind.

"Yeah . . . Why don't y'all find a bedroom? Cal will chew my ass out if you keep fucking her in front of everyone."

"All right, but join us, man. Her pussy is tight, and she wants a cock up her virgin ass, which she saved for you."

Kimber recoiled. She was pretty sure that the blonde wasn't in her right mind at the moment and couldn't possibly know what she actually wanted.

After a surreptitious glance in her direction, Jesse shook his head. "I'm going outside with Kimber, bro. Find a bedroom."

Ryan rolled his eyes and grumbled, but he stood and lifted the blonde up, keeping her impaled on his dick and urging her to wrap her legs around him.

God, she really couldn't stay here. Kimber shook her head.

As the door to the suite slid shut behind them, humid summer air wrapped around them, hot and restless.

Jesse curled his arm over her shoulder and sighed. "I'm so glad you're here."

"We need to talk." Kimber turned to him with a serious stare. "That engagement announcement totally took me off guard. I—I thought you'd ask first."

With a shrug, he said, "We'd talked about it before. I just assumed it'd be cool." Something on her face must have shown her shock and denial, because Jesse grabbed her hands and pulled her against him. "We'll make it work. I need you, babe. You know I do. I don't want to go back to that"—he made a sweeping gesture to the party in the room behind them.

Kimber's gaze followed the motion. Someone opened another champagne bottle. The lines of cocaine were gone, replaced by three roadies all clustered around the barely legal girl, who was now positioned on her hands and knees, a hard penis in her mouth, a man under her devouring her nipples, and another behind her, plowing into her sex with punishing strokes. Kimber flinched, wondering how much of this the girl would remember tomorrow.

"See, I'd be one of those guys right now if it wasn't for you."

Kimber blanched. "Why? Walk by. Say no. You don't need my help to do that."

"I do! Without you, I'm weak. But I want to be better for you. I don't want to disappoint you. I don't want to ruin you."

Ruin? Before Kimber could respond, Jesse jerked her against him and swamped her with a desperate, open-mouthed kiss. His tongue lashed at hers, tangling, dominating. Begging by force.

Not arousing her in the least.

She tore herself away. "Stop!"

He gripped her arms in a tight hold, his frown dissolving into something damn near tearful. "Don't push me away. Please. Since you've been here, there's been something on your mind. Something holding you back, acting as a wall between us. What's going on? I've tried to wait and be patient . . ."

Deke. Damn him. Even Jesse, as absent and self-involved as he'd been, could see where her heart was. And her body.

"Jesse. It's not simple. Before I came here, things happened. The men I learned ménage from, they affected me. One of them"—she paused, frowned—"I haven't been able to stop thinking about him."

"Then this marriage will be good for both of us. But you've got to give me a chance. I can help you, and you know I need you."

Kimber shook her head. "I've been realizing over the last few days that I don't love you like that. You're a friend—"

"Fuck being friends! Do you know how many women would kill to be my wife? Hell, I have them lining up after a concert just to get fucked. Or to let me watch them get fucked by someone else. Or both. I want to give that up for you, and you want to be friends?"

She'd hurt his feelings, said everything the wrong way. "I didn't mean to upset you. You mean a lot to me. It's me. I don't think I'm cut out for this life. And don't you want a wife who loves you and you alone?"

He blew out a harsh breath. "Someday you might. I just want you to give me a chance. I really can help you get over your . . . tutor. As good as you think he is, I can be better. Babe, I know so much about pleasing a woman. I can turn you to butter, make you melt at my feet, then lick you right into a screaming puddle. Let me try. Please."

He sneaked a glance at the tableau inside. The barely legal girl still had a man pummeling her sex, but now the man at her breasts had eased under her and moved his mouth to her clit, devouring her as if it was his last meal.

Kimber risked a quick glance down, and noticed that the more the men worked the young woman into a frenzy, the harder Jesse got. His head might want to give up this life, but his dick wasn't on the bandwagon yet.

Suddenly, a scowling Cal stepped in front of the glass, blocking their view. Jesse cursed and whirled away, allowing his manager to open the door and step outside.

"That journalist from *People* magazine is waiting in the suite. Get him the hell out of here before the foursome fucking on the floor takes center stage. As it is, they're gathering a crowd. Are you sober?"

"Haven't had a drop." Jesse sounded bitter.

"You haven't been smoking, snorting, sniffing—"

"No."

"Then get out there, find the journalist, and grab the opportunities while they last. Fame is fickle and fleeting."

"I can think of another f-word for it at the moment."

"You hired me to help you be a megastar. I'm doing my job. Go do yours."

Jesse's jaw clenched, and he shoved his shaggy dark hair from his face. "C'mon, Kimber." He reached for her hand.

Cal stopped him, his mouth tight with barely restrained fury. "Just you. Make the magazine focus on you, not your romance. That's not the angle we've been playing to the press. Try to avoid mentioning this . . . engagement if you can."

He sent Kimber a regretful glance. "You're a first-class bastard, Cal."

The older man's smile filled with sharp, artificially white teeth. All she needed was the theme music to *Jaws*. "That's why you pay me."

Grumbling to himself, Jesse grabbed the door, yanked it open again, and disappeared inside.

An awkward silence passed over the balcony. Cal stared, and Kimber met it, wondering why the hell he seemed to be accusing her of something without saying a single word.

"Thank you for trying to help Jesse," she said finally. "I know he doesn't appreciate you like he should but—"

"You're a nice girl, and you shouldn't be here. He's going to screw up your life, and you're definitely going to ruin his image. Tell me how much you want and where you want to go. I'll take care of everything."

"What?" Was he . . . buying her off?

"Don't play stupid." His voice turned angry. "You don't belong here. You don't belong with Jesse. How much to end this engagement and go away?"

Kimber had planned on leaving, but not like this. She sent Cal an incredulous stare. "You're bribing me?"

Cal glared with cool blue eyes. "I'm paying you to go back where you belong, while sparing you a lot of heartache and public humiliation."

"I don't want money," she insisted. While she had no intention of marrying Jesse, she wasn't about to give Cal the satisfaction. "You *are* a first-class bastard, just like Jesse said. This decision is between him and me, and whatever we choose for our lives is our business."

"This engagement is going to kill his momentum. His new album is due to release soon. We want people focused on the music and the mystery behind the man who lives in the fast lane. We don't want people wondering if you're going to wear Vera Wang for the big day and how skilled you are in bed to have lured him to the altar. Don't ruin his career."

"Don't run his life. He's a grown man—"

"With his brains in his dick. If you don't want money, then for your own sake, get smart and get out before you get hurt," Cal growled as he returned inside.

Shaking with anger, Kimber waited until she was sure he'd gone before sliding the heavy glass door open. She climbed back into the air-conditioned chaos. A glance around the suite showed the people still partying in force. The quartet on the floor had finally finished their group shag and lay in a panting heap. The girl looked as if she'd passed out, in fact. A pretty fan with silky dark curls doused the front of her white shirt in champagne like a wet T-shirt contestant. The cloying smell of marijuana hung all around the room, making her cough. An object came flying through the room moments later and landed six inches from her feet. Someone's bong. *Great.*

Sighing, she looked around for Jesse. If he'd finished with the journalist, they needed to talk. About their futures, this marriage that couldn't happen. And she needed to warn him about Cal. He probably already knew that his manager was a manipulating son of a bitch, but just in case . . .

But where the hell had Jesse gone?

Maybe it was better if she didn't find him right away. This way, she'd have time to pack. Then she could talk to him, lay her feelings out on the table, and go. Clean and easy. She only hoped he wouldn't see it as desertion at a time when he desperately needed her. If possible, she wanted to remain friends. But she couldn't lie to Jesse and tell him she wanted to be his wife.

Difficult, closed-off Deke had somehow squeezed her heart between his massive hands and refused to let go.

She let herself into her bedroom. Surprisingly, it was empty. She'd expected to see complete strangers in here doing the nasty. Being alone was a nice, pleasant bonus.

Shoving clothing and personal items in her suitcase, Kimber mentally prepared a speech. She'd tell Jesse that she cared about him, recommend that he find a good counselor. She'd strongly suggest he watch his back with Cal and fire Ryan, who was only encouraging Jesse to be his worst. And she'd volunteer to be a part of his support system while he cleaned up his life, absolutely.

With a last look around, Kimber realized she had everything packed away. Grabbing her toothbrush from the adjacent bathroom took care of the last task. When she unpacked next, she supposed it would be at her dad's place, and she'd have to explain this mess. After spending the next week or two with her dad before he jetted off to whatever assignment was next on his list, she'd return to her own apartment and figure out what to do with the rest of her life.

Sighing, she shook her head. Nothing had turned out as expected. A quick tutoring from Deke and his cousin only revealed her deep fascination for the soldier and opened her heart up wide to the man, even as he slammed his own closed against her. And her time with Jesse . . . yes, it had ended with the desired marriage proposal—but she no longer desired it.

Rolling her suitcase behind her, Kimber scanned the suite's main living area. Lots of partying, no Jesse.

Traveling back down the hall, she opened the door to the main bedroom.

And stopped short with a gasp.

Ryan was thrusting into his blonde's mouth with slow, lazy movements. She wriggled her hips from side to side, then grabbed Ryan's cock in her hand so she could stare over her shoulder with wide, wild eyes . . .

At Jesse, who knelt behind her, chugging a fifth of Jack Daniel's— and shuttling his cock deep in and out of her previously virgin ass with ferocity that stunned.

Oh, God. Shock washed over her. Icy. Sickening. She had to leave. *Now.*

Before she could turn and get the hell out, Jesse caught sight of her, pulled free of the blonde's ass, and shoved the bottle aside with a creative string of curses.

Kimber didn't wait to see if he was going to dress first or chase her down the hall wearing nothing but a condom.

She made it to the hall before he came at her, white bath towel around his waist, and pushed her back into her empty bedroom.

"Shit, babe. Oh, hell. I—"

"Don't say anything." She closed her eyes, but still kept seeing the scene in her mind.

"I'm sorry. This doesn't mean anything. She doesn't mean anything!"

Kimber flashed ahead to her future. If she actually married Jesse, she had a feeling she'd be hearing those words a lot. And he'd actually mean them . . . in his way. But she couldn't change a man who, deep down, didn't want to give up his wild-child ways. He'd see that when he was ready, and she could only hope that he wouldn't hate her in the meantime.

"It does mean something." Kimber wheeled her suitcase out the bedroom door. "It means we weren't meant to be and I'm leaving."

"No. I don't love her. I don't even know her name! I was horny and she was available and I didn't want to ruin you. Because you—you I need."

"You don't," she countered. "What you need is to look at yourself and decide what you want your life to be. It's best if you do that alone. Call me if you're serious about changing yourself, and I'll be your friend. But I won't be your crutch, and I won't be your wife." She leaned in to kiss his cheek. "I'm not angry, but I have to go. Good-bye."

* * *

THREE days later, her cell phone rang. Again. Kimber lifted her head from the couch in the family room at her dad's house after dozing. Four o'clock in the afternoon. Wow, a whole eight minutes since the last time the phone rang. A quick peek at the caller ID revealed an unknown number.

Damn it.

Shaking her head, she flipped it open. "No comment."

"Reporters?" her dad asked as she slammed the phone shut again.

"I assume so. I don't talk long enough to find out."

"No one threatening has called, have they?"

She shook her head. "How about you?"

Dad rubbed the back of his neck, where he kept all his tension. "A voice mail and a fax in the last three days. This asshole is a loon. I just don't know how serious a loon."

"Are you worried?"

He hesitated, grimaced, shrugged . . . then finally confessed, "Yeah. My gut tells me he's real serious. I really want you to be careful when you leave the house."

Kimber sat up. Her dad was hardly ever worried. Cautious, yes. But worried . . . This was a bad sign. Very bad. "What does he say in his messages?"

"Oh, the usual. Payback for busting him and testifying so that he did time. He missed out on his little girl growing up, blah, blah, blah."

"Does that tell you who you're dealing with?"

Her dad shook his head. "It could still be one of a dozen loons. Remember, I've been in business for nearly fifteen years. If you get a threatening call, you tell me. But I'd feel better if you just turned your phone off."

Before she could respond, it rang again. Another unfamiliar number.

"No comment." Kimber sighed and shook her head. When would these reporters get a clue?

"You'd probably feel better if you turned the phone off, too. Hell, girl. Those people are going to keep calling all day and all night as long as they know you'll answer." Her dad sounded every bit as irritated as she was.

"I know."

"Then turn it off. Or are you keeping it on so that you can take another call from Jesse?"

Kimber grimaced. She really didn't want to discuss this with him. "Dad . . ."

"I know he called again last night. Sounded like he begged you to come back."

It had been three days since the engagement announcement and her departure. Since then, he'd called day and night, nearly as often as the reporters trying to get the scoop on their relationship and why she was no longer on tour with him. Just last night he'd called drunk and confessed that he was sleeping next to another girl whose name he didn't know. And he was miserable.

"He'll stop eventually."

"Kimber, honey, underneath that tough exterior that Logan and Hunter beat into you as a kid, you have a soft heart," he said warmly—a side of him he didn't show to anyone but her, and it never failed to make her feel loved. "You need to tell that boy to move on with his life. Be firm."

"I am, but it's not that simple. He needs a friend right now. I'm it."

"You can't save him from himself."

"I told him that."

"So why are you keeping that phone on?"

Because she'd made a decision. Being with Jesse had shown her the difference between a crush and real love, between a girl's hopes and a woman's wants. She wasn't a girl anymore, and she wanted Deke. Luc was a big part of his life, and she cared about them both. That's where she belonged. Everyone knew it but Deke.

She'd let him run her off. Time and perspective had helped her to understand that Deke hadn't meant an ugly word he'd hurled at her that night. But she'd let herself feel the hurt and dashed off. *Stupid, emotional decision.*

Despite her mental bravado, Kimber couldn't bring herself to call their house. If Deke answered and rejected her . . . No, she wasn't voluntarily signing up for pain. He'd give her plenty of hell later, when she tried to ingrain herself back in his life. But Luc would call. Soon. And that's why she left her phone on. He'd want to know the scoop between her and Jesse. When she told him it was over, maybe he'd tell Deke. Maybe it would make a difference . . .

She grimaced. God, that sounded so high school. If she wanted something, it was up to her to make it happen. Kimber knew that. She'd known it when she'd seen her doctor and started taking the pill two days ago. She'd known it yesterday when she left a message on Luc's cell phone and indicated that she wanted to talk to him.

"By the way, who the hell is Luc?" her dad asked.

Kimber's head snapped up. "How do you know about him?"

"When you turned off your phone late last night, he called me to ask if you're okay. Why does he care and how do you know him?"

"Luc Traverson, the chef."

"The one with the cookbooks? How did you meet him?"

"He's Deke Trenton's cousin." She didn't offer more information. She didn't dare. Her dad would figure it out anyway.

His eyes narrowed. "You didn't tell me how you met him."

"Dad, it's really not important."

"Bullshit. The reason you don't turn off your phone when these reporters are hounding you has something to do with this guy. Why? You couldn't have met Luc while you were away at school."

Kimber pretended rapt interest in the TV. It wouldn't be long now, and she wished desperately that something fascinating would flash on the screen and distract her dad. A beer commercial, despite the big-breasted blonde, wasn't going to do it.

"You could only have met him through Deke. Why would you see Deke? He always had a hard-on for you and treated you like hell for it. Years ago, I told him if he touched you, I'd cut his balls off."

Why didn't that surprise her? She wished that was the reason Deke had refused to make love to her . . . but she knew better.

"You know what sort of sex Deke is into, right?"

Kimber winced. *Here it comes . . .*

"Of course you know. Before you went to Jesse, you . . . talked to Deke about it? Or did you more than talk?"

"Dad, I'm not seventeen anymore."

"*Shit!*" The Colonel sighed, raking fingers through his salt-and-pepper hair. Even at forty-eight, he had the look of a warrior. He prowled the family room like a caged animal. Dad was a man of action, and all this talking had to be grating for him. Kimber tried to hide her smile.

"This isn't funny," he warned.

Clearly, he was not amused by the knowledge that she'd seen Deke and possibly partaken in a ménage. "I didn't imply it was."

Jesse's face flashed across the TV screen as part of a montage previewing a popular entertainment show.

Then her face.

"Oh my gosh." Kimber stared at the image of them at the concert, shortly after Jesse's engagement announcement. She grabbed the remote and turned up the volume. What the hell was going on now?

Then, it got worse. The screen flashed the face of another woman. Young. Artificial blond hair. Artificial tears. Something about her face was familiar . . . The girl was claiming to be Jesse's longtime lover and pregnant by him.

Suddenly, Kimber placed her.

"She's lying," Kimber murmured. "Jesse met her the night I left. I found him and one of his band members having sex with her. He didn't even know her name."

"He had sex with her after announcing to the world he intended to marry you?" Her dad all but growled the words.

She nodded, hoping to hear the announcer's next words.

"Why didn't you tell me?"

"Why bother?" she asked. "You can't fix it for me. I have to do that."

The Colonel just sighed.

The announcer voiced over a series of pictures of Jesse, then cut again to the artificial blonde. "Jesse McCall is the father of my unborn baby," she cried. "The announcement of his engagement to Kimber Edgington was a shock to me . . ."

More tears. Kimber's stomach lurched. Then came a video, grainy, jumpy, a bit dark, of Jesse and the girl. Despite the pixilated blur of various parts of their bodies, it was clear that they were naked. Kimber knew it was Jesse because the bedroom had been his at the Houston hotel suite and he had that exact birthmark on his shoulder. Apparently, Ryan, who enjoyed home movies, had shot this footage. In the video, the girl lay on the bed, on her back, legs spread. Jesse, with his back to the camera, climbed between them.

Kimber quickly realized that must have happened directly after she'd caught him with the other two and left. She shook her head.

Cut back to the artificial blonde. "His proposal to this other woman is both unexpected and heartbreaking. My baby needs a father . . ."

Could this get any worse?

The show cut again to a clip of Jesse on a late-night talk show host's sofa. The TV personality sent him a wry glance.

"So tell us about your fiancée. And if she knows anything about your pregnant girlfriend."

"That girl in the video is not my girlfriend. When you're a celebrity, people make claims . . ." Jesse waved away the rest of the host's question. "Right now, I'm focused and eager to be a full-time fiancé to Kimber."

Kimber flinched. Damn it, she'd made it clear that she wasn't going to marry him. Why didn't he get it?

Jesse just went on. "You know how it is when you meet the ultimate woman for you, man. That's it."

The talk show host, who'd been happily married for many years, nodded. "What do you say about the rumors that your fiancée left the tour the night you proposed?"

"She left to spend time with her family before the wedding. The press has blown it out of proportion. The rest is just a misunderstanding." Jesse's mouth wobbled so slightly, probably no one noticed but her.

"I don't call sleeping with another woman a misunderstanding," her dad snarled, looking ready to lunge at the TV.

Raking his hand through his signature shaggy hair, Jesse recovered his smile. "She'll be back. Are you watching, honey? I miss you."

Then he broke into a few bars of song, something he'd written himself, she guessed, with a sappy melody and lyrics about needing her. It ended with a plea to come back.

She flinched again.

The entertainment show cut to the "pregnant girlfriend" again, holding yet another press conference, now surprisingly dry-eyed. "Jesse McCall is not the father of my baby. I'm a great admirer of his, but I have never met him. I deeply regret if my desire to get his attention caused any harm."

What? "She's lying again. She did meet Jesse. That's them on the video."

Cal, Jesse's manager, appeared next. *Grim* would have been a pleasant description of his expression when asked to comment about Jesse's appearance on the talk show.

It hit Kimber then that if Cal had tried to pay her off to make her go away, he'd likely done the same thing to this girl, who'd apparently tried to blackmail him with Ryan's home video footage.

On TV, Cal cleared his throat. "Jesse McCall's private life is private. Right now, we're focused on the upcoming album and his current tour—"

"Did Ms. Edgington leave him? Did she end the engagement?"

"No comment. We're adding a second show in Atlanta. Tickets will go on sale this Saturday. These are the kinds of things fans should be focused on."

"Jesse indicated a wedding this fall. Will that still happen?"

"Nothing has been decided yet except that the new album will be out then and he'll be in full support of it," Cal snapped.

Oh, he was pissed. Anything that focused media attention away from Jesse's music and too much on his personal life would not please Cal.

Then the announcer returned, asking in the most lurid voice possible what the truth was and asking viewers to stay tuned while they got to the bottom of it.

Kimber sat back. How had she missed all this? Because she'd been busy making decisions and starting her plans, not watching TV for the last two days.

She shook her head. *What a mess!* God, she needed some fresh air. And for all of this to die down.

Flipping the TV off, Kimber got up off the sofa, grabbed her phone, and headed toward her dad's office.

"What are you doing?"

"I'm putting a stop to this crap with Jesse."

She marched down the hall and plopped herself in her dad's office chair, booted up the computer, and waited. At the log-in prompt, she typed the password. At the desktop, she opened a web browser and signed into her e-mail account.

Then she began typing. A few minutes and a few quizzical stares from her dad later, she asked, "What do you think of this:

> *"Mr. McCall and I have chosen to end our engagement, as we're both focused on our respective careers and other matters. I'm still a great fan and a great friend, and I wish him all the best in future endeavors. At this time, I'm asking for privacy while I pursue this next phase of my life."*

"That sounds good," her father praised. "Who are you sending it to?"

Kimber hesitated. *Good question.* What was the fastest way for this news to both reach Deke and Luc, and give the reporters enough so they'd eventually go away?

Suddenly, she smiled. "The world."

It took nearly an hour, but she drudged up e-mails to every major news outlet she could think of. Then pressed Send.

* * *

TWO hours later, Kimber sat out on the back patio, enjoying the sunset, despite the summer heat, when her phone rang for the umpteenth time, finally displaying the name and number she'd been hoping to see.

"Luc?"

"Sweetheart, is that really your statement on the news, the one about the engagement being over?"

So he *had* seen it. And he sounded damn hopeful, too. She smiled. "Yeah."

The question was, had Deke seen it?

"When did you decide to break it off?"

She sent him an ironic laugh. "The night he announced to the world we were getting married without asking me first."

"He never *asked* you?"

"We'd talked about it in the past, so he assumed . . . I called you yesterday to tell you my plans."

"I hate that I missed your call. I had to take a quick trip."

At the mention of his trip, he sounded . . . distracted. No, upset. *Hmm, something.* "Everything all right?"

"Yes," Luc finally said after hesitating. "Just something in Louisiana . . . It—It's no big . . . It's not important. What's more important is you breaking the engagement. Tell me, did you call me because you want to come back here, to be with us?"

Kimber bit her lip and steeled herself to hear the worst. Luc would welcome her, but Deke . . .

"Yeah. I was hoping to tell you first." Her stomach jumped, coiled into unrelenting knots. Sitting here worrying wasn't going to solve anything. "And that you'd tell Deke and get his reaction."

"Deke heard the news about your engagement when I did." Luc hesitated again, this time for longer. "He was furious. He thought you'd said yes to Jesse. Slept with him. Were in love with him."

If he was furious, that meant he still cared, right? "What do you think his reaction will be when he finds out none of that is true?"

"None of it? You weren't in love with Jesse?"

"I thought I was, before you two. I realize now it was every bit the schoolgirl crush that Deke accused me of having."

"You didn't have sex with Jesse?"

"No. No real interest on either part, to be honest. Him because he wanted to keep me a 'good girl' so I could save him from his depraved life, and me because . . . he wasn't the man on my mind. I didn't want him."

"Oh, sweetheart." Luc's happiness vibrated across the phone. "You don't know what a relief that is. What a relief that will be to Deke."

"Do you think so?"

"Yes. Not that he'll admit it." Kimber heard the irony in Luc's voice.

"Do you think he'll welcome me back?" Kimber stood and paced across the front porch. She couldn't just sit and wait for this answer. Too much of her future was riding on it.

"He won't be able to say no. I think he's regretted forcing you out the door a thousand times." Luc paused. "He's afraid."

"That he'll be emotionally vulnerable to me?" Kimber held her breath, waiting for an answer. She didn't want Deke to feel threatened. But until she figured out exactly what was stopping him from exploring their relationship, she was going to have to go on the offense.

"That's part of it." Luc sighed. "Look, Deke's shutting off the shower now, so I can't talk long. But he knows that if you come back, he's going to want to make love to you—in every way."

"I hope so."

"Yes, but it's complicated. Deke isn't going to be whole until he tells you his story. It has to come from him."

"I understand." Kimber hated it, but she would respect it.

"Will you be back with us tomorrow?" Luc's voice told her that he wanted her there that quickly.

As she sat under the setting Texas sun, it was stunning to think that shortly after the sun rose tomorrow, she could be back with Deke and Luc, in their arms and in their lives . . . if Deke would have her.

"I'd love that. I hope that—"

Kimber never finished the sentence. A massive explosion boomed like thunder directly behind her. The force of it threw her down onto the planks of the old wraparound porch, scraping her palms and knees. The phone skittered out of her hand. Heat, as strong as a thousand suns, lashed her back. The ground shook beneath her.

She whirled around in time to see the house burst into a fireball.

"Dad!"

Chapter Twelve

JUST under two hours later, Kimber paced the cold hospital waiting room, chewing on a ragged fingernail. God, her insides jumped and shivered so badly, she was about to come out of her skin. She shot another worried glance toward the operating room, where they'd taken her dad.

No one had emerged yet to tell her whether her father was going to live or . . . No, she wouldn't think that. *Deep breath. Hang tough. Pray.*

Good advice, but she kept reliving that terrible moment. One minute she'd been sitting on the porch talking to Luc, the next, her father's house had exploded with him inside. The fire had been everywhere, she realized in retrospect. That fact hadn't really occurred to her when she'd run in and found him unconscious, about to be consumed by encroaching flames. Upon finding the doorknob too hot to handle, she'd saved time by simply knocking his chair through the glass door to the backyard and dragging him out.

The firemen who'd responded to the emergency had told her that her dad would never have survived if she hadn't thought fast and saved him from the growing inferno. But he was injured pretty badly. What if she hadn't done enough to save him?

Kimber glanced at a long row of empty chairs in the waiting room perched on brownish indoor/outdoor carpet and surrounded by dusty silk plants. No, she couldn't sit, couldn't stop moving.

Couldn't stop worrying.

Damn, what had caused that explosion?

Behind her, the automatic doors whooshed open. Absently, she turned.

Luc charged in. Looking harried and worried, he scanned the room and sighed with relief when his frantic gaze landed on her. Crushingly glad to see him, tears stung her eyes as he darted toward her, then enveloped her in warm, strong arms.

With her chin tucked against his shoulder, she inhaled, breathing in comfort, feeling a blessed moment of joy. Then she opened her eyes.

Deke!

He stood behind Luc, blue eyes so dark with concern, their expression damn near resembled panic. His stare delved into her, needing reassurance that she was alive yet offering support all at once.

Her stare collided with his, and Kimber felt the impact reverberate inside her, tightening around her stomach and squeezing until she could hardly breathe.

He'd come. He'd put everything between them aside and come to her.

Tears spilled over, onto sooty cheeks. Watching her, Deke grimaced as the tears fell, as if seeing her upset was physically painful.

She reached out a hand to him. He grabbed it in a fierce grip, then he used it to pull her out of Luc's embrace and into his. She crashed against his iron-solid chest, and he hooked a strong arm around her waist. They stood close, body to body. The comforting beats of his heart melted her, and she threw her arms around him, until not even the tiniest bit of air came between them. His solid strength enveloped her, just like his scent, earth and rain and all male.

"Kitten," he muttered into her hair in a concern-rough voice that rasped across her senses.

Lifting her chin, Luc caught her gaze and diverted her attention from his cousin. "Are you okay?"

Deke stepped back and watched her face with undivided attention.

She nodded. "I'm fine. My dad—"

Kimber couldn't finish the sentence without falling apart. A fresh batch of tears splashed onto her cheeks, scalding and painful. A sob wrenched up from her gut.

She tried to be strong. Tried hard. But the reality of this situation made her dissolve into tears. Deke enveloped her against the warm breadth of his chest again. Luc stroked her hair and whispered assurances.

"Shh." Both men soothed her, and she didn't know exactly who spoke. But it didn't matter. With them here, she finally began to believe things might be all right.

"I'm so glad you came. Thank you."

"We wouldn't be anywhere else," Luc murmured, then kissed the top of her head.

Deke dragged her to a chair and sat her on his lap. Luc sat beside him. They both looked at her with such tenderness. Joy lightened her burden for a moment, and her heart twisted with something bittersweet. More tears tracked down her face, and Luc wiped them away with his thumb. Deke's arms tightened around her.

"What happened?" he prompted.

The interrogation. She knew how these military men operated. They wanted answers, needed to assess the situation. Then they'd act accordingly. She wouldn't get any more emotional responses out of him until he knew what he was dealing with and if everyone was safe. She had to get her head together and answer him.

Kimber drew in a shaky breath. "I don't know. A-an explosion of some sort . . ."

She hedged, but she wanted answers, damn it! What *had* happened? And where the hell were the doctors with the news about her father's condition?

With a soft palm rubbing up and down her back, Deke soothed her. "After Luc heard the explosion on the phone and you didn't answer anymore, we hauled ass to your dad's house. One of the firefighters on the scene was an old army buddy of mine. He said you went into the house and got your dad out?"

She nodded.

"Oh my God," Luc muttered. "The place had to have been engulfed in flames."

"I had to do it."

"I know." Deke's gravel voice softened, caressed her. "We're just glad you made it out in one piece. How's your dad?"

"He—he's in surgery. They haven't said anything yet. I don't know . . ."

"When did you last eat?" Luc asked.

Who could recall? God, the thought of food revolted her. "I'm not hungry."

Luc frowned. "Soda? Coffee?"

Kimber just shook her head. Not now. She couldn't take anything on her tumbling, topsy-turvy stomach.

Deke grabbed her face in his hands, snagging her attention again. "Where are your brothers?"

Frowning, she swallowed. Damn, her throat hurt. Inhaling smoke had turned her insides raw, like she'd been drinking turpentine. Her lungs ached, but her pain was minor compared to what her dad was suffering. The doctors had already treated and released her.

"I don't know. I think Hunter is out of the country on some assignment. Logan . . . He called to ask questions about my engagement a few days ago, but never said where he was."

Arms tensing, Deke's grip around her tightened. "Have you called Logan since the explosion?"

No. She'd thought about it. But her father's life had depended on every tick of the clock. Then once she'd gotten him to safety, the fire department arrived. Then the police. Questions—lots of them—as they stabilized her dad for the ambulance ride. She'd gone along, holding his hand, hoping he knew that, even though they weren't geographically close, he was still her parent, her only parent, and she loved him dearly. Then at the hospital, forms and questions, then the waiting began, tense moments of brittle fear splintering her composure . . .

"Kitten?" Deke prompted.

"I don't know where my phone is. Destroyed, I guess. I don't know . . ."

"Okay. I'll call Logan. Just relax for me." He kissed her forehead, then stood and set her in Luc's lap as if she was more valuable than hundred-year-old china.

Kimber watched as Deke flipped open his phone and spun away.

For a long moment, Luc did nothing but hold her, and she basked in his warmth and caring, even as anxiety tore at her insides. How much longer would the doctors be? She needed news about her father now. Sooner than now, or she'd go insane. *God, what if . . . No.* She wouldn't think the worst. Refused to think it.

"We're so relieved you're all right," Luc murmured against her cheek, interrupting her inner turmoil. "My heart stopped when that explosion occurred. I knew you had to be right in the middle of it."

"I don't understand . . . I have no idea what happened."

Deke returned then and sat in the chair beside them again. "Logan will be here in fifteen minutes. He'll also get in touch with Hunter."

She breathed a sigh of relief. "Oh, good. Thank God. Logan and dad are so close . . ."

With gentle fingers, Luc wiped away new tears she wasn't even aware had fallen. "I know, sweetheart."

"Kimber." Large hands enveloped hers, warm and strong. Deke.

She blinked, stared, drinking in the sight of him, the solid safety he brought.

"I need you to focus," he demanded. "The fire department told us that explosion was no accident. It wasn't a gas leak or anything natural."

Not natural? "What are you saying? It was deliberate?"

"Very deliberate. It was a bomb."

Kimber's jaw dropped. A thousand thoughts screamed through her head, but she couldn't settle on one long enough to speak the words. *A bomb?* It made no sense. Who? Why? When? What did the asshole who set it want?

You mean besides everyone in the house to die? an acerbic voice in her head whispered.

"When you first visited our place, you mentioned that someone had been after your dad," Deke prompted.

Stunned mute, she nodded.

"Know why?"

She frowned, trying to recall. "Not exactly. Just that some psycho my dad helped thwart and put away was bitter about missing his daughter growing up."

"Had he threatened you?"

Hesitating, she paused to think. "Dad told me that this wacko mentioned me. Dad thought the guy would hurt me to hurt him."

Luc and Deke exchanged a glance full of gravity and instant agreement.

"Once Logan gets here," Deke began, "you have to go with us."

"G-go?"

"Away from here. Someplace this twisted asshole who probably blew up your dad's place won't suspect. Someplace remote and safe."

Kimber heard his logic, but . . . "My dad. He needs me here. I can't just leave."

"Logan will stay here, keep us posted on his progress, but until we know who and what we're dealing with—"

"He's my dad. I have to know if he's going to make it. I have to talk to the doctors. I can't . . . just leave. Logan has all the sensitivity of a doorknob, and Dad will need me."

Deke's face twisted into grim lines. "He might want you here, but he'd want you safe and alive more. You're distraught and not thinking straight. That makes you easy prey if this sick bastard wants to kill you. I'm not letting that happen."

She sagged against Luc. Was it possible she was as much a target of this wacko's terrible plot as her dad? It made so little sense. In all the years her father had been in this business, they'd never had a serious brush with a vengeful criminal. Lots of threats, a few minor incidents. But nothing like this.

But as Dad frequently said, there was always a first.

If her father, who knew how to protect himself and others against nut jobs and stalkers, was on an operating room table fighting to survive, did she stand a chance if this guy came after her? No, but could she just leave her dad in what might be the last moments of his life?

"But—"

"No buts." Deke looked as if he'd reached the end of his patience. He thrust his fingers into her hair and used his leverage to make her meet his stare. "I'm taking you away from here. Period. It's not a fucking negotiation. You won't argue, wheedle, or sweet-talk your way out of this."

Rebellion rose up inside her hot and eager, jumpy to get a word in. Logic tamped it down. The explosion had been a bomb. Someone had been threatening her father. If this psycho planted the bomb, he was sophisticated and he'd done it when people were home. Which meant he was likely watching the house. And he'd known she was there.

Hell, he'd probably consider killing her a bonus. Or maybe it was his goal. And her dad would never want her to put herself in danger.

Kimber sighed, long and ragged. "Okay."

Luc wrapped his arms around her and laid his cheek against her back. Deke tensed, fingers pulling at her hair, then he cursed and laid a harsh, possessive kiss on her mouth.

At that moment, the hospital's double doors opened. Kimber saw Logan prowl inside, scan the room.

When he spotted them, he stopped.

She broke away from Deke's embrace and jumped up from Luc's lap. But Logan had seen. Fury didn't come close to describing the expression that flashed in his eyes.

Swallowing, he approached her and grabbed her arm, dragging her away from Deke and Luc.

"Any word about Dad?" Every word was tight and clipped.

Damn. He was restraining himself and his wild temper. *Big-time.* But he wouldn't for long.

Kimber refused to flinch. She wasn't a child, and he wouldn't treat her like one anymore. "Nothing. We're still waiting."

"How long has he been in surgery?"

She shrugged. Time had been meaningless since the explosion. "Over an hour, I guess."

"Deke tells me a bomb exploded at the house?"

"According to the fire department, yes."

"And you pulled Dad out?"

Would it please him or piss him off? This answer could go either way, and Logan was unpredictable at best.

"I did." Her stare challenged him to give her crap about it.

"Brave. Stupid," Logan pointed out as he dragged her into a brotherly embrace, "but damn brave. Good going, little sister."

"I had to. You would have done the same."

Logan knew he couldn't argue that point, so he didn't try. "Has a doctor looked at you yet?"

"I'm fine. I had two stitches in my arm and three in my leg. Just scratches . . ."

"I'm glad you weren't seriously hurt."

He glanced at Deke and Luc sitting a few feet away and nodded. Controlled. Restrained. Deceptive. Logan could be a bad son of a bitch when he wanted.

"So," he went on. "Necessities aside . . . What the fuck are you doing with these two?"

As Logan's tone exploded with anger, Deke rose and came to stand behind her. Kimber felt his big body envelop her back and give off heat. With a glance over her shoulder, she saw him meet her brother's enraged gaze. In silent reply, Deke wrapped an arm around her waist. Hell, he might as well have branded her as his like a calf. Logan's eyes flared again.

A pair of nurses passed in the nearby hall, obviously in the midst of a shift change, and paused to stare at the tableau taking place.

Great. An audience. Before things could erupt, she held up her hands to ward off Logan. "This isn't the time or place to do this."

"They weren't just comforting you, little sister." He glanced up at Deke. "You want to tell her about the way you fuck women, or should I?"

If they hadn't had the nurses' undivided attention before, they surely had it now.

Deke tensed behind her, and Kimber knew she needed to diffuse the situation now.

"Logan, keep your damn voice down. I know."

Her brother looked at her as if she'd lost her mind. "Then why the hell are you letting them touch you?"

"Goddamn it," Deke snarled behind her. "Don't you—"

"Let me handle this. Please."

Deke hesitated, then backed off—reluctantly. Kimber sighed. She didn't want to do this now. Dad's very survival was up in the air, and she was so damn tired. But she knew better than to think that Logan would be put off.

"I know from experience the way they have sex," she snapped in low tones. "Not that it's any of your business. I'm a grown woman, and I make my own choices. You can either live with that or shut up. But I'm not going to hear another word about this."

Logan looked ready to drop his jaw. "You and . . . both of them?"

His attitude was grating on her last nerve. "Don't pretend you've been an angel your whole life. I've heard plenty about you over the years, so let's consider it even and drop it."

For a long moment, he didn't speak. What could he possibly say? She'd heard rumors for years that he was one hell of a dom, particularly gifted in giving the kiss of the whip and making a woman love it. He'd better not say a damn word.

Logan's jaw tensed. "You were engaged three damn days ago to someone else."

"Now, I'm not."

The answer agitated him, but he stopped arguing. Instead, he shot Luc, then Deke, a venom-filled glare. "If you hurt my sister, I swear I'll peel the flesh off your fucking bones slowly and let you bleed to death."

"We have no intention of hurting your sister," Luc soothed as he rose and pulled her from between Logan and Deke, wrapping her in a protective embrace. "Ever."

"And every minute you stand here yakking off your jaws is another minute she's in danger," Deke snarled.

"What the hell does that mean?" Logan demanded.

"There's a big chance the asshole who blew up the Colonel's house is trying to hurt your sister. We're taking her away, getting her under wraps."

Logan looked ready to protest.

Deke didn't let him. "You know I can protect her. It's my goddamn job."

Her brother took a deep breath, then regarded her with a flat expression. "Is that your choice?"

"Can you stay with Dad and take care of him, keep me posted, until this is over?"

He looked like he wanted to say no. But he didn't run from the truth. "Yes."

"Then, yes. I should go with them. This psycho blew up Dad's house. I think he knew I was there. Given the way he's been threatening, he's not going to quit, not until he's caught."

After a long moment, Logan gave her a jerky nod, then turned to Deke. "You'll keep me apprised?"

"Yes."

"Miss Edgington?"

The sound of her name from across the room startled Kimber. She whirled around. A youngish doctor stood there, shoulders heavy. He looked exhausted. Her belly knotted and flipped. *Oh God, oh God, oh God.*

She raced across the room. The testosterone posse followed.

"My father . . . Is he going to make it?"

The doctor looked at Luc, Deke, and Logan, then again at her, silently asking if he could speak freely in front of the men.

"Yes," she said impatiently. "My brother and my . . . boyfriends." Frankly, she didn't care what the doctor thought. "Tell us."

The doctor was momentarily startled, but quickly smoothed his expression. "He's suffered a lot of head trauma. We stemmed some internal bleeding. We hope that was the extent of the internal damage. He's strong, and that's the only reason he came through such a surgery. He hasn't gone into shock or slipped into a coma, so those are good signs. We're trying to keep him stable, but the next twenty-four hours will be critical. We'll know more then."

* * *

"DEKE!"

Startled out of his misery, he stepped out of the little boat at sundown the next day, onto the dimly lit dock, and turned to find Morgan Cole standing there, all fiery red hair and a huge smile.

He mustered up a smile as she neared, then kissed her cheek. "Hiya, doll."

"Good to see you. Jack told me you have someone to protect? A friend."

Kimber was way more than that. Racing across a hundred miles of Texas, wondering if she was dead or alive, had slammed that fact into him like a fastball to the stomach.

For Morgan's benefit, he shrugged. "Something like that. Jack here?"

"Inside turning on the generators and security equipment." She laid a comforting hand on his arm. "You know Jack's cabin is one of the safest possible places, right?"

Deke agreed with a slight nod. "Yeah. No one in their right mind travels this deep into the swamp unless they know their way around."

"Or the gators swallow them up," Morgan agreed, easing her arms around his neck and giving him her sweet brand of comfort in a gentle squeeze. "It'll be fine."

Damn it, he hoped so. Deke didn't want to think about the alternative, didn't want to relive the pure cold-sweat terror of wondering if some sick bastard had ended Kimber's life.

Suffering the painful, gaping hole in his chest at the thought she might be gone forever.

The thought of putting a name to the emotions those symptoms pointed to made him sweat.

"Hey, you pervert," Jack called, stepping out the rustic cabin's door. "Get your hands off my wife. You're not getting the opportunity to fuck her again."

Behind him, Deke heard Luc help Kimber up on the dock at that moment. And he couldn't miss Kimber's little indrawn breath of shock.

Shit! Deke closed his eyes. Something cold and sludgy and dreadful washed over him. *Shame.* He recognized it for the first time in years. In that moment, knowing that Kimber could see firsthand exactly what his life had become . . . Suddenly, he hated the choices he'd made.

"Jack!" Morgan scolded her husband and flushed twenty shades of angry red.

"Oh, hell. I'm sorry." Jack slapped him on the shoulder, his face contrite. "I feel like such an ass."

"You are," he growled. What else could he do? Jack hadn't known his someone to protect was a female. He hadn't known Kimber was within earshot when he'd opened his mouth. At the end of the day, none of this shit was Jack's fault, Deke acknowledged.

It was his own.

Jack reached out a hand to Kimber, steadying her as she stepped onto the little wooden dock. "Welcome, miss. I know you're going through a tough time, but Deke is one of the best in the personal security business. Here, in the middle of nowhere, with him . . . there's nowhere safer."

With a reluctant, wide-eyed nod, Kimber shook Jack's hand. He reached around to her elbow to guide her up the little platform, illuminated in the humid, hazy evening by a single sixty-watt bulb.

"Thank you," she said finally.

Jack shook Luc's hand briefly, then helped Kimber inside. Deke watched the little party head indoors and wondered what the hell would happen next. Now that he had Kimber away from this bomb-building asshole, he had to face reality. One, he cared about her far more than he should. Two, she'd apparently broken off her engagement, which his hungry cock told his easily duped brain made her fair game. Three, he and Luc were going to be confined to this four-room cottage with her for days, perhaps weeks. Four, he wanted Kimber more than he had ever wanted anything or anyone in his life.

This has disaster written all over it.

Wiping a hand across his weary face, Deke reluctantly moved toward the cabin. A soft hand on his forearm held him back. Morgan.

At one time, Deke had wondered if he wasn't half in love with the vivacious, submissive redhead, even though she was strictly Jack's and they'd been married nearly three months. In the past, anytime he entered a room Morgan occupied, she'd get a rise out of him, and he'd feel the bite of desire in thirty seconds or less.

Three minutes ago, watching Kimber, despite her wariness and shock, he'd forgotten Morgan was even in the same state.

Again, it spoke volumes—and he absolutely didn't want to know what those tomes said.

"God, I'm so sorry Jack opened his big mouth. That girl, she's more than a friend."

He looked away from Morgan's searching blue gaze. "It doesn't matter."

"The hell it doesn't. Do you love this girl?"

"I can't."

"You don't want to. But do you?"

Deke cursed, refusing to even think of the answer.

Damn, why did Morgan insist on dredging this up? He'd rather string himself up by the balls with barbed wire.

"You're turning slightly green, so I'll take that as a yes," she said dryly. "Does she know about you and Luc and . . . ?"

"Yeah, she knows." He swallowed. "And I've got to stop thinking about Kimber. It's just wrong for me to want her."

"If you recall, I thought the same about Jack not too long ago. As it turned out, he was exactly what I needed."

True, but happy endings weren't going to happen for him. He'd been around the block enough to know that fairy tales could turn to nightmares in the blink of an eye.

"I'm not what she needs." *Far from it.* He sighed. "It might be hours, or if I'm really strong, days before I can't resist anymore. But this bastard threatening her has put me in a corner too, and it's not likely she'll be a virgin much longer. Once that happens . . . I'll destroy her."

Surprise filtered across Morgan's sweetly freckled face. "Or you might make each other whole. If your heart is drawing you to her, there's a reason. Maybe you should just see where it leads."

* * *

KIMBER woke after a few hours of sleep in the cabin's lone bed, cuddled against Luc's solid warmth. Deke was nowhere in sight. Last night, like the days she'd stayed with the guys in East Texas, he'd slept elsewhere.

He wasn't detached; he was scared. Something, feminine instinct maybe, told her that. He wasn't avoiding her as much as he was trying to hold himself at arm's length.

She wished to hell she knew why and what to do.

But now that the guys had brought her out to the middle of nowhere, she had lots of time to figure it out, she supposed.

As soon as she could find some peace of mind. As soon as she had some news about her dad.

Jack Cole, the cabin's owner, had explained last night that getting a cell phone signal in the middle of the swamp was nearly impossible, so she was welcome to use the cabin's phone.

Rolling away from Luc, who grunted in protest in his sleep, Kimber rose and padded into the kitchen. Predawn filtered dingy gray light through the cabin's huge picture windows. Deke wasn't on the couch he'd insisted sleeping on last night. But she spied him out on the patio, looking out over the swamp, coffee in one hand. A frown dominated the sharp angles of his face.

She sighed. *Later.* She'd have to deal with him—her heart wasn't going to let her turn her back on the problem, but first things first.

Lifting the receiver, she called Logan's cell phone. He answered on the first ring.

"Kimber?"

"Hi, Logan."

"You okay?"

"Fine. How's Dad?"

"Stable so far, thank God. His injuries would have killed a lesser man, but he's proven very hardy these first critical hours. They're cautiously optimistic."

Kimber let out a huge sigh of relief. "Oh, that's fabulous news. Wonderful. I worried all night."

"No need. Deke called me a few hours ago to check status. He didn't tell you?"

"I . . ." She wasn't about to admit to her brother that Deke did everything humanly possible to avoid her. "I was asleep."

"So you're where? I'm getting no display on my caller ID."

"Somewhere in Louisiana. In the middle of a swamp. That's all I know."

"Deke said something similar when I talked to him. Honey, I know it's none of my business, and I had no right to treat you like a teenager, but I have to know . . . are you going to be okay with the two of them?"

Who knew? It all depended on how badly Deke broke her heart.

Tears stung her eyes, squeezing out the corners. She was tired and over-wrought and ached so badly for a man who refused to want her and wouldn't say why.

"Fine. If anything changes with Dad's condition, call here."

"Ten-four. Likewise, call me if you need anything. *Anything.*"

His offer of counsel was implicit, but impossible. With a murmured thanks, she hung up the phone. Even her sigh shook, she noted wryly. This week had been a killer . . . and it wasn't over yet.

"Everything okay back home?"

Luc. Kimber whirled to face him. He looked sexy and sleep-tousled, and her heart melted like chocolate in sunshine when she saw him. More tears filled her gritty eyes.

"Fine," she managed to get out between sniffles.

"Come back to bed, sweetheart. You need more sleep."

Maybe. But she didn't think it was that simple. "Would you just hold me?"

His face softened. "Anytime."

Tucking her hand in his, he led her back to the darkened bedroom, eased her onto the soft, creamy sheets, and cuddled her against his body. This close, chest to chest, legs tangled, she couldn't miss his erection.

She tensed.

"I'm not going to touch you," he promised. "Not if you don't want to be touched."

Relaxing against him again, Kimber couldn't deny that she was oddly relieved. It wasn't Luc. He was sexy, sweet. In bed, compelling. He had this . . . intensity she saw flashes of—so far removed from the nice guy he seemed to be on the surface. There were layers here. Hidden but so obvious. Lord knew he could make her dissolve, set her on fire, make her feel as if she'd crawl out of her skin for satisfaction . . . right before he delivered.

But at the moment, Kimber had another man on her mind.

"You're thinking too hard and not sleeping." He kissed her temple. "What is it?"

She hesitated. Would talking too much about Deke and her confusion hurt Luc's feelings?

"Okay, I'll fill in the blanks," he said into her silence. "Your dad is going to be okay, based on your phone call. Right?"

"I think so. It's a big relief."

"Good. So the next thing screwed up in your life is all this crap with Jesse. But you left him; he didn't leave you. If you ended the engagement, it's because you don't love him. It doesn't seem like you had a hard time giving up Jesse as a potential life partner."

"I didn't. His life . . . I couldn't live like that. I quickly realized that he didn't love me; he loved the *idea* of me. My purity and innocence was somehow supposed to save him from his out-of-control, rock-star existence."

"And you knew better. Smart girl." He kissed her mouth gently, almost in praise. "So once the press latches onto the next bit of celebrity gossip, the reporters hounding you won't be an issue anymore."

"Probably true."

"You're not upset about Logan's reaction to Deke and I being with you at the hospital. You told him that your personal life is none of his business. You're too smart to take any guilt he might give you."

"He's fine with it now. He more or less apologized this morning."

Luc nodded sagely, soft fingers brushing her hair away from her face. "I doubt the status of your nursing exams would have you near tears."

"No," she admitted, trying to hold back even more tears.

"So, you're not telling me that you love Deke because you're afraid it would hurt my feelings."

Kimber bounced a shocked gaze up to Luc's indulgent smile. Damn, the man was smart.

"It's fine. You've known him longer. It stood to reason that you'd fall for him first. In time, I think you'll come to love me, too. For now, I take your feelings for Deke as a good sign."

"It's bad!" she cried against his chest. "My feelings don't matter. Once the immediate crisis of the explosion was over, Deke went back to business as usual. He refuses to be in the same room with me, so what does it matter if the man has my heart?"

"You know he wants you. I'm pretty damn sure he loves you, too."

God, how she wished that was true. But wishing wouldn't make it reality, and she had to come to grips with the chasm he purposely kept between them. "I think he cares. But he's not going to act on it. Something . . . some fear, it stands in his way."

Luc nodded. "Yes, but you can make him face it and get over it."

Had he suddenly turned stupid? "How? I don't know what it is."

"You don't have to know," he soothed. "He'll tell you. Get him to make love to you, and before too long, he'll tell you everything."

"But I can't get him to make love to me." More tears came, and Kimber shook her head. Damn, she hated this crybaby stuff. It wasn't her style. But she'd never had such an emotional week. "I laid under the man, nearly naked, and offered—begged—him to make love to me. And he didn't. His will is stronger than his desire."

Luc dropped another soft, soothing kiss on her mouth. "Not true. He's just . . . hung up."

"Yeah, on my virginity!" She sighed and wiped hot tears off her cheeks. "Maybe . . . if he knew I didn't have it anymore—Maybe if you took it . . ."

He groaned. "Oh, you're killing me, sweetheart. *Killing* me." As if to prove his point, Luc rolled her to her back and nudged his hard cock against her. "I would *love* to be your first and be honored . . . You don't know how much. But I think Deke *needs* this."

Kimber opened her mouth to question Luc, but he placed a finger over her lips to silence her. "Again, his story to tell."

"Then we're doomed," she snapped. "Because that man is not going to give in."

"He will. I think he's on the edge right now."

Luc paused and propped himself up on his elbows and looked down at her with a solemn expression. "The minute I told Deke what had happened, he grabbed his car keys and ran out the door. I had to run a footrace to make it to his Hummer before he peeled out of the garage. The entire trip to your dad's place he made phone calls, cursed, prayed. He drove a hundred miles an hour, at least, and gripped the steering wheel so tightly, I was surprised he had any blood flow left in his fingers. I thought he was going to come undone before we reached you and found out you weren't seriously hurt."

What did that mean? Kimber looked up at Luc, lashes fluttering, mind racing. In her book, that indicated that he cared. More than cared. But how much more?

"I've never seen him like that," he added.

Luc was trying to tell her that Deke loved her. Why? Everything seemed hopeless, since Deke himself would never tell her that.

"Let's pretend for a minute that he . . ."

"Loves you," Luc supplied, cutting into her hesitation. "Okay."

"It seems like time and patience is the only way out of this dilemma."

"Maybe not." Luc shifted, rubbing her lower lip with his thumb. "I have an idea, but it's a gamble. A big one," he admitted. "To agree to it, you'd have to trust me completely."

"I do. But wouldn't it just be easier for you to tell me his secret, and I could pretend I didn't know?"

"You couldn't pretend your way around this. Besides, that wouldn't help Deke deal with it, and he needs to."

Kimber was curious as hell, but point taken. "All right. If I took your gamble, I'd have to trust you. What else?"

A small smile. Another soft kiss. "You'd have to be totally committed. And willing to deal with the consequences if he doesn't take the bait."

The gravity of Luc's words grabbed at Kimber's stomach and pulled hard. He was deadly serious.

She let loose a shaky breath. "Could it backfire?"

His expression said that he didn't want to admit the truth, but he wasn't going to lie. "Yes."

"But you think it will convince him to overcome his fear of being with me?"

For a long moment, he fell silent. "No guarantees, but I think it's our best chance."

Luc wasn't pushing, but Kimber could tell he was definitely hoping she'd agree to his grand plan. "If I do this, what's in it for you? Deke said once you were hoping I'd stick around for marriage and babies."

"Guilty." He had the good grace to flash her a sheepish smile. "I'd love those things, and I think you'd be perfect in our lives. But ultimately, if you disagree, I think you can at least help make Deke whole. Besides being my cousin, he's also my best friend."

And he didn't have to say that he loved Deke as both a family member and a friend. Concern and caring softened his dark gaze. Kimber didn't need to think twice. "Then fill me in on the details. Let's go for it."

Chapter Thirteen

THE summer afternoon baked inside Jack's swamp hideaway. Deke's shirt clung to his skin. It was humid, hot. Very hot.

And not just the weather.

In deference to the heat—or just to drive him insane—Kimber drifted around the kitchen dressed in a little white robe, so thin it was damn near see-through. Auburn hair streamed down her back in soft waves that begged his fingers to tease them. The air of no-nonsense, afraid-of-nothing challenge that she wore like comfortable clothes turned Deke on. That same quality infused her gaze now. Half of him respected the hell out of her for it; the other half wanted to show her exactly why she should lose the bravado and be very afraid.

Unfortunately, Kimber wasn't just unique, daring, or smart. She was downright mouthwatering, too. Her peaches and cinnamon scent lingered every time he got near her. It made him hungry, hard.

And he was getting damn weak.

Blowing out a shaky breath, he walked into the attached den to escape Kimber's come-hither stare and the temptation she represented. It was going to be a long few days or weeks until Jack and Logan could get to the bottom of this situation with the Colonel's bomb-setting freak.

And until then, for her protection, Deke knew that he, Kimber, and Luc weren't leaving this place.

Her sudden, sweet laugh carried across the room and snagged his attention again, latched onto his cock. Resisting the urge to watch her was impossible.

With a curse, Deke turned back. She talked to Luc, who, shirtless and smiling, chopped something Deke assumed would be part of dinner eventually. And Kimber was lapping up his every word, flirting, her gaze licking at the bulge of his shoulders, the solid slabs of his pecs.

In return, Luc nuzzled her neck, whispered something in her ear. Kimber shivered and curled against his cousin.

Goddamn it—he didn't need this!

But he was lying. He did need this—sex—her. The reality was, *she* didn't need it. It was up to him to be the grown-up and exercise control. Save her from herself and what she only half understood.

Deke turned away and flipped on the TV, determined to distract himself and the erection screaming for her. Whatever Kimber and Luc did, they could do alone. It was no big deal to him. If they wanted to make googly eyes at each other, fine.

Brave words. But all through *Seinfeld*, Deke kept glancing over his shoulder. Luc and Kimber together . . . it wasn't fine. It was twisting his stomach, whipping up fury. The same old lies he'd been telling himself weren't working anymore.

Luc finished chopping whatever green stuff he'd been making into edible pieces and set it in a bowl. He stored it in the fridge, then closed the door with a sway of his hips and a salacious smile for Kimber.

If that wasn't enough to make Deke want to break something, Luc drew her into his arms, his fingers making their way down her narrow back to the soft curve of her hips. Then he kissed her, a sexy linger of lips on her neck, a slow layering of his mouth over hers. Kimber melted, molding against him, arching her head back into his waiting hand and baring more of her graceful neck. Luc took full advantage of her tempting skin under his lips and nibbled at her. She moaned in his arms.

Deke's balls hurt. His chest hurt. Even his fingers hurt. He looked down to see that he was practically crushing the remote control. In the few minutes since they'd distracted him, *Seinfeld* had ended, replaced by *Friends*. When the hell had that happened?

Damn it, he couldn't take this. With a curse, Deke flipped off the TV and bounced to his feet. He opened his mouth to say . . . what?

Not say, do.

March across the floor, drag Kimber into his arms, and carry her off to the bedroom. His mind spun with that fantasy. Deke wanted to give her pleasure, watch her take it. All that . . . but even more. He wanted, more than anything, to get deep inside her, take a part of her she'd never given to any other man, and stay there.

He wanted to claim her.

At that thought, all the blood rushed out of his brain, to his cock. Damn, lust hit him in the chest with such force, he almost couldn't breathe. Between one gasped breath and the next, his dick became hard enough to bust concrete, and his resolve weak enough to allow X-rated images of himself thrusting into Kimber's tight body to bombard him without mercy.

Bad, bad, bad!

Desire wasn't a want anymore. It had grown to need. He *needed* to touch her. Needed to know that, no matter what, he was somehow imprinted on her, the way she was on him. When had that happened? Why?

Torn, he stood there staring at Luc and Kimber sharing the intimacy of wet kisses in the kitchen, hungry, gaping—going out of his fucking mind.

Then Luc added fuel to the fire, trailing a hand from her jaw, over her collarbone, then down inside that little white robe. With a smooth slide of skin on skin, Luc edged the cotton aside and off her shoulder, baring the side of her breast to Deke's gaze. And her hard, blushing nipple.

What little blood had been in his brain jetted south to join the rest, like a flood running down a mountain.

With a velvety glide of his thumb, Luc stroked her plump nipple, prodding it, soothing it. She gasped, shifting closer to him so her thighs brushed his.

God, what he wouldn't give to be there next to her, turning her to face him, delving down into her mouth, possessing her sweet pink tongue as he tore that nonexistent robe from her body.

He took a step forward.

Neither one seemed to notice. Instead, Luc skated his fingertips down the side of Kimber's bared breast, then anchored his palm onto her hip. He sent his free hand into action, sweeping the robe off her other shoulder. Completely bare breasts. A pair of lush nipples begging for attention Deke was dying to give. Luc ignored them. Instead, he tugged gently on the belt still tied at her waist. He didn't unknot it . . . just dragged her closer. With a graceful sway, she curled her body around Luc's and lifted her rosy lips for a kiss.

Even in profile, the desire softening her face punched him like an uppercut in the gut from a prizefighter.

Sweat drizzled between Deke's pecs, down his back. Damn, just looking at that woman did him in. Watching her as arousal dawned across her face and flushed her body was imploding his sanity.

Luc stepped back and sank into one of the little chairs around the kitchen table, then wrapped his hands around Kimber's hips, engulfing them. Damn, sometimes he forgot what a little thing she was. Fragile. Breakable. He should think of her as untouchable.

He didn't.

Over her bare shoulder, Kimber shot him a coquette's gaze. *Zing!* That one glance tugged on his cock before her lashes fluttered, drifted back open.

But it wasn't just sex she made him crave. He'd been horny plenty of times in his life. This was different. Totally new. It scared the hell out of him.

Their gazes remained fused, and the electric power of it kept slamming him and shimmying through his body. He felt the jolt of her stare all the way down to his balls. The sensation bounced up again to the middle of his chest and squeezed when she bit her plump lower lip, looking shy, uncertain. Aroused.

Then Luc pulled her onto his lap, gave her a long, lingering kiss, and whispered against her mouth, making Deke edgy, angry, needy.

To hell with this! He took a handful of steps closer.

As he did, Luc turned Kimber to perch on his thighs, plastering her back to his chest, so they both faced him now. So Luc did know he'd been watching them? The challenge in his cousin's gaze to do more than be a spectator was a dead giveaway.

Kimber's stare held pure invitation. Deke stopped short.

This was bad. Really bad. They'd lured him in, set him up. Even though he knew he should turn away, walk outside, get the fuck out, their gazes still set his balls on fire. He didn't move a muscle.

The speed at which Luc undid the lacy little belt circling Kimber's lean waist could only be called prolonged torture. In absolutely no hurry, he unknotted the top half of the belt in a slow unwinding. He trailed the silken tie against Kimber's knee, edging it up beneath the hem of the robe until she gasped and her nipples peaked. Her areolas were dark and ridged and enticing.

"Should I?" Luc asked him, hands poised on the last fold of the tie at her waist.

Deke swallowed. If Luc did that, Kimber would be naked, completely. Her body would be exposed to his ravenous gaze, available to Luc's thorough touch.

No one spoke, breathed, moved . . . except one of Luc's fingers inched down between Kimber's legs to brush over what had to be the sensitive area just above her clit.

Deke shot his cousin a questioning glance. What the hell was he doing? What *would* he do? Luc merely answered with a smile, a raised brow . . . while that damn finger worked little circles right above Kimber's pussy.

Silence stretched, punctuated by Kimber's occasional jagged breath. Slowly, Luc withdrew his finger and wrapped both hands around the tie again.

It was impossible to miss the little wet spot on the robe right where Luc's finger had been.

That little dot of moisture told him how completely wet Kimber had to be. The sight nearly brought him to his knees.

"Should I?" Luc's hands tightened a bit more on the belt of Kimber's robe.

Deke knew he was going to hell for this. "Yes."

With a glittering smile of triumph and an erotic sweep of his hands, Luc brushed the fabric away from her body to hang on either side of his thighs.

And Kimber was totally, stunningly naked.

Deke was barely able to do more than gape and feel the impact of her nude beauty all through his tight-strung body before Luc wrapped his hands around her thighs and gently pulled, spreading her legs wide. Kimber drew in another ragged breath as Deke took in the view of her pussy.

Juicy, swollen, ripe. Perfect.

She looked every inch a wanton goddess as Luc skimmed a fingertip up the inside of her leg and paused to rub the soft, musky skin where her thigh and torso joined. If Luc moved half an inch, he'd be touching wet flesh and soft reddish hair with nothing but wanton intentions between them.

Oh God . . .

Luc's other hand meandered its way up the flat of her belly, up, up—slowly—until he cupped one breast and flicked the taut nipple once more.

Deke clenched his fists and tried to look away from the unfolding scene. Maybe if he turned away, their in-his-face fondling would end. Lord knew, if he watched too much more, he'd join in.

Once he did . . .

No, he couldn't think about the fact he'd get Kimber flat on her back, make sure she was seriously wet, and—

"Look at her," Luc invited, his voice challenging.

Deke swallowed. God, how could he do anything but stare and ache to have her? How could he possibly look at anything except the woman he desired above all else?

He wanted to shut his eyes to shut out the thought, but running from the truth wasn't worth missing an instant of her, so abandoned and sensual. So fucking beautiful and brave.

If she only knew the truth, she'd be terrified.

Tell her, the scared part of him prompted. *She deserves to know why you can't be with her this way.*

"Are you looking?" Kimber teased, low, sultry.

Why were they taunting him, baiting the wild animal inside him? Tempting fate?

"You know I am." He cleared his throat, but knew he'd still sound like he had a hundred rocks rattling around in his larynx.

Why can't you have her? another part of him asked. What happened in the past, with Heather, wouldn't happen again, right?

Likely not. Not for the world would Deke hurt Kimber intentionally. But what if he was cautious? Luc would be here, be responsible—hell, he'd insist on it . . . just in case.

Nice rationalization.

"Feel her," Luc invited.

"Please," Kimber breathed, spreading her thighs just a little wider.

She glistened, wet and rosy and needy.

Deke was in such a giving mood.

Still, he couldn't just pounce on her. He had a decision to make first: push her away . . . or crash into her life permanently. The thought of hurting her, fucking up everything in her world, tore fear through him.

The situation was like sitting on a case of live grenades. He had to do something, and he didn't have much time to decide. Pushing her away again with hateful words, tearing at her tender feelings and spitting on them—it wasn't an option. Watching his words crush her once before had damn near killed him.

Clasping her to him with all the lust rushing inside, fueled by all his electrically charged feelings—Deke wanted nothing more. He felt that combination jacking up his system, like rocket fuel with a 180 proof chaser. Potent. Undeniable. He shouldn't even think about her and the sizzling urge she incited. If he touched her—at all—his restraint wouldn't just crumble, it would combust into a million little pieces.

But his chest lifted in harsh, aroused breaths. His palms itched with the urge to take Luc up on his invitation, despite knowing that once he touched her, he'd take her. It would be irrevocable.

"If you don't touch her, you'll miss out . . ."

And to remind him of exactly what he was missing out on, Luc inched the hand on Kimber's thigh inward, tracing lazy patterns through her pussy before he slowly dipped inside. Deke watched her hungry body swallow his finger, and he couldn't help but think that finger plunging deep, deeper into her wet heat could be his own.

With a moan, she rested the back of her head on Luc's shoulder and arched. Deke watched his cousin penetrate her with one finger, slowly fucking her, before adding another and resuming the leisurely rhythm.

On his lap, Kimber writhed and thrust down. Luc answered by sliding the hand at her breast south to her hip, then delving into her slick curls. He teased the tangle of nerves between those pretty, spread thighs without pause. Without mercy.

Light pressure, a few swirling circles with those long, sensitive fingers, and Kimber gasped, thrashed, flushed, mewled.

Desire ratcheted inside Deke, coiling tight. He felt ready to launch, to explode.

God, she'd be fabulous to fuck. The thought of directing all that energy toward his cock, toward satisfaction, was so damn erotic. But it wasn't just about getting off. Giving pleasure to the woman he needed as much as his next breath, hell yes. That way, he could express all the foreign feelings coursing through him without a word . . .

Deke took another step toward them, edging into the kitchen.

Kimber, on the verge of orgasm, whimpered, gyrating her hips toward Luc's caress. He kept her there like a maestro, expertly taking her to the precipice, then backing away whenever her body revved and fluttered. After a short respite, he'd return to inflame her anew.

Spellbound, he watched as Luc used his hands to bring her close, then deny her, once more . . . again and again and again. Ten minutes later, her whole body was tense, flushed. Even after a brief rest, the mere slide of a finger inside her depths, a brush of skin over her clit, and Kimber teetered again between heaven and hell.

Damn, this was killing him. Deke adjusted the hypersensitive length of his steel-hard cock in his jeans. Even that little touch made him groan.

Kimber's eyes flashed open, dilated, hazel dominated by green, pleading.

"Deke, touch me . . ."

Her words were a machete to the gut. He closed his eyes, trying to block the scene out, but her scent, cinnamon and fresh peaches, all sugary and ripe, enticed him. Her hitching breaths and the way she called his name and stared, as Luc brought her to the edge once more . . . almost too much to take. He clenched his fists and realized he was shaking. Trembling like a fucking teenage boy.

"Deke." Luc again, with that damn taunting, challenging voice.

Slowly, he opened his eyes. His hot gaze traveled from the rosy patches staining Kimber's fair-skinned cheeks and splashing across her chest, down her rapidly rising and falling breasts. His visual thrill ride continued over her narrow waist, the soft curves of her hips . . . then to the slick flesh that swelled and pouted for attention. The flesh Luc pointed in his direction so he couldn't miss an eyeful.

The bastard had planned this . . . but that fact didn't make Kimber less potent or easier to resist.

"Luc, stop," Deke growled.

His cousin continued on as if he hadn't heard. "Taste her."

Shit! Deke's knees nearly buckled at the suggestion. All that sweet need, just for him, hot on his tongue . . . The knowledge that he could give her pleasure, that with a few hungry licks, she would surrender all to him, offer the rich cream of her essence to him, made his cock throb, his balls tighten.

His heart swell.

How the hell did a man fight that?

He'd nearly lost her twice in the last few weeks, first to Jesse McCall, then to a psycho-bomber. The evidence of the latter still showed in scattered stitches and bruises. If he walked away now, would he ever have another chance or would the separation be forever?

Even the possibility was too painful.

"Please, taste me," she begged softly, easing Luc's fingers away and trailing her own through her glistening cunt.

Then she held up one wet finger to him like a tempting treat.

Before he could breathe, think, Deke took another step closer, fell to his knees. He grabbed her wrist in his fierce grip and brought that finger to his mouth, sucking it like a man possessed. He groaned at that complex, musky taste he hadn't forgotten.

Fresh, salty-sweet, delicate—even after the flavor of her musk was long gone, her skin lingered on his tongue. It was so . . . her. So perfect.

Deke gripped her hips, eager to slide her ass to the end of the chair and dive into her like a dessert buffet.

"No." Luc's fingers brushed over her clit again, then covered her mound, denying Deke a full taste of Kimber's cream.

He gritted his teeth, watching as his cousin pressed down on her rhythmically until she clawed the arms of the kitchen chair and whimpered for the release he again denied her.

"Fuck her." Another challenge from Luc.

The ultimate one.

Deke's head snapped up. Luc was serious. Completely.

He gazed at his cousin for a heartbeat. Luc wasn't saying anything that Deke hadn't been thinking—and wanting more than his limited caveman vocabulary could express right now.

"Please . . . Oh, please!" Kimber broke into his thoughts, her voice high and tight. "I need you."

Blowing out a breath, Deke stared as she pleaded. His mind raced. Hell, he wanted to give her what she needed. Everything she needed. God knew he did. But . . .

"Now." Luc clarified, demanded.

Deke grabbed the chair in desperate fists. "Luc—"

"Fuck her," Luc cut him off. "Or I will."

Oh, shit. Shock lashed him.

Sucking in a harsh breath, Deke shifted his glance back to Kimber. He couldn't ignore the writhing, pleading, rosy-flushed woman watching him with hungry, half-focused eyes.

"She didn't say yes to this."

"Do you think she wouldn't in this state? She needs to come. I made sure of it."

"She should be thinking clearly before she agrees to sex. Ramping her up to wrench a yes out of her—"

"Kimber said yes before we came into the kitchen. Before I laid a finger on her. She wants us to make love to her. The only question is, who will be first?"

Luc had backed him in to a corner, for chrissake. Why? For the sake of his precious fucking picket fence fantasy, no doubt. *Damn him!* But Deke had no illusions. If he didn't take Kimber, Luc would.

"What's it going to be?" His cousin demanded.

"I'm thinking." But how much was there to ponder? If Kimber had already said yes, and Luc would fuck her if he refused, how could he say no when he wanted to be her first lover and claim her so badly?

"You've got thirty seconds."

"Do *not* back me in a corner, asshole."

"Too late."

"Why the fuck are you doing this? Why not just let things ride? Let me get her off with my mouth. That would ease her."

Luc scoffed. "Today. But what about tomorrow? Or the day after? She's a full-grown woman who deserves a rich, happy sex life. We've discussed it. She's on the pill and she's ready. More than ready. God, she's dripping all over my fingers. She cares about us. We both adore her."

Deke felt himself sweating. "What you're suggesting . . . It's permanent."

"Which is exactly what you want. What I want. Don't let fear hold us all back."

Deke squeezed his eyes shut for a moment, but it didn't block out the truth. "You planned this, you son of a bitch, to force my hand."

"I was beginning to wonder if we'd be old and gray before you found the balls to make love to her." Luc glanced at his watch. "So now I'm going to find out. Your thirty seconds is up."

Deke said nothing as Luc's arguments chased one another in his head. Kimber did deserve a sex life that included . . . well, sex. She wanted this. She wasn't underage or mentally unstable. And he cared about her—more than he wanted to admit. If she got away again, her departure would crush him.

But what could he give her besides a scarred past, a paranoid present, and a future most people would see as depraved?

Impatient now, Luc lifted Kimber onto the old round surface of the kitchen table, then shucked his jeans, kicking them across the floor. He stepped between the V of her spread legs, gripped her hips, and took his cock in hand.

"What the fuck?" He pushed at Luc, shoving him away from Kimber. "It's her first time and you're going to bang her on a kitchen table?"

Luc shrugged. "Okay, I'll take her to the bed and fuck her there."

Dumbfounded, Deke watched Luc hold out a hand to Kimber. She hesitated, lifting a wide, questioning gaze in his own direction.

Would he be her first? that gaze asked him. Did he care about her? Did he need to be inside her now? Be the first man to sink into her and take a part of her no other would ever have?

Yes, yes, yes, and yes.

"The hell you will," Deke snarled. Then he lifted Kimber from the table, up against his body. Her legs automatically wrapped around his waist as his mouth crashed down on hers, every sweep of his tongue desperate. He wanted to crawl inside her and stay as he wrapped his arms around her, supporting her with a hand under her bare ass. The sweet juice of her cunt seeped onto his wrist and through his jeans.

Good damn thing she was wet. She was going to need all that lubrication.

Inside the darkened bedroom, Deke shifted aside the mosquito netting and laid her across the antique tester. She looked perfect there. Beautiful and gleaming, like the bed itself, with lean, clean lines.

"You sure, kitten?" he rasped, his voice thick in the air.

Kimber nodded, writhed. "Yes. Please. Now."

"Is that you talking or arousal? Luc jacked you up—"

"I wanted this, wanted you, before he laid a hand on me. Please," she whispered, inching a slow hand between her legs to tease her clit—and driving him closer to insanity.

Deke's knees buckled even as his cock leapt in approval, but he grabbed her wrist and pulled it away. He wanted to give her this orgasm. Him and his aching cock.

He swallowed. *Fuck it.* He was going to do it. Forget everything but now and make love to Kimber. Fuck her. Be her first lover. Claim her. He couldn't stop it, didn't want to.

"I pushed you away before, said terrible things I didn't mean . . ."

"I know. I forgive you."

The breath whooshed out of him. How wonderful was she, to understand he hadn't meant that crap? He didn't deserve her, and hoped like hell he didn't fuck up her life. But he couldn't fight what they all wanted anymore. And that wasn't just her body, but closeness. He needed to feel as joined to her as two people could be.

"Thank you." He turned to Luc, his heart firing faster than an M60. "Condom?"

"No." The small, feminine word pinged shock all around the room, all through his body.

"She's on the pill," Luc reminded.

Deke looked back to her, stared, couldn't resist placing a hungry, wet kiss across her mouth, thumbing her stiff nipple. "Is that true?"

Kimber arched into his touch. "I saw a doctor after I left Jesse. I hoped this would happen."

The information sank into his churning blood and made it sing. *Safe.* She was safe. Bless her! He rewarded her with a nibble to her other breast. She hissed in response. Not only could he be deep inside her, but he could be bare and deep inside her.

Not smart, another part of him shouted. The pill wasn't totally effective . . .

"Give me a condom," he told Luc. "Just to be sure." Then he brushed a soft hand over Kimber's hair. "I don't want anything to happen to you."

"I don't want anything between us. Please . . ."

Oh, hell. Stupid, crazy, impulsive. But something primitive inside him erupted, shouted *hell yeah*, at the thought of being inside her with nothing between them. He wanted to have Kimber in a way he'd never had any other woman. The pill was safer than condoms, and he knew from experience that condoms weren't foolproof.

Deke couldn't keep his eyes off of her. This time, though, his gaze latched onto her healing stitches and fading bruises. They reminded him that he could have lost her before he'd ever claimed her. That would have been a goddamn travesty. He needed her. In the most elemental way possible, he had to have her.

"Kitten," he rasped. "I promise I'm clean. I have regular physicals. I've always been careful. I've ne-never . . ." He swallowed. "Be sure."

"I am." Smiling, she caressed light fingers down the length of his back. He shivered and sucked in a breath at the sudden rush of sensation. "Then I can be your first in a way, too."

Like she could be claiming him. Need raised another notch. He downshifted his brain and turned it off. Everything he did with her tonight would be pure instinct . . . all heart.

"I want that." He shoved his jeans down his hips and crawled up on top of the bed, lowering himself beside her.

Diving into the sweet heaven of Kimber's mouth, Deke lost himself in her taste, unique and clean. Her kiss was strong, demanding. Without words, she told him that she expected him to give her everything, hold nothing back.

For as long as he'd wanted her, as much as he cared for her, could he even begin to withhold a single, scintillating thing he wanted to do to her? She'd already proven hearty enough to meet his needs with other varieties of sex. They'd be perfect together.

As he clasped the back of her head to bring her deeper into the kiss, Deke felt Luc climb up on the bed and take up position on Kimber's other side.

He broke the kiss, then stared at Luc. Opened his mouth, then snapped it shut.

How had he forgotten about his cousin? He, who hadn't had sex alone with a woman in twelve years? But he had forgotten. Now he had to face the fact that Kimber would be not just his lover, but Luc's.

The thought stabbed him with immediate denial, complete rejection. Deke shoved the instinct away, forcing logic into his lust-hazed brain. He needed Luc here.

He might be willing to slide into Kimber without a latex barrier between them. Oh, fuck it—he was dying to feel her bare flesh gripping him. But he wasn't willing to forego all precautions. He couldn't be the lone man responsible . . . just in case.

Giving into that fear meant that he had to share. And no matter how much something inside him railed, he couldn't be the only man she made love to.

Shoving the thought from his mind, he watched as Luc's tongue swirled around one of Kimber's stiff nipples. He took the other, laving, nipping—thrilled at her quick response, the automatic parting of her thighs.

Deke slid a reverent hand down the soft skin of her abdomen, then continued down into her pussy. A wet haven, drenched, swollen. She gasped at his very first touch.

Under his fingers, the hard knob of her clit pulsed. Damn, she was beyond primed. Knowing that, Deke was, too.

He slid lower, sliding one finger inside her. *Tight. Oh, hell . . . so damn tight.* Gasping. Her body closed around his finger, silently begging. Adding a second finger, he plunged deeper. Good damn thing he'd jacked off twice already today, or the moment he got inside this vacuum of sultry heat, he'd explode.

But getting his cock inside her, it was going to hurt her. Deke hated that fact. With his fingers, he scissored, trying to spread her open, minimize the pain.

"More," she demanded.

Snapping his gaze up, he stared at Kimber. She wasn't talking to Luc, who was treating her nipples like a cross between a lollipop and something his Hoover would attack. She was talking to him.

"Deeper?" Deke's voice cracked as he asked the question, while he thrust his fingers inside her up to the hilt.

Her breath hitched as she shook her head and nodded—virtually at the same time. "Deeper. More. I want to be full of you."

Deke nearly staggered at her gasping, starkly honest answer. "I want to fill you, kitten. I don't think I've wanted anything more in my whole life."

"You're making the right choice," Luc whispered, dusting little kisses up her jawline.

The nipples he'd left behind were red. No other way to describe them. Swollen, well worked, beyond hard. They'd be tender tomorrow, but given the way Kimber arched to Luc and led his head back to her breasts, she wasn't feeling it now.

The only thing she felt was ready.

Easing off the bed, Deke stood at the side and, caressing his way up her thighs, to her hips, he pulled her to the edge of the bed, curving her thighs around his hips.

"Deke?"

He leaned down and placed a soft kiss on the flat of her tummy. "I'm not leaving. In this position, I can better control the angle and the pressure. If it hurts too much, I can back off."

At least he hoped he could. What he really wanted was to charge into her like a riled-up bull with a red cape in its face. Deke forced a full lungful of air in, held it, centered.

"A little pain won't break me."

"I'm leaving Luc a little room to work here, too." His hands wandered up the sleek lines of her torso, then back down, pausing to swirl around that candy-button clit. "But trust me, by the end of the night, you'll feel well fucked."

Kimber wrapped her legs around his waist, trapping him in. "Promise?"

That one taunting word arched through him and went straight to his dick. Deke glanced at the ceiling, looking for some self-control. He wanted Kimber to feel well loved, too.

"Yeah," he croaked. "Oh, yeah."

She answered with a stunning smile that only ratcheted up his anticipation. His control snapped.

Taking his stiff cock in hand, he guided himself to the small, swollen opening. Very small. And he wasn't a small guy. He was going to have to fight his way in. The thought had him breaking out in a fresh sweat.

Deke leaned forward a fraction and eased the head of his cock inside her. *Oh, damn. Already so hot and tight.* Under him, Kimber thrashed, lifting, forcing him in an additional inch. Gripping her hips, he forced his way in another.

Right up against her barrier.

"Don't stop," she pleaded.

He couldn't have stopped if he wanted to. But a million thoughts slammed through him. What if . . . he hurt her too much, or she didn't like the feel of him deep, or she wasn't as ready as she thought?

Or worse, what if history repeated itself?

"You're overthinking this," Luc murmured. "You want each other. Unless I miss my guess, you love each other. She's protected, and I'm here. It doesn't get more perfect than this."

All his arguments were hang-ups, his problems. Luc was right about that. Worrying about her pain or readiness—even the future—were just excuses.

After twelve years, it was time for him to take a chance again.

Chapter Fourteen

WITH his left hand, Deke gripped Kimber's hip. With his right, he skated his way to her pussy and rubbed in soft, slow circles, his fingertips providing friction on the little bead of her clit. He stroked her until she gasped. Until she gripped the sheets, and a fresh flush washed over her fair skin.

After being denied climax so many times, she pleaded, "Please, Deke. Now. God, now . . ."

She was right on the edge. He wasn't going to refuse her again.

Deke reared back to her opening, gathered power and, teeth bared, he pushed inside her with one hard thrust.

Her flesh yielded to him slowly. Though his heartbeat drummed in his ears, her scream rose above it, clutching at him. There was no stopping. He slid into her. Then he lifted her hips, tilted her toward him, leaned over her, and moved in another half inch.

Finally, he was in. Completely.

Shaking so damn hard, Deke realized he'd never had a woman feel so perfect, like . . . home. Until Kimber, he hadn't missed it. Now, in some elemental way, Deke knew she was his.

Under him, she twisted on the pale sheets and watched him with hazel eyes now so green and glossy with unshed tears. Maybe the "Band-Aid" approach, dealing with it quickly to put the hurt behind her, hadn't worked. Guilt for her pain raked him.

"I'm sorry," he choked.

"There's a good part to this, right?" She panted. "If there is, don't you dare stop."

She was certifiable if she thought he could walk away now. But he was determined to void the pain with pleasure.

Forcing himself to remain still, despite the sweat and ground teeth it cost him, Deke rotated his fingers over her clit again, soothing, cajoling. It took a moment to coax her, as if her body had recoiled from the shock of his flesh tearing through her. His balls boiled as her sheath enveloped his cock, but he didn't move an inch. Luc seemed to understand his goal and helped him out with a gentle caress of her nipples, soft, deep kisses across her mouth.

Soon, Deke felt her swell around him even tighter. Flutter. Gasp. Explosion was imminent. Damn, she was amazing. He wanted her to have this one . . . just in case the rest was too painful this first time.

Under his fingers, her cries became mewls. The mewls turned to pleas, then the pleas to a shout of spectacular release as her entire body bucked under him and her pussy gripped him like a desperate fist, nearly milking him of self-control and seed.

God, she looked beautiful, joined with him, surrendering all control to the pleasure . . .

Deke tensed against the promise of ecstasy teasing his cock. He barely managed to hold off. But he'd waited too long to be inside Kimber to treat it like a ten-yard dash. She'd waited too long for her first time for a rush to the end. Somehow, he had to make it special. Memorable. Even if she left him after the danger to her had passed, he wanted her to remember him. He wanted to be in her heart the way she was in his.

Once her peak of pleasure subsided and the walls of her sex caressed him with a slow pulse, then he drew back, all the way to the tip of his cock, and eased in. He set a pace like molasses—sweet, slow, designed to dazzle. From the very first stroke, she responded, gasping, tightening, staring at him in wonder.

"Deke. You . . . This . . . Ohmigod!" she panted. "The friction . . ."

"That's right, kitten." He felt it, too. Without the latex between them, skin slicked across skin, providing the most heavenly sensations. But it wasn't just physical; it was knowing he could feel her everywhere, in every way, that turned him inside out. He wanted to turn her inside out, too.

It was hard to imagine that he was going to manage to make her come again. Virgins often didn't orgasm from intercourse the first time they experienced sex. Kimber had just detonated in a killer climax. And he was working on a short fuse—and getting shorter every time the bare head of his cock glided its way up her walls and settled against her cervix as she gripped him in welcome.

But damn if he wasn't going to try to give her one last burst of pleasure.

Bending his knees, Deke made sure he scraped the tip of his dick against that upper wall of hers, coasting in until her breath caught, until she tightened. Her G-spot. *Gotcha!* he thought with a smile.

"Want to come again?" he asked, prodding that bundle of nerves.

She gave him a shaky nod and tightened on him again. "What about you?"

When he plunged in again, the friction nearly had him cross-eyed. "Oh, I'll get there."

Luc caressed her damp cheek, brushed sweat-slick hair from her temple. He settled next to her, burying his face in her neck, and started crawling inside her mind.

"You look amazing," he whispered in her ear. "So open. You surrendered to every inch he gave you so perfectly. I want to see you come again. Can you do that for me? Please . . . Just the sight of it unravels me. I can only imagine what it does to Deke."

Damn, his cousin was good at inciting a woman's brain. A mental frenzy of desire always led to a bodily expression of ecstasy. And just in case . . . Luc shoved Deke's fingers away from her clit and replaced them with his own.

"Aaahhhh." Kimber didn't say much, but the frantic nod of her head said they were overwhelming her again.

Hell, Luc's little speech was even getting to him. That and watching the thick span of his own cock tunneling inside her, seeing her unfurl for him, take him completely. As he delved deep into her stare while he plumbed her body, Deke knew that she welcomed him inside her so freely because she cared.

The thought nearly made him burst.

"Do you like the feel of him inside you, sweetheart? Like being full?"

Another frantic nod of her head as he nudged the hot spot inside her again with his cock, while Luc stroked the little bead of her clit. She grabbed at his arm, at Luc's hair, and cried out.

"I love to watch you like this, so accepting and aroused," Luc muttered.

Deke swallowed against his rising need to come and focused on Kimber, her body, and its signals. She couldn't be far away. Please let her be close. *Please . . .*

"When you're on the edge, your nipples are so beautifully flushed and hard." Luc bent to lap at them, nibble, suck. Slow, leisurely, as if he had nothing else to do all day long.

Around Deke, Kimber tightened, rippled.

She reached out to him with her stare, those bright hazel eyes pleading, panicked.

Deke encouraged her. "Yes, kitten. That's it. Come for me. I gotta feel you . . ."

"Kiss me," she entreated.

After a quick glance at Luc, who nodded, Deke leaned over and lowered his belly onto hers. Then chests connected next. At the sizzling contact, Deke sucked in a breath at the vicious, breath-stealing sensations. Then he ravaged her lips, fusing their mouths together. *Oh, damn . . .* The heat both inside and out. Sweat slicked both their bodies, providing friction at every point of contact. Those hard little nipples slid across his chest, and she sucked in a loud, staccato gasp.

Deke drove as deep into her body as he did her mouth, bracing his hands against her hips for each possessive thrust. She wrapped her legs around him and accepted him even deeper. He slammed into her again . . . again. Writhing, Kimber moaned louder. Blood roared. Hearts drummed. Accelerated. Pounding. Desperate.

Kimber screamed into the kiss. Her body buckled beneath him, and Deke held on with all his might, pumping his way into the tight clasp of her body as it rhythmically squeezed him without mercy.

Then, white-hot light and heat engulfed him, sizzling his whole body. The sweet burn revved from the base of his spine, tingled. His balls were so damn tight, and he held his breath. In the next instant, sublime pleasure exploded through his cock, prying something in his chest wide open, as he erupted inside her, flooding her with passion, semen.

Something that felt suspiciously like love.

* * *

EARLY gray morning slanted through the little window to her left. Kimber blinked, looked around the unfamiliar room. An antique bed, an equally old, lovingly cared for dresser, a large, empty rocker in the corner.

Then everything rushed back at her. Louisiana. The bomb. Her father. Jack Cole's hideaway. And last night . . . Deke deep inside her. Luc watching every moment, urging her on.

After that, she didn't remember a damn thing.

"Morning," Luc murmured in her ear.

He cuddled closer, heat pouring off him in a searing rush. Something about the way he greeted her, or the way he curled his arms around her to drag her close, told Kimber that Luc had awakened eager and ready for more than a casual greeting.

"Hi." She dipped her head shyly.

Crazy to feel any reticence after everything she'd done with and around him.

"Sleep good?" He planted soft butterfly kisses on her neck, across the curve of her shoulder, the swell of her breast.

"Hmm. I crashed. You?"

Luc inched closer, so the front of his body was plastered against her side. So the steel length of his erection prodded her hip in a silent question.

"Not so good."

Really? Luc usually slept good, especially after . . . Oh, but he hadn't come last night. She'd made love with Deke and fallen asleep.

"I conked out on you, didn't I? I left you . . ."

"With blue balls?" He smiled, letting her know it was okay.

"I'm sorry."

With another sultry smile and a flick of his thumb over her slightly sore nipples, he quipped, "Want to make it up to me? That is, if you're up for it."

She hesitated, knowing that Luc wanted to make love to her. How did she feel about that? How would Deke feel?

Kimber had known from the beginning that they'd share her. Deke and Luc had never stated otherwise. If their intent had changed, Deke would have thrown his cousin out of the bedroom last night. Right?

But she hesitated. Last night hadn't been just sex. Even she knew that. Deke had taken her with such feeling and passion . . . and he hadn't denied loving her. Did that make her exclusively his?

If so, why would Luc be the man lying next to her now, especially when Deke knew that his cousin always woke up in the mood?

Given all that, Kimber doubted the three-way part of their relationship had changed.

Besides, Deke seemed to want him here, almost like a security blanket. If she wanted to lull Deke and encourage him to open up to her, spill his secret, saying no to Luc wasn't a wise option.

Not that he was a hardship. She might love Deke with everything in her heart, might have even fallen for him when she was seventeen and barely able to process the unruly demands he pushed her body into feeling. But if keeping Luc here somehow enabled Deke to stay with her, it was a small price to pay. Besides, she adored the sexy, sultry chef. His way with words—and his hands—were always sublime.

Kimber wiggled, shifting, testing. "I'm sore, but not too sore. If you're gentle . . ."

"For you, sweetheart, yes."

"Um, I need a quick bathroom trip first." She definitely felt every one of those ten hours of sleep in her very full bladder.

"Of course. I'll wait. Impatiently," he teased. "But I'll wait."

She dropped a kiss of thanks on his cheek and rolled to her other side, intending to crawl out of bed and across the hall to the little bathroom.

Instead, she encountered Deke.

He was awake now, but he looked sleep-rumpled and tangled in the sheets.

Her heart tripped. "You slept here?"

Deke tensed. "Yes."

She couldn't help the smile breaking across her face. "Next to me?"

"Yes." Because he hadn't wanted to be parted from her, his gaze said. A first. Something new. Like . . . he'd given a bit more of himself.

Kimber didn't stop, didn't question her urge; she simply hugged him and planted a soft kiss on his mouth. The connection that had forged them into intimacy last night leapt between them again, immediate, strong. He wrapped his arms around her and rolled her on top of him, right onto his hearty erection. When he pressed right against her, everything between her legs that had slept all night awoke with a vengeance.

"You all right?" he asked.

"Are you?"

Those blue eyes of his looked stormy, troubled by her question.

She tried to rephrase. "If Luc and I . . . ?"

He cast a quick gaze over at his cousin, now stroking her back. In that flash, she caught hesitation, then resignation. "Yeah. We share. That's no secret."

It may not have been a secret, but his acceptance of her doing the wild thing with Luc seemed questionable. She wanted to press Deke further, but nature called—insistently.

While she tossed on her white robe and dashed across the hall to take care of necessities and brush her teeth, she pondered Deke's reaction. It seemed like he wasn't sure he wanted to share her, but felt compelled to for some reason she didn't quite grasp.

She wanted to talk to him. Luc had been convinced that if she could persuade him to make love to her that he'd tell her about his past. But her feminine intuition—and having lived many years with military men— told her it wasn't going to be that easy. Special Ops types were trained not to divulge classified information under duress or torture. Even at her teasing best, she didn't think she could get him to break his silence.

Now what? Kimber shook her head. It seemed she had nothing to do but go with the flow and see how everything played out. Not her favorite strategy. The Colonel always preferred a careful plan, but tough times called for tough measures . . .

Storing her toothbrush in the nearly empty drawer again, she dashed across the hall. Luc lay in the middle of the bed like a pasha, waiting for a woman to come pleasure him. It would be easy to imagine him as some sort of desert prince with his long, dark hair, those wicked chocolate eyes with their intriguing tilt. And miles of rippling golden skin.

"Come here, sweetheart," he murmured, opening his arms to her.

A little ache took up residence in her body—part affection, part stirring of desire. Poignant. She cared about Luc, utterly adored him. Would she ever come to love him with that same wildfire, all-consuming whirl of emotion that seized her when Deke was near?

Hesitantly, she stepped into the room. She felt Deke in the corner, then turned and saw him standing there, watchful, silent.

She reached for his hand. He clasped it in his grip and swallowed.

"Deke, if you don't want—"

"Luc waited all night for this, for you. He needs you. God knows I'm not touching him."

Kimber smiled at his attempted humor, but she could tell he was torn by this. Why share her? Duty? Loyalty? She didn't quite understand.

But she also knew that if she asked him point-blank, he'd never answer.

"Guess it's up to me, then."

Releasing Deke's hand, she climbed up on the bed and gifted Luc with a soft kiss of greeting. With the most gentle touch, he palmed the crown of her head, petting his way down to her neck, her shoulder.

"You're so soft, sweetheart. I'm going to be so careful with you."

Sweet. That described Luc through and through. She caressed his face. "That sounds wonderful."

He brought her down for another kiss, this one longer, a more involved exchange of breath, a soft brush of lips, a soft slide of tongues. Minutes later, Kimber lifted her head and realized that, just from his kiss, her heart pounded like a platoon of cadets marching up and down a field. And parts south were already . . . moist.

But something was missing.

She turned to Deke. "Are you joining us?"

Barely an instant passed before he took two huge, ground-eating steps forward and bounded onto the bed beside her.

"I'll take that as a yes."

Deke pushed her to her back and covered her mouth in a ravaging kiss like a starburst—fiery, intense, quick. Then he turned her to face Luc, tore the sheet away, and urged her toward his cousin's cock.

"Suck him. Gently. It's a tease. Don't let him come."

Expressionless, his face like granite, Deke barked the order. Kimber really wanted to pursue the reasons for his insistence and reticence, but he wouldn't talk now, and she knew it. Besides, she wanted to keep Luc on her side, which meant keeping him happy. And okay, being honest . . . Deke had her heart completely, but she'd bet money that Luc was stunning in the sack.

Still, she wasn't about to let Deke do this reluctantly. She wanted him fully committed to touching her.

"And what are you going to do?" she challenged, swiping her tongue across her lip.

"Last night, Luc brought you within an inch of your sanity before I fucked you. You're going to repay the favor."

Before Kimber could reply, Deke gave her a nudge on the back. Luc slid his hand into her hair and lured her down, lowering her to his waiting cock.

After overhearing Ryan and Jesse discussing the merits of a great blow job, Kimber had a little more fuel to add to the fire with Luc.

Smiling, she skimmed her fingers up the insides of his thighs, slowly creeping her way toward his balls. He moaned as she fitted a hand under his testicles, lifted and cupped them. Gently rubbing her thumb across the soft surface, she turned her attention to the stiff length of his erection. Large. No denying the man had size. In that, it was clear that Deke and Luc were related. And wow, was he ever hard. The head was so engorged it looked like a plum, all purple and delicious.

Using just the tip, Kimber ran her tongue up his length, from base to crown, laving her way around the glans, finding a sensitive spot on the underside that made him gasp. Meanwhile, she found the sensitive, baby-smooth skin just beneath his balls and press-rubbed.

Luc gasped and nearly came out of his skin. "Holy . . ."

As he tried to hold back, she sensed Deke watching the show over her shoulder. To test her theory, she flicked her tongue along the length of Luc's cock, and Deke's hands on her tightened.

Finally, he set her on her knees, ripped off the robe and blanketed her back with his body. Naked body. Impossible to miss the iron-slabbed chest on her back and the bare erection pressing against her ass.

"Kimber, sweetheart . . ." Beneath her, Luc lifted his hips to her teasing tongue. "Put your mouth on me."

"Soon," she taunted, pressing kisses to his belly, drizzling her fingertips along his thighs, across his hips. On his abdomen, she traced the outline of his cock with her tongue.

He sucked in a sharp breath. "You really are going to try to pay me back for last night."

It wasn't a question; he knew the answer. Kimber gave Luc credit for lots of smarts.

Still, she played dumb. "What? Deke said to tease you."

She skimmed her fingertip up the length of his shaft with all the pressure of a whisper. He gnashed his teeth and tried to hold back.

"Damn it, not to the point of insanity."

"Oh, you need to come?" she asked, backing away.

"It would be nice," he gritted out.

"I'm sure. But since you nearly brought me to climax *eight* times before denying me, that makes me cranky and you fair game. And you've got seven more frustrating cooldowns coming your way."

With those words, Luc came out of his sensual haze and opened his eyes. Dark, hungry, endless, his stare focused on her and promised payback if she continued down this path.

Hadn't he already treated her to his torturous worst? That wicked stare said no. Kimber shivered.

Luc threaded his hands in her hair and grabbed a fistful. "You don't want to taunt me, sweetheart. I can't be gentle if you do that."

Behind him, Deke concurred, guiding her down again. "Just suck him deep. I'll tell you when to stop. If you quit too soon, you'll find out Luc is a pussycat compared to me when it comes to denying your orgasm."

Kimber didn't doubt for a moment that Deke could make good on that threat.

Licking her lips, she sent a sultry stare Luc's way and sucked his cock inside her mouth, all the way to her throat.

Stuck somewhere between placated and aroused, Luc settled in with groans and whispered encouragement. She was gratified when a film of perspiration broke out across his chest, and he began to fuck her mouth with measured lunges of his hips.

Damn, the man was simply delicious.

But Deke wasn't content to watch. At all.

Still behind her, he covered her back with his chest and fondled her breasts, squeezing her sensitive nipples between his thumbs and forefingers and gently twisting. His hot breath on her neck made her shiver.

Then he started to speak. "Keep sucking him and feel me . . . here."

Here turned out to be a wide palm covering her sex, the heel of his palm pressing right onto her clit. Her sex cramped with desire. Immediately she went from moist to dripping.

With insistent hands, he spread her knees wider, and his fingers went to work.

"I can press you hard and *nearly* get you off," Deke growled in her ear, "but the trick with you is a varied touch. A firm circle around your clit, then a soft swipe of my finger just barely over the top, so light you wonder if you imagined it. Right?" He demonstrated as he spoke. At her whimper, he continued on. "Then between two fingers, I'm going to trap this sweet little thing and rub the sides."

And he did. Kimber gasped. A totally new sensation converged as he trapped her clit between his index and middle fingers and stroked the sides in a friction-filled slide that ignited her all over.

"Now I'll start at the beginning again and throw in lots of contact with the rest of that hot, dripping pussy . . . but not enough to get you off."

In the next three minutes, he proved how deadly effective his technique was. With a cry, she squirmed each time he changed the touch. Every time she knew she was a stroke or two shy of coming, he'd change his approach, let his fingers wander elsewhere—drive her insane.

The more aroused Kimber felt, the more voracious she was with Luc's cock. She moaned around his thick erection, swiping her tongue across the fat head, curling her fingers around the base and squeezing up. Then she teased the underside of his balls, traced her finger around the crown, rubbed her nipples across the surface.

"Damn, sweetheart . . ." Luc looked both sweaty and speechless. "Where the hell did you learn all that?"

Kimber didn't answer that. No point. Besides, she didn't want to stop licking every delicious inch of Luc.

The sexy chef drew in a bracing breath. "No more teasing. I can't take it."

It was up to her to show him differently.

But Deke moved his hands again, changed the pressure of his touch, this time right across the ultrasensitive knot of her clit. A slow skim of flesh on flesh brought her closer to the edge than ever. A pass over the top, then another, then a third. Oh . . . The pleasure grew so intense, it damn near broke her apart. Now close to a thunderous orgasm, she gasped and jerked—and lost her grip on Luc's cock.

As she did, Deke eased off his electrifying touches, and tears of frustration—of need—seeped from the corner of her eyes.

"*No!*" she wailed.

"Yes," Luc countered, thrusting a gentle but insistent fist into her hair and forcing her to meet the hunger in his stare. "I can't wait to feel you around me when you come."

He gripped her hips and pulled her toward him, yanking her from Deke's grip, and straddled her right over his waiting erection.

As Luc pulled her down, he arched his hips. In he slid, up, up, up. And suddenly, Kimber was filled to the brim with his incredibly hard flesh.

Long and loud, he groaned. And still he kept tunneling into her, steady and deep until she swore she could feel him at her tonsils. Sex this way definitely maximized the penetration, nearly to the point of pain.

Above him, she whimpered, tensed, her thighs tightening to stop him from sinking inside anymore. They both came to her rescue.

Easing her back up his shaft, Luc murmured, "Painful?"

She gave him a shaky nod. "A little."

Behind her, Deke urged her back down onto Luc's cock with a line of teasing kisses across her shoulder. "Just a little. Just at first. You can take him, kitten. Take all of him. I want to watch you come."

Before she could even answer, his fingers delved back into her wet folds, honing in on her begging clit.

Luc pressed home. Deke pressed her hot button. Kimber's cry became a moan as Luc ground against a sensitive spot deep inside her. Deke teased with a flick of his fingers. They shoved her closer to heaven . . . before they both withdrew like some perfectly synchronized stunt show.

"Harder. Now. More!"

Gritting his teeth, Luc entered her again, slowly filling her, a torturous drag of the head of his cock over her G-spot. Deke took his time stroking slow circles over the one spot guaranteed to send her reeling, soaring.

Sizzle became burn. Pressure became an unrelenting ache. It all gathered, centered, concentrated. Kimber gasped, clutching Luc's shoulders for support and so thankful for Deke's anchoring arm around her waist as the sensations took her breathlessly upward.

Then she rocketed into ecstasy, soaring, weightless and breathless. High, higher, she climbed until the red heat burst. Kimber shuddered, her body clutching at Luc still buried hard and tense inside her while pleasure pulsed, spread through her body like a potent shot of pure alcohol.

In degrees and slow moments, she returned to earth. Eyes closed, Kimber struggled to draw in a breath. Perspiration filmed her.

God, she was tired. Limp. She didn't think she could take anymore. Another orgasm like that and she'd lose consciousness.

But the drive of hard male cock inside her sex all the way against her cervix brought her back to the moment with a gasp. Luc gritted his teeth and gripped her hips. He wasn't done.

With a desperate edge, Deke pushed at Kimber's back. She fell onto Luc's chest, and he grabbed her and urged her lips apart to tangle her tongue with his, dominating her mouth with a ravenous kiss.

Before she could even assimilate Luc's assault, Deke made his move, probing her back entrance with a pair of lubricated fingers. The forbidden thrill of it sent fresh tingles shooting to all the right places. Nerve endings she would have thought dormant for the day awoke. She felt so full, both front and back, stretched taut.

Clearly, Deke wasn't done with her, either.

Tossing her head back and baring her throat to Luc, he took advantage, nipping his way up her neck to tug on her lobe with his teeth and breathe shivers over her shoulder.

A rip, a tear. Oh, God, she knew the sound of a condom wrapper. Surely, Deke didn't plan to . . .

The sinful smile on Luc's face told her that Deke did.

"Hold still, sweetheart." Luc gripped her hips to ensure she did.

"But Deke . . . He's going to—"

"Fuck you while Luc fucks you," Deke growled into her ear, the aroused gravel in his tone making her hot and shivery. "Welcome to ménage, kitten. Get ready to know the meaning of multiple orgasms."

The hot promise in his tone dive-bombed her with another burst of desire. Those detonated in her belly, in her sex, spreading like a molten river down her legs, up to her nipples. But that wasn't all. Desire mixed with anxiety. Taking them both at once—huge potential for ecstasy . . . and pain.

"Don't tense," Luc whispered, soothing her.

Easy for him to say. He wasn't about to be penetrated twice—simultaneously.

"The condom is lubricated to ease his way. He'll make it nice and smooth. Just relax."

Sweat broke out on Kimber's back. Deke began to probe her back entrance, sliding the head just inside.

"Push back on me." His voice was barely more than a rough pant.

She did as he reached up her body, grabbed her shoulders, and used the leverage to push his way past the ring of muscle—and beyond.

After an initial twinge of pain, Kimber gasped. Then Deke began to fill her up, zap forbidden nerve endings with sudden, scorching life. Then he was completely inside and shoving that last fraction deep in her rectum.

Oh, damn, did she feel full. Stuffed full of hard male flesh. So packed even drawing in a deep breath exacerbated that overflowing feeling.

A thin bit of flesh separated the two cocks. When they started moving, she could only imagine what that would feel like. Friction? For sure. Pleasure? Damn straight.

"Can you take it?" No mistaking the tight control in Deke's sandpaper-on-asphalt voice.

Before she could even answer, they both did their best to seduce her into a *yes*, Deke by nipping a line of sweet kisses from her neck to shoulder while he skimmed a teasing finger across her clit, Luc by kissing the side of her neck and toying with her tender nipples.

There wasn't anywhere they weren't touching, weren't igniting with thick, syrupy pleasure that drizzled through her body, drowning her fears.

But they didn't move.

Kimber frowned, wondering. Then she realized they were waiting for her answer. They had to be in hell—not that both didn't deserve it for teasing her within a breath of losing her sanity—but neither moved until she gave them the green light. Considerations like this—and like the pair of them racing across Texas when they thought she might be injured or in need after the explosion—told her that they cared.

She wriggled her hips. Nerve endings jumped, practically began to cha-cha. A hint of the bliss to come slid across her senses, and Kimber knew she couldn't wait another second for this experience.

"I can take it. Can you dish it out, boys?"

"I don't recommend taunting us." Luc's voice sounded strained.

She wriggled again, and flashed him a come-hither smile. He hissed in a breath.

"I'll stop taunting if you'll start fucking."

"Deal," Deke growled, even as he eased back—then plunged forward in a killer stroke, punctuated by a little pinch of her clit.

Kimber yelped, but it did no good when Luc's mouth covered hers and he teased her with a slow, friction-fantastic withdrawal just as Deke surged all the way inside her ass. Then they reversed, Deke drawing back, Luc arching his hips and shoving into her swollen sex with every inch he had.

They repeated the process again and again, their mouths, fingers, and cocks relentless.

Like a well-oiled machine, they worked her. Clearly, they had done this before—lots. They knew exactly how to work with and around each other to maximize everything she was experiencing. She no more than had an inkling that something would feel good before one of them was all over it, making it happen . . . making it blindingly sublime.

In minutes, sensation overwhelmed her. Her whole body shook as the ache swelled between her legs, grew, expanded, multiplied faster than she could deal with. Breathing nearly came to a stop as she used all her energy to move with them and handle the onslaught of pleasure they kept throwing her way.

"You're about to come," Luc whispered against her mouth. "I'm dying to feel you again."

She was dying, period. Overwhelmed, overpowered. The sensations were huge, almost frightful. Everything inside her fixated on the hot rhythm of the two cocks working in and out of her body, insistent fingers plucking and twisting, two mouths breathing, laving, biting . . . demanding.

"You're not going to outlast us, kitten," Deke vowed.

Luc stroked deep inside her, until she felt him nudging her womb, shooting off a new barrage of sparks that battered her self-control. Deke included a gentle pinch of his thumb and forefingers to her clit, then a blindsiding little rub that spelled the demise of her restraint.

Sensation shot her straight up into the stars. Her body shivered, bucked, as her womb convulsed, her sex contracted, and pleasure torched her body. She spun into a realm beyond her imagination. Her throat stung, and she realized suddenly it was because she couldn't stop screaming. Orgasm was always a fabulous experience, but this wasn't just a big O, it was ginormous, threatening to consume her as the pleasure poured all over her.

"Oh, damn . . . Hell! I—"

Luc didn't have to finish his sentence for Kimber to know that he was about to follow her in orgasm.

"No! Suck it up," Deke growled to his cousin. "We've waited too long to lose it like teenagers."

After a sharp peak, climax let Kimber down gently. The warm honey of languor spread sweetly.

Luc wasn't so lucky. As she regained her wits, she watched him in fascination as he tensed, shook, sucked in a harsh breath, and fought with squinted eyes and clenched fists. Tendons striped his neck. His cock had never felt so hard inside her.

Finally, he let out a shaky breath. "Bastard."

"As long as you hold it in and fuck her until she comes again, you can call me whatever the hell you want."

* * *

"AGAIN?" Kimber gasped. "Deke, I don't think I can—"

"You can. I know your body. You're like a temperamental car. Once your engine is warmed up, it's easy to rev you repeatedly. It's getting your motor to purr the first time that's a bitch."

And he was damn determined to make her motor purr like it never had. She might have regrets later about the choice to give him her virginity and engage in full ménage with them, but until then, he intended to take her every chance he had to give her so much pleasure that any regrets would be all tangled in it.

Maybe then he'd have a chance of keeping her when the truth came out. *Maybe.*

Knowing that Luc's self-control wasn't on his side and that his own was fraying too fast for comfort, Deke started the dance into Kimber's body again. Luc followed his lead. With each stroke, he gritted his teeth, fighting the crushing sensitivity. He'd never felt so rigid and engorged. His thrusts grew rough. And Luc . . . he kept rhythm, but now wracked by tortured need, he wasn't nearly as gentle as he had been. Deke hoped that worked in their favor.

As they began their efforts again, Kimber responded with pleasant moans and sweet *ahs*, like she was in the midst of a lovely afternoon, bathed in spring sunshine. Like she thought the sex was warm and enjoyable. Nothing earth-shattering.

Totally unacceptable. Time to turn up the heat.

Deke leaned over her back and delved his fingers back into the slick flesh of her clit. As he had earlier, he used that alternating pressure—light on the top, friction on the sides, hard circles above. In the span of a heartbeat, her body drew taut. Her clit swelled, hardened. She gave them a throaty growl between pants. *Ah, yes. God, yes.*

She writhed, trying to accommodate him and Luc deeper into the silken perfection of her body. She moved with them as Deke slid every hard inch across the electric hot zone inside her that begged to be stroked. And despite Luc hanging on by his fingernails, he was, no doubt, doing the same.

Kimber struggled against the quicksilver change in her body; Deke wasn't having any of that. He wanted her drowning in pleasure.

"You don't know how many times I imagined you between the two of us while we fucked you from anxiety to arousal, from arousal to orgasm," Deke whispered in her ear. "Once wasn't enough. Give it to us again. Take us with you."

Kimber glanced over her shoulder at him. A flush spread across her fair complexion. Her hazel eyes looked unfocused, dilated. Needy. Beautiful.

Sweat trickled from his temples, filmed his chest. His insides burned with determination. She was going to come again, damn it. He wasn't giving up until she did.

"Damn," Luc panted. "The more my cock swells, the more friction I feel from you. And she keeps closing in on me. It's mind-blowing."

"And it's only going to get better. Give her everything you've got now."

The look of relief on Luc's face would have been comical if Deke had been in the frame of mind to do anything but tunnel into Kimber over and over, to compel her into perfect surrender.

Luc grabbed her hips, Deke her waist. They unleashed the well-practiced rhythm he knew would bring them all to climax.

But this was more. Last night, inside her pussy, the sensations had been different. He'd been swamped, like a soldier on a mission with tangos all over him. Overtaken. The sensations hadn't all been in his dick.

Kimber hit him square in the chest, and everything he felt there splintered through his body, melding with the physical gratification that being inside her gave him.

Today was no different . . . except it was more intense. *Holy hell.* Being buried inside her, exposing his heart to more of her, was so damn dangerous, like walking a tightrope above a swamp full of hungry gators. He was only going to fall more every time he touched her. And someday . . .

She tightened around him, killing his train of thought, as she demanded, "Harder. Please. Hurry!"

The last bit of his restraint snapped. With Luc's next wild thrust, Deke knew the same had happened to his cousin. He filled her once, then again, hoping, imagining that with each lunge inside her, each hard press of his body, she could feel how much more was behind the act than lust. That she could feel how much he cared.

Saying the words scared the shit out of him.

Her breathing began to shut down until it dissolved into quick pants. She trembled hard and braced herself, fingers clutching Luc's shoulders.

Deke felt her begin to flutter, squeeze his cock, a moment before she cried out. Clawing at the bottom sheet, she thrust back at him, even as her body wrapped around him so tight he had to fight to move at all.

With a toss of his head and a shout, Luc tumbled off the cliff, losing his grip on control.

Hearing his cousin lose it and the hoarse groan that blasted through the room ripped a new hole in Deke's restraint. Inside his balls, the need to come built up with every rasp of his flesh over Kimber's. Damn, he wasn't going to last . . .

Finally, Kimber cried out, a long moan of surrender. Deke basked in it, drowned in her total acceptance of the ecstasy they gave her.

And he let go, releasing everything he was and had deep inside her as pleasure knifed him, carving straight into his heart. If his inability to fuck Alyssa hadn't been a big clue, this feeling right now sealed the deal.

For better or worse, forever, he loved Kimber.

And Deke knew that if she walked away now—or his nightmare came to life—either would kill him.

Chapter Fifteen

DEKE nursed a cup of coffee in silence, listening to the sound of the shower running in the bathroom, the splash of water hitting Kimber's naked skin, then dripping onto porcelain. Across the table, Luc stared out the picture window at the early morning sun shining over the swamp.

Once the night was gone and the desire temporarily spent . . . that's when the second-guessing started. The regrets.

This one was a killer. He'd fucked up. No ifs, ands, or buts about it. But he hadn't been able to keep Kimber at arm's length anymore. Twenty-nine, and he'd finally fallen. Hard. She was his now.

God help her.

He glanced at his cousin and sighed. Well, Kimber was his and Luc's. And given Luc's goal of getting her pregnant and his own of preventing it, the truth, his past—it was all going to come up, likely in one big chunky-puke pool.

What then?

"You did the right thing," Luc said suddenly.

"Making love to Kimber?" He shrugged. "Time will tell. I doubt it, but I'd sure like to be wrong."

"She loves you."

"That's not going to help much when she finds out the truth."

"Heather wasn't your fault."

Of course she was, at least in large part. Everyone knew it. Her father had certainly laid the blame at his feet. He'd had Deke beaten, arrested, harassed. Deke had taken it numbly. He'd deserved it. Only Luc insisted differently.

Yeah, it took two to tango, but Heather . . . hadn't been able to think past her emotions. Kimber didn't seem off-kilter like that, but under those circumstances . . . Who knew? Over the years, he'd realized that combat showed how unpredictable soldiers could be. Life's battles revealed the same about civilians.

"We've been over this. Let's not rehash it again."

Luc gritted his teeth. "You're going to have to get over this before you hold back so much you destroy everything with Kimber. She's an all-or-nothing girl. You're not giving your all."

"What the fuck am I supposed to do? Get down on one knee and propose in the next ten minutes?"

"Soon."

It was on the tip of Deke's tongue to tell Luc to propose. But after last night, he knew better. Luc would do it, and if he didn't want Kimber to belong to his cousin in the eyes of the law, he'd better shut up now. Sharing her was hard enough. Necessary for normalcy, but a bitch. Watching her become Luc's wife . . . Deke swallowed against the unwelcome pain crushing his chest.

"To start with," Luc went on, "I think you should tell her everything."

"Are you out of your fucking mind? It'll all come out soon enough, and she'll probably run screaming. Call me stupid, but I'd rather delay the inevitable."

"Until you do, you'll keep holding yourself back from her, and it's hurting her."

"I didn't hold back last night."

"I don't mean just sexually. You won't tell her you love her. She's given up so much to be with you: years of believing that she belonged with Jesse, her pride, her virginity. You won't tell her one little secret."

Deke stood, his chair scraping across the wooden floor as he shoved it back. "Back the fuck off."

Holding up his hands, Luc signaled surrender. "Your funeral. But I'll tell you now, if she's going to be alienated about anything, it won't be the past. It will be the fact you didn't trust her enough to tell her and didn't believe in her strength enough to see that she wouldn't suffer Heather's fate."

Fists clenched, Deke took a step toward his meddling cousin. Luc stood, meeting his challenge. Deke hadn't swung a punch at his cousin in twelve years. At the moment, he wasn't sure if he could stop himself from decking the son of a bitch.

In the background, the shower turned off, and water stopped flowing through the pipes.

The men stood in silence, staring in angry standoff.

"You don't want to keep pissing me off," Deke warned.

"Yes, Mr. Special Ops, I realize you know twenty ways to kill me with your bare hands. But if you want to *try* to beat my ass for force-feeding you some honesty and common sense—"

"You want to try common sense and honesty? Okay. Tell me why you didn't return Alyssa Devereaux's phone call. She clearly wants to talk to you, and you avoided her so you didn't have to face the fact you lost your precious self-control."

"Alyssa isn't the subject of this conversation," Luc bit out.

"It's a comparison. Work with me. Why won't you explain to Alyssa the reason you went all caveman on her for six hours?"

"I'll be honest with Alyssa as soon as you're honest with Kimber."

"Stay out of my business."

"Stay out of mine." Luc returned. "You want to make love to Kimber all by yourself?"

That was a low blow. *Bastard.*

"I can get in the little boat outside right now and go home, leave you here alone with her for hours. Days . . ."

And leave Deke fully responsible.

"Stop." Restraining a new urge to pound Luc's face, Deke swallowed. "Just stop. I'm not ready to say anything to her."

"Don't expect her to have unlimited patience. She's given to you, stripped herself bare for you. If you don't reciprocate, she'll be gone."

Deep down, Deke feared—knew—Luc was right.

Down the hall, he heard the sound of the bathroom door swinging open. Kimber stepped out.

"Did I hear shouting?"

Deke glanced at Luc, who stood and crossed the room to her.

"TV," his cousin muttered, then kissed Kimber's freshly washed cheek before exiting the room and stepping out on the wraparound porch.

Leaving Deke alone with Kimber.

For long moments, neither said anything. Silence ripened, stretched. She cast suspicious glances at the television, clearly too smart to fall for Luc's BS. But she didn't pursue it.

"Is there any more coffee?"

With a nod, Deke turned and poured. He added two sugars and a dash of milk.

"You remembered?" She smiled, looking . . . touched.

God, what would it be like to bask in that smile every day? To know she reserved such beauty for him and no one else?

It would be nothing but trouble.

He shrugged in answer. "You know we Special Ops types pay attention to details. Sometimes, they save your life."

Her smile wilted. "Of course."

Damn, he sure knew how to put his foot in his mouth. He'd likened her to a terrorist, rather than a girlfriend. *Smooth* . . .

She took the cup, sipped, sat in the seat Luc had vacated, and retreated into her own world. And Deke couldn't stand it.

The silence, as if everything last night and this morning had been nothing. From her perspective, she was probably hoping for affection and closeness. At the very least, kindness.

So far, he hadn't really given her any of the above. And he doubted he was capable of those in any long-term sense, and hated himself for it. But for her, he'd try. The reality was, learning to do something besides fuck and leave was going to take time.

He sighed and approached her, not at all sure what he was going to say or do.

Kimber looked up as he approached, surprise and wariness dawning across her face as he crossed into her personal space.

"What?"

Deke didn't say a word. Instead, he bent and picked her up, sat in the nearest chair and cradled her on his lap. He smoothed her damp hair away from her face, and she lifted her gaze to him.

"I'm not very good at talk. I . . ." How did he sum up the jumble of everything he wanted to say into the right words? "I loved being with you last night."

He pressed a soft kiss to her mouth, insanely proud of himself. That sounded perfect.

Kimber broke away. "If you loved it so much, why did you fight it so hard?"

How did women do that? In two-point-two seconds, cut right past the postcoital talk and sweet words and get knee-deep in shit?

"Kitten, not now."

"Yes, now. Despite my limited experience, I understand that twelve hours in the sack doesn't entitle me to make demands, but there's something going on with you. I—I want to know what."

"It's in the past. It's not important—"

She pushed off his lap. "If you had to be bullied into sleeping with me, then it's obviously important and not in the past."

Hell, hadn't he just had this conversation, more or less, with Luc?

"Because I'm an idiot with noble ideas who didn't want to just snatch your virginity without you being really sure. Can we just enjoy being with each other now, rather than getting into all this?"

Deke reached for her again. She backed away.

"No. Whatever it is you're not telling me is the reason you didn't want to have sex with me. It's the reason you fucked Jack Cole's pretty wife."

Blood rushed up his cheeks. "Actually, that was at Jack's request. I didn't—"

"But Jack thought of you because you only do ménages. And this mystery reason is the cause. It's standing between us, and I don't know what it is."

Damn, she was right. So right. When had she pieced all that together? She might be younger and less experienced, but she excelled at people.

"One day at a time, huh?" He sighed. "I'm here with you now. I'm not going anywhere. What's that cheesy movie line; you had me at 'hello?' That's pretty accurate here. Part of me is stubborn and didn't want to fall in line, but I have. We're together. Let's just accept that for now."

Kimber crossed her arms over her chest and pressed her lips together. That wasn't the end of this conversation, not by a long shot, but she was tactically retreating for the moment. He let out a big sigh of relief.

"Fine."

It wasn't fine, but he hoped he could . . . distract her from the subject. If he told her the entirety of his screwup, she'd run screaming.

Treading softly, he closed the distance between them and wrapped his arms around her. She stood stiff, those arms still crossed. Clearly, she'd learned how to battle on her terms. She couldn't fight him physically, but her stubborn will was a more than worthy adversary, he'd bet.

He ignored her resistance and simply felt her. With a soft hand caressing her back, he dropped a kiss on her forehead, brushed one across her mouth, lingered at her neck. *Heaven.* He couldn't remember the last time he'd kissed a woman without any intent to fuck her in the next ten minutes. Just standing here and breathing in her scent, her presence, was a treat.

"You fight dirty," she grumbled, tilting her head to give him better access to her neck.

"This isn't fighting. It's giving you affection. You got a problem with that?" He slid his thumb over her bottom lip.

Before she could answer, the phone rang. Deke jumped. Only one of two people could be on the line, and both represented news about the explosion and its aftermath.

"Yeah," he barked into the line.

"Deke." It was Logan. His voice sounded heavy.

Turning away, Deke held in a curse. "I'm here."

"It ain't good." He sighed. "Kimber . . ."

"Tell me."

Logan did, and Deke couldn't hold in a rush of four letters.

"What is it?" Kimber asked.

"I'll let her know," Deke promised.

After a long pause, Logan replied. "Thanks. Any news from Jack?"

"Not yet. The police?"

"What is it?" Kimber demanded.

Deke shook his head at her. He wanted to give Kimber his undivided attention when he gave her this news.

"Nothing concrete," Logan answered. "Lots of questions. No answers. But it's weird, man. No one at the hospital has even twitched the wrong direction. Nothing suspicious here at all. Lots of phone calls from some guy, though, wanting to know where Kimber is. I tried to figure out who he is, trace the call, keep him talking. Too smart. He disconnected."

Fear struck a cold bolt down in Deke's chest. The psycho-bomber hadn't moved in on the Colonel's hospital room. That sounded like he was fixated on Kimber instead. It could be the press, looking for a slant on Jesse's ex and the latest drama. But the same person calling over and over?

"Shit," Deke muttered. "Call us if anything changes."

"Will do. Give Kimber my love."

"Yeah." Then he hung up.

"What the hell is it?" She looked pissed and desperate. She wasn't going to be brushed off or let this be glossed over.

Deke took her by the hand and led her to a chair, then sat her down. He drew in a deep breath. What the hell to say?

"Tell me now. Oh my God . . ." Her voice shook. "My dad. Tell me he didn't . . ."

"No. No, kitten. He's alive." He kissed her palm, trying to soothe the blow to come. "But they did some extra tests yesterday and realized he had something foreign lodged in the back of his head. It was causing swelling. They had to operate this morning, and he went into shock. He slipped into a coma."

Kimber dissolved. No other way to put it. Tears filled those hazel eyes, and Deke found himself wishing he had some way to take her suffering away. He'd gladly put it on his shoulders so she wouldn't have to bear it. But life didn't work that way.

As he reached to draw her into his embrace, let her cry on his chest, she surprised him by standing and drying her tears. "We have to go to him. Right now."

Deke froze. "Kitten, I know you're upset, but we can't do that without careful planning. There's still a psycho on the loose who may be after you—"

"I don't care! My father might die, and I might not get to say goodbye."

"No one said anything about him dying."

"He's in a goddamn coma! Now I'm not a doctor, but in nursing school, I learned that's bad and that some people go from coma to death."

Her sarcasm was understandable, but not helpful.

Softly, he said, "And some people come straight out of it."

"I'm not taking a chance that I'll never see him alive again." She ripped off her robe in the middle of the kitchen and marched for the bedroom.

Deke watched the sway of her bare ass as she retreated into the shadowed room and started rummaging around the sheets for her clothes. He marched in the room and grabbed her shirt and underwear out of her hands.

"You're not going now, especially not by yourself."

"The hell I'm not. You can't stop me."

"If I have to wrestle you to that bed myself and tie you to it to keep you from presenting a public target to this maniac, don't think I won't."

Kimber marched toward the door. "I'm an adult and I make my own decisions. You don't own me."

He grabbed her arm and pulled her against him. "Last night, I claimed you, remember? I took what you'd given no one else. In my book, that makes you mine. I'm not letting you be used for target practice. You're safe and hidden. You're going to stay that way."

"You son of a—What are you doing?"

Deke dragged her across the room, toward the bed. She wasn't listening, wasn't going to hear logic.

He tossed her onto the bed and held her down as gently as possible—keeping all his force behind the grip. "Keeping you safe."

A quick glance around the room proved futile. *Damn!*

"What is going on in here?" Luc demanded, taking in the scene with a horrified expression.

Deke explained the phone call. "And now Florence Nightingale here thinks she's going to the hospital on a mercy visit in the next ten minutes."

"You can be such an asshole," Kimber groused, struggling to break his hold. "Luc . . ."

"Sweetheart, he's right. Call, talk to Logan, have him put the phone to your father's ear so you can speak to him for now. But you can't just leave and risk the danger of exposure."

"So now I'm being held captive?"

"That's not my intention, but if that's the way you want to look at it . . ." Denying her troubled Deke, but he wasn't backing down. "Either way, you're staying."

"I'm sorry, sweetheart, but I agree." Luc crossed his arms over his chest, and Deke was damn glad for the backup. "Promise us you'll stay put until we can work out a plan, and we'll let you up."

Kimber pressed her lips together mutinously and said nothing.

"You know the minute we turn our back on her, she's going to try to sneak away."

Luc hesitated, glanced at Kimber, and nodded. "It seems."

But Deke had an idea. Master Jack's cabin came fully equipped.

"Hold her down."

Luc shot him a curious glance, but crossed the room to take Kimber's wrists in his grip. He straddled her as Deke made for the door and disappeared around the corner.

"I may not have been an Army Ranger, but that doesn't mean I haven't learned a few tricks over the years," Luc warned her. "You're not getting away."

Satisfied she was in good hands, Deke fished a set of keys out of his pocket and unlocked the door to Jack's secret room at the end of the hall. He wound his way past the computer and desk, to the door at the back of the room, and flung it open.

A dominant's paradise with every manner of toy, paddle, dildo— and, of course, restraint—known to man.

He grabbed a pair of velvet cuffs and some silken ties to wrap around Kimber's dainty ankles. He paused to contemplate a pair of nipple clamps.

Focus, he told himself. *Keep her safe. Right now, she's going to be too pissed to fuck you.*

Putting the toys in his pocket and in the *later* category, he rushed back down the hall to see that little had changed. Kimber was questioning Luc's parentage and masculinity with insults she'd probably heard from her brothers over the years. Luc looked unfazed.

"I'm sorry you feel that way, sweetheart. How much worse would I be if I cared more about your name-calling than your safety?"

Rushing back into the room, Deke reached Kimber's side, took her wrists from his cousin and cuffed her in two seconds flat. He quickly discovered that the silken ties were plenty long to reach from her ankles to the thick posters on the antique bed.

Only when she was fully restrained and spread out on the bed did Deke realize she was also totally naked.

And at their mercy.

Deke had never been a huge fan of bondage; he could take it or leave it. At the moment, the idea held appeal. He stifled the impulse.

"Okay," he said, dragging his gaze away from her breasts. They really were beautiful, and the memory of their tender nipples . . . Damn, he had to focus! "I don't like letting you out of hiding yet, but I understand it. I will find a safe way for you to visit your father. Give me a day or two."

"What if he doesn't make it that long? Please." Her eyes teared up, and it tore at him. "Can't we go now?"

Deke wished he could say yes. But he couldn't give in to his wish to be the good guy. His job—his responsibility—was to keep her safe. "No, but as soon as possible. I promise."

"But—"

"If your father was awake to put in his two cents, kitten, you know he would agree with me."

She sighed with resignation. "Please hurry."

Deke stepped out of the room. Damn it, he didn't want to do this, but she was close to the Colonel. Denying her was hurting her, and he couldn't do that. With a sigh, he picked up the phone and called Jack Cole and Logan, along with another buddy. He was gone five minutes, tops.

When he returned to the bedroom, Kimber was no longer tied up. She lay in Luc's arms, listening to his whispered reassurances.

Deke couldn't help but look at her, and he was sure his eyes glazed over with lust. Damn, he had to get his mind off sex and on protecting her.

"Jack and Logan will contact us soon. You'll see your father. We'll have a plan quickly, I promise." He kissed her mouth gently.

With a cry, she opened to him, arched to him. Deke hesitated, surprised. Then he dove into all the kiss offered and tasted her thanks, as well as her desperation for reassurance.

He lifed his head. "Kimber?"

"Hold me. Please."

The pools of tears gathering in her eyes tore at Deke's heart. He wasn't really good with cuddling, but how could he say no to her now? Why would he, when he'd take any excuse just to be near her?

He relaxed his body at her side again, nuzzling his face in her neck, his arm across her middle. "I'm here."

"Touch me."

If he touched her any more, he'd be groping her, and his mind—along with all the blood in his body—would go south. But she needed comfort, so he stroked her side in a soothing caress. Or tried. He just wasn't good at being a cross between a teddy bear and just a friend. He got lost lost in her eyes, her scent, that sexy-soft skin. He couldn't be around her and *not* get hard. Feeling like a perverted shit, he closed his eyes.

"Deke," she murmured.

"Yeah, kitten?"

"Make the worry go away for a while. Please." She arched her hips toward him. "Love me."

God, temptation. The offer of fucking paradise. Deke swallowed. "Kimber, honey . . ."

"I know what I'm asking for. Touch me. I know you can. Make it better."

On the other side of the bed, he glanced at Luc. His cousin didn't say a word, but he went hard in an instant.

Kimber noticed, too. "See. You want me."

Always. But she was upset now, and only a class-A prick would take advantage of her now, right? On the other hand . . . distracting her might take the edge off her worry.

Yeah, he was probably rationalizing because she was naked and whenever he gazed at her, he was horny. But it was either sex or watch her cry, agonize, and panic over something she couldn't change.

Deke voted for sex.

In wordless seconds, he stripped. He didn't have to look up. Just the rustle of clothing told him Luc was doing the same.

"Kitten, if this is what you want, I'll get inside you and touch you so deep you won't remember your name."

Deke stretched out on the bed, raised himself above her, and stared. She was so fucking beautiful, she hurt his eyes. The ache in his chest torqued up.

Luc crawled onto the bed, stopping when he reached her other side, and his palm took up residence at her breast.

"I need this, need you . . ."

"We know. You need to feel alive, sweetheart. We'll take care of you, in all ways."

With that, Luc skimmed his thumbs across her nipples, and they hardened, flushed. Pretty and alluring, a sight Deke couldn't resist.

It was a race to see which of them could get his mouth around a tempting bud first. Deke was pretty sure he'd won. It sure felt that way when she drew in a sharp breath and arched toward them.

Her poor little nipples had to be sore. And he tried to be gentle.

Difficult when the sweet tips just kept getting harder against his tongue. Every time he laved, sucked, or nipped at her, they hardened more.

"You guys are *so* good," she moaned.

Yeah, her voice was losing its starch. It sounded low, a little scratchy. *Perfect.*

As much as he enjoyed the hard berries tipping her breasts, he was dying for a real taste of her.

Glancing his way down her body, he was startled to see Luc's hand between her thighs, her hips surging in search of his cousin's teasing touch. With a hard-on that wouldn't quit, he watched as her breath grew harsh. Her panting filled the room. Luc continued to taunt her with his fingers, brushing over her clit, sinking into her channel, caressing the pouting lips around her sex, delving deep inside her sex to rub her G-spot without mercy.

Deke smelled her, peaches, brown sugar, musk. It drove him insane. Impatience strangled him.

"Hurry the fuck up and get her off."

Without breaking stride, Luc raised a brow. "I'm having fun."

"This isn't about you."

"It isn't about you, either. It's about keeping her mind elsewhere."

"Oh, trust me. I will."

Luc paused. Kimber whimpered, writhed.

"You want to be inside her again?"

No shit. "Among other things," Deke answered.

"Stop talking and do it!" she demanded between rough breaths.

His cousin responded to her command by reapplying himself to his task. Deke watched, aroused beyond belief. God, she was gorgeous. Those rosy cheeks, parted lips, eyes drowsy with need. Men had written sonnets about women like her, and now he knew why. But she wasn't just beautiful. She was ballsy, too. She walked her own road. Deke respected that. Understood it. She didn't cringe from his profession—or get turned on by it. He'd had both sorts of women before and couldn't get into either. Kimber . . . she was just her, and she took everything in stride. Sure, she had emotional moments, but she didn't fall apart. Silk with a steel backbone—that was his woman.

His.

Deke swooped down and plundered her mouth with a desperate kiss. She opened to him, mewling. His lips vibrated with the sound. His cock throbbed in response.

The impatience to have her taste on his tongue again bombarded him. He broke off the kiss and whispered in her ear, "Come for Luc, kitten."

She gave him a shaky nod and raised her hips, not quite there . . . but close.

He pushed her closer to the cliff. "That ache building? Burning? Yeah," he answered for her. "And the minute you let go, I'm going to get down there and lap you up. He's just making you nice and juicy for me." He nipped at her lobe. "Once I get down there, you'll give me more cream, right?"

"Yes. Yes!" she shouted as her body bowed in climax. She thrust her head back, arching her neck, pushing the red peaks of her breasts into the air as she wailed out satisfaction.

Luc was on her nipples in an instant, sucking, squeezing . . .

Just to make sure Kimber didn't think about her troubles any time soon, Deke reached into his pocket and dangled the clamps in Luc's face. "Know what these are?"

Luc's hungry gaze fastened on them, and he grabbed them from Deke's hand excitedly, like a kid with a new toy.

"I thought you might." Deke grinned at his cousin.

Then he kissed his way down Kimber's body.

Deke didn't tease her or make her wait. He spared her that. Or maybe he spared himself, so damn eager for her taste again and those sweet little hitching breaths she made when arousal began to take her.

Bending her knees, Deke parted her with his thumbs and dove into her rich cream. *Hmm.* And he took her with his mouth, holding her thighs wide, throwing his shoulders into it with every lash of his tongue. Life didn't get much better than this moment.

Suddenly, she stiffened and gasped—not all from pleasure. With a pissed glower, he lifted his head to watch her adjusting to the clamps biting into her nipples.

"They look more vicious than they are," Luc assured. "Give her two minutes."

He looked at his cousin reluctantly, then turned his attention to Kimber. "This hurting you too much, kitten?"

Her eyes drifted open, edgy . . . but heavy with arousal. She bit her lip, holding in a cry.

"Kitten?"

"Inside me," she gasped. "Get inside me now."

He frowned, then licked his way from slit to clit. "But I wasn't finished—"

"Now!"

Kimber was demanding when she was horny. Deke loved it.

Crawling up the bed, up her body, he slid inside her in one smooth stroke that had her groaning so long and loud, the sound went to his balls and squeezed. Apparently, it did the same to Luc. He cursed.

"*Yeesss.*" Kimber watched him with a serious fuck-me stare.

Deke was totally happy to oblige.

Before he could get down to business, she shot Luc a demanding stare. "Over here." She gazed at the spot on the mattress beside her.

Luc quickly complied—and she rewarded him by turning her head, parting her lips, and taking his cock to the back of her throat.

The sight tortured Deke—with both resentment and arousal. The sublime look of ecstasy on his cousin's face wasn't something he could pretend didn't exist.

Deke knew exactly why he engaged in ménage. But not for the first time, he wondered what Luc got out of the arrangement. He would—and did—fuck women on his own. But he'd insisted for years that he wouldn't marry one, wouldn't be just a couple with a woman. He wanted a committed triad, had long sought a woman both he and Deke could happily share. *Why?*

Kimber whimpered.

"Take her," Luc instructed. "Fill her."

God, his voice was so solemn, as if . . . it meant something to him beyond great sex.

Was he in love with Kimber, too?

Likely, yes. But Deke couldn't pursue that now, not when she lifted her hips to him, tightened, and desire shot up his cock in the form of pure, liquid need.

He reared back, plunged in, cranked up on the feel of her around him. Damn, she was silky perfect. He'd never known anything like this, like her. And he'd bet his soul he never would again.

Deke gave to her, everything he had—pumping, filling, sweating, stroking. The urge to come snuck up on him, tightening his balls. He gritted his teeth. She was going first, damn it. If he had to bite his way through his tongue to keep himself from coming, he'd make sure she found satisfaction before he did.

Luc fisted her hair in his hands. The angle had to hurt her neck, and yet she just kept deep-throating him.

"Yes. Yes. God, yes!" Luc started to chant.

Deke related perfectly.

Kimber moaned in return, lifted to him, swelled, tightened, rippled.

Oh, holy mother of—there was no fighting the tidal wave of sensation that ripped across his senses, stripping him of defenses. He thrust into her, stroke after single-minded stroke. And she met him.

Despite teetering on the edge of madness himself, Luc watched her hold her breath, tremble. Just as she started to shudder, he unclamped her nipples.

She screamed.

Then her pussy undulated around him like nothing he'd ever felt, not just encouraging him to come, but demanding it. Deke surrendered—sweat, need, love.

Somewhere in the middle, he heard Luc's shout of satisfaction, and Deke found himself desperate, determined to get deeper inside her. He thrust up against her womb as the last of his seed spilled.

And he gave his very soul to her.

* * *

TWO hours later, Kimber was sulking in the bedroom. Not the most mature behavior she realized. Screw maturity though; she was worried about her dad and pissed that Luc and Deke weren't driving her to the hospital.

Okay, so those make-her-panties-melt men were right—rushing off to the hospital might be dangerous. But now that they'd finished distracting her, reality rushed back, and she was scared; this was her dad. After talking to Logan, she was scared all over again. Terrified she'd lose her only remaining parent and a man she loved so much, afraid she'd experience more of the nightmares she'd had each night since the explosion, anxious that there was actually someone after her.

None of that changed her wants, however. She wanted to go to the hospital and visit her father. See him. Touch him. Say good-bye . . . just in case.

Deke and Luc were hardly letting her go to the bathroom without escort.

To make matters worse, she couldn't hate them for it. They had her safety in mind, she knew. And they knew how to give a girl mind-bending pleasure. And after . . . Deke had wrapped her tight in his arms and held her while she cried out of release, anger, frustration, fear.

How could she be pissed about his cautious approach to a hospital visit when he acted like he cared so much?

"Want some lunch?" Luc said softly from the bedroom doorway.

"No."

He shuffled into the room and placed soft hands on her shoulders. "Sweetheart, you have to eat. You skipped breakfast."

"It slipped my mind."

Luc cleared his throat. "You've been upset for a while. You're tearing me up. Can't you cut an old man some slack?"

Old man. She snorted. Yeah, he might be pushing thirty-five, but Luc was prime.

"I'll throw in an apple crisp with brandy butter for dessert."

Oh, the man knew how to play dirty. But she was going to stay strong. Besides, every time she thought back to her dad lying in a hospital bed, connected to IVs, tubes, and monitors, her empty stomach nearly heaved. She could only imagine the results if she filled her stomach with Luc's rich cooking.

Stubbornly, she shook her head.

More footsteps. She turned to find Deke shouldering his cousin aside and stepping into the room. He braced his hands on his hips. "Here's the deal. You eat some lunch, at least something light that will help you keep your energy up, then we'll talk."

"About what? We've already conversed today—twice—in the language you're most fluent in: Fuckese."

Deke fought a smile. "You probably meant that as a slur, but somehow I'm complimented."

"You would be," she muttered.

"See, Morgan, I told you, she's terrible company."

Kimber turned her head around so quickly, she nearly got dizzy. Yep, there stood Morgan Cole, the wife of one of Deke's best friends, a woman she knew he had taken to bed. And Deke imagined that she wanted Morgan's company? Even without knowing that her man and the gorgeous redhead had played hide-the-salami, she would have resented Morgan. Pretty, daintily curved, feminine, not to mention a celebrity, and a great dresser. Probably smart and witty and admired by every man she met.

Sometimes, life just sucked.

"Bite me," she murmured.

"Okay, where?" Deke asked, then went on. "Never mind. I've got some enticing ideas of my own."

Kimber groaned. "Go away."

Out of the corner of her eye, Kimber saw Deke lean toward Morgan. In a stage whisper, he said, "She probably doesn't want to play dress up with you and go to the hospital."

The hospital?

She charged to her feet and ran to him. "Did you say—"

Deke grabbed her and laid a hard kiss on her mouth. "The hospital. Yes. We're ready to take you, but there are rules," he stressed.

Kimber nodded eagerly. She didn't care what they were. She'd get to see her dad. Get to squeeze his hand, talk to him, kiss his cheek, and hope that her being there would help him.

"Anything."

"Oh, that's interesting. I'll save that for later." He winked. "Morgan will help you disguise yourself. She brought wigs and makeup and clothes. You won't arrive there until after sundown. If anyone asks, you'll say you're visiting a friend in maternity. You'll have fifteen minutes, no more. I'll be there. Logan and Jack will be there. Hunter may even be there, recently arrived from an undisclosed location so secret, he'd have to kill you if he told you. We're not deviating from plan. We're not taking chances. We're not letting anything happen to you. Agreed?"

"Yes." More tears burned her eyes, even as a bolt of pure love pierced her chest. He was willing to let her have her way, even though letting her go to the hospital clearly worried him. God, she was crazy in love with the man. Would he ever open up and share his soul—his past—with her? Ever love her back?

Kimber didn't consider herself a coward, but that was one question she wasn't sure she wanted the answer to.

Chapter Sixteen

KIMBER, wearing a wig of dark brown hair in a swinging bob and casual, conservative clothes that made her look as if she'd just stepped out of a Lands' End catalog, wended her way into the hospital with Morgan beside her. Jack and Deke trailed, low-key in shades, but still looking mean enough to remove the limbs of anyone who screwed with her.

She was pretty sure they were being more than a little over the top. No, make that paranoid. Who would want to hurt her? Why? Yes, it was weird that someone had been calling for her from an untraceable phone and refusing to leave messages, but did that necessarily have to be sinister? Truth was, Dad had way more enemies than she did. And if someone really wanted to do her in, why blow up her dad's house? Those calls were probably just some pain-in-the-ass reporter wanting more dirt on Jesse.

But for the sake of Deke's peace of mind and to see her father, she played the game.

Nothing escaped Jack and Deke. *Nothing.* Kimber was used to men aware of their surroundings, but this . . . She wouldn't have been surprised if they'd made note of the orderly's shoe size or the brand of the fluorescent lights in the ceiling.

Apparently, they'd consulted blueprints of the hospital in advance or something. After entering the building, they went straight to the maternity ward, wound through some back stairs, and hijacked an employee-only elevator. A guard stood outside the authorized-personnel-only hallway they emerged from a few moments later and quickly shook Deke's hand.

Then they were down a short hall and inside her father's room.

Kimber nearly crumbled at first sight.

He looked so . . . fragile. Still sporting muscle and the remnants of his summer tan. But all the monitors, tubes, and machinery surrounding him in that sterile bed . . . The beeping drowning out his light breathing. His salt-and-pepper hair had been shaved completely. And so unlike her dad, he hadn't moved a muscle in the two minutes she'd been staring.

"It's okay, kitten," Deke whispered, sliding a protective arm around her shoulders. "We'll do this together."

He led her to the room's lone chair. Kimber had a sense of Jack drifting out the door, whether to stand guard or give them privacy, she wasn't sure. Morgan fell into step beside her husband, leaving Kimber and Deke alone with the Colonel. Deke sat and pulled her into his lap.

She would not cry. It would only piss the Colonel off if he was conscious. And it wouldn't do him a damn bit of good, no matter how tempting her compulsion was. Instead, she reached out and took his lax hand in hers and squeezed.

"Hi, Daddy. I hope you can hear me. Get better soon, please. Life isn't the same without you barking orders." She tried to smile.

Kimber faltered when there was no response. Not that she expected one. Well, in one tiny corner of her heart she'd hoped that he'd magically snap out of the coma upon hearing her voice, but that was the stuff of fairy tales.

Lately, her life was anything but.

Still, it was good to see him. A relief just to watch his chest move up and down.

"Sir," Deke addressed him with respect. "I'm watching over your daughter."

"What else are you doing with her?" came a sharp voice from the doorway.

Hunter.

Her oldest brother was everything Kimber wasn't. Coolly controlled. Extremely serious. Apparently lacking a sense of humor. Hunter always knew exactly what he wanted out of life, what he didn't, and how he was going to conquer any obstacles in his path. He didn't make many friends, but people always feared and respected him.

Normally, Kimber herself fit into that category. At the moment, his sharp question just pissed her off.

"Well, hello to you, too, big brother. Nice to see you. It's been what . . . four months? And the first words out of your mouth aren't even to me."

A normal person would have scowled. Hunter looked completely unruffled.

Secretly, Kimber had dubbed her brothers Fire and Ice. Logan raged out of control, blowing hot, his temper like an inferno. Hunter . . . he was always too glossy and cool. No one could see under the thick surface.

"Hello, little sister. I'd be more welcoming if I could figure out exactly why you're wearing a wig and sitting on a depraved son of a bitch's lap."

Underneath her, Deke tensed.

Kimber stood. "Stop. I'm not doing this here and now. In fact, I'm not doing this ever. I've explained myself to Logan, not that my sex life is anyone's business. If you haven't talked to our dear brother—"

"I just flew in this afternoon."

"When I'm gone, he can fill you in. Until then, shut it. I've only got a few minutes to be with Dad, and I'll be damned if I'm going to spend them arguing with you."

"A few minutes?" Hunter leaned against the wall, crossing biceps the size of her thighs across his chest. "That as long as Trenton and his cousin can let you out of bed?"

Deke didn't give him a verbal whipping, she was sure, to avoid starting a fight here in the hospital. Thank God one man in her life had some brains at the moment.

"Look, Edgington. I think she's in danger. Logan can fill you in. He agreed that having her with me, well hidden, is the best course of action."

Hunter didn't miss a beat. "Now that I'm back, I'll see to my sister. I take care of my own."

Deke slipped an arm around her waist. "How do you know she's not mine now?"

A muscle ticced—once—in Hunter's cheek. "Kimber?"

"Deke is protecting me. I'm here to see Dad. I'm not discussing anything else with you right now."

"Do you know what you're getting into?"

Kimber shot him a glare that was much more self-assured than she felt. "Perfectly well, thank you."

"Want to tell me why, if I've seen Jesse McCall making an ass of himself all over the media about you being his bride and future pop queen, you're cozying up to Mr. Ménage?"

Was Jesse *still* going on about marrying her? Having been tucked away in the middle of a swamp and very . . . busy, she hadn't paid that much attention to the news. God, Jesse must be desperate to change his life, but hadn't yet realized that she couldn't do it for him.

"You saw that overseas?"

"It's everywhere."

Shaking her head, she explained, "I broke it off. Apparently, he hasn't accepted it yet. He doesn't need a wife; he needs a spine. And I don't want to discuss it anymore. Now, what do you know about Dad's condition?"

Hunter hesitated briefly. Knowing him, he was waging an internal debate over whether to let the subject of her love life drop or not. Finally, he said, "Logan phoned me briefly this morning when I was headed back Stateside. I stopped to talk with the doctor on my way here. There's been no change since this morning."

Yeah, that wasn't a stretch of the imagination. A coma was still a coma.

She sighed and moved closer, sitting on the edge of the bed beside him. "Daddy, get better soon. I couldn't stand it if . . ."

No, she couldn't say that, as if saying it might somehow make it true. Instead, she kissed his cheek, then whispered "I love you" in his ear.

Jack poked his head in the door. "Kimber, time's up. New shift is coming. Dark has completely fallen. We need to slide out while we can."

Now that the time to leave was here, Kimber was reluctant to go. "Is all this precaution really necessary?"

"Yes," Jack and Deke said in unison in voices that indicated they weren't backing down.

Kimber sighed. She hated being coddled and hidden away, but doing it kept Logan, and now Hunter, free to watch over Dad, rather than standing guard over her . . . just in case.

"Fine. You win."

After dropping another kiss on her dad's cheek and getting a stiff half hug from Hunter, Kimber allowed Deke to escort her out the door.

On the way out, they crept through the hospital, taking a different route. It whipped them past the hotel's gift shop, complete with current magazines and newspapers. And there on the front of a magazine was a picture of her and Jesse the night he'd announced their engagement on-stage in Houston. The headline screamed "Is the Wedding Off?"

Before Deke could drag her away, she slipped into the store and grabbed the magazine and started skimming. The pictures themselves showed him smiling—almost frantically so—and denying the breakup, insisting she was "the one." There was a brief news item about the explosion, almost as a throwaway. The magazine was far more concerned about whether Jesse had really reined his party ways and whether his up-coming album would do poorly now that he appeared to be both taken and unstable. A picture of him scrambling across Jay Leno's desk, look-ing frenetic and off-kilter, confirmed that the merry-go-round of Jesse's behavior went on.

Hell, he looked like he'd lost touch with reality.

Deke snatched the magazine out of her hand and put it back on the rack. "Don't read that shit. You, of all people, know it's not true."

"What the hell has he been doing? I called off the engagement. I copied every press organization I could think of."

Deke gritted his teeth as he led her out of the gift shop and toward the car. Jack flanked her, holding Morgan's hand.

"Some of the press disregarded your e-mail as a hoax."

"Damn it! I copied Jesse himself. I broke things off with him. He knows I sent that e-mail."

"Yeah. Well, he ain't telling."

Kimber bit the inside of her cheek as Deke urged her into the car, his ever-observant eyes scouring every inch of the parking lot, probably seeing every ant that lived in the cracks of the concrete. Jack clapped Deke on the shoulder and took off with his beautiful wife.

What the hell was she going to do? She couldn't do anything about Jesse's massacre in the press . . . When she left the swamp, she didn't want the vultures with cameras at her door night and day. And this couldn't be healthy for Jesse.

"Whatever you're thinking," Deke warned as he sat in the driver's seat and backed out, "the answer is no."

"I have to do *something* to stop all this."

"No."

"But—"

"No."

"Damn you. Why not?"

"We've worked long and hard to protect you. Jesse's made his own fucking bed. I stood there and watched while you went to him. He couldn't make it work. You're not going to risk your life to drag his stupid ass out of this mess because he's a head case."

"But—"

"You want to go back to him?"

Damn. Way to back her into a corner with just a few words. "No."

Deke flashed her a look with those wild blue eyes she couldn't quite decipher. "You okay with me and Luc?"

"I don't like hiding out in the middle of nowhere and having to be away from Dad."

"Answer the question."

Was big, seemingly invincible Deke asking if she was happy and wanted to stay with him and his cousin? It seemed to matter to him. She repressed a smile. The question seemed almost . . . sweet. It spun a sugary hope inside her.

She reached across the SUV and put a hand on his thigh. "You know I am."

He nodded as if that ended the conversation. "Then no more about that prick. Ever."

* * *

THE next week passed by slowly, a mixture of euphoric highs in Deke's and Luc's arms and wrenching lows hearing about her father's unchanged condition. Hunter's chilly disapproval blared through the phone every time she talked to him, adding to her tumult.

As if sensing her confusion and sadness this morning, Deke had awakened her with soft kisses on her neck—and demanding fingers inside her sex. Luc had added the talent of his tongue on her nipples and those clamps he was so fond of. Within minutes, they'd driven all thoughts from her head except the need for them inside her. Naturally, they'd obliged, taking her again to heights she could barely comprehend.

Now, in the early morning glow, Luc pressed a soft kiss to her forehead and rolled from the bed, toward the shower, leaving her alone with Deke. The big blond warrior held her against him, their damp skin pressing together, breathing in unison.

Kimber fought tears. She didn't know if her father was going to make it, if her choices were going to estrange her from her oldest brother. If anything would ever come of her love for Deke. Here in the swamp, life was like a bubble. Not real. No going back or forward until something happened and they achieved some closure with her father's health and the bomb-wielding asshole.

"Kimber?" Deke stroked a wide palm up and down her back. His way of asking if she was okay.

Do you love me? She was dying to ask. Kimber knew better. And maybe she didn't want the answer. Deke wanted her. That would have to be enough for now. The men were always touching her, sitting her in their laps, kissing her . . . getting her between them two, three, four times a day. It was a miracle she wasn't living in an orgasm-induced stupor. And she wasn't complaining . . . except she had no idea how Deke felt about her. He'd never said a word, and she still knew nothing about the past that haunted him.

"I'm fine," she lied. What else was there to say?

He shifted, rolled to his side and looked down into her face. God, the man was gorgeous. Not perfect. Not pretty. A slight bend in his nose told her it had been broken somewhere along the way. But those blue eyes of his jumped out of that golden face. Military-short hair only accentuated the hard, Germanic features that all shouted *male!* What was she going to do if this was nothing more than a huge fuckfest to him?

"You're too tense to be fine." He smoothed a hand down her belly, toward her sex. "You need more, kitten?"

She grabbed his wrist to stop his downward progress. God knew he could sweep her away. But he wouldn't make love to her by himself. And he wouldn't tell her anything about his feelings. If he even had any. Luc insisted that Deke loved her, but who knew?

"No more." She rolled out from under him and started to rise.

Deke curled a beefy arm around her waist and brought her back down. "You need to call Logan again, hear about your dad?"

"It's barely six in the morning. They won't be at the hospital yet. I worry about Dad, but there's nothing I can do at this moment."

"Then tell me why the hell you look like you're about to burst into tears."

He can tell? Kimber bucked under him, trying to break his hold. But he was like iron.

Damn, she wasn't doing a great job of hiding her feelings. And if she didn't get away, she was going to lose it altogether and do something stupid, like tell the man she loved him.

"Gee, I'm under a little stress, don't you think?"

"Yeah. But something more than the usual is eating at you. What?"

Desperately, she tried again to wiggle free of his hold. He had her pinned better than a WWE champion. A scream of frustration rose up inside her, and she barely clamped it down.

"What the hell do you want? You want me to bleed and pour my heart out? I don't see you eager to do that for me."

"One thing at a time, kitten. Talk to me."

"Fine. Here it is: I have no idea if this means anything to you." She gestured to the bed. "Every day, I pour my heart into my body, hoping you'll get the message. I love you!"

As soon as the words were out, she put her hands over her mouth, wishing she could take them back. Above her, he stiffened. His eyes narrowed.

"A few weeks ago, you loved Jesse McCall."

"A few weeks ago, I was a girl who didn't know the difference. But don't worry, I know you have some big, bad past that keeps you from really giving a shit about me. You'll protect me and—"

"I love you, too."

Shock pinged through her body, like pure voltage from a live wire. A thick rush of joy followed. Had she heard that right? "What?"

He sighed, smoothed her hair from her face, then leaned in and kissed her so gently, Kimber damn near wept.

"I love you. I wish I was . . . better for you. My personal life and my head, they're fucked up. Sometimes . . ." He paused, swallowed. "I hate sharing you."

Wow, that was a first—and a surprising one. Kimber blinked. Then stared. He'd wished Luc was absent from their bed. Secretly, she'd had the same wish. She had a ton of affection for Luc . . . but it wasn't love.

"Then don't. I would love to be alone with you, just us. Please."

A long sigh. Shaky. "I can't. This is the only way I can be with you."

But why? Kimber bit the inside of her cheek. Maybe . . . maybe if she tread carefully here, he would tell her his secret. Maybe she'd finally understand what was holding him back from simply being with her. "If you could tell me why—"

"It wouldn't matter."

"Maybe you're wrong. We're both accepting a situation we don't really want for a reason I don't understand. It's possible that if we just talked—"

"It's complicated, and you playing shrink isn't going to change a damn thing. I'm just . . . wired this way now." He shrugged like it didn't matter, but the anguish in his frown told her that it mattered very much. "Take it or leave it. Your choice."

That was it. His way or the highway. He wasn't opening up. The past would not be a topic of discussion.

Deke was shutting her out.

Kimber turned her back on him, rolling to her side. She resisted the urge to curl up in a ball and cry. High highs, followed by low lows. Deke loved her, but wouldn't confide in her. He couldn't—or wouldn't—stop sharing her with his cousin.

Neither moved, and she could feel him staring at her back. The moment ached. Kimber had no idea what to say. To do.

The shrill ring of the phone in the background burst into the tense air between them. Still, they didn't move an inch.

"Someone going to get that?" Luc sounded annoyed as he padded into the kitchen with damp feet and a towel around his waist. "Hello?"

He paused, listened, nodded. As Kimber watched, the wet strands of his inky hair clung to the strong width of his shoulders. Finally, Luc turned. Kimber sat up and looked right past Deke, over at Luc.

"It's for you, sweetheart. Logan."

Nodding, she made a show of rising from the bed completely naked with both of them looking on. If Deke intended to continue sharing her, then she had nothing to hide from either man. They'd seen it all, touched and tasted it all.

Out of the corner of her eye, she saw Deke bend and retrieve her little white robe. He tossed it in her direction. With a pointed glance, she let it fall to the ground.

"Why bother?"

His face tightened. Kimber didn't feel any hollow triumph. She didn't feel anything but despair as she grabbed the phone.

"Hi, Logan."

"Hi. Good news, little sister. Dad's conscious! And he's perfect."

Another jolt to the system. This one the best. From low to high again.

Something must have shown on her face because Luc was right beside her, holding her hand. Deke wandered closer, hovered.

"When?" she asked.

"About twenty minutes ago. They're going to run more tests on him today. But if all goes well, he could be out in a few days."

"Oh my . . . Oh, wow." She couldn't hold the tears back. "That's amazing! I'm so . . . God, thanks for calling me. Can I talk to him?"

"They just took him away to do an MRI. He should be free in a few hours. We'll call back then."

"I can't wait. I'm so thrilled . . ." She sobbed into the phone.

"Wait, sis. No crying. There's more."

"More?" God, could she take it? She felt splintered by the emotional divergence. How would she hold herself together?

"We're pretty sure we nailed the asshole with the bomb."

"What?! You caught him?"

"Yep." Logan's cheer pepped up his voice in a way she rarely heard. "We'd seen this asshole casing the hospital a few times in the past ten days. This morning, he was sniffing around the halls. He snuck into Dad's room dripping weapons. Hunter was in the corner and surprised him before he could empty his thirty-eight into Dad's head."

Kimber's heart all but stopped. "Ohmigod. Is he in custody now?"

"Absolutely. Hunter is down with the police. At the moment, he's denying the bomb, but he's been made. I think it's just a matter of time before he 'fesses up. What else can he do?"

"Yeah," she murmured. And all sorts of implications raced through her brain.

Someone had tried to kill her dad. He was not only alive, but conscious and out of danger. *She* was out of danger. They could leave the swamp. Today! No more hiding or worrying or . . .

Staying under one roof with Deke 24/7. He loved her, he claimed, but he wasn't ready to be with her. Just her. She either had to decide to leave him or stay and hope that things between them—the three of them—changed.

But she couldn't think about that now. Today had to be about Dad.

"This is great news, all of it! It's like someone poured miracle juice on us." Her voice cracked; she couldn't keep it together.

"You okay, sis?" She could hear the frown in Logan's voice. "It's not like you to cry."

"Just really . . . happy." *And miserable at the same time.* She squeezed her eyes shut, but damn, they still leaked.

"Okay." He didn't sound convinced. "We'll call you later and let you know for sure about Dad's discharge. Cool?"

"Absolutely. Thanks."

"Take care, sis." Then he hung up.

Kimber followed suit, sagging against the kitchen counter, barely noticing how cold the wood was against her skin.

"Your Dad is awake?" Luc prompted.

"They caught the psycho threatening you?" Deke demanded.

"Yes." Her voice shook as she looked at both of them. "Yes."

Luc wrapped his arm around her waist and brought her against the clean, steely flesh of his torso. He covered her mouth softly with his own, lingering, then whispered, "That's great, sweetheart. I'm so thrilled."

Deke stood. Watched. Unblinking. Unmoving as Luc kissed her again and leaned her against the cabinet, then covered her body with his. The erection at her belly was impossible to miss. The way his lips brushed, teased, aided by his tongue—it was like art. She felt the stirrings of desire. Luc was amazing, and he could make her want. But not love.

Why, damn it? Why couldn't she love the man who was prepared to be with her and only her?

Kimber broke off the kiss, trying not to cry. Luc interpreted it as emotional overflow.

"Hey, no tears. This is all good. We can leave this swampy paradise, go home, and get back to normal. You, me, Deke." He framed her face in his hands and offered her a gentle smile. "I can't wait."

Then he kissed her again, deeper, with a hint of demand. As he did, Kimber opened her eyes. Deke's stare was glued to them, harsh, vivid, angry, but still aroused.

Backing away, Luc took her hand and headed for the bedroom. "Come with me. I want to celebrate by loving you."

God, did she have it in her? If Deke tagged along, could she share herself, knowing that he considered this a status quo that would never change? Or take the chance he'd simply sit there and watch, so that sharing didn't become an issue? Either way, she had to make him see this threesome wasn't a workable, long-term solution.

Kimber stood on her tiptoes and planted a long drugging kiss on

Luc's mouth, until the man grabbed her hips and brought her right against the hard staff of his cock. When he groaned and ripped away his bath towel, baring himself completely in the kitchen, she backed away with a vixen's smile. "Come with me . . ."

Deke didn't say a word; he watched her with burning eyes, his fists clenched at his sides. So he didn't like it. *Good.* Now it was time to fuck Luc so thoroughly, Deke could no longer stand to watch. He'd better get ready for one hell of a show.

* * *

KIMBER had yet to look Deke's way—not once since Luc had suggested they celebrate horizontally and she had agreed. Damn it, he should be glad that she was willing to accept something he couldn't change. But looking at Luc run big, bronze hands all over her body, sliding over stiff nipples, gliding into damp crevices . . . That just wasn't acceptable. Not when the news about the Colonel being conscious and the whacked-out freak responsible for the bomb behind bars made a hell of a reason for all of them to celebrate together.

In the middle of swamp central, what better way than sex and lots of it? It was a hell of a way to climb down this three-week adrenaline rush he'd been on. Except it went deeper than that. Deke *had* to touch her before they returned to civilization and her family. And not just touch her body. He'd done that plenty. This time, his mission was to touch her heart. Infiltrate and capture, if possible. He had to bond with her.

He had to make her understand that, even if Luc touched her, she was *his.*

Sure, she said she loved him. He prayed like hell that was true. He'd even stripped his own defenses and admitted out loud that he loved her. But a woman like Kimber deserved a whole man. He wasn't it. But he was too fucking selfish to just give her up.

"I want to hold you, sweetheart," Luc said. "I'm—"

"*We,*" Deke cut in. "We want to hold you."

"Absolutely." Luc caressed her cheek. "We are every bit as relieved as you are. Thrilled. We can't wait to express our gladness with you."

It was partly true. Mostly, Deke just wanted to get Kimber under him so she could feel him, see and taste and smell him. He wanted to seep into her pores so that if she really was rethinking her part in this ménage, she wouldn't just turn her back and simply walk away.

How big would the hole in his chest be if she left and never looked back? So huge, it would make the Grand Canyon look like a tiny pinprick.

His best bet was to remind her—vividly—about all the positives of being with him. And even though she'd rather be an exclusive couple, Deke knew for a fact that he and Luc managed a hell of a one-two punch on her libido.

Luc beat him to the bed and sprawled across it, arms open. Kimber hesitated, for just a moment. Deke put a hand at the small of her back, and even though the thought of letting his cousin around her—inside her—was like scraping his balls on a rusty blade, he urged her forward.

With a furious glare over her shoulder at him, she dove onto the bed, onto his cousin. The neon temptress inside her burst out, full of sizzle and come-hither, and shined her bright light all over Luc. She curled her body around Luc's, and didn't waste a second before plastering her lips over his, seeking, hungry, desperate. Kimber pushed her way into Luc's mouth with her tongue, purring with feminine moans that both stroked Deke's cock and ripped at his heart.

She straddled him, fisting Luc's dark hair as she sank even deeper into their rough, frenzied kiss. *Holy shit!*

Surprise passed across Luc's face, but it didn't last long. Desire hit his cousin like a tornado, whirling him up in the promise of mind-blowing sex that dripped from her kiss. Luc met that kiss with every ounce of finesse in his arsenal and clutched the curves of her body—breasts, waist, hips—as he poured himself into answering the raw demand radiating from Kimber.

Moaning, she placed herself right over the length of his cousin's cock, which was already more than hard for her. And with female hips swaying, she undulated, rubbing her soft, wet pussy all over Luc's cock and letting out a high, pleading groan that asked him to make it better. To make her come.

The sounds, the view, *his* woman gyrating her clit over the head of another man's cock . . . He swallowed. It was hard to watch.

Bullshit! He ground his jaw. Seeing Kimber turn her back on him and flash Luc the raw, raging need burning in her eyes, seeing her kiss, which demanded he satisfy her hunger . . . that was a tearing pain, like ripping his motherfucking entrails out with his bare hands. God, he couldn't watch.

But Deke forced himself.

Watching the slide of Kimber's pussy against Luc's cock quickly became a wet, silken torment. She broke the kiss on a gasp and tossed her head back.

"That's it. Rub yourself all over me," Luc growled as she ground down on him. "You feel how hard I am for you?"

Kimber whimpered, and the sound stabbed at Deke like a hot blade in the balls.

"Yes," she mewled, a violent flush spreading across her skin. "I'm wet. So wet. Luc . . ."

"You want to come?"

A wild nod sent her auburn waves tumbling across the pale skin of her back, her breasts arching. Damn, she was so fucking beautiful—and so fucking aroused by another man.

They looked perfect together. And he'd encouraged her right into Luc's arms. Deke suddenly wanted to break those arms.

Not for the first time, Deke wondered why Luc stayed in this ménage relationship when he was a whole man who could easily take a woman to bed all by himself. But seeing Kimber and his cousin together, Deke feared he knew the answer.

He stood frozen. It was like rubbernecking a traffic accident; he knew he shouldn't watch, and yet he couldn't tear his gaze away.

Perched on her hands and knees over Luc's body, she rubbed her clit over the head of Luc's shaft. Sweating, trembling, she looked back down into Luc's eyes.

"Tell me you want to come," Luc whispered, clutching at her hips to hold her still until she answered.

Her cry of protest and need pounded down on Deke. He took a step forward to give Kimber what she needed, to make that building orgasm his, to tear her out of Luc's arms so that—

"Yes," she shouted. "Yes. Make me come!"

Then she went wild on Luc, arching, wriggling, crying out, until her whole body trembled for release. Kimber clutched him, dragging her sweet pussy—the one that belonged to Deke—all over Luc's dick, doing her best to find the wild release Deke knew he should be giving her.

No more. Deke couldn't take it. She was his. This orgasm was his to give.

He reached out to drag Kimber off of Luc, throw her on the bed, and mount her. He needed to give her the spinning, explosive sensations of a whirlwind climax. Before he touched Kimber, her body jolted, as if she'd been shocked. She let out a long, harsh cry of guttural satisfaction. And she screamed something guaranteed to destroy him:

"*Luc!*"

Deke's guts imploded as she came in a fiery tirade of need. *For another man.*

His insides bubbled, like he'd been filled up with acid. A need to fuck Kimber and claim her all over again warred with a violent urge to beat the living shit out of his cousin. He'd gone volatile. Felt unstable. On the fucking edge of something he couldn't predict. He'd never experienced this wild and uncertain violence.

Deke tried to deep-breathe through it as Kimber collapsed against his cousin's chest, a panting mass of sweat-slick arms and legs. She held Luc tight, buried her face in his neck.

Suddenly, she let out a wail of tears that split the air with anguish. She looked so damn sad. Defeated.

It snapped Deke out of his trance.

As she dragged in a jagged sob, hot tears flowed down scalding cheeks that burned rage and helplessness through him. He wrenched her from Luc's embrace and against his own body.

"You don't fucking touch her without me," he snarled to Luc. "She's mine. *Mine!*"

Immediately, she started fighting him, struggling and writhing to break free. Sobs overtook her, but Deke understood what she didn't ask. How could he allow another man to touch her body?

Oh God, what had he done to her?

Shame crashed in on Deke, crushing and bleak. Fury—mostly at himself—followed.

Deke suddenly knew the meaning of the phrase "seeing red." The whole bright, blood-sharp color filled his gaze, saturating logic. Rational thought—gone. Instinct ruled as he lowered Kimber to the bed, took her thighs in his hands, and spread her wide.

Glistening, sticky-sweet, and oh-so-wet, she was spread out before him. The pink petals of her flesh had gone red, swelling with arousal. Those folds still looked full and aching for more. And she made him so goddamn hungry just lying there.

"I'm not just yours. I'm his, too," she flung at him.

He raised his head from between her thighs and drilled his stare deep down into her tear-drenched eyes. Bravado. Anger. A silent *fuck you*.

Oh, he'd fuck her, all right. He'd make sure she understood that, no matter who touched her, she belonged to him.

In one leap, Deke covered her body, gathered her legs above his hips, and slid the aching-hard length of his cock deep into her pussy. To the hilt.

She gasped. Out of surprise, pleasure, or pain, he didn't know. Probably all three. The feel of her closing around him like a hungry little mouth burned away anything that might have resembled a conscience.

He bared his teeth in a semblance of a smile. "You're going to learn differently, kitten. Right now."

Chapter Seventeen

With long, harsh strokes, Deke groaned out a rough breath as he plunged deep into Kimber, stretching her around his cock, moving against her cervix. Under him, she bucked, gasped, softened.

He wasn't close enough, deep enough. He had to envelop her, fill her. Easing his arms over her shoulders, between her back and the mattress, he lifted her chest against his and pressed in. Panting, frantic, fucking on fire, he fused their mouths together and surged deep into her once more. She responded again with a jerk and a groan. And still, it wasn't enough.

It never would be.

Hard, fast, the slick slide of his flesh over—into—hers was both heaven and hell. Exquisite torture. Every rasp of her clasping cunt sent him careening closer to oblivion. She was everything he'd ever wanted, never believed existed or that he deserved. And he wasn't leaving this bed until she exploded in orgasm and shouted a hoarse cry in his name.

"Deke," Luc's voice broke into the wild rhythm of his shuttling in and out of her. "Deke!"

"What?" he snarled.

"Be gentle."

Gentle? *Shit!*

Deke thundered a heavy stare down at Kimber. His gaze met her dilated hazel eyes and an arc of electricity zinged right up his cock, punctuated by her needy, restless moan. "Am I hurting you?"

Yeah, he sounded like he gargled with sandpaper. *So fucking what?*

Before she could answer, he had to level another long stroke to the end of her channel. The motion lit up nerves and set off a blaze of sensation, based on the way she scratched her nails into his back, arched to him, and her sensitive walls clasped him tighter.

"Am I?" he demanded.

"No. More. God, more!"

Her words peeled the veneer off what little civility he possessed. Hammering into her like a lust-crazed maniac, Deke held her against him, immobile, forcing her to accept the brutal need of his every thrust as he took possession of her mouth in a desperate kiss.

"It appears you don't need me here after all. I'll just . . . go," he heard Luc say over the roar of his heart.

His cousin rose and made his way across the room, to the door.

The impact of Luc leaving him here alone with Kimber . . . Deke stopped. Froze. Like someone had put a choke hold on his pleasure and squeezed the life out of his arousal. Blood rushed away from his erection. It dwindled, dread replacing arousal.

What the . . . ? This had never happened. Panic stole into his veins like sharp, stinging needles. *No, no, no!* This wasn't supposed to happen. He wanted to make love to Kimber, have her all to himself.

His body had other plans.

Holy shit! His erection . . . gone.

How? Why was this happening suddenly?

He squeezed his eyes shut, trying to focus on everything sexual, anything that would bring his cock back to life.

Nothing.

In that instant, Deke knew he wouldn't be able to finish this if Luc left.

Goddamn motherfucking son of a bitch! What was wrong with him? Maybe he should just ask Heather. Oh, wait. She was dead.

Mortification slammed as he wondered with a sick frustration how his body could let him down. All this time he'd been afraid and psyching himself out about it, thinking he was just screwed up in the head in his refusal to fuck a woman alone. But it was physical, too. He couldn't even stay hard without his cousin here to hold his hand. He felt like half a man. Like a freak.

"Stay!" Deke demanded, choking the word out. "For chrissakes, come over here and be gentle. I can't."

Luc hesitated.

"Please." It physically hurt to spit the word out, but Deke knew, *knew*, he wasn't going to be able to finish staking his claim on Kimber if Luc left the room.

And didn't that speak volumes about how fucked-up in the head he was?

With a defeated sigh, Luc padded back to his side of the bed and crawled on. Biting the inside of his cheek so hard he tasted blood, Deke rolled to his side so that Kimber's back nestled to Luc's chest.

His cousin placed his hands on her shoulders and kissed the damp crook of her neck. "You look beautiful in pleasure."

All was normal again—or his definition of it. Seeing Kimber relax against Luc, and his cousin's mouth travel over her flushed skin, his cock sprang back to vital life.

Taking hold of her hips, Deke pressed as deep inside Kimber as he could. "You *are* beautiful, kitten. I've never wanted anyone the way I want you."

Fresh tears clawed out of Kimber's eyes as she threw her arms around Deke's neck. Her pussy fluttered around him. With another hard stroke into her, he pushed against her G-spot, ground up against her clit.

And Kimber came apart, roaring out a tortured cry of satisfaction so wild, unlike any Deke had ever heard from her. *"Deke!"*

Her untamed pulsing all over his cock, her cries of whimpering pleasure ringing off the walls, sent him straight into a crash of ecstasy that clenched around his heart. Sobbing out a masculine growl, sensations gathered up inside him like a fireball, dangerous and consuming. In a few powerful spasms, he poured it all out into her. Everything—his love, his need, his hopes, his soul.

Kimber accepted it all inside her with a long cry. Their gazes connected, and the connection latched, locked into place. He couldn't have looked away to save his fucking life.

Timeless moments later, the tumult ended. Kimber stilled, then broke their connection as her body sank into the mattress and she clambered away from him, rolling away—right into Luc's arms with a sharp cry and jagged tears.

Luc closed his arms around her, but his gaze met Deke's. *Confusion.* There was no other word to describe it. About Deke's physical reaction. About Kimber's emotional one. From Deke's complete inability to perform, then straight to orgasm. From her immersion in ecstasy to razor-sharp despair. Now, Deke was spent. Kimber sobbed. Luc had no idea what was going on with either of them. Deke wasn't totally sure himself. But he was focusing on Kimber for now.

"Kitten?" he rolled closer, leaning over her. "What?"

For endless minutes, she refused to talk. He asked. Luc asked. No answers. Just more of those hysterical tears that ripped a sword of excruciating pain right through the middle of his heart.

He did the only thing he could do. And Luc joined him. They simply rubbed her, soothed her, telling her everything would be okay.

Deke knew for a fact that every word out of his mouth was bullshit.

"No more," she sobbed. Then she closed her eyes against him.

Moments later, she went still, as if the peaks of body and emotion were too overwhelming. She sank into slumber, curled in a fetal position. Deke looked down as he realized that he'd slipped his hand into hers at some point and she still clutched it.

The roaring climaxes that had wracked her body thrilled Deke, but all the tears . . . It wasn't a coincidence they'd come after Kimber had told him that she loved him and he'd confessed in kind. And after she'd told him that she didn't want to be shared again, then it became obvious that he couldn't love her by himself.

"No more what?" Luc asked, looking tense. "Is she talking about what I think she's talking about?"

Shit. Here came the part where he had to be honest with Luc about a truth he could hardly process himself.

A truth that would change everything.

Deke sighed. "You know I think of you like a brother."

Something guarded and angry entered Luc's dark eyes. "Yeah?"

"Keeping it real, my brother? We can't keep doing this to her. She doesn't want to be shared anymore."

"What? You're going to fuck her by yourself?" Luc challenged. "You didn't seem exactly able a few minutes ago."

Observant bastard. Deke had no idea how sex was going to work. Today had proven beyond all doubts that he was half a man, that he couldn't make love to a woman without another man being near. Even if, like this morning, Luc didn't fuck her, too. Simply knowing that someone else had his back, just in case . . .

Luc kept on. "You told her you were going to claim her for yourself. How are you going to make that happen?"

"They're big words you know I can't back up alone," Deke choked, sounding as ripped apart about that as Luc looked. "Even so, this, the three of us . . . it has to stop."

"Goddamn it!"

"C'mon. She's not built for this. Can't you see that?"

"I need this! You need this. What the hell are we supposed to do?"

With a frown, Deke studied his cousin. "Why do *you* need this? What do you get out of it besides getting off?"

"Plenty. I'm not giving up on you two. Until today, Kimber did fine with us. Perfectly. This is just some anomaly—"

"It's not. You saw her sobbing her fucking heart out!"

In some ways, he wished Luc was right. But the reality was, Kimber probably felt unloved, maybe abused, when he said he loved her and still let his cousin touch her. And he could barely stand to see Luc's hands on her anymore.

"What the hell changed?"

Oh, another hard truth. Deke resisted the urge to wince. "She says she loves me."

"She's told me as much before." And Luc didn't sound jealous in the least.

Which confused the shit out of Deke. "I told her I love her, too."

"And now she wants to be exclusive?" The tight, bitter smile told Deke this could get ugly fast.

He shrugged. "We both know I'm not built like that. I can't"—Deke looked away and buried his face in his hands—"I feel so fucking broken. What the hell kind of man needs a buddy to hold his hand when he's making love to his woman?"

"Do you think she understands that? Knows why?"

"No." Luc started to open his mouth, but Deke shut him down. "Telling her won't change facts."

"That's bullshit you tell yourself so you don't have to spill the truth to her."

Maybe. But he wasn't willing to test the theory. Oh hell, she was probably going to run screaming from him no matter what he did. So why vomit his past all over her? "Drop it."

Luc shrugged, clearly pissed. "So what's next?"

With a sigh, Deke looked down at Kimber. *Good freakin' question.* "We spend the rest of the morning driving back to our place and tell her there, after dinner, that there are no more threesomes. Then . . . I guess, we'll let her decide what she wants."

"You mean who?"

Half a man or the man she didn't love. Hell of a choice. Deke raked a tense hand through his hair. "Yeah."

Funny, when Kimber had first come to their place to ask him to teach her all about ménage, she'd asked how they handled jealousy. His answer had been bullshit and ignorant lies. The truth was, he'd never dealt with it before. None of the women he and Luc had fucked together had ever mattered. Now that he'd felt the bite of covetousness, he hadn't handled it well.

And he'd probably lose her in large part because of it.

*   *   *

THE guys were eerily silent the rest of the day, which suited Kimber just fine.

She awoke that afternoon to find herself alone and exhausted in the swamp cabin's big bed. Luc brought her lunch, but she couldn't bring herself to eat it. Deke announced they were headed back to Texas. She supposed she should be happy. But happy just wouldn't come.

Whether Luc's brown or Deke's dazzling blue, their eyes seemed to see through her, and they were heavy and worried. She had a feeling that some sort of reckoning was coming . . .

Listless and queasy from crying overload, she quietly packed her suitcase. In the kitchen, she heard Luc loading up the appliances and supplies he'd brought. Deke . . . who knew where he was?

Kimber had the oddest urge to find him—now—ask if he still loved her. Ask if excluding Luc from their bed was going to end their relationship. She had a bad feeling about the answer, especially after experiencing his reaction to Luc's attempt to leave the bedroom earlier that morning. It seemed wild, nearly unbelievable, that a man as virile as Deke couldn't make love without another man in the room, but what if it was true?

The fact that he refused to tell her why was shredding her insides, and frankly, pissing her off.

And now she had one other complication she just hadn't expected . . .

Silence filled the trip back to East Texas. She consoled herself with the thought that she was one step closer to seeing her dad—and figuring out where her life would go from here.

They'd barely stepped foot in Luc's house before Deke announced that he had to leave to take care of business. God, he was distancing himself from her already. He might love her . . . but it sure felt like he wasn't going to try to overcome whatever was bothering him. Was his sudden exit supposed to be her cue to leave?

The minute Deke left, Luc approached her looking like he had something on his mind. "You need something, sweetheart? Coffee? Food? I'll make you anything."

At the moment, she just wanted to be alone, especially if he had any ideas about acting on the heat in that dark chocolate gaze of his, currently melting all over her. "I need to grab a few things at the store. Can I borrow your car keys?"

With a frown, he agreed. "Could you be back by six? I need to put in an appearance at a restaurant downtown tonight."

With a nod and a gutful of relief, Kimber escaped the quiet house—too packed with memories for comfort—and drove.

It didn't take her long to pick up some supplies. Picking out the get well/I miss you card for her dad was easy. Securing a new cell phone didn't take long, either. She called Logan and Hunter to check in, and they said Dad would be released day after tomorrow. She even had the opportunity to talk to him for a few short minutes.

Ecstatic about his quickly recovering health, Kimber picked up the rest of the items on her mental list, trying to push away the reality of it all.

Kimber returned to Luc's house a little after five.

Looking sinfully sexy with his long hair loose, charcoal slacks, and a long white linen shirt, he pressed a lingering kiss to her cheek. "I won't be gone long. Can you wait up? I think we should talk . . ."

She didn't love the man the way she loved Deke, but the feel of Luc's hand cupping her cheek was somehow such a comfort. "He's done with me, isn't he?"

"What happens next is really up to you." He kissed her again, this time a sweet press of his lips over hers, a soft slide of tongue—then he was gone.

With a huge sob, she sat on the sofa and unloaded again. Tear after tear streamed down her face, hot and annoying and creating the mother of all headaches. When had she ever been this emotional? All the crying was exhausting her. And the sex. The two happening multiple times a day, it seemed, was making sleep her new hobby.

At least she hoped that's all it was . . .

Damn, she had to leave this pity party. Get some answers, get her head straight, talk to the guys, figure it out. Things just couldn't go on like this. She couldn't go on like this.

Picking herself up, she made herself a bowl of soup and flipped a few channels, trying to think about nothing, Staged laugh tracks didn't work. She drifted off to sleep.

A car pulling up into the driveway awoke her. Deke had returned.

Dark had fallen. Kimber didn't think she was ready to handle conversation, ultimatums, or hard choices. She grabbed her shopping bags and her newly charged cell phone and headed to the bathroom.

* * *

WHAT a fucking nightmare, Deke thought, sliding into the house. An afternoon conferring with Jack about business—and personal—matters. Business was fine. Healthy, in fact. Jack had done a great job at keeping everything running while he'd been protecting Kimber from the psycho-bomber. It was the personal stuff he couldn't seem to untangle.

Now he had to wait for Luc to come home, so they could hash it out. And hope they didn't come to blows over it.

Luc called to say he was on his way home. He'd be there by nine. Still plenty early to get all this shit out in the open. *Great.* He was looking forward to it—about as much as he would castration with the jagged lid of a tin can.

Sucking up his jangled nerves, Deke went in search of Kimber. Before Luc came, he needed to say a few things. She was smart, so he didn't doubt she'd already figured out that he needed a crowd to get down. In order to make choices for her future, she needed to know that might never change . . . along with the other thing he couldn't give her. And why.

Time to rip open the scar of his past. *Oh, goodie.*

Trekking down the hall, Deke heard her talking and followed the sound of her voice. Who the hell was she talking to? One of her brothers? Her father? A girlfriend?

"It's good to talk to you, too." Pause. "I agree we have some things to talk about."

Frowning, he leaned against the wall outside the bathroom and listened as she sighed, crossed the room. Deke supposed he should have some compunction about eavesdropping on her. He didn't.

"I know. I've had to protect myself, which is one reason I was hiding and not available. But the guy who set the bomb at Dad's house"—she broke off, only to start again—"He's fine. I'm fine. Just really tired. Maybe we could talk tomorrow."

Deke scrubbed a hand across his face, a sneaking suspicion sinking into his gut.

"No, I'm not trying to blow you off. I've just had a hell of a day." A pause. Then a giant sob. "Please, let me go. You don't love me, Jesse. You want redemption or saving or something, and I can't do that for you. I can't even manage to help myself."

So his suspicion was right. *Jesse.* The fucking pop star pretty boy was still calling her? And wanting what? He ground his teeth. The prick was making her cry.

Deke prepared to charge into the bedroom, grab the phone from her hand, and tell Mr. "MMMBop" to get fucked.

Before he could, Kimber screamed. "Damn it, not now! Stop!"

He'd never heard her so out of control. Never heard her so close to hysterical as he had today. He'd also heard enough.

Charging into the bathroom, he saw red again as he grabbed the phone and growled into it, "You keep calling and upsetting my woman, and I'm going to break every fucking bone in your body, you pansy-ass falsetto son of a bitch."

Resisting the urge to throw the phone against the wall, he stabbed a button with his thumb to end the call. Then he powered it down and tossed the phone on the counter. In a lunge, he grabbed Kimber and pulled her into his arms.

Shit, she was shaking. Not a gentle tremble, but an all-over body shake, shoulders rattling, breath hitching, body jolting.

"Kitten. Baby . . ."

He stroked her hair as gently as he knew how. Tough when he wanted to go find Jesse McCall and pound on him until his face was as flat as a slab of concrete. Deke was much better at fighting than soothing. But Kimber needed gentle right now.

In the distance, he heard Luc pull into the driveway. For the first time today, he thanked God for his cousin's presence. Luc would know how to deal with her emotions. His cousin could calm her.

"Let me get Luc . . ."

"No." She clutched him tighter. "Deke, I'm scared."

He was both relieved and anxious that she wanted him. If she wanted him, rather than Luc, she had to still care about him, despite the hard truth they still hadn't faced.

"Don't be afraid of Jesse. If I need to personally talk sense into the bastard—"

"That's not it."

She started sobbing, again so uncontrollable, he freaked. If she didn't stop, she was going to pass out or throw up or something. He sat on the edge of the tub and pulled her into his lap, his thoughts racing.

"Then what? If it's about this morning, I'm sorry, kitten. Really sorry. Take a deep breath and—"

She lifted tear-drenched, frightened hazel eyes to him. That look stopped him cold.

"I'm pregnant."

Her words were like a battering ram to the gut. He jerked out from under her and bounced to his feet. And he stared. The blood left his head in a sick rush. Had he heard . . . ?

God, please. No!

"Pregnant?"

Slowly, Kimber stood and reached into the pocket of her shorts, withdrawing a plastic white test stick. With two blue lines running right down the middle.

Swallowing, Deke backed away. This couldn't be happening. It couldn't. He was going to puke everywhere.

"How the fuck . . . ? The pill. You—How?"

"The doctors at the hospital gave me antibiotics in case my stitches got infected. I forgot they weakened the pill's effectiveness . . . Oh, God. You look green."

He felt green. So sick. His worst fucking nightmare come to life.

His past all over again.

"I can't do this." He shook his head. "I should never have taken your virginity. I knew better . . ."

Deke turned away and darted out of the room. He heard Kimber's cries behind him, fading in the distance. Before he could get out the front door, he saw Luc standing there.

One look at his cousin, and Deke knew Luc had heard every word.

Luc grabbed him by the shoulders. "Take a deep breath."

"You fucking heard her. She's goddamn pregnant!"

Of all people, Luc should get it. Why did he look so freakin' calm?

The urge to hurl rose up inside Deke again. *Pregnant.* Why the fuck hadn't he worn a condom? Because he knew from past experience, they didn't work. What was he going to do now? Keep watching her day and night? How could he be assured everything was okay when he wasn't even sure himself?

"I know." Luc spoke in his most soothing voice. "Deke, I know you're upset. But it's a blessing—"

"Yeah, it was such a fucking blessing for Heather."

"Who's Heather?" Kimber asked from the threshold, wrapping her arms around herself like she was clutching her stomach.

Deke whirled to her. Her eyes were so red in her ghostly pale face. Her haunted expression ate at his gut. For chrissakes, that look . . . it was as if he'd struck her.

Luc sighed. "Heather—"

"She's the reason I'm no good for you—or any other woman," Deke cut in. "The reason I can't fuck a woman without another man in the room. And I'm the reason she's dead."

With unseeing eyes, Deke groped around and found the couch. Shaking, he sank down into the leather and cradled his head in his hands. "And now history is going to repeat itself, and it's going to be all my fault again . . ."

"What do you mean?" she whispered.

His head snapped up and he stabbed her with a sharp stare. "I was going to tell you the ugly truth tonight, anyway. But not like this."

Kimber backed away to sit in a chair across the room, her face hesitant. Now she was unsure of him. Too bad she hadn't been before the damage was done.

Deke took a deep breath, sinking down into the past, drudging up his pain. "Heather was my girlfriend in high school. We started dating when she was a freshman. I was a sophomore. We'd been dating a little over a year when"—*Damn, this was hard. Really hard*—"When we started having sex. She was barely sixteen. A virgin."

"She got pregnant." Kimber didn't have to guess.

"Yeah. I was scared shitless. Not even eighteen. Her father was the local sheriff. He'd never liked me."

"So she died. Giving birth?" Kimber's horrified whisper barely crossed the room.

"No." He folded his hands. Unfolded them. Forced himself to look at her. "She committed suicide."

With a horrified gasp, Kimber covered her mouth. But he could still see the shock in her hazel eyes. Was she condemning him? Probably. He deserved it for knocking her up, then not knowing what to say. For not being a whole man.

"Sleeping pills, a whole bottleful of them. In her suicide note, she said that her family hated me and she'd been stupid to let me touch her. Said I'd be a terrible father." He choked on the words. Fucking choked.

"Deke, no. You were both so young—"

"But she was right. Me and my stupid Energizer Bunny dick might as well have poured the whole bottle of shit down her throat."

"She made a choice," Kimber insisted.

"Yeah, *after* I got her pregnant. I swore to myself this would never happen again. And now look." He tossed his hands up in the air.

Hell, his life was going to shit faster than he imagined possible. And he had no idea what to do.

"Never? You were *never* going to have children?" She looked appalled. "Deke, you can't imagine that every adult woman was going to react the same as Heather. I certainly . . . Are you freaked out because you thought I might end it all now that I'm having a baby?"

Yeah. The thought had crossed his mind. More like stomped in, camped out, and took a pickax into his soul.

"Kimber, you only just found out. How are you going to feel in a few weeks when you're retching up your toenails? Or in a few months, when your shape changes and your body isn't your own anymore?"

She looked . . . betrayed. There was no other word for it. And Deke was totally confused.

"Pregnancy isn't the end of the world. I'll deal. If you think for an instant that I'd do a damn thing to endanger myself or this baby in some fit for attention, then you don't know me very well. At all." Tears squeezed from her eyes, down her cheeks.

"You say that now—"

"I'll say that until the day I deliver," she vowed.

God, he wanted to believe her. But after the hysteria in the bathroom, all the drama of tonight . . . What if it caught up to her? What if she decided she didn't want the baby, him, or life?

Heather's death and the guilt had crushed him. He'd been a walking zombie for at least two years. Barely finished high school. If it hadn't been for Luc and the army and his introduction to ménage . . . there'd been times he was tempted to join Heather in her fate.

"At least this makes so many things clear. You took up ménages after Heather's death, didn't you? Then if any woman got pregnant, you always had another man to blame."

She'd figured him out fast. Exactly. She was exactly—Wait!

His gaze snapped over to Luc. "Maybe you're the baby's father. Maybe—"

"I'd love to take responsibility for this." Luc dropped to his knees in front of Kimber, lifted her T-shirt, and placed a gossamer kiss on her still-flat belly.

Deke waited for the relief. And waited. But watching Luc's reverence as he stroked a soft hand over Kimber's stomach, he could only feel sick at the thought of his cousin creating life inside *his* woman. The possibility made him want to retch and break something at the same time.

Then Luc stood and looked at him with not just sadness, but tragedy in his dark eyes. "But I can't take responsibility, Deke. The baby can't be mine."

"You fucked her, too. Both of us did."

"True." Luc crossed the room and sat beside him, clapped a hand across his back. "But I can't have children. I'm sterile."

Kimber gasped. Deke barely heard.

Instead, he stared at his cousin, barely able to process those words. A second bomb tonight—the first, Kimber's news, like Hiroshima, the second, Luc's confession, Nagasaki. Nuclear. Devastating.

"You can't . . ."

"No." Luc gazed away, stared out the window. "When I was about fourteen I got some virus. Really high fevers for days." He shrugged. "Apparently, it killed nearly all the swimmers."

Was he hearing this right? Deke couldn't comprehend. "What?!"

"You're sure, Luc?" Kimber asked.

"The first few years, I was tested and retested and tested again. I saw specialists. They said my sperm count was so low, it's pretty much statistically impossible that I could get anyone pregnant."

"And you never told me? *Me?*" Of all people.

Luc shrugged. "I begged my parents not to tell the family."

"But you didn't tell *me*. Why the fuck not?"

"You know how people are, always wanting the one thing they can't have." His smile was tight with self-deprecation. "I wanted a baby who shared at least some of my own blood. A baby that might have a chance of being a little like me. I wanted to know its mother. Be a part of its family. Feel connected to the conception and pregnancy, the birth, the raising. I would have asked you to simply . . . donate, but I knew you wouldn't want to accept the responsibility of a child."

Luc's whole MO came into focus with startling, sickening clarity. "You've been waiting around for twelve years for me to get someone pregnant?" Deke could hardly close his gaping mouth. "That's why you were always pushing for the wife and the picket fence? That's why you cornered me into taking Kimber's virginity?"

Deke had thought of Luc like a brother, a best friend, the closest family. All this time, Luc had thought of him as a sperm donor?

"You would have taken her, anyway. Be honest about that."

Grinding his teeth, Deke silently admitted Luc was probably right. But he wasn't about to give his manipulative cousin the satisfaction now.

Luc sighed. "Deke, there are a lot of reasons I've hung with you for years. But I have to admit, hoping we could eventually find a woman and have children was a big one. I never hid that."

"You knew the last thing I ever wanted was to get anyone else pregnant!"

"But I also knew that someday, you'd be whole again and want kids.

You believed it, too, somewhere deep down. If you hadn't, you would have had a vasectomy. I know you."

Deke didn't want to think too hard about that. He'd considered a vasectomy. He'd even had an appointment once. Then . . . something had stopped him. He'd never known what. Never looked at it too hard, figuring condoms and ménages would cover his bases.

"But since you never got snipped, I was sure you'd find the right woman—"

"Knock her up, take off, and leave the ready-made family to you?"

"No. I never intended to cut you out. I figured you—"

"I can imagine what you figured," he snarled. "Congratulations, you got your fucking wish. Now you've got a pregnant woman living under your roof who will pop you out a baby. And you," he pinned a stare on Kimber, "you got a whole man who's eager to marry you and have the perfect little family. Consider each other my wedding gift to you."

Chapter Eighteen

ON his way out, Deke slammed the front door. A minute later, his Hummer left the driveway in a squeal of tires. Like he couldn't leave fast enough. Kimber closed her eyes and tried to stop shaking.

In the wake of Deke's departure, a terrible dread smothered her. She hadn't expected him to be happy about the pregnancy, but in her worst nightmare, she couldn't have imagined the scene that had followed.

Luc sat beside her and wrapped a supportive arm around her waist, offering a shoulder to lean on. "Are you okay?"

Well, she was pregnant by a man who was scared shitless she was going to do herself in and had handed her over to another man. All in all, not her idea of a great day. "I think I would have preferred being hit by a Mack truck. Faster and less painless."

He brought her against his chest and stroked her back. "I'm sorry. The way he acted must have hurt. I don't know what to say to help explain his reaction."

"I don't expect you to explain him." Deke was a big boy, responsible for his own actions. And she'd be pissed as hell at him if his fear hadn't been so real and tangible. So obviously painful.

Instead, she just felt hopeless.

"Deke is just . . . He never healed."

"Got that, loud and clear."

"After Heather's death, he took on so much guilt. And her family didn't help. Her twin sister spread a rumor around the school that Deke had encouraged Heather to kill herself. Her mother worked as a teacher at the high school and made sure that most adults on campus believed he'd been responsible for the death of a sixteen-year-old girl—and treated him like a stone-cold killer. They lived in a really small town, so there were no other schools to transfer to. He could barely leave the house without one of his parents. One time when he did, Heather's dad picked him up for supposedly speeding, hauled his ass to jail, and threw him in a cell with a violent adult offender, even though Deke was a juvenile. The bastard denied him a phone call for six hours. If Deke's dad hadn't figured out quickly where his son was and showed up at the jail with his lawyer, I'm pretty sure Deke would have been raped."

Kimber's heart stuttered and wept all at once. "Oh my—That's terrible."

"What's worse is, I think Deke believed he was solely responsible and heaped the guilt on himself. I think he still does. And I think he's been terrified for years that he might be responsible for another woman's death."

The story was awful. Beyond tragic. A waste of a young girl's promise, her grieving, vindictive family, the fracturing of a young man's sense of self and worth. No one healed.

And now she was bringing a baby into the picture.

"Thank you for telling me."

"You're not angry with me?"

"For being honest about Deke's past?"

He winced. "For not being honest about my . . . issue sooner."

Mad? No. She had no real cause to feel betrayed. His inability to have children was something that shamed him. Even in the midst of all the drama of Deke and Luc's argument, she'd seen the humiliation on his face and felt more than a pang of his hurt and loss for something he wanted so desperately.

"You didn't owe me any explanations."

He hung his head as if he heard her implied words. "I owed Deke one."

No way she could refute that. "Why did you keep the truth from him? You're his best friend, his rock. He cares about you, relies on you—"

"I—I thought we'd both win with this arrangement. I've always believed that, someday, we'd meet the woman who could help make him whole again. Then he'd be okay with her becoming pregnant. One of us would marry her; we'd all be happy . . . I thought going through all that would help heal him and give me the family I want so badly."

Luc had guessed wrong. "I guess the fact I was a virgin was an added bonus."

"For Deke, yes. I thought taking you would be a catharsis for him, get him past one of his mental barriers. And when he did, I really thought he'd grown. It was more about you, though. The way he responded to you was, from the beginning, totally different. I think he was half in love with you when you walked through the door. You looked half in love with him yourself. And I thought you were sweet and wonderful the first time I met you." He smiled sadly. "I didn't see how any of us could lose."

"I guess on the surface it would have looked good." But everything had gone to hell, and Kimber had no idea where to go from here.

With a finger under her chin, Luc turned her toward him. "Oh, sweetheart. I'm so damn sorry. You look so lost, like you're wondering what the hell to do." He placed a soft, lingering kiss on her mouth.

"Sometimes I swear you're psychic."

He tapped her nose with a fingertip. "Sometimes you're easy to read."

She rolled eyes, raw from crying, and tried to laugh. "Good point."

"I like that about you. I like a lot of things about you." He took a deep breath, then cradled her face in his hands. "Marry me."

What? That had come out of left field. Yet it shouldn't have. Luc wanted a baby of Deke's seed, since he couldn't have one of his own. She had the power to grant him that request. But . . .

"It's a logical offer. You'd have a baby. I'd have a husband . . . except we'd just be saying 'I do' for the wrong reasons. You don't love me."

"That's not true."

Kimber looked in his eyes and saw love reflected in those dark depths—but the same kind of love she had for him. "Luc, I won't deny that we have hot sex—"

"Very hot sex." He smiled.

"But you don't *love* love me. You love me like I love you, as a friend. Over time, the hot sex would wear off."

"Maybe not. And a lot of people start with less, and we could grow more in love together. We'd be a family. Please think about it before you answer." He was damn near pleading.

Damn, she didn't want to hurt him, but if she said yes, she'd only hurt him more later when it didn't work out. "We'd always have Deke between us. He'll always be the father of this baby, and I'll always *love* love him. As years pass . . . I don't think you could live with that."

"I'd be fine—"

"I see how much you want this baby and a family of your own. I have no doubt you'll be one of the proudest uncles ever to my baby, but I don't think marriage is a good idea."

"Please . . . This is my last hope. I'll be thirty-five this fall. Deke is never going to share with me again after tonight—not you or anyone. Fathering a baby is the one thing I can't do for myself. I've achieved success in my career. I managed to buy a house, make close friends. I've got more money than I'll ever spend. But . . . this is the one hole in my life I can't fill."

And her heart ached for him. "Have you considered adopting?"

He grabbed her hands. "I want a part of me, even if it's a small part. You're carrying a small part of me with you. Deke is not going to come play daddy. This baby needs a father. I'll be a good husband."

"I have no doubt you would." To the woman he really loved, he would be golden. But that wasn't her. "And I know Deke isn't going to change his mind. I just don't think it would be a good idea to add another mistake on top of all the others."

"Think it through before you say no."

"I have. You'll be a big part of the baby's life. But if you marry me, rational or not, your relationship with Deke will be destroyed. I don't think you want that. I know I don't want it on my conscience."

Luc's shoulders fell as he pulled away from her with a heavy sigh. "I know you won't, but if you change your mind . . ."

"I know where to find you."

Kimber leaned forward and kissed Luc. Softly. A brush of lips and an exchange of sighs. A whisper of good-bye. Desperate fingers latched into her hair as he nudged her lips apart and stroked inside, his kiss begging. As if he'd decided that if words didn't convince her, maybe sex would.

Damn, the man could flat out kiss. The finesse . . . wow. The way he raked his tongue across the roof of her mouth sent a shiver through her. Then he nibbled erotically on her lip. A tilt of his head later, and the kiss changed, deepened, as he swept through. He had full command of her mouth now, and she tingled, felt . . . taken. It would be easy to melt against him.

But it would give him false hope.

She pulled away. "I'll be leaving in the morning."

Luc's fingers tightened in her hair, and he looked like he wanted to argue. Instead, he gritted his teeth and released her. "Where will you go?"

"I need to check in with my brothers. My dad should be coming home from the hospital soon, and they'll bring him to Logan's place when he's released. They'll need my help. My place isn't too far from his, and my poor neglected apartment . . . Bet all my houseplants are dead."

"Will you leave me a number? I want to be with you. I want to be as involved as you'll let me."

She smiled. "Sure. I have no doubt I'll need a hand to hold along the way, and neither Logan nor Hunter can be classified as warm guys. It'll be fitting if you're involved. Even if we're not married, there's still a little bit of you inside me, and I'd never take that from you. Ever."

* * *

THREE a.m. *Shit.*

After five hours away and a half-dozen whiskey shots chased by a handful of beers, Deke still couldn't outrun the barrage of emotions shredding his guts.

He quietly let himself into the house, bracing himself for the sight of Kimber in Luc's arms, in his bed. Better get used to that. Once they got married, he'd be confronted with it—and know exactly what he was missing—for the rest of his fucking life.

Unless everything that had happened with the baby, the arguments, the revelation, had driven Kimber over the edge of sanity. Panic flashed like the stab of a cold blade into his heart.

No, Luc wouldn't let that happen. Luc would save her. Even though he couldn't father children, of the two of them, he was the whole man.

Even so, knowing that they were a couple, that Luc had the right to touch her, stroke her, fuck her . . . God, it was going to eat him up.

It's for the best. Suck it up and get over it.

Swallowing, Deke set his car keys in the foyer, locked the front door behind him, and started the long walk down the hall toward the bedrooms. Every step felt like one closer to his execution. His gut twisted in tight knots, strangling his stomach into something painful. His palms began to sweat.

Oh, hell. The house seemed still, but what if they were having sex? Or were naked and entangled and had obviously had sex tonight?

You'd better get used to it . . .

He reached the open door to Luc's room, drew in a deep breath, and braced himself for the worst. Instead, he found his cousin sprawled out across his king-sized bed in an obviously restless sleep. *Alone.*

Relief and fear both sucker punched him at the same time. Where was she? His knees buckled, and he tore down the hall toward his room.

Please be there. Please be okay.

Deke rounded the corner and charged into his room. And came to a dead stop.

Wearing some pale-colored tank top that showed the graceful slope of her shoulders, Kimber slept in *his* bed, with her head on his pillow, clutching one of his T-shirts in her hands.

He braced himself against the doorframe and stared at the gentle rise and fall of her chest, visible by the streetlamp's glow slanting through his bedroom window. A million thoughts assailed him at once.

Had she turned Luc's marriage proposal down? Deke had no doubt that his cousin had issued one. Maybe she hadn't answered. Or maybe Luc had given her last night to deal and would ask her today. Yeah, that seemed likely. And maybe Kimber had stuck around just to give him the ass chewing he deserved for getting her pregnant in the first place, then handling it so badly.

Whatever the reason, he didn't deserve her, and he knew it.

How had life gotten so fucked up? No, life wasn't; he was. And that wasn't going to change. It was what it was, and Kimber was better off with Luc. Even if seeing the two of them together was going to kill him.

She whimpered in her sleep. Pushing aside all the reasons he should leave her alone and let Luc take care of her now, Deke stumbled across the room, to the edge of the bed.

A glance at her red nose and the silvery paths down her cheeks told him she'd been crying.

Damn, he'd rather be punched in the stomach for a week by the heavyweight champ than see that.

And despite everything, he wanted nothing more than to crawl up in his bed beside her, tuck her against him, and sleep. Then wake slowly with her, stretching together, kissing, maybe . . .

No. It wasn't going to happen. Unless Luc participated, there was no way Deke could make love to Kimber. Would it make a difference if she was already pregnant? Maybe . . . but he wasn't sure. Maybe the mental crutch of the ménage was just too embedded into his psyche. Even if he could make love to Kimber alone while she was pregnant, what about after the baby was born? She didn't want to be shared anymore, and Deke couldn't picture calling Luc again to join the party.

After last night . . . there wouldn't be any more parties with him and Luc and this luscious woman— or any other. With Kimber, they'd shared their last. He'd come to that conclusion after about his fourth beer. He'd have to find someone else to share with and make sure every woman between them was utterly meaningless. But after Kimber, he didn't think the last part would be a problem. Eventually. The utter disinterest in sex he'd experienced with Alyssa wouldn't happen forever, right?

He was also going to stop being a chickenshit and get a vasectomy. Ensure there'd be no more issues. Ensure he never fucked up another woman's life again.

And he was going to have to move. Leave Tyler, Texas. He couldn't see Luc and Kimber together day after day, year after year. After he ensured that she didn't take the pill-bottle way out of life, leaving was the only way he could deal.

And there was no fucking way he could watch them build a life together.

Even now, when he knew all was well and that he should leave them, he couldn't make himself walk away from her.

Instead, he knelt by the bed. Kimber's sleep-lax hand was right in front of him, and he took it gently so he didn't wake her. But even he felt the desperation in his touch as he brought her fingers closer to his lips and pressed a bittersweet kiss to the back of her hand, trying not to crush her.

God, he loved her. Somehow, even when he'd worked for the Colonel and she'd been seventeen, some part of him had suspected that she'd be his weakness. Now, not only was he going to have to do without her, but know she belonged to a man he regarded as a brother.

And the sad fact was, Kimber was better off without him.

With that harsh realization, emotion rattled in his chest, exploded inside him. Damn, he hated this shit, but he couldn't stop it. The sting of tears attacked his eyes with the subtlety of an ice pick. Then they were falling and wouldn't stop. Deke drew in great big lungfuls of air, trying to get on top of the tears and shove them back inside. But his breath stuttered as he tried to inhale. He closed his eyes as liquid heat poured down his face and he gripped Kimber's hand in his.

What was he going to do without her? Looking back, she'd given him her complete trust, her tart sense of humor, her ability to be tough when necessary and soft when he'd needed it. He loved that feminine way she asserted herself, the way she could make him hard with just a smile.

Deke buried his face in the blankets next to her thigh and let the sobs happen. Quietly. He didn't want to wake her. Didn't want anyone to know. But, oh fuck, he was bawling like a goddamn baby, and he couldn't stop. His life had been one giant screwup. For years, Heather had been top on his list of regrets. Now he could add Kimber. She was going to hurt like hell for years to come, and he had no idea how to make the situation any better.

Except have the most rational discussion they could about the child growing in her belly, then leave her in peace.

Chapter Nineteen

IN Luc's car, Kimber floored her way into Dallas by eight that morning, the same tiny suitcase in hand that she'd left with.

Only now, she had a broken heart.

When she'd awakened shortly before five a.m. alone to find Deke crashed on the sofa in their "man den," Kimber couldn't help but get the picture. After all, she'd been sleeping in his bed, which was big enough for the two of them if they cuddled. Instead, he'd chosen the leather couch at the other end of the house. Kimber didn't need him to draw her a picture; she understood the implication perfectly.

Sniffling as she eased the car from one highway, across the interchange, to another, Kimber turned on the radio and determined to think of the future—without dissolving into tears.

She was going to have a baby. She was going to be a good mother, a nurse, live near her family. Her he-men father and brothers would no doubt hit the ceiling when she eventually announced that she was having a baby and not getting married. They were horribly old-fashioned. But they'd get over it. If they insisted on beating the crap out of someone for knocking her up and not "doing right by her," she'd simply point out that Luc had proposed and she'd refused. They'd have plenty to say about that. The fact Deke was actually the baby's father was none of their business.

As she approached home, she called Logan. She didn't really want to deal with him, but he was the information source about her dad and his release from the hospital, especially since Hunter was still behaving with all the warmth of a glacier.

He answered on the first ring and barked out, "Kimber?"

Lord, spare her caller ID. "Morning."

"Where are you?"

"Nearly back to my apartment."

"Really? You finally found your brain and left the tag-teaming two-some in Tyler?"

No, she'd finally gotten in over her head and ruined the lives of two perfectly wonderful men, one of whom she'd never get over. "It's over. By my choice. Let's leave it there."

She'd tell him about the baby later. When she was stronger. When Dad was better. When they weren't on the phone. And not until she was absolutely ready to face them all.

"Glad to hear it."

His tone intimated that she'd finally done the right thing and hadn't it been obvious. *No.* She felt wretched, and Logan's attitude stomped all over her last nerve.

"Why? What did you have against them?"

"You're kidding me, right? You, of all people, should know exactly why I wouldn't want those kinky bastards anywhere near my sister. I want to throw up every time I think about the things they probably did to you—simultaneously, no doubt. The same things they've done to dozens of other—"

"Kinky?" Oh, Logan always knew the perfect way to hop up her temper, and she shouldn't take the bait but . . . "That's rich coming from you. Do you have to whip a woman and cause her pain to feel man enough to have sex with her?"

"Fuck," he snarled. "No. That's low, damn it! And it has nothing to do with"—he took a deep breath—"We're off topic. You left them and you aren't going back?"

Kimber felt more like arguing, but figured that hitting his sex life was every bit as low as him hitting hers. In both cases, it was uncalled for. The realization deflated her. In the wake of her anger, she didn't feel anything but crushed and damn tired.

"Right."

She parked the car and collected her mail from its overstuffed box.

"Sorry," Logan finally muttered. "I know you're an adult. Deke and Luc were your mistakes to make. I'll try to stop being a prick."

"Thanks. I'm sorry, too. How's Dad? When is he coming home from the hospital?" she asked as she let herself into her apartment. It was stuffy and had that closed-in smell. Though the morning was muggy, she opened a few windows for air.

"It's looking like tomorrow. We'll get some more test results back today, which will give the doctors a clearer picture of his condition." He paused. "Dad would appreciate a visit."

"Now that the assbite who set the bomb is locked up and off the streets, I'm free to see him."

"I don't know how much longer they're going to be able to hold Ronald Fusco Jr. That's his name. Dad helped send him to the big house about ten years ago. Ronny keeps saying he didn't set the bomb. There's no physical evidence tying him to it. There *is* a shitload of evidence to support the fact he was harassing Dad, but nothing more concrete."

Alarm jumped under Kimber's skin. "Do the police still think he set the bomb?"

"Depends on who you talk to. Besides, doesn't matter what they think, only what the DA can prove. Right now, they don't even have enough evidence to get an indictment, much less go to trial. The guy might walk."

"Damn it . . . What do you think? Is he guilty?"

"Could go either way. But my gut . . . he didn't set the bomb."

"So we could still have a psycho out there after Dad?"

"Or after you. While you were in the swamp, we got a couple of phone calls on Dad's cell, some guy asking where you were and how to find you. He always used private, untraceable numbers and never talked long. I never knew if he was a reporter or a criminal."

She frowned. Surely, he was overreacting. It had to be the press trying to get ahold of her and bite into the big juicy story of her and Jesse's busted relationship, which seemed like a lifetime ago now. . . . She'd assumed all the unavailable numbers and mute voice mails on her cell phone were all members of the press, too.

"I haven't made any enemies."

"That you know of."

True. Kimber sighed. But unlikely. Had to be the pesky press not knowing when to leave a story alone. "Go with me to the hospital later today, just in case?"

"Yeah. Let me know what time. Could I . . ." He hesitated. "I gotta ask, are you okay? You sound like shit."

She felt like it, too.

"I'm tired. The last two days have been really tough. I need a little space and rest. I'll be fine." She hoped.

"Okay." Logan didn't sound like he believed her in the least, and she didn't care. "Call me later."

"Will do."

After she disconnected the call, Kimber sorted through her mail. A lot of junk. A few bills she needed to pay. Later today, she'd call the manager of the restaurant where she'd been waitressing during nursing school and sweet-talk her way back into her job so she could pay said bills. Right now, she couldn't face the future.

Another envelope caught her attention. From the State of Texas. Her NCLEX results. God, could she take another shock if she hadn't passed her nursing exams?

Trembling, she tore into the envelope and scanned the page. Relief hit her. She'd passed easily. Kimber exhaled. Whew! All her hard work had paid off, and she had one less thing to worry about. Now, she and her baby would be assured a secure financial future. No doubt her family and Luc would all want to help. She'd rather not be beholden to any of them if she didn't have to. And after Deke's reaction . . . she assumed he'd rather pretend she didn't exist.

The very thought made tears threaten again, but she refused to let them flow. One day at a time. Today was about righting her apartment and her family interaction—and putting the past behind her.

Kimber exited her apartment again, into the humid July morning.
As she was pulling her suitcase out of Luc's car and trying to decide how
best to return the vehicle to him, her phone rang.

She looked at the caller ID and groaned. But if today was about putting her past behind her, that meant she had to take care of this, too.

"Hi, Jesse," she greeted as she dragged her suitcase across the hot
asphalt.

"Just hi? I've been worried out of my mind! Who was the caveman
that threatened me and called you his woman? And what did he mean?"

Never mind that she'd been crying hysterically last night and was
obviously upset about something. Had she ever really believed herself
in love with him? Such stupid, girlish fantasies, borne of painting her
memories of him with rosy brushstrokes and her complete inexperience
with the opposite sex.

Deke had been right about that.

"Just . . . no one who's going to bother you again."

"He sounded like a fucking barbarian. I was just trying to talk to
you, and the guy sounded like he would have reached through the phone
to strangle me if he could have."

That was probably accurate, but no need to freak Jesse out more.

"Did you need something?"

"I went up to Oklahoma City and St. Louis, put on shows, gave
interviews—"

"In which you said we're still getting married. What the hell are you
thinking?"

"Don't be angry, babe. I'm back in town for a few days. Can—can
we meet somewhere for lunch? Quietly. I need to talk to you. Please.
You're like the lone voice of sanity in my crazed life."

"Jesse, you're the only one who has control over your crazed life,
not me."

"See, I'm not sure that's true. I just . . . Please."

Kimber wanted to refuse him and knew she should. But given last
night's call and this early morning conversation, she didn't think he was
going to get the picture over the phone.

She sighed. "One o'clock."

"Great. Thanks!"

She rattled off the name of a hole-in-the-wall deli with a great little patio. It would be hot out there, but they'd be alone. And she could finally end this chapter of her life.

* * *

DEKE nursed a cup of coffee and a hangover when Luc came barreling into the kitchen.

"Where is she?"

He took a sip from his cup, ingesting the bitter brew. "Gone. She took your car."

"Damn! She said she was leaving, but I thought she'd at least say good-bye."

"You want to tell me why she left? Why she spent last night in my bed, instead of yours?"

Luc shot him an incredulous stare. "You really are one screwed-up bastard. Would you rather that I'd spent all night beside and inside the woman you love?"

God no. He was fighting between the rational part of him that knew pairing her with Luc would be best for them both and the emotional beast lurking within him that wanted to kill any man who laid a finger on her ever again.

"I may as well get used to it now." He smiled cynically.

"Don't bother. Kimber won't marry me."

Deke flinched. Clearly, Luc had proposed. And the pain of losing the right to be her baby's father was all over his face.

What a horrible fucking mess. But Deke couldn't bring himself to tell Luc that he was sorry Kimber had refused him. He was surprised, though. She seemed too practical to turn down a catch like Luc and raise a baby alone. God knew he was too much of a head case to help.

"She loves you, man. She'd rather be alone than be with anyone else," Luc said.

How damn tragic was that? Deke shook his head.

"So it's all up to you."

Deke blinked and looked at his cousin as if he'd lost his mind. "Up to me to do what? I think I've done plenty here, and none of it good. If I do any more, things are likely to go from fucked up to catastrophic."

Luc set his cup of coffee aside and yanked Deke from his chair, to his feet.

"What the hell are you doing?" Deke demanded.

"Resisting the urge to beat the hell out of you. Barely."

"Bring it on," Deke snarled, itching for a fight. Anything to take his mind off this shit.

"And give you what you want? No. I'm going to screw your head back on straight. You are not going to leave Kimber alone and pregnant when you could make—"

"Could make what? Love to her? Not without you or some other chump there. I know my boundaries, and she deserves more than I can give her. She'll get smart and eventually accept your offer."

"You better hope to God she doesn't because I'll break land-speed records to run her to the nearest Justice of the Peace." He frowned. "If you don't want that to happen, fix it."

From that, Deke wondered if Luc would keep pursuing Kimber until he wore her down. He could be damn persistent.

"What the hell are you saying?"

Luc grabbed him by the shirt. "Get over your shit. Is that plain enough for you?"

"My shit?" He jerked away. "I'm just supposed to forget that I caused the death of a sixteen-year-old girl? Poof. Just put the guilt out of my mind and everything is hunky-dory again? Let's throw a fucking party."

"After twelve years—"

"After twelve years, Heather is still dead and it's still my fault."

"Goddamn it, it isn't!" Luc growled. "I'm not going to win Kimber, but you still can. And you belong with her. She can heal you. You just have to face some realities about Heather and your involvement in her death."

"I know the realities," he said through clenched teeth.

"You know the crap her family fed you. You swallowed it whole. But think about it. About her. She was messed up. Getting pregnant was just one of her issues."

He shrugged. "So she had problems. Who doesn't? But being pregnant was the biggest problem."

"Wise up. What about her drug use? Or the fact her parents were divorcing? Wasn't she failing school? Two days before she swallowed that bottle of pills, she'd failed her driver's test, right?"

"She wasn't a drug addict. Her parents didn't end up splitting. She could have turned school around, and retaken her driver's test."

"She could have ended the pregnancy, too. It wasn't like she hadn't already told her parents. They'd offered to pay for an abortion. She didn't kill herself because she didn't want her parents to know you'd had sex. And she didn't do it because she felt she had no other options."

"You don't understand how Heather was."

"Yeah, I do," Luc shouted. "The girl craved attention. I'm sorry she's dead. It's terrible and tragic. But she didn't want to untangle her life. She was determined to punish everyone for not loving her the way she wanted to be loved. Her sister was a bitch to her. Her dad never had time for her. Her mom took so many antidepressants, I wonder if she even knew Heather's name anymore. If you look in the dictionary under *dysfunctional family*, their picture should appear."

"Yeah . . ." Deke sighed. "But being pregnant sent her over the edge."

"No. What put her over the edge is anyone's guess. She'd known about the pregnancy longer than her parents' divorce, school, or the driver's test. Any of those things—or none of them—could be the final reason she committed suicide. She was a volatile, immature girl. You can't keep being her martyr. You didn't force the bottle of pills down her throat."

That was true. If he'd been there, he would have stopped her. Somehow. But from all accounts, she'd been distraught about the pregnancy and determined to end it all.

"Your biggest part in this was an unfortunate condom and the way you behaved after she told you the news. It wasn't as bad as the way you treated Kimber . . . but close."

Deke froze. "What are you saying?"

"You reacted with fear and fury. You rejected her. Not the way a woman wants a man to behave when she says she's going to have his child. If you're worried about Kimber . . . leaving her to another man or to face this alone isn't the way to ensure her emotional health."

Put like that . . . no shit. There was a big, heaping pile of reality.

"But more than that," Luc went on, "are you really going to walk away from the woman you love and your baby because of a death you didn't really cause over a decade ago?"

God, Luc made it all sound so simple, like he'd just been one tiny part of Heather's messed-up life, but not the whole reason. Deke sat at the table again, grabbed his coffee, and stared into the black liquid swirling in his cup. Was it that simple? Years had gone by. Who knew? Not him; he'd resisted thinking about it too much.

He'd never seen her suicide note, just believed the crap he'd heard. Heather's mom had been the kind of woman who would have shifted blame to someone else so she didn't have to look too hard in the mirror. Heather's twin, Haley, had been a carbon copy of her mother. Maybe . . . what Luc was saying had *some* merit.

At the very least, the last twelve hours had proven how much Kimber was unlike Heather. After discovering she was pregnant and he'd handled the news badly, Heather had gone on an all-night bender, gotten shit-faced drunk, and slept with one of his best friends to spite him—then made sure he found out to punish him. Kimber had refused Luc's marriage proposal, cried herself to sleep in his bed, then quietly packed her bag and left. She was a lot more . . . together and practical. She simply went on with the business of living and rolled with the punches.

But knowing that still didn't solve his problem. Even if he could just swallow all the guilt, that wasn't going to make him normal. What if he couldn't make love to Kimber, one-on-one, like a typical man?

But he owed her conversation, assurances that he'd be a father and a friend and provide anything she needed financially. In time, she'd find a great guy. Deke winced at the thought and shoved it away. Okay, one day at a time for him, too. Until she made him face the reality of another man in her life, he'd probably pine for her, think of her as his.

And wish he was a better man who deserved her.

"Why are you trying to make everything better between Kimber and me?" Deke turned his attention back to his cousin. "To make up for manipulating us? To get closer to the baby?"

Luc closed his eyes. "I deserved that. I . . . influenced you both to get what I want. I thought it was in everyone's best interest, not just mine. Now, I'm trying to talk some sense into you purely for your own good. Like you said a few days ago, I regard you as a brother. You should be happy. You deserve it after all this time and shit."

Deke swallowed. That was probably the nicest thing Luc could have said to him in that moment. He wanted to believe it. He almost did . . .

"Thanks."

* * *

AT one o'clock, Kimber sat on the patio of her favorite deli. The area was shaded by live oak trees and bordered a quiet side street, which would help with privacy. She plucked at the tank top wilting against her skin, hoping that the heat would ensure that if they were gawked at, it would be purely through windows in the deli's cool interior.

Ten minutes later, Jesse pushed his way out the door and onto the patio. He turned and waved. Kimber frowned, until she saw a scowling Cal through one of the windows.

"He insisted on being around, in case a crowd follows. He'll stay inside, though. This lunch is just for us. Damn, it's hot!" Jesse stripped off his checked collared shirt, which he'd worn over a wife-beater tee that shouted "Life Sucks" in bright blue letters and enough bling to blind her. He didn't remove his sunglasses.

Kimber sighed, then spotted the waitress coming their way with two glasses of water. "Everything here is good."

The young woman in low-rise shorts pretended not to recognize Jesse while she took their order, but the way her body tensed with excitement and her eyes kept cutting in his direction . . . it was obvious.

"A turkey sandwich with sprouts and double cheddar on a baguette and a cola. Sure, Mr. McCall." Her voice was high and thin with thrill.

Trying not to roll her eyes, Kimber ordered egg salad on wheat and a side of fruit. Then, reluctantly, the waitress left them in peace.

After a long pause, Jesse took a sip of water, then fingered the condensation on the exterior of the glass. "Thanks for agreeing to see me."

"This is the last time until you accept the fact we're not getting married. What possessed you to make that announcement without asking me first?"

"I just thought . . . we'd talked about it before. You're a good influence, and I don't like where my life is going."

"Then *you* change it," Kimber suggested. "I can't do it for you."

He looked at her over the tops of his sunglasses. Wounded, bloodshot eyes pleaded as he took her hands in his. "You can help me. I'm stronger with you. You make me want to be a better person."

"You have to want to be a better person for yourself. Not having me around is just an excuse not to change your life. If you really want to clean up your act, fire Ryan. He's trying hard to make sure your life is every bit as screwed up as his. Stop the parties. Start listening to Cal. He might be gruff and dour, but he's trying to prevent you from self-destructing." While perpetuating Jesse's bad-boy reputation, which would sell lots of CDs and iTunes downloads, but that was another story . . .

"I'll do it," he vowed. "See, you're smart. With you, I can handle things."

"You can also handle them alone. You have to."

He tore off his sunglasses to reveal a tired, crestfallen face. "I don't blame you for not wanting to help me. I behaved like a shit when you toured with me. I shouldn't have fucked the blonde with Ryan. And the video . . . God, I felt so stupid. I'm sorry. Really. It's just . . . being near you made me crazy, but I didn't want to touch you. Every time I thought about it or tried, I felt like . . . a child molester or something. Like I was going to ruin you, and you're too innocent—"

"I'm not. Not anymore."

Jesse froze. "The asshole on the phone, you gave him your virginity?"

"I fell in love with him, Jesse. I was in love with him before I came on tour with you. He did his best to push me away—"

"Sounds to me like he pushed his way between your legs," he growled. "And where is he now?"

Kimber sighed. "Sometimes, things just don't work out. Like with us."

"Don't say that. Come with me. We'll take care of each other."

"No. You'll be fine without me. Just think smart. Do what you know in your heart is right. You got sucked into too much fame and money too young. What would your parents have wanted you to do? What do you want to be able to tell your children about this part of your life? Certainly not that you saw people snorting coke and having group sex in your hotel room. Or that you and one of your bandmates had anal sex with a total stranger. Do things you'd be proud of."

"You're really not going to change your mind, are you?"

She shook her head. "I'm always available by phone or e-mail. When you come through town, we'll meet like old friends. I'll always care."

Looking sad, like someone had shot his dog, Jesse stood and made his way around the table, plucked her from her seat, and drew her into his arms. "You're a special woman."

Kimber smiled. Jesse covered it softly with his mouth. A kiss of friendship. Of good-bye.

Suddenly, an electronic *whirr* crashed into the quiet. Footsteps—lots of them. Another electronic *whirr*. A flashbulb. Squealing girls.

Pulling away, Kimber blinked, stunned to find she and Jesse surrounded. A handful of photographers frantically snapped pictures. Young women looking barely legal jumped up and down, several proving themselves braless, as they stared at Jesse in worship.

"Can I have your autograph?" one asked.

"What are you doing here?" the waitress asked, horrified. "It's supposed to be a secret!"

"I had to see him!" protested the fan with the autograph book.

"Are you really going to marry *her*?" Another female fan looked at Kimber with disdain.

Neither one answered.

The photographers kept taking shots of Jesse as he autographed the girl's book and handed it back to her with a smile as phony as the huge gold loops dangling from her ears.

"Could you leave us alone?" Jesse said to the press. "We're trying to have lunch here."

"Answer the girl's question," shouted one reporter. "Are you marrying Ms. Edgington?"

"I'm so sorry," the waitress babbled.

Jesse ignored her and scowled at the photographers. "You've had your pictures. There's no story. Get the hell away from us."

"Public property," one quipped, then captured the shot of anger mutating Jesse's face.

As if to underscore the point, more people wandered down the side street to investigate the growing crowd. The number of passersby swelled. The sound became a cacophony of voices and cameras. A van stopped a few feet away. One of the local news stations. *Great. How did they receive word so quickly?*

Someone reached out to grab the shirt Jesse had draped across the back of his chair. She yelped with excitement and sniffed it. Actually held it to her nose and inhaled. Kimber could barely pick her jaw off the floor as Jesse reached out to grab it back, but she darted through the crowd. Other girls chased her, grabbing at the shirt, too.

Holy cow, how does he put up with this everywhere he goes?

Cal appeared beside Jesse and murmured, "The crowd is only getting bigger. I think you should go."

"How did they find out I was here?"

Cal shrugged. "Probably the waitress. Doesn't matter. This is going to get out of hand if you don't leave now. You take the car back to the hotel. I'll make sure Kimber gets home safely."

Jesse looked pissed, as if he was being forced into a position he didn't want and impotent to do anything else.

"It's fine. It's for the best." She touched his arm in reassurance.

More cameras clicked, capturing the moment.

"Are you going to marry Ms. Edgington?" the pushy reporter asked again. "And what do you say about the entertainment industry's prediction that marriage would ruin your career?"

"If he gets married, I'm not buying any more CDs," one bitchy fan snapped.

"Knowing he's tied himself to some other woman kills the fantasy," Kimber overheard another girl telling the reporter.

He ignored everyone and looked at Kimber with regret. "You going to be okay?"

"You heard Cal. He'll follow me to make sure I reach home safely. You get out of here before this turns into a bigger circus. Call me when you're free and we'll talk."

He sighed with acceptance, then whispered into her ear, "I really do love you."

In his one-sided way, she believed he did. But now it was time for him to stand on his own two feet, just like she'd have to do. "Take care."

Jesse kissed her cheek, and Kimber did her best to ignore the clicking of cameras. Yikes, this was likely to be all over the front page. If it was . . . could it really hurt his image, his career? If so, that was yet another reason he'd be better off without a wife right now.

As he turned away, Kimber watched. He jumped the little fence and darted for his car. The horde followed him, cameras bobbing, girls screaming.

An eerie quiet settled over her and Cal in his wake.

"That's crazy," she said as the last of the mass disappeared down the street.

"That's showbiz."

"Would people really stop being his fans if we married?" The whole idea seemed inconceivable to her. They either liked his music or they didn't, at least in her mind.

"You heard it yourself. Most of his fans are women who see Jesse as the ultimate catch. If you've already caught him, they're out in the cold. You ready to go home?" Cal asked.

"Sure."

"I'll follow you, just to make sure no one else does."

Emotionless. Expressionless. Cal was all business, all the time. Right now Jesse needed that. Kimber just hoped that he'd listen.

As they turned toward the parking lot, a sleek, black Maserati Spyder convertible zoomed past them, tires screeching as it turned out onto the main drag. Then Jesse was gone. Probably forever, and she could live with that. They each had their own lives ahead of them. And his would be what he chose to make of it.

Chapter Twenty

KIMBER curled up on her bed in the fetal position, her pillow bunched beneath her head, and tried to drift back to sleep. No luck—and no wonder. Her life could make a soap opera look tame these days. *Love triangle, check. Surprise pregnancy, check. Possible psycho-stalker, check.* Gosh, throw in a good catfight or aliens from outer space and she could rival any daytime diva's dilemmas.

Lack of sleep, no surprise there. True, she'd been tired most of the day, a symptom of pregnancy, she'd heard. She sighed. In a few days, she'd see the doctor, have them confirm everything, give her a due date, explain what would happen over the next nine months. Then she'd have to tell her family. Kimber cringed at the thought of Logan's and Hunter's reactions.

Turning over, she punched her pillow, wrestled it under her a bit more. Why wasn't this position any more comfortable than—

Tap, tap, tap. Pause. *Whoosh.*

What the hell was that? Those noises were totally foreign, and seemed to be coming from her living room. Yes, it was her first night back at her apartment, but Kimber had lived here long enough to recognize the usual sounds. None of those fit that category.

The people above her had kids who usually ran around until close to eleven. The newlyweds next to her had sex every night—at least once—and she could hear their bed banging against the wall every time. But this sound . . . It was subtle. Like someone trying to be quiet.

In fact, it sounded a whole lot like someone forcing one of her windows open.

Easing out of bed, Kimber got to her feet, nervously grabbing her cell phone off her nightstand with a damp palm and smoothing her tank top over her jumpy stomach with the other. She approached the hall, intending to investigate the odd noise when she heard footsteps on her hardwood floors. Soft footsteps, like someone creeping slowly. There was no mistaking the sound.

On bare feet, she whirled and darted into her closet and eased the door shut. Then she dialed 911 and whispered her address quickly. The operator wanted her to stay on the line and wait for the police.

The ever-closer footsteps let her know that waiting around for the cavalry wasn't an option. She was going to have to defend herself.

Suddenly, she was damn glad for every self-defense skill her brothers had insisted she master, every time they'd roped her into being their martial arts sparring partner, and every male endurance/fighting/general toughness contest they had put her through.

The footsteps entered her bedroom, paused, wandered around, then headed to the closet.

As Kimber braced herself against the wall behind her walk-in closet's door, her hand came into contact with something solid, wooden. She smiled. And she was damn glad that she'd been on the apartment complex's co-ed softball team.

Wasn't this shithead in for a surprise?

* * *

DEKE'S palms had sweated for the entire one hundred miles into Dallas.

Nearly twenty-four hours after Kimber had dropped her bombshell, he was ready to talk to her. No, he *had* to talk to her. So he'd driven west, into the thick, inky night, with his insides jolting like he was hooked up to jumper cables.

Luc had spoken a lot of truths. A dozen years ago, Deke had been guilty of many things. Having sex with an emotionally unstable girl. Thinking with the wrong head. Letting the abundance of Heather's emotions—and her family's—drown out his logic.

What he hadn't done, as his cousin and Kimber had pointed out, was force Heather to swallow the pills. A hard fact to accept, but the truth. She'd chosen that path herself . . . for reasons he'd probably never understand, but weren't all related to the pregnancy.

Facing his grief again had brought Deke right to the source of his guilt—and he was finally seasoned enough to understand where he'd most fucked up with Heather. He'd let her go before he knew what could have been between them. He'd been seventeen and terrified by her pregnancy, then furious that she'd fucked someone else to spite him. They hadn't spoken for nearly three weeks . . . then she'd ended everything permanently, leaving him with nothing but questions and gut-wrenching remorse.

Had he loved Heather? Maybe he'd been too young to know what love was, but he hadn't been ready for their bond to be broken, especially by Heather's suicide. In retrospect, what he'd been most guilty of was being too stupid and scared to fight for what might have been.

He was *not* making that mistake with Kimber, especially since he *knew* he loved her.

If she wanted to end their relationship, the choice would be hers.

Unfortunately, Deke had no illusions; he'd behaved like a deranged moron after Kimber had announced her pregnancy. Like Luc had said . . . he'd treated her worse than he'd treated Heather. The revelation of his cousin's secret hadn't contributed to his overall good mood or mental health, either. But now that he'd had time to process all the shocks and talk himself off the emotional ledge, it was time to make things different. Or at least try in his way.

Looking up Kimber's address on the Internet had been too easy. He'd have to talk to her about protecting her personal information a little better. Later.

He cruised the apartment complex's parking lot, trying to find her building in the dark. It wasn't well marked, damn it. Deke frowned as he glanced around. The units were far apart, with a park-like area in the middle. A lot of trees all around. Lots of dark, shadowed corners. No guard gates around the place.

Why was it that women, the more vulnerable sex to attack, never thought about security before they settled into a place to live?

Maybe after tonight, she'd leave here and go with him, so the lack of safety measures here wouldn't be an issue. Yeah, he could handle that. Hell, he craved it.

First, he had to find out if she'd have anything to do with him.

He spotted Kimber's building toward the back of the complex, butting up against an empty field and surrounded by big trees casting shadows under the moonlight. She had a ground-floor unit. And on his first pass by her apartment, he could see that her window was wide open.

With a ripe curse, he parked his Hummer, wondering why the fuck she hadn't just locked up tight and turned on the air-conditioning. Why had Logan and Hunter let her move in to such a hard-to-defend place? Why hadn't her brothers lectured her within an inch of her life about the fact that a single woman leaving doors unlocked and windows wide open was a fucking engraved invitation to violent sickos who looked at rape and torture as entertainment?

Locking the vehicle behind him, Deke jogged to her door and knocked. And waited in the still night barely broken by crickets chirping.

Nothing.

He frowned. Maybe she was fast asleep. Or maybe she wasn't here. *Ever think about that, asshole?*

He'd heard on the radio today that she'd been spotted at a cozy little deli having lunch with the prick with the falsetto pipes. Was Kimber having feelings for Jesse again? Deke could hardly blame her after the way he'd treated her, but God, the thought made him want to throw up.

He whipped out his cell phone and called her. No answer. She had caller ID, so she was avoiding him. Had to be.

Deke wanted to beat the fucking phone against her door. Frustration boiled inside him, shooting upward like some science experiment coiling up a test tube and about to blow. But he wasn't giving up. It was hotter than hell tonight, looked like it might rain. But that meant shit. He'd camp on her front door step all night—days, if necessary—until she came home.

Deke's shoulders sagged. He couldn't pretend that knowing she didn't want to talk to him didn't hurt. And if he didn't stop walking this mental territory again, he'd start bawling like a baby. Again. He wanted to be a man when he faced her, so he could look her in the eye and promise he'd do everything he could to be the man for her.

But could he be the man she needed? Self-doubt lashed him like a vicious whip.

Pressing his forehead to her door, Deke resisted wrestling with his inner demons, but the fuckers just kept coming after his hope. Fisting his hands against the door, he wished she was here, that he could hold her. He loved her so much . . . Her no-nonsense approach. Her quick wit. That surprising naughty streak. The way she rolled with the punches and handled life with aplomb. Her ease with her emotions, the times she'd shared them so totally when he'd been with her . . . inside her. God, let her come back to him.

A sound—a grunt?—ripped through his thoughts. Faint, but . . . out of place. A man's grunt coming from Kimber's place.

He frowned and drifted over to the window. Another sound he couldn't place. A crash, like something hitting the wall.

What the fuck? Anxiety clawed at his gut. Was she . . . spread out under some other man, maybe Jesse, in her bed? No. He would not believe—No, not Kimber. She wasn't Heather.

But Deke still didn't know what the noises were. He only knew they were out of place.

Crawling inside the window, Deke withdrew his SIG SAUER from his shoulder holster, just in case. He crept around the sofa, past the galley kitchen, then down the hall, gun in the lead. He fought the urge to charge like a bull. Slowly, carefully, until he knew what the fuck was going on.

A high-pitched scream ripped through the night, stabbing up his spine. *Kimber!* Fuck, careful.

Charging down the hall to the source of the sound, he reached her bedroom. Dark, empty. Bed mussed. *Shit.*

The sounds of a struggle through the bathroom made him whip his head around. It was coming from behind the closed door inside the bathroom. The closet?

If the son of a bitch had harmed a hair on Kimber's head, he'd be eating for the rest of his life through a straw—after just the first punch. If Deke got in a second one . . . the fucker would have no need for a straw—or food—period.

Creeping toward the closed door, Deke tried to listen. He didn't want to endanger Kimber by jumping in like an idiot.

"Put the baseball bat down," growled the man. "I don't want to cause you pain."

Whoosh. Thud. Grunt.

"Bitch! That hurt."

Kimber had nailed him. Good. The bastard wasn't at his best, and she was still alive. All good news. Deke knew he might not ultimately win her, but he could goddamn save her.

Suddenly, Kimber cried out.

"Damn you, die like a good girl."

"No!" Her terror dripped down the walls and slashed at Deke's gut.

Deke uncorked the bottle of his emotions—the fear, guilt, frustration, rage—and let them fly as he blasted the door to the closet aside and rocketed into the room. It was damn dark in the little closet, but he saw the outline of Kimber's body going down, the sick thud of her head striking the wall. Blood gushed down her front.

Oh, no. Hell no! God . . .

Pushing panic away for fury, Deke whirled, grabbed the intruder by the neck, and pushed him against the wall. The glint of metal arcing in his direction caught his attention. He swerved his torso out of the way and tightened his fingers around the man's throat. With the other hand, he pointed his gun right in the asshole's forehead.

"Toss the knife to my feet."

The intruder hesitated. Deke could hear his harsh gasps, smell his fear, feel his trembling. It wasn't enough. He wanted to see the bastard bleed, writhe in pain, twist under his fingers as he begged for mercy.

Welcome to your inner caveman.

Shoving the thought away, Deke sent the man a lethal glare. "I don't need much of a reason to blow your head open, motherfucker. Drop the knife."

Hesitation, indecision. Deke inched the gun forward, pressed his palm into the asshole's windpipe. Still, he didn't cooperate.

And Deke had no idea if Kimber's life was bleeding out onto the closet floor at this very moment.

"I'm done jacking with you." Deke's finger tightened on the trigger.

The intruder finally sensed that Deke meant business and tossed the knife down. It landed at the toe of Deke's left boot.

Stepping on it so it couldn't come back into play, Deke tried to come down off his aggression high. Kimber needed him now.

Deke pointed to the farthest corner of the closet. "Sit here on your hands. Don't move. If you even twitch, you and my friend SIG SAUER are going to get to know each other real well, you got me?"

Under Deke's palm, the man swallowed. Then nodded.

Resisting the urge to crush his windpipe for the hell of it, Deke backed away, aimed his gun at the assailant, and watched as his shadow went to the wall and sank to the floor. Without looking away, Deke tucked the knife away and flipped on a light.

Mr. Intruder was wearing a ski mask. How TV show of him.

But that was the only thought he could spare as he sank to his knees in front of Kimber, searching for the source of her blood with one hand, training the gun on the asshole with the other.

Oh, damn. Oh, God . . . Let her live.

The panic rose in him again. He slammed the lid on it brutally. Logic. *Think. Suck it up and be smart.*

Deke looked her over quickly. Kimber was out cold, but her heart was beating at a steady pace. She breathed. There was a cut in her forearm. Deep. Would need stitches ASAP. He pulled a shirt off a nearby hanger and applied pressure to the wound. It had likely come from the intruder's knife. Probably from putting her arm in front of her to defend herself. And he could only imagine the terror she must have been feeling watching that knife come at her . . .

He speared the intruder with a stare of cold fury. "If she dies, you die. You got me?"

The head under the ski mask gave a shaky bob.

He couldn't find any other stab wounds on her. But panic rose. Why the hell was she unconscious? She'd hit her head on the way down. How badly?

Deke flipped open his phone and called 911. He gave them Kimber's address.

"Police units are already in progress to that location, sir. About two minutes away."

Kimber had called. Smart girl, his kitten. *Hang on, baby.*

"I need an ambulance, too. She's unconscious." Then he hung up.

"Did you drug her?"

"No," the voice cracked.

"Rape her?"

"No."

"But you wanted to kill her, you sick fuck," he growled. "Take off the mask."

The guy hesitated, and Deke raised the SIG. "Now!"

Off it came . . . and Deke could only stare. "What the . . . ? You're at least fifty-five." Wasn't he a little old for the thrill of home intrusions?

He cleared his throat. "Sixty-two."

"You get off on hurting women, Gramps?" The thought made him want to retch, then strangle the vile son of a bitch.

"No. Nothing personal. I didn't want to cause her pain. I just wanted her out of the way."

His hand on the gun tightened. "Out of the way of what?"

Silence.

"You better fucking answer!" Deke shouted. "I'm at the end of my patience—"

"Of Jesse McCall's career. She'd tried to end it a few times, and he wasn't taking no for an answer. He's been all over the press . . . He's self-destructing. Imploding. He's going to destroy his career and everyone who's invested in him for this woman."

An old guy focused on Jesse. Given everything Kimber had told him and Luc about Jesse's situation, this had to be the manager. What was his name . . . Cal?

"I'm too old to start over again." The man's voice trembled.

The old guy was whacked. Stupid to think that killing Kimber was going to solve his problems. If Deke didn't get the cops over here soon, he didn't know if he could hold his fury and itch for vengeance long enough for the police to need anything but a body bag for the scum. Even if he managed, the old guy would be starting life over inside a cell.

"Keep talking," he told the old man. "Cal, isn't it?"

"Yes," the old man said cautiously.

"What do you mean, start over again?"

He hesitated. "I'd better not say anymore without my lawyers."

* * *

WITHIN three minutes, pandemonium erupted in the apartment. Police units stormed the place. Deke led the suspect out by his nape and prodded him forward with the barrel of his gun. After the police verified Deke's credentials, they were cool. And he turned all his attention to the EMTs working on Kimber.

He detailed the cut on her arm calmly. "Why the hell is she still unconscious?"

"You family?"

Oh, this shit. "I'm her . . ." *Boyfriend? Fiancé? Father of her child?* "She's mine."

"Your wife?"

"Not . . . yet."

"Sorry. No information given out to nonfamily members," said one as they carried her out on a stretcher.

Deke couldn't resist touching her face, her shoulder, as they passed. He followed them out to the ambulance. "Let me ride with her."

"I'm sorry, sir. Family only."

Fuck family only! "Where are you taking her? And don't tell me family only. I can get her family there."

The EMT rattled off the name of a hospital. Deke didn't know where it was, but he'd find it.

"I'm following you."

"If you can keep up."

Deke resisted the urge to snort. He'd crawl naked across broken glass to make sure Kimber was okay. Driving fast was nothing.

He watched as they shut Kimber away in the ambulance. Through the small windows in the back doors, he could see they were working on her, stabilizing her. She'd lost a lot of blood. She still hadn't come to.

Someone fired up the engine on the ambulance, and Deke scrambled to the Hummer, leaping into the driver's seat and hauling ass across the parking lot to track with the ambulance down the lonely street, to the hospital . . . and an uncertain prognosis for Kimber.

She hadn't pulled her own trigger the way Heather had, but if Kimber was lost to him, too . . .

Gripping the steering wheel, Deke willed the thought away. *No. Fuck no!* He loved Kimber. Wanted her. Always. Even with the baby. Lots of them if she wanted them. He'd try his best. Anything. Everything.

Just as long as she lived . . .

Chapter Twenty-one

DEKE slung his Hummer into a parking space at the hospital and hauled ass across the parking lot to the emergency room. Damn, his palms were sweating. When would Kimber wake up? How extensive were her injuries? Having no answers balled a roaring frustration in his chest. And fear. Couldn't forget that.

Even at this distance, he could see the EMTs unloading Kimber out of the back of the ambulance . . . and her brothers standing there watching.

He'd called them on the way to advise. Logan lived just a few blocks away, so they'd beat him to the hospital. Hunter's grim eyes tracked Kimber's progress out of the vehicle, through the automatic double doors, and into the hospital's cool interior. Logan looked ready to crawl out of his skin as they followed the gurney.

Deke caught up to the guys, and they nodded absently in greeting.

"Are you the family?" a fiftyish nurse asked them.

Hunter pointed to Logan and himself. "We're her brothers."

She cast a pointed glance at Deke. *Oh shit.* The whole family thing again. Hunter had the power to cut him off at the balls on this one . . .

"He saved her life. He stays."

Deke breathed a sigh of relief.

"Anything I should know about her medical history?"

"No."

"She allergic to anything?"

"Sulfa-based antibiotics."

The nurse jotted that down, then regarded Hunter again with kind blue eyes. "Is she taking any other medications right now?"

Hunter shrugged stiffly, seemingly annoyed with himself. "I don't know."

Deke cleared his throat. "No."

The brothers turned to look at him. They'd always given him a wide berth before but now . . . they looked downright grateful.

Yeah, they were thankful he'd saved their sister from Cal the killer right now, but he doubted their appreciation was going to last.

"Thanks," Hunter murmured.

"History of head trauma or concussions? Seizures? Passing out?"

"No."

"Anything else?"

Deke swallowed, waiting. Both brothers shook their heads.

They didn't know. *Oh, shit . . . Mother humping son of a bitch.*

The nurse started to turn away. Deke reached out to grab her arm. "One other thing." He drew in a deep breath. "She's pregnant."

"You lowlife snake!" Logan lunged at him. "I'm going to rip your eyes out of your skull and force-feed them to you, you bas—"

"Not here. Not now." Hunter grabbed his brother and restrained him—barely.

"No fighting in the hospital. You take that outside," said the salty nurse. Apparently, she'd seen it all in her time.

After another efficient notation on the chart, the reed-thin woman in blue scrubs turned away.

With a huff, Logan backed off. But he still had broiling murder in his eyes. Green and alive with fury, they promised pain. Hunter's, on the other hand, were a glacial blue and vowed revenge—in his time, in his way, to his satisfaction.

Great.

"Is the baby yours or your cousin's?" Hunter asked quietly.

"Or do you even know?" Logan sneered.

"Mine. I'm not going to apologize. I love your sister. I went to her apartment tonight to talk to her. What happens next is up to her, and between us. But you *dare* upset her while she's recovering . . ." *If she recovered*. Deke turned to address Logan. "I'll cut off *your* balls and force-feed them to you. You got that?"

The younger brother bristled and looked ready to keep the verbal war going. A grudging respect entered Hunter's icy stare as he interceded again.

"Thanks to you, she's more likely to live long enough to have that conversation. The rest we'll sort out later, once Kimber is up to it and Dad is out of the hospital."

With a terse nod, Deke turned away and sat in a slightly padded, circa-1977 orange chair with chrome arms. The brothers sat two chairs away. No one spoke for hours.

Logan paced. Hunter sat stock-still, looking eerily placid, but the way his gaze cased the room and lingered on the clock hinted at his inner turmoil. Deke related. Maybe he and Kimber's brothers would never have any sort of lovefest, but he respected them. In their shoes, he'd be pissed about a pregnant sister who'd been in the middle of a ménage. Hunter in particular . . . one cool customer. Faring much better than Deke himself was, in fact.

Deke glanced at his cell phone again, checking the time. *Over three damn hours.* Why hadn't the doctor come out to report? What the hell was going on?

Enough time had passed for Luc to scrounge up a car and haul ass to Dallas from Tyler, he noted as his cousin swept into the waiting room, looking stiff and anxious. And still no word. *What the fuck is taking so long?*

* * *

AT five minutes until nine the next morning, Deke felt ready to climb walls, bash heads in—anything to make all the folks in white let him in to see Kimber.

Near five that morning, the doctors had come out to report that she had awakened. They'd stitched her arm, run a few tests, and were awaiting results. So far, all functions looked normal, and it appeared as if she'd suffered a concussion, bruising, and a mild case of shock.

Logan and Hunter had gone in to visit her about two hours ago, then left to retrieve their father, who was due to be discharged after recovering from his injuries following the bombing. Vaguely, he wondered what the Edgington boys had said to their sister about the fact they were going to be uncles. If they were smart . . . nothing.

Nonfamily members weren't allowed in until nine. Shitty-ass rule. He glared at the clock. Had the fucking thing moved in hours?

"Take a deep breath," Luc murmured. "Calm down."

"What?" Deke shrugged, annoyed. He'd hardly moved. He knew because he'd been using all his self-control to sit still.

"I can feel waves of worry and impatience coming off you. She's fine. Hunter said so on his way out. They're going to release her today."

But he hadn't seen her for himself. He didn't know with his own two eyes that she was all right. Until then, he couldn't stop the worry.

With two minutes to spare, a nurse approached them. Young, cute, blond, with a pink bow mouth, big tits, and a welcoming smile. He wasn't interested. Luc glanced, lingered, then let it go.

"She's up the elevator. Third floor. Room 321. If anyone asks, just tell them Missy said it was okay." She pointed to the nametag just above her left breast.

Subtle. Deke refrained from rolling his eyes, but only because he was already jogging toward the elevator. Luc followed.

The ride up seemed long. If he'd have known the elevator moved slower than a herd of geriatric elephants, he'd have taken the stairs. He clapped his hands in front of him, noticing that Luc didn't look nervous. But he did look troubled.

"Cough it up." Deke didn't want to do this now, but figured—hoped—he'd be too busy with Kimber later.

Luc met his stare. "This is damn awkward. I guess I should just . . . Have you decided to hate me?"

Hate him? "For keeping your . . . um, issue a secret?"

"My sterility," Luc supplied.

"I was shocked that night. Said some things I shouldn't have. You're like my brother. Too much between us for hate."

Looking relieved, Luc reached out for a brotherly handshake, a rap of knuckles. He passed it off as casual, but Deke knew it meant a lot to him. Hell, he felt the same.

"Thanks. For what it's worth, I'm sorry. I never intended to deceive or manipulate anyone. I love you, and I'm sorry I screwed up."

"Apology accepted. And that's about as mushy as it needs to get between us."

Luc did a crappy job of repressing his smile. "Big surprise there. So what's next for you? You're going to get with Kimber, aren't you?"

Deke shrugged, but the uncertainty around that answer gnawed at his gut like a hungry chain saw. He wished to hell he knew the answer. Damn, right now, he just needed to hold her, know that she was all right. "We'll see. What about you? What are you going to do now?"

"I don't know."

"I know your road isn't easy, wanting a baby of your own and being unable . . . Straight up? You're a good guy. You'd make a great father. I'm sorry for you."

Luc let loose a long sigh. "It sucks to be able to fuck for hours, until you're covered in sweat and every muscle in your body screams in protest, until the woman is damn near incoherent . . . and know she'll never be pregnant by you."

Yeah, he could see where that would suck for Luc. "Just my advice, man, but I think you should forget about babies for a while and call Alyssa Devereaux. I suspect you feel more for her than you've wanted to admit. Even if you two will never have little ones together, it'll be a hell of a good time practicing."

"I'll think about it. I owe her a favor for agreeing to hook up with us in the first place."

Finally, the elevator doors opened. Deke racewalked to Kimber's room. He would have flat out run if he was sure they wouldn't throw him out. Impatience at the slower pace, the winding hallways, chafed him.

Deke found her door. He hit the threshold and stopped.

From her bed, Kimber stared out the wide hospital window, through sterile white miniblinds, at the parking lot and sunny summer day beyond. As if suddenly aware she wasn't alone, she turned to face him. *Them,* he realized as Luc stopped just behind him.

A bluish bruise flared across her cheek. A scrape raked her jaw. But what jumped out at Deke most were her swollen eyes and red nose. They shouted the fact she'd been crying.

"Kitten . . ." Deke darted across the room. "Are you in pain? Do I need to find a nurse to get you something?"

Wrapping her arms around her middle, she shook her head and looked at him with eyes so pain-filled and empty.

He sat on the edge of the bed, worked around her IV, and dragged her against him. "Hey, it's fine. All fine. Cal is behind bars. He's not going to hurt you again. I won't let him."

"I know. Thanks for coming to my rescue," she whispered. "Jesse has already called three times to apologize."

Oh, the goddamn pop star. There was a subject guaranteed to send his temper into the stratosphere.

"I hope you told the bastard to leave you alone," he growled.

"He just called to explain why Cal tried to kill me."

"The Lance Bass in leather had to call you to explain that Cal was whacked?"

"He told me that Cal had lost another star about a decade ago to marriage. He couldn't name names, but he said the guy let a promising career fade away so he could play house with his new bride."

"The pansy-ass pop star was making *excuses* for his manager?"

"No, just filling in the gaps."

Deke relaxed. Or tried to. "So . . . what? Cal was going to off you so that Jesse wouldn't be distracted by you anymore, could keep making his silly-ass CDs, and the old guy could rake in all that money?"

"Cal's getting old and apparently felt like he couldn't lose his nest egg." She shrugged. "Even though I'd turned Jesse down, Cal was worried by Jesse's pressroom antics and convinced he wasn't letting go of me, so I guess Cal figured it would be better to eliminate me before Jesse self-destructed."

"That's twisted." Luc shook his head as he walked to the other side of the bed and took her hand. "Hi, sweetheart."

Kimber looked at Luc and fresh tears tracked down her face. She turned her watery gaze to him and started sobbing again.

"Hey, Cal is going to be the senior citizen of the swinging singles' prison scene," Deke joked. "You're not going to cry for him, are you?"

She shook her head. "It's not that. I have to tell you . . . I-I'm not . . . There's no baby."

Shock blindsided Deke. *No baby?* What about all the unprotected sex when the pill wasn't at full strength? What about those damn double blue lines?

Luc sucked in a breath and looked like he'd been punched. Suddenly, Deke knew exactly how he felt.

"I'm sorry . . . I thought—I'd never done a pregnancy test before. I guess it was a false positive. There never was any baby. The doctors told me this morning."

More tears. Endless drops of the hot, salty things making their way down her face. It tore Deke's heart out. "Shh. Don't be sorry. It's fine. All fine."

"No, it's not! I'd grown attached to the idea of having your baby. I *wanted* that baby. I didn't know how much until—until I wasn't having it." She looked at Luc again. "I'm so sorry. You w-wanted this . . ."

Understatement of the century.

Kimber withdrew from Deke and curled her knees up to her chest, wrapping her bandaged and stitched arms around herself. Shutting him out. Shock was still ricocheting through his body. No baby. No . . . nothing. He frowned and glanced at Luc.

Damn, his cousin was fighting tears so hard, he looked ready to shatter with a single touch.

"It's okay, sweetheart. It's not your fault. This . . . curse is mine to bear, and I haven't done it very well. I pushed both you and Deke, hoping . . . Well, you know what I hoped. If anyone should be sorry, it's me. Put me and my problem out of your mind. Focus on being well and happy." Luc kissed the top of Kimber's bowed head.

"You be happy, too." She looked at him with apology swimming in her eyes.

The expression on Luc's face said that wasn't possible. And damn if Deke didn't feel sorry for his cousin all over again. What would it take for him to make peace with himself?

With a reluctant glance at Kimber, Luc slapped him on the shoulder. Then he was gone.

Deke had no idea what to say into the silence. *No baby. Wow.* The breath whooshed out of him. He waited for the relief to come. And waited.

Nothing.

And Kimber wasn't talking. In fact, she was sobbing quietly, given the way her shoulders shook. That tore the blood-pumping guts out of his chest and made him want to beat something and weep himself all at once. He realized she was mourning.

Damn it, something hollow and painful had taken up residence inside him. *Yeah, sadness.* Regret. Sorrow. In a way, he was grieving, too.

He stroked a hand down her back. "Kitten, don't be so upset."

"Don't be upset?" Her incredulity was like a slap. "I'll leave the happy stuff to you. Hey, no baby means you have no more worries now. Go out and have a party."

Fuck that, he started to say, then bit it back. Gentle. Easy. She was hurting.

"Stop. Kitten . . . I'd come to your place last night to tell you I love you. Still love you. I want to be with you. Baby, no baby, that hasn't changed. My head has been screwed up for a long time, and I let Heather's death drag me into a mess of shit. I dragged you into it, too. I can't tell you how damn sorry I am. I still think you can do better, but I'm not going to let the past stand in our way. If you still want me, I want to make it work."

Her head snapped up, and the need in her eyes was like a jagged blade sawing at his heart. God, she was going to tear him up with that stare all stuffed with pain and hope and yearning.

Her shoulders dropped in defeat. "What's the point? I love you, but we don't want the same things."

"What things?"

"I want babies someday."

Deke waited for the panic at that thought to arrive. Instead, he saw a mental image of Kimber round and smiling, glowing, happy. With her, he could handle babies. With her, he would love it.

"I'm up for them. I can't promise that I'll be perfect. Hell, I don't even know if I can . . ." He blew out a breath. Had to be honest. Had to. "I don't know if I can make love to you by myself. But I'll try. And keep trying until it works. You don't want to be shared. I don't want to share you. I just want to love you for as long as you'll let me."

Kimber opened her mouth, and the doctor walked in the room, chart in hand.

He paused, as if he realized he was interrupting something. But with a professional mask in place, he flipped through Kimber's chart, then flashed one of those practiced smiles. "Everything looks in order. All your tests came out just fine. Your concussion was mild. I'm writing you a prescription to help with any headaches you might have. Follow up with me in a week. Other than that, you're free to go. Any questions?"

Kimber shook her head.

"Who will be taking you home?" he asked.

She gulped as fresh tears glassed her eyes. The look on her face . . . God, she'd never been more beautiful.

Sending Deke a radiant smile, Kimber murmured to the doctor, "He is."

*　*　*

THREE days later, after her father had come home from the hospital and settled into Logan's place, after some of the media fervor over Cal's murder attempt had died down, Deke knocked on Kimber's door at exactly seven o'clock, just as she'd asked. He held tissue-wrapped flowers in one hand and tried to keep his goddamn tie from strangling him with the other. But he wanted to look good for her, treat her right. Do his best.

Tonight was going to make or break them.

She opened the door wearing a filmy red top designed to make his eyes bulge. Halter, low cut in the front. A black skirt flirted with her thighs. *Oh, hell.* If he had to look at her over the dinner table wearing that, the meal was going to be sheer torture.

"Hi." Kimber took the flowers from him, stepped back, and invited him in.

Doing his best not to shake like a pansy, Deke stepped inside and shut the door behind him. The table was set with candles, the room piped with subtly sexy music. Something smelled really good. Italian. But when Kimber turned away to find a vase for the flowers, he got a load of the nonexistent back of her blouse—and his need to touch her kicked into overdrive.

Even so, nerves raked up his spine. What if . . . he couldn't do this alone? He wanted to, God knew, but . . .

Before Deke could continue the destructive trail of thought, he grabbed Kimber's arms and pulled her back against his chest, caressing his way down her hip. No doubt, she'd feel instantly exactly how hard she made him.

"Did you wear that little number to drive me insane? It's working."

She sent him a saucy glance over her nearly bare shoulder. Deke didn't think he could get any harder. Kimber proved him wrong.

"Hmm. I have a favor to ask you."

"Favor?" Like what? Her expression gave nothing away.

She set the flowers on the counter, then turned in his arms, cozying up very close to him—and raising his temperature another twenty degrees. Oh yeah, the desire to make love to her was there. That was never a question. Just the . . . follow-through.

"I want to learn about the way you like to have sex." She stroked her hand up his abs, over his chest, then his shoulder. "With just me."

Deke swallowed. A few weeks ago, when she'd first come to Luc's place seeking assistance, she'd spoken very similar words. He'd thought then it was an insane request, and she'd spoken as if his sex life had come from a foreign planet. Now . . . it did. At least for him.

He hadn't made love to a woman by himself since Heather.

Tonight, he had to try. For her sake. For their sake.

"I'm not sure what that is." The honesty hurt, but he had to say it.

"We'll figure it out together. Dinner first or . . ." She glanced down the shadowed hall.

Candlelight glowed golden in the room. And damn, Kimber smelled downright edible. Still, he hesitated. He wasn't in a hurry to have his failures exposed, if that's the way the night went. *But eating dinner first isn't going to help you keep your dick stiff if you freak out, either.*

Deke exhaled, searching for calm. "Or. Definitely or."

"Good call. Let me turn the oven down . . ."

Kimber disappeared for a few moments. He heard her in the kitchen, adjusting dials, opening the oven, closing it again. When she emerged again, she handed him a cold beer and held a glass of wine in her hand.

Taking the bottle from her, he downed half of it. Kimber gnawed on her bottom lip as she watched.

"We could talk first."

"Nothing to say that's going to change the outcome of tonight." He just needed to wrap his head around the fact Kimber was exclusively his and act accordingly.

Determined to make their first time alone together as right as he could, Deke set the beer down, plucked the wineglass from her hand and set it next to his bottle. Then picked Kimber up and stalked down the hall to her bedroom.

More candles everywhere reflected off the shades of cream, sage, and cinnamon on the bedspread and walls. Really nice. Really her.

And they were really alone.

He pushed thoughts of everything but Kimber aside as he eased her down to the mattress. Her hands fluttered nervously, one landing across her stomach, bringing into focus the row of neat stitches across her forearm. The sight sobered him.

Kimber had been through so much: a ménage that wasn't her heart's desire, attempts on her life, a pregnancy scare, his subsequent blowup and revelations about Heather—and she was still strong, so amazing. What could have happened with Cal served as a stark reminder that life was too short not to reach out and grab the woman he wanted and loved. All he had to do now was touch her, take her, and never let go.

In about two seconds, he had her out of everything but thigh-high stockings and a smile. His own clothes were casualties of the ache inside him in the next heartbeat.

But once he laid his hands on her bare skin, he began to shake again. What if he was an utter fucking failure?

Letting out a troubled breath, Deke covered her body and kissed her feverishly, sinking deep into her mouth, branding her. Failure wasn't an option. Truth was, he never wanted to be anywhere else. Never wanted anyone else with them or near her. He was going to have to make this work. She was his.

The enticing creamy skin, his.

The pretty berry nipples, his.

The addictive taste of her cream on his tongue, his.

The cries of delight when she gripped the sheets while he licked her into bliss, his.

All his. Just his.

Working his way back up her body, Deke sighed over her delicate female curves, then groaned as her hand suddenly enveloped and stroked his erection. Hell, she didn't need to prime him. He felt hard enough to drill through concrete.

But he wanted to caress her, celebrate the fact she was in his arms, protect her, shelter her. Love her.

He also wanted to fuck her—in every way he could. He took that as a good sign. Fear edged the arousal . . . but not the usual fear. It wasn't the panic of worrying about an unexpected pregnancy. This was the fear of letting her down. But every other cell in his body was focused on the scalding need to be inside her and the burning determination to make that a reality.

Easing into the cradle of her thighs, he brushed his lips over hers, then sank in, sampling the desire and hope on her tongue. He seized her mouth again. And again. Damn it, one more time because he couldn't taste her enough. Couldn't believe his good fortune after a decade of believing himself unworthy of a woman of his own, much less one this wonderful.

All he had to do now was claim her . . .

"I—I want to make love to you tonight. Every night, kitten. I'm glad you're mine. I feel so damn lucky."

"I'm the lucky one. When you look at me like that, I feel loved."

"You are." Deke gently worshipped her mouth. "You are."

"Feel like demonstrating that?" She lifted her hips to him in blatant invitation.

"God, yes."

Kimber nipped at his shoulder, kissed her way up his neck. "I'm still on the pill, but if you'd rather . . . condoms are in the nightstand."

They were really going to do this, just the two of them. He hesitated, fearing the nasty sideswipe of panic. But it didn't come. "Whatever happens we'll handle it together, right?"

"Yes."

The reassurance in her voice went straight to his chest, where he felt all damn mushy. The rest of him . . . taut, tense, every bit rigid. Everything from his shoulders to his toes was juiced with adrenaline. Nerves. Anticipation. He'd never needed and feared something so much at once.

"For three days, I've been thinking about nothing except how you'd feel inside me."

Then she lifted her legs high on his hips. Damn, her pussy pressed right against his cock. And she was wet. *Oh, hell.* Deke started to sweat. His heart took off like a jet trying to reach new speeds. He'd thought about her, too. Obsessively. What would it be like to finally take her alone? Claim her as his very own?

Kimber nipped at his lobe, sending a new shiver across his skin. "You're going to feel so good. I've missed you. I look at you and I ache."

Yeah, he knew exactly how that went. He reacted to her the same way. He was reacting that way now, so damn hard he could swear most of the blood in his body had flooded the same nine inches of flesh. He grimaced, then probed until the head of his cock held right against her entrance.

Shit. Sweat poured off of him now. Deke swallowed. Kimber had to feel the heavy pound of his heart against her chest, couldn't miss the harsh grip of his fingers on her hips. He meant to ease off, be gentle . . . but every muscle in his body was wired.

"I can't wait to have your hard length inside me, stretching, driving me insane."

Didn't she know her words were only ramping him up more? He was going to lose the last threads of his sanity if she went on like that.

"The feel of you deep inside me . . ." She groaned. "I need it."

It was all he could do not to groan with her. Yeah, he remembered. How the hell could he forget how perfect she felt all around him? *Not in this lifetime.*

She lifted to him again, and the head of his cock eased inside her. *Oh, damn. Oh, wow!*

"Then you nudge that one spot, and I scream for you. Every time, you make me come apart."

Just like those hot words of hers were doing to him—dismantling his reserve, his hesitation, arousing him past thought.

His head swam with her scent, her whispered come-ons, and the feel of her pussy trying to latch onto his dick. He couldn't stand it. God, he couldn't hold out. Couldn't wait . . .

Deke gripped her hips and slid home in one delicious, endless thrust, sealing their bond. All the way to the end, as tight against her cervix as he could.

He drew in a shuddering breath at the wild sensation that pounded at him. Tight, wet, hot, silken, perfect; Kimber was everything. What he didn't feel was panic or worry about being responsible for whatever happened. As she cried out underneath him, Deke realized that he *wanted* to take care of her. More than anything.

The very thought of doing that felt almost as good as making love to her.

As he retreated then sank deep again, Kimber moaned once more. Around him, she tightened.

Home. His.

"Hush, and I'll make you come now," he murmured, fitting his hands underneath the firm cheeks of her ass and lifting her tighter against him.

Then he took her mouth, filling it with his kiss at the same time he filled her sex with his cock. Slowly. Even, measured strokes. *Oh, hell yes!* Friction was definitely his friend. His best damn buddy, in fact. Every rasp of his flesh against hers was like an electric charge running through his body. All the sensations burst through him, short-circuiting any thoughts he might have had. It was all body, baby. The ever-tightening clasp of her sheath, her nails in his back, her bucking hips under him, her breathless begging in his ear. The way his heart wrenched at each one. The thrill of knowing he was pleasing her.

Moments later, she cried out . . . His name. That was it, and in the same sentence with God. Her words were a litany, a plea. And he felt her pulse down on him, milking him, melting him. He careened out of control, racing toward the finish line too rapidly to stop.

Deke grabbed her, his arms tightening around her, like a lifeline. She *was* his lifeline.

Damn, he felt like a volcano. The pressure brewing in his balls stopped his breath. The amazing pleasure stunned him. After years of shared sex, having Kimber to himself completely was like a revelation. An amazement. He almost expected the heavens to part and start singing or some shit.

Instead, ecstasy ripped through him with such force, he thought his body would explode into a billion pieces. He clutched her, cried out for her, emptied himself inside her in a series of jolting spasms that devastated him. Changed him. *Forever.*

* * *

UNDER the hard protection of Deke's body, Kimber clasped him tighter. He'd already owned her body tonight.

There was no question he owned her heart.

Tears seeped from the corners of her eyes.

Still panting, he raised his head. Sweat clung to his temples, rolled down his neck. Veins bulged, muscles bunched. He looked so big and invincible. Except when he opened his eyes and looked down at her. Every vulnerability lay bare in those dark blue eyes, and her heart opened for him even wider.

"Hi," she murmured.

"Hi."

"That was . . . beautiful. You moved me."

He grunted. "Yeah, I'm really trying not to cry like a baby here."

Kimber couldn't help but laugh as her heart lit up. Had she ever been happier?

"Just the two of us, was it difficult?"

"Not as much as I thought it would be. Once I convinced my mind it was you and I focused on how I felt about you . . . everything was all right."

"It was perfect," she corrected with a caress of her fingers up his cheek.

"It was."

"You know, when I came to you for help, I was a girl stupidly chasing a boy for some silly daydream that didn't exist. You gave me something real. You treated me like a woman, taught me about sex, showed me love. Thank you."

"Thank *you*. I put you through hell, and I hate that. But you still healed me and cared about me. You didn't give up on me. I love you so damn much, kitten. I always will. You going to marry me someday?"

Clearly, the question surprised her—pleasantly. "You going to ask someday?"

"Yeah." He brushed auburn curls away from flushed cheeks.

She pressed a soft kiss on his lips and teased, "I don't know. When I first asked you to teach me about sex, you said there would be no emotional bonds."

Deke snorted. "I was an idiot. I need the bond between us. It's essential like air, baby. I've got to have it." He pressed a soft kiss to her lips. "I-I'm hoping you still want to have babies with me someday."

She nodded. "I'm glad we can, that you never, um . . ."

"Had a vasectomy? I really thought about it. Hard. But Luc was right; I didn't because I couldn't give up on the hope of someday being a father. Somewhere in the back of my mind, I didn't want the past to have that kind of power over me for the rest of my life."

"You took a huge step tonight in letting go of the past. Would it be too weird if I told you I was proud of you?"

A flash of tears glossed across those denim blue eyes. He did his best to blink them away. "Nah. Hell, I'm proud of me, too," he joked. "And now you're mine. All mine. Just mine."

Under him, Kimber smiled. "Yours. Always."

The author of sizzling contemporary, paranormal, and erotic romances, **Shayla Black** is the pseudonym for a prolific, award-winning author. She lives in the South with her husband and daughter, juggling the many roles in her life: writer, mother, wife, and all-around laundress. In her "free" time, she is a reality TV junkie and enjoys reading, obsessively studying all things Harry Potter, doing step aerobics, and listening to an eclectic blend of music.

Shayla's first book, *Wicked Ties*, was an Amazon Top 10 Hot Erotic release, and she loves hearing from readers through her site, www.shaylablack.com or www.myspace.com/shelleybradley.

A writing risk-taker, Shayla enjoys tackling writing challenges with every book, as well as writing emotionally based relationships and hot love scenes from the heart.